24 HOURS

CLAIRE SEEBER

Published by Bookouture

An imprint of StoryFire Ltd.
23 Sussex Road, Ickenham, UB10 8PN
United Kingdom

www.bookouture.com

ISBN: 978-1-910751-57-2
eBook ISBN: 978-1-910751-56-5

ACKNOWLEDGMENTS

I'd like to thank Nicola Smyth; always the front-runner.

I'd like to thank the team at Bookouture; particularly Rhian McKay for her careful attention.

Most of all, I'd like to thank Keshini Naidoo, for not only her editorial eye, but also her friendship, enthusiasm and encouragement.

DEDICATION

To the home gang; especially, this time, the big man.
The right place.

Occasionally, one must be unworthy, simply in order to be able to continue living.

Carl Jung

When the fight begins within himself the man is worth something.

Robert Browning

THIS DARK LOVE

We see what we want to see.

My husband taught me that. It was always Sid's catchphrase: sometimes we see, and sometimes we simply choose not to look. Sometimes we just close our eyes.

This is a story of how I didn't look.

Of how love did not win the day, or conquer all.

How can you see love anyway? Love isn't clear or clean-cut. Sometimes, sure, it's gentle – but it can also be strange, intangible, amorphous. And too often, love isn't about love at all. The lines get blurred and it becomes simply about survival. It folds us in its warm embrace, then flings us to the floor.

Is it a blessing, or a curse? A moot point, I'd say. Up for debate. So, I can't tell you the answer, but I can tell you this …

This is a story of an ugly, brutal love: the kind that blinds.

The kind you may not survive.

NOW: HOUR DOT

Light is breaking on the horizon behind the hills as we pull into the hospital grounds, but the day already looks grey.

There cannot be any hope for this day.

My eyes are hot and gritty: they sting with exhaustion and smoke. I rub them, but it only makes them worse.

The woman next to me in the ambulance says something, but it doesn't seem to make any sense. I can't understand the words she speaks. I would answer, but I can hardly even swallow. My head throbs; my throat is like sandpaper; my mouth tastes of ash and guilt.

The woman is still wearing a dressing-gown; it is pink velour, although hardly pink any more. She is pale and bewildered; tear-stained, soot-marked. I imagine I look similar.

I don't care what I look like.

I just want to know where Emily is.

No one has been able to tell me anything. There has been nothing but chaos; no one to ask, or explain – just confusion and panic. The police who eventually arrived at the scene were too busy, trying to corral everyone into the lane outside the grounds. We watched with mounting desperation as the flames grew, so high they were visible above the fences, thick black smoke billowing across the tree-tops, burning debris flying on the breeze. We watched until they forced us down the road into some kind of village hall where we waited for the ambulances to arrive.

The paramedics assure us that all will become clear soon; that, at the hospital, news of our friends and family will be available; that we should just 'hang on. Keep hanging on, there's a good girl.'

I am terrified. I have a nagging pain in my stomach that gnaws at me. I need to find Emily, and then I need to go. To get the hell out before I am found.

I am more terrified that I will *not* find Emily.

Last night reels through my head again and then stops; freezes; rewinds. Plays again. And again. Flames lick against a wall; smoke seeps under doors. The heat; the lack of air.

I hold my pounding head in my hands to stop the images that flicker remorselessly – but it's impossible.

'All right, love?' the balding paramedic holds his hand out, gently pushes my face up so he can look at me.

'Yes,' I croak. It's not the truth. 'Thank you.'

'Hand hurting?' he indicates my bandaged hand.

'A bit. My throat hurts and my shoulder's really sore.'

Talking makes me cough. He studies my face. He has short stubby eyelashes I stare at, like toothbrush bristles.

'Anything else? Feeling odd? Light-headed? Headache?'

I want to grab his hand and keep holding it. I might float away if I don't. 'I'm fine, really.'

I have never been less fine in my life.

'Well,' he releases my face. 'Go slow, okay? You're in the right place now. They'll check you out for smoke inhalation.'

But I am in entirely the wrong place.

The fluorescent lights of the hospital A & E are blinding as they open the back of the ambulance to let us out. I screw my eyes up and clamber down, disoriented.

I am reminded of sheep in a truck, blindly following on, tumbling clumsily forwards. A solitary bird sings and then stops. It is not a day to celebrate.

There is a news crew already at the doors of the hospital. I walk inside, following the herd. In my mouth, an acrid taste; the taste of smoke.

At the foot of a stairwell that everyone now starts to climb, I stop a nurse in blue uniform, hurrying down. She looks fraught.

'I'm looking for Emily Southern,' I say. 'Can you help me?'

'Who?' she frowns.

'My friend. The fire.'

'I'm not sure,' she shakes her blonde ponytail. 'Sorry. You need to stay with your party. Someone will come and talk to you soon I expect.' She hurries on.

I sit in the room with the others for a while until I can bear it no longer. My hand hurts and no one has come yet; one young, bemused-looking healthcare assistant keeps us company. Keeps us captive.

'The police will be here in a moment,' he keeps saying, looking increasingly harassed. The woman from the ambulance is crying now. A big man is hissing into his mobile. 'Just come and get me,' he is saying.

The healthcare assistant tries to ring someone; no one can help him apparently.

'Please,' I say to the weeping lady. 'Don't cry. It'll be all right.'

But I have a feeling it won't be. Someone brings us tea, but I don't want it. Fear sits in my chest; I'm on the verge of hysteria myself. I imagine flames licking at the door. I stand and then sit again a few times, until eventually I know I have to get out of this room.

I have the clothes I stand up in, which include Emily's hoodie and my pyjamas. I have my mobile phone, which has long since run out of battery. I have nothing else.

I open the door.

'Please, stay here, miss,' the young man says. 'Someone will be along in a minute to talk to you.'

'I just need the loo,' I lie.

'Okay,' he shrugs. 'It's just down the hall.'

Outside the room, I turn a corner: two policemen are talking to a white-coated woman further down the corridor. Their business is private; my instinct is to hide. I move backwards, holding my breath.

I wait a beat, then peer cautiously round the wall.

One of them holds a list.

'Right. So that's Peter Graves. Poor sod.' He marks something down. 'And Laurie Smith, you said?' he says now.

'Here,' I am about to shout. I step forward—

'Laurie Smith is dead?' he says, looking up from his list at the woman. 'You're sure?'

I freeze.

'I'm afraid so,' the woman nods, her neat bob swinging. 'DOA. Not pretty.'

The policeman writes again.

'And her room-mate?' The other squints at his list. 'Emily South-something, I think. If this bloody list is right, anyway. That hotel was unbelievably slack.'

'Only one female,' the doctor swigs from her coffee, wipes her mouth. 'And the two men we've already discussed. Plus the housekeeper is still up in the ICU. We'll know one way or the other in the next few hours, I would think.' She is perfunctory. Scarily so. 'It's quite quick, normally.'

From my vantage point, I see the ginger-haired policeman writing. 'It could have been worse, I guess,' he says. 'A fire that size.'

'Yes, thank God,' the doctor agrees. 'A few walking wounded, but really. Could have been a *lot* worse.'

My heart races so fast I think it might explode. I press myself against the wall before I fall.

Laurie Smith is dead.

But I am *not* dead. I am standing here, in this hospital corridor. So that means, that means …

It's Emily. It must be Emily.

'Have you contacted the families?'

'Not our job, thank Christ,' the policeman says. 'We've been waiting for some kind of confirmation. It's a total bloody mess at the moment to be honest. Guv doesn't know his arse from his elbow.'

'We shouldn't even be involved,' the other man sticks a little finger in his ear and wiggles it. 'We're traffic.'

'Going to have to move fast now.' There is a modicum of excitement in the man's voice. 'The press have got hold of it already.'

'The help-line's up and running, at least,' the small one says, as if it is a huge consolation. He checks the finger he's just withdrawn from his ear for goodies.

'Don't envy you the families.' The doctor's pager begins to beep. 'Hardest part of the job, I find.'

'I don't know,' the ginger policeman takes off his hat and rubs his forehead. 'It's the kiddies in car-smashes I can't bear.'

The doctor checks the pager at her waist, begins to hurry away. 'I'm needed upstairs. It might be four after all, I'm afraid.'

So painful; so routine. The policemen look rueful, pondering life and death.

Then they move off, taking their list with them.

I walk round the corner and into the ladies' loo.

I lean on the washbasin. The tears do not come yet; my eyes are so dry and sore it seems impossible. Instead, I splash my face with water; sink to the ground, back against the wall.

My best friend is dead. Emily is dead; and yet they think it is me.

I took her jacket. It was the nearest, hanging on the back of the hotel door. She'd woken me, almost crying; she had such a bad headache, she said, apologising, one of her migraines, could I bear to fetch her Migraleve from the car? Disoriented, half-asleep, I'd stumbled around, lost in the unfamiliar half-lit corridors, fumbling around in the dark car, not finding the blessed painkillers anyway – and then as I made my way back, to ask reception if they could help, the fire alarms went off. Shrill and brain-piercing.

The alarms went off – and I couldn't get back into the room. The door wouldn't open.

I think the door was wedged shut. I banged my weight against it, but it would not give.

Perhaps they are wrong? Perhaps they have got her mixed up with someone else.

But I know they are right. She was wearing my necklace; the locket with '*Laurie*' engraved on the back; it went with the peacock blue dress she wore at dinner. We have swapped jewellery and clothes since we met during our A levels. Last night we laughed about how the locket drew eyes downwards. Not that she needed any help.

'You are bad, Laurie Smith,' she said, as I prodded her bosom gently after fastening the necklace.

'Not bad. Jealous,' I said. 'Polly did for me.'

And I know the bedroom door did not open. I was trying to open the bloody thing from outside and it was stuck. I was there, smashing my shoulder against it, until the heat forced me to run, to find someone to help.

But no one could help; no one came. The smoke was indefensible.

I stand again; I wash my face of the soot. My eyes look enormous in my pale face. Fragments of the terrible night are still filtering back to me.

Emily. My beloved Emily.

And the worst thing is, I know it shouldn't have been her.

It was me they were after.

Everything adds up: the fear and stress of the past few months have led to this.

Staring in the mirror, I have a moment of clarity. She is giving me a chance. In death, as in life, my best friend is trying to protect me.

I have to go. Before they realise they are wrong. Before they realise I am still alive, and whoever wants me dead knows too.

I walk out, down the stairs, towards the daylight.

THEN: SPAIN

It was so hot. I don't know what I was expecting but it wasn't the intense sunshine that knocked us backwards as we stepped out of the airport building. Brightness that made us both scrunch our eyes against the glare.

'Wow.' Beneath the spike-topped palm trees I squeezed Polly's hand tighter. 'We're going to get a brilliant sun-tan in this, aren't we, Pol?'

The look she gave me was impressively disdainful for a six-year-old.

'Sun-tanning isn't good for you, Mummy. Just like cigarette-ing.'

'Wow!' I repeated, stumped. When did my daughter join the moral majority? My mother must have got to her.

Sid would be horrified.

Polly was fumbling around in her rucksack as I unlocked the tiny hire car and slung the bags in the boot.

'All right?'

'I am now,' she agreed solemnly, placing pink heart-shaped sunglasses on the end of her snub nose. I hadn't taken my own shades off for most of the flight in case anyone noticed my puffy eyes; mere slits in a pale and horribly woebegone face. I told Polly I was pretending to be a big star. She pondered this information for a moment.

'Like Taylor Swift?' she asked.

I had no idea who that was. 'Yes,' I agreed. 'Exactly like him.'

'Her,' she corrected.

'Fabulous,' I said now. I felt very far from fabulous; very far indeed. I put the car into gear; it took a massive bunny-hop forward. 'Whoops! Sorry, Pol.'

'That's okay,' she said kindly. 'You can't help being a rubbish driver.'

Shades of her father.

'No, well,' I wasn't going to argue. I was all done with arguing. This was our new beginning. Tentatively I put the car into the correct gear. 'Let's go and have an adventure.'

The adventure would have started a lot earlier if it hadn't taken me three laps to find the exit from the airport, and four attempts to find the right junction off the motorway, trying simultaneously to map read whilst also driving a left-handed Hyundai. But eventually, sometime around dusk, we wound our way up to the small white-washed town perched on the very top of the hill.

After a hair-raising episode squeezing the car through tiny Moorish streets so I could unload near the house I'd rented from my colleague Robert, during which time various Spanish men shouted at me a lot about things I chose not to understand, we finally reached our destination.

Unpacking, we marvelled at the pretty little house; at the lemons growing in the courtyard, the tiny marble pool just big enough to dunk yourself in. We bought eggs and bread and water from the shop at the end of the street and after supper, when it was cooler and I could breathe again, I bought Polly ice-cream at the bar in the square whilst I drank a cold beer. I clasped her solid little body against mine and thanked God she was here with me.

But when she went to bed that night, I sat beneath the lemon tree and opened a bottle of white Rioja and tried desperately not to succumb to the overwhelming sadness that I had felt for the past three and a half days; the past three and a half months. The past three and a half years.

I failed.

Lying on a sun-lounger in the dark, the sky a canopy of speckled silver above me, the sadness won.

The tears slid noiselessly down my face and collected in pools in my ears.

I had spent every last penny I had coming here; my refuge from *him*. I had saved Polly and myself – temporarily at least – so why did it feel so horrible and sad?

Because a great crack had been riven in me, one that could not be fixed or filled; not now, maybe never. I could pour the wine in, I could fill it with cigarette smoke – but the gap would still be there.

Desperately I searched the heavens for a shooting star to wish on. But that night, there were none.

NOW: HOUR 1

9am

As I reach the ground floor, two nurses walk past.

'Did you see the news crew outside earlier?' one sniffs. 'And the photographers. Bloody vultures.'

'They offered Lisa McCormack fifty quid to tell them what state the bodies were in.'

Trying desperately not to imagine Emily now, or the condition she may well be in, I follow them through the swing doors, towards signs to the exit.

As the dawn predicted, it is a bland, colourless day here.

I don't even know *where* here really is. Only the tiny sliver of sea I glimpsed from the windows upstairs says we are probably still in Devon.

'Did she take it? The money?'

'Joanne!' The other nurse laughs, digs her friend hard in the ribs. 'What do you think?'

'What? She might have been tempted! We can't all be angels.'

'I think they're bloody bastards.' The nurse shudders. 'Probably hacking everyone anyway. That's what they do these days.' Turning towards a ward, she offers Joanne something. 'Polo?'

I need to catch my breath.

I sit on a chair in the corridor and try to think, but I am so tired and shocked, I can't get my thoughts straight. I squeeze my head between my hands, attempting to force back memories.

Fear. I remember fear. Pure and unadulterated: believing I was about to die. About to suffocate in the smoke.

I stand and head towards the exit.

I am not meant to be here. I am meant to be dead. I know without any doubt that my life is in danger.

And crucially, most vitally: I have to reach Polly before hers is too.

I have to get somewhere safe before Sid arrives here. He has been so angry since I stopped him seeing Polly. I am sure this is to do with him somehow.

Because they *will* call Sid, undoubtedly. If they realise that I am not dead. That the body in the mortuary is Emily's, not mine.

How long do I have?

I am not dressed for the cold outside, and I have no money.

At the end of the corridor a door swings open; in the main reception waiting-area, a television talks to itself in the corner.

The morning papers adorn the news-stand outside the little shop. I read a headline.

BLAZE AT FOREST LODGE SPA KILLS THREE

My scalp prickles. I pick up the paper, my hand shaking almost uncontrollably. I scan the article.

> *Two victims of the Forest Lodge fire have been named as businessman Peter Graves and night porter Jeff Leigh. Two as-yet unnamed women are thought to have been the third and fourth victims; police are hoping to identify them today.*

'All right, love?' the fat girl behind the counter looks worried. She is taking money from a man for a Kit-Kat; ringing it up in her till. 'You look a bit wobbly.'

My mind is working furiously. The man thanks her and leaves. The till must be full of money. Her coat is over the back of the chair.

'Actually, I don't feel too good.' I hold a hand to my head. I am not lying. 'Could you fetch someone for me?'

She puffs up like a great robin redbreast in her scarlet jumper, validated by the task in hand. 'Of course, my love, don't you worry. You just sit there and rest.'

'Thank you.' I am treacherous.

She bustles off down the corridor. I glance around. At the information desk fifty feet away the receptionist is on the phone, oblivious to me. Otherwise it is eerily quiet.

Quickly I stand and press a few buttons. To my infinite relief the till opens immediately. I help myself to the notes: I wish my hand would stop shaking. I take the voluminous navy coat off the chair and wrap it round me. 'Sorry,' I mutter to no one. I hurry to the sliding doors, then outside, where the cold hits me.

At the tea-stall across the road, a small gaggle of photographers are gathered, cameras slung round their necks as they smoke and banter. I walk very fast to the taxi rank; I throw myself into the back of the first cab. At least my pyjama bottoms could almost pass for the latest trend of baggy trousers. Nevertheless, I pull the coat closer.

'Can you take me to the nearest town please?' It's such an effort to speak, my voice is still barely more than a whisper.

They explained the pain in my throat was caused by smoke inhalation; they promised it would wear off gradually. But it hurts.

'You're *in* town, love.' The driver glances at me as if I am mad. I probably do look like I've escaped the asylum.

'Oh,' I say, looking behind me. A multi-pierced teenager in a wheelchair and spotted dressing-gown smokes furiously beside the doors, but no one else goes in or out. 'Of course. Can you take me to the nearest shopping centre then please?'

The driver sighs as if I've just asked him to take me to Timbuktu.

'My bag got stolen,' I offer.

He turns the radio up, pulls away, uninterested.

I have a sudden thought. 'Actually, can you wait one minute?'

I get out and run to the photographers at the tea-stand. They look faintly amused at my dishevelled appearance; my hair all sticking up on end. One of them offers me a cigarette. 'No,' I shake my head. 'I'd rather have a cup of tea. Did you hear the news?'

'What news?' the one with psoriasis perks up. Someone orders me a tea.

'That artist's wife. The famous one. Sid Smith.'

'The one that did all that religious porn? Won the Booker prize?'

'Turner Prize,' I correct him absently.

'Whatever,' he scratches at his inflamed cheek. 'So?'

'His wife's dead. Laurie Smith. In that fire.' I turn to go.

'Is she? In the Spa? Poor cow,' he says. 'He gave her the right old run-around, didn't he?'

'Did he?' I feel shaky again.

'Ran off with that singer.' Someone hands me a cup of tea. 'The young half-caste. Dead fit.'

'Well, she's dead and gone now.' I take the tea. 'Laurie Smith. Poor cow,' I agree sadly.

But they have lost interest in me; already reaching for their phones, calling news-desks and editors.

I get into the car and, warming my cold hands on the cardboard cup, sit back for a moment. There are so many things I need to do, I don't know which to do first. I need to speak to my mother, to make sure Polly is safe; I need to get clothes; I need to speak to Emily. She'll know what to do.

I can't speak to Emily.

Horror crawls through my head as realisation hits me afresh.

I can't speak to Emily ever again.

My best friend is dead and I killed her: I might as well have done.

Inadvertent or not, I killed her: because it was meant to be me in that mortuary.

THEN: SPAIN

No one gets married thinking it's going to fail.

Do they?

My wedding day was a start, I thought; the seal on something precious, a beginning, and the best day of my life, before Polly was born. On a hilltop on the south-eastern tip of Cornwall, overlooking a becalmed turquoise sea, I married the man I had fallen so deeply for the year before. We ate local lobster and chips off long trestle tables in the sun, and afterwards we had a party in Sid's studio. We had no money but it didn't matter: we decked it out with wild flowers, pinks and yellows and blues, and Emily twisted the same blooms through my loose hair. I wore a simple flowing silk dress, all bare feet and obvious euphoria, utterly lost to love.

'You are beautiful,' Sid whispered as we stood before the registrar but when I met his eyes – eyes the colour of the sea – he seemed distant, almost as if it hurt him to say as much.

I just held his hand tighter, my poor lost boy. I knew he was scared.

How scared, I didn't realise yet.

'I've never seen you so happy,' Emily said. It was gallant, because I knew what she *really* felt. 'Shame for the poor lobsters though. Pair for life, they do.' She pulled a face at me, puffing out already-round cheeks. 'Till you served them up as lunch.'

Typical Em. My mother, on the other hand, didn't say anything. She just cast her eyes to heaven at my inappropriate hair and lack of shoes, but she too was high on adrenaline. Sid was most charming when he chose to be, and despite his lack of income, she'd decided eventually, and of her own accord, that his potential might be huge.

And the best thing was, everyone we loved was in that place. Apart from my father, who had refused to come. It was no surprise; I'd only asked him out of duty in the end.

On our wedding night, whilst people still danced to the local skiffle band and drank cheap rosé under a crescent moon, Sid took me out to the tumbledown old barn where he kept his motorbike and the sit-down lawnmower that had packed up the first time he'd used it. He pulled the tarpaulin off a painting that leant against the wall; a small oil I'd had no idea he'd been working on. I stood, speechless, staring at it.

It was a nude of me sleeping, curled safely in the middle of a bed.

'Sid's Bed', he'd called the picture.

It turned out to be the one truly loving gesture of the entire relationship. That, and my eternity ring.

But I didn't know that yet.

I loved that painting. Not through any kind of vanity but because, fool that I was, I thought it symbolised what I meant to him. Because I thought he saw me differently than anyone else had ever done. Truly, I couldn't believe my luck. I'd married a man I believed was a true genius – and he loved *me* beyond all else.

I had lost myself entirely.

In the early hours, when everyone had finally left, Sid stood me in the middle of the darkened studio and studied me.

I had felt something building in him as the night had darkened; something I did not understand, but something that I was aware existed in him. Something I had glimpsed only once or twice before.

He reached forward and pulled the straps of my dress roughly from my shoulders until the dress fell in a puddle of silk round my feet.

He didn't speak – his expression was inscrutable, and so I followed his lead, paralysed by his gaze. There was something deeply unfamiliar about him as he stared at me, standing there in a pool of moonlight, until eventually I felt more naked than I ever had before.

Then he picked me up, right off my feet, and for a moment he held me so tight I felt I couldn't breathe. I made a sound, some kind of protestation.

In response, he threw me backwards onto the studio bed so hard I hit my elbow on the wall, crying out in pain. Still almost fully dressed himself, Sid tugged at my underwear until he ripped it, tearing the sheer lace, tearing my skin – and it was not an act of passion. It was more frightening than that.

An act of ownership, perhaps – and it was as if he had disappeared into himself. Sid wasn't quite there; in his place was a man I had no real understanding of yet. I was overwhelmed, but I was obsessed, and I relinquished myself willingly; gave myself up to him so completely that, by the end, I was almost crawling on my knees.

When I fell asleep, near dawn, I was utterly spent and slightly deranged. And deep down, I couldn't say that it was entirely a shock; this savage side of my new husband. He lay next to me on the single bed in the studio, smoking, staring at the ceiling. And he did not hold me or hug me, though he grasped one of my wrists tightly between his long thin fingers.

The next morning I was bruised and sore, and I could not quite meet his eyes when he opened his; I turned back to the white-washed wall. But he rolled me over gently and kissed me tenderly; made me look at him; made love to me so slowly I was shaking – and so I thought it would be all right.

Six weeks later, I found with shock that I was pregnant. It wasn't meant to happen; I hadn't even been sure I could actually conceive, having suffered with endometriosis from adolescence. But I was quickly elated by the idea of our baby – too quickly, it turned out.

In retrospect, the pregnancy only marked the beginning of the end. Sid didn't want to share; Sid liked things his own way. My new husband, the genius. His star was in the ascendant, though it was a painfully slow trajectory that took its toll on both of us, for varying reasons. Yet to become the *enfant terrible* of the British art scene, he was still unequivocal, brilliant and passionate – and eventually, when success came later than expected, utterly spoilt. Where did a baby fit into that? Into a life honed specially for his 'talent'?

Sid's Bed. I came to hate that painting. But I had been right about one thing: it did symbolise what I meant to Sid. He painted me, therefore he owned me. I was on *his* bed; he thought I was his possession to do with what he pleased; to pick me up and lay me down again.

He picked me up and laid me down again one too many times.

The week in the Spanish sun after Sid and I finally split was a sort of tonic, I supposed, and against the odds, maybe, Polly and I still managed to have some fun. We sat on the windy beaches of the Costa de la Luz and tried not to swallow the sand that was blown up by the incessant gusts. We looked for tall ships out on the headland where the Battle of Trafalgar had been fought (not, as Polly insisted, in Trafalgar Square).

We drove along the coast to pretty Tarifa where I was not reassured to read that the town had the highest rate of suicide in Spain – 'because of the winds' apparently. Enough to send anyone mad, being constantly buffeted – although the surfers seemed to like it. We ate strange-coloured tapas in the bars on the small square near our house, and Polly was welcomed by everyone. Wrinkled old Mires in particular loved her. She had worked for Robert, the owner of the house, for years, and she was an amazing force of life, despite her prehistoric appearance.

And at the very least, we were away from the fights and re-criminations and the awful crushing sadness that came with seeing the man I'd once believed I would spend my whole life with, knowing that, actually, everything was falling apart. That everything was irretrievable.

But during those long Spanish evenings, I would stop pre-tending things were fine. I'd switch on my mobile to see that Sid still hadn't called me and promptly switch it off again. And then, whilst Polly slept, I drank too much, chasing oblivion. I hadn't drunk properly for years, not since the incident after the Turner Prize that ended with me falling badly. That ended with a midnight dash to A & E.

But now I drank until I collapsed across the old four-poster, desperately seeking sleep's sanctuary. I dreamt strange, vivid dreams, often about Sid, often about looking desperately for something I'd mislaid: something nebulous, intangible. And worse, sometimes about happier, far-gone days that had slipped through my grasp.

I kept drinking until the morning Polly found me asleep outside, sprawled on the sun-lounger, wine glass smashed on the tiles beside me where it had fallen from my hand. Groggy, gazing blearily at my daughter's chubby face, I knew I had to get a grip of myself before the alcohol did – again. Full of self-loathing, I pulled Polly onto my lap, kissing her shiny head that smelt of sun-tan lotion until she struggled to get away.

'All right, Mummy!' she protested. 'I am a bit old for kisses, actually.' She was all of six, her tummy a gentle swell above the frilly skirt of her green swimsuit. Sensing my sombre mood, she relented a little, patting my hand kindly. 'You can kiss me again later if you need to. I'm going for a swim.'

As she splashed into the tiny pool I felt a huge stab of guilt. I swept up the glass and in the dark little kitchen I brewed strong coffee and chucked the rest of the wine down the sink.

On our last day, it rained. It seemed a fitting end to the week, somehow; it was still warm, the rain was gentle and the air velvety. After breakfast, we sat on the swirly iron bench under the lemon tree and drew pictures, 'for Daddy'. I had a nasty moment when I realised Polly had drawn in Robert's posh leather visitors' book, but we managed to change the sandcastles into a kind of calling-card, incorporating our names and address, which Polly insisted on writing in full. '*London, NW5 1HX, the World, the Universe. Very lovely ice-creams*', Polly wrote laboriously, her tongue stuck out in concentration. '*We will come back for more.*'

Mires hugged Polly fiercely when we left and I tried to give the old lady twenty euros, but she refused, and I was worried I'd offended her.

'Send me a photograph,' she asked in her broken English, pointing at my daughter, and I promised I would.

England matched my mood that night, dark and chilly. As we stood shivering on the platform for the Stansted Express, I longed for the warmth of Vejer.

As the train pulled in, my phone finally rang.

It was Sid.

'Hi.' I felt strangely nervous.

'Hi.' Long pause. 'Put Polly on.'

'Oh.' I swallowed. 'Is that it?'

'Yep.' Shorter pause. 'That's it.'

'Right.' I looked down at my small daughter who looked so like her father; at her tangle of dark curls, the smattering of freckles that had come out in the sun. Only her eyes were like mine, a dark blue that Sid called cobalt. 'Hang on a sec. We're just getting on the train. Maybe I should ring you—'

'Don't be difficult, Laurie,' he sounded infinitely bored. 'I know you love to be, but really. Don't bother.'

Oh God. I had not missed *this*. Sid was the only person in the world with this strange power over me; so quick to rile me. And God knew, he tried to. I bit my tongue against my retort and pulled my daughter onto the train, depositing her in the first seat available.

'Oh, and while I've got you there, I should probably tell you now,' he drawled. 'You'll only see it in the gossip rags tomorrow.'

I felt a stab of pain.

'What?' I said quietly.

'Jolie.'

'Who?' I slid our case under the rack.

'Jolie Jones.'

'Who?' But I knew who he meant really.

'You met her at Randolph's. She sang.' Randolph was Sid's agent – born without a soul, apparently, or any sign of conscience, and no compunction about showing his contempt for me. A Northern oik made upper middle-class: and my nemesis. I think his real name was Rick. 'She is a singer?'

'Oh yes.' I pictured the tall young woman, willowy and beautiful, a brown-skinned beauty. I'd only met her once or twice at parties I'd felt out of place at; twice my height, wandering around in tiny dresses with a shimmering Afro or multi-coloured braids down to her waist. Skinny-ankled, fragile-framed; she looked like she needed a man to literally hold her up. 'The one who cried at your *Eve* show. What about her?'

'We're together.'

Perhaps she did need a man to hold her up.

'*Together?*' My mind refused to process this.

'Yeah, together. Put Polly on. I don't have much time.'

I passed my daughter the phone, shepherded her into a double seat, sat beside her, furious tears blurring my vision. Randolph must be overjoyed, I thought bitterly. A media match made in heaven – and not me.

'Daddy. We went on a plane and I had Pringles and Coca-Cola in a tiny can, and a lady got locked in the loo and shouted a lot.'

I stared out of the window, savagely blinking away tears before Polly noticed.

'The uniform man said she was a … a mother's ruin.'

I could hear Sid laughing on the other end. So this was how it would be from now on. Him – and me. Him, and Jolie. And me.

'Yes,' Polly nodded seriously. 'It was hot, but I weared a hat.'

Pause.

'I'll ask Mummy. Next weekend?'

She passed me the phone. I couldn't talk to him again.

'I'll call you back,' I mumbled. I switched it off.

I had loved Sid so very much, although sometimes, God only knew why; and I had fought so hard to make my marriage work and when it didn't, I felt lacerated with guilt – mainly on Polly's behalf.

Separating was the hardest thing I had ever experienced. But no one, not even my worst enemy, could say I hadn't tried. Now I had to try harder to get over him.

NOW: HOUR 2

10am

On the outskirts of the town that I've learnt is called Paignton, in the middle of a nondescript high street full of beige people and pound shops, I stand by the only pay-phone that still works. I will not attempt to switch on my own phone, buried deep in my coat pocket. I have no way of charging it and I also have an idea that, the minute I do use it, someone will trace me; someone I don't want to find me.

I have a handful of change from the till – but I realise that, other than my mother's landline and Sid's mobile, I don't know a single number off by heart. I don't even know if I can reverse the charges, or if there's even an operator any more. There are no humans, just automated systems and—

I am starting to hyperventilate; I don't feel well. I sit down on a bench outside New Look, from which I have just bought myself a stripy jumper and a pair of ill-fitting jeans. I have survived the smirks of the somewhat alarmed shop assistants with thick painted eyebrows as I changed out of my strange outfit in their fitting rooms. Now I need to save my money; it's all I have and where will I get more?

I try to collect myself. My hand throbs. My throat hurts. The painkillers are starting to wear off.

Think. Think, Laurie, think.

I think of Mal.

I remember Sid's hand round his neck.

A huge wave of nausea washes over me.

I ring my mother, even though I'm pretty sure she is still on her way back from France. I am struggling to remember if I knew her timings; when she was catching the Eurostar with Polly. My head feels full of cotton-wool.

There is no answer. I leave a message.

'It's me. Laurie. I am not dead. Don't worry, Mum, if you read the papers, I'm not dead. But oh God, Mum, I need to speak to you. Is Polly okay? I'm in Devon. There was a fire and Emily's ...' I hear the catch in my voice; it has taken all my breath to even speak the words. I cannot afford to break down now. 'Emily's gone. I haven't got a number to give you. I'll call you again. Do not let Polly out of your sight. Whatever you do. Promise me. And do not speak to Sid.'

I get off the phone and I have a sudden idea. Of course: how stupid. I find the nearest phone shop and I buy the cheapest pay-as-you-go phone, and a charger for my own mobile. It costs £22.50 altogether. I buy £10's worth of credit. I only have £34.76 left

I ring directory enquiries. It costs me 70p to ask for Pam Southern's number in Lincolnshire – Emily's mother. But when I get the number, I can't bear to call it. What will I say? 'So sorry, Pam, but actually it's Emily who is dead'? And anyway, they must be on their way to the hospital. To see Emily. To see me ...

How long will it take someone to realise it's Emily lying there, and not me? To gaze on that beautiful destroyed face, so honest and open in life, that spark of mad energy doused forever. How long do I have to find out who actually killed her, before they find me and kill me too?

I sit again on a bench outside a hardware shop selling mops and brightly coloured plastic.

I can think of nothing but Emily.

She swept into my life one windy autumn day in '93, assigned to show me around the sixth-form college I had just joined. Transferring late from the private school I'd attended briefly whilst my father was actually in funds, I was infinitely relieved to be leaving: I hated the girls, the snooty teachers and the stuffy timetable. But I was very nervous that first day in the new place; shy; out of my depth. And there were boys.

I wasn't good with boys.

Achingly cool, all blue-tipped peroxide hair, glittery rings and bangles up her plump arms, chewing Juicy Fruit dramatically, Emily was quite obviously everything I was not. Quietly, I followed in her wake, too frightened to speak in case I said something stupid; in case my voice came out too loud. It always came out too loud in my head; I always said something stupid when it counted most.

Emily didn't care if her voice was loud. She had a presence already. Everywhere we went in that building, everyone knew Emily: why would they not want to? Kids called out to her, particularly the boys, and she blew kisses back. I was impressed: far too naïve to find it affected. And anyway, it was just Emily. It came naturally to her.

Occasionally, she'd ignore someone, muttering beneath her breath, and I'd glance back at their crestfallen face. I wasn't quite basking in her light yet – but I was realising it would be desirable.

'Do you like The Charlatans?' Fluffing her hair in the mirror, she threw the question over her shoulder as I filled in a form for my own locker.

I wished I knew the right answer.

'Er, yeah,' I ventured. 'Love them.'

'God, *really?*' her disdain was impressively dramatic. She leant on the desk next to me, beads clicking on the wood; she smelt of sandalwood and cigarettes. 'They're so, like, over. It's Nirvana now. The gorgeous-io Kurt Cobain.'

'Oh,' I stared at her, discomforted, first test failed. 'Well, I love them too. More. Like, "Teen Spirit".'

She stared back, hardly blinking.

'And he's well sexy.' I sounded idiotic, but I ploughed on valiantly. 'Kurt. I like his – his teeth. His hair.'

His teeth and hair? Oh God.

Her eyes were like a tiger's as she gazed at me.

'What's your name again?'

'Laurie.'

'Well, Laurie,' she affected a Scottish accent, for what reason I wasn't sure. 'It's "*Smells Like Teen Spirit*". You'd be as well to learn that. Honestly, if you are the crème de la crème, my girl, I'd hate to see the skim of the milk.'

Later, I learnt she was channelling a character called Miss Jean Brodie; as likely to slip into another persona as to be herself. Ever the drama student, Emily relished showing how versatile she was.

But now, I just goggled at her, utterly thrown.

She gazed back, unwavering.

And then she began to laugh, heartily.

And slowly, I began to laugh too; slowly, as I realised she was laughing with me, not at me.

Somehow that day, against every odd, our friendship began to be forged. It was sealed a month or so later when her dad walked out for the last time, disappearing for good. Girls with similarly feckless fathers, we were bonded for life over her tears and milky coffee in the café on the corner. Secretly, I hated coffee, but Emily drank it, so I did too.

Where Emily led, I followed, until eventually one day I caught her up. I didn't live in her shadow exactly, but I was comfortable being warmed by her light.

She had a lot of light, my lovely Emily.

A toddler bumps against my knee running from his mother, and I force myself back. Right now, more than anything, I need to get to London.

I don't ring Pam, coward that I am – but I do ring my mother's answer-phone again and leave my new number. Then I buy a cup of horrible tea and I ask the woman, whose toddler is now screaming as she hauls him into the buggy, where the nearest petrol station is.

It is drizzling. I walk down the road towards the motorway clutching my lukewarm tea, wrapped in the stolen voluminous coat, and I look out for lorries. I haven't hitched since I was seventeen and trying to get to Edinburgh to see my first boyfriend who had gone up to the Festival with a ridiculous mime show. I got all the way there and then I found him in bed with a girl with no pubic hair. When I'd rung Emily, sobbing down a pub pay-phone, she'd said 'I did tell you so. He's a knob-end. Come on, Laurie. Pull yourself together. Next!'

I look desperately for someone who might give me a lift now.

As I walk, I see great flames that lick the walls; I smell the noxious black smoke that billowed out over the once-white building; I hear the chaos: the shouting and the pandemonium that ensued.

As I walk, I repeat over and over to myself, *It will be all right, it will be all right.*

But I am not sure it will be. Something has gone catastrophically wrong.

A lorry passes, flicking me with spray. My feet are already soaked.

The lorry slows. I start to run.

How did it come to this?

THEN: AFTER SPAIN

That first weekend after our holiday, I had to let Polly go and stay with Sid. There was no good reason why she couldn't; his behaviour towards her had always been entirely loving, and I knew it was the grown-up, responsible thing to do, shared parenting, even though all I wanted to do was hang on to her, kicking and screaming.

Reality was closing round me with a horrible snap. I found myself craving refuge again from it, but there were no other options. In Spain, there had been a chance to forget, but back home in London's Dartmouth Park, it was down to earth with a bump. Back to work, back to a new regime – sharing my daughter.

On the Friday, Sid collected her from school so I didn't have to see him, which was simultaneously a relief and another stab in the heart. Part of me wanted to know if Polly would be spending time with the ethereal Jolie, but I couldn't bear the answer.

Instead of rushing home from the Centre to cook Polly's tea, I went to the cinema with Emily. Unfortunately, the light-hearted comedy about lesbian mothers was sold out, so we sat through three interminable hours of Scandinavian gloom about the impending end of the world. By the time it finished I felt so depressed, I wished it really would end.

'I'm sorry about that, babe,' Emily said, dropping me home afterwards. 'Maybe not the best choice of film ever.'

'No,' I agreed. 'But … interesting.'

'Yeah, right,' she looked at me, feather earrings swinging wildly. 'Interestingly suicide-inducing.' And we both laughed. But I didn't really feel like laughing. I just felt infinitely sad.

'Do you want me to come in?' Emily said nobly, but I could feel her itching to go. She had checked her phone incessantly in the cinema. It irritated me almost as much as the film, but I understood there was a new man in the offing. Who was I to stand in the way of romance?

'Go,' I instructed, waving from the front steps as she lurched off down the road, reapplying her red lipstick as she drove. And watching the tail-lights disappear round the corner, I was only the tiniest bit jealous.

On the Saturday morning, I tried my utmost to stay asleep but of course I was awake at seven, watching the pale autumn light seep slowly through the curtain. My house had never felt so empty or sounded so quiet. First Sid had gone, and now Polly …

I attempted one of Emily's Buddhist mantras to stop those thoughts, but I just felt ridiculous saying *Om*, and anyway I kept thinking of Polly waking up on the other side of town. And of Sid and Jolie, and how I was alone, and they were not. I didn't want Sid, but it didn't mean I wasn't struggling with the idea of another woman.

I got up and drank tea at the kitchen table, staring at the garden that was turning golden-brown as autumn arrived properly. I walked the rooms. I watered the peace lilies. I fed the fish. I talked to them a bit. Could they hear? Did fish even have ears? I looked closer. One of the pretty blue ones was belly-up on the surface.

Oh God. Everyone left me.

I was getting maudlin. Where was Buddha when you needed him?

Polly would be back tomorrow night, I reminded myself. But her bed looked so very empty. I straightened her duvet and plumped up Toy Bear on the pillow. Perhaps I could take Toy Bear round if she missed him– I stopped that train of thought promptly.

I flushed the fish down the loo and rang Robert to ask him what to do with the key to the house in Vejer as he hadn't been at work this week, but really it was just because I wanted to hear another human voice. He didn't answer the phone. It was too early to ring Emily. She never rose before eleven at the weekend, and God only knew where she was anyway.

I tried my hardest not to, but finally I gave into a few pathetic tears. Then, resolutely, I wiped my eyes and dressed, pulling on my warmest jumper, hat and scarf, and walked across the square to Robin's Café. Other people; warmth and light.

It was very busy in the fugged-up little café but I managed to bag the last tiny table in the corner. I grabbed the last bit of the newspaper in the stand, realising too late it was the sports section. I read it anyway. It was amazing what I didn't know about golf – didn't know and could have happily lived a good while longer without learning.

I was halfway through my scrambled eggs and an article about the Australian Grand Prix when a voice asked if it could join me.

'Sorry, it's just there's nowhere else to sit. Except the garden, and it's a bit cold out.'

'Sure!' I leant over to retrieve the hat and scarf that I'd thrown over the other chair. The scarf trailed through the tomato ketchup on my plate and down my white jumper.

'Oh God,' I was starting to feel a bit flustered now. 'Stupid.'

'I'll get you a napkin,' the voice said.

'Thanks.'

I looked up at him now as he passed me the paper serviettes. He had a nice open face, slightly ruddy from the cold; tawny hair. He looked … I couldn't think of the right word for a moment. Sort of *solid*, in a comforting kind of way.

'That's so annoying, isn't it?' he indicated the mark.

I looked back down at my jumper, at the ketchup stain, almost flushing. 'Very typical of me,' I grimaced. 'Rarely get my food near my mouth.'

He laughed and my stomach shifted very slightly. I concentrated hard on dabbing the mark. He was sitting down now; I could feel the cold coming off him. He smelt of fresh air. Chucking the serviette away, I buried my head in my cappuccino and kept trying to read about someone called Räikkönen.

Our knees touched under the tiny table. I almost jumped. This was ridiculous. Bravely, I looked at him and we both grinned.

'Bit small, isn't it?'

'Don't worry.' I finished my coffee. 'I've got to get going anyway.'

'Oh please, don't go on my account.' He looked worried.

'No, well, honestly, I think I've read all I can read about the Grand Prix anyway.'

'Fan of it?'

'Definitely not.' I shook my head vehemently. 'I've never watched one in my life, and I'm happy to keep it that way.'

'It is a bit of a specialist sport, I think. Not for the masses really.'

'Too noisy for me.' I looked round for Robin to ask for my bill. 'And is it really a sport? Girls with long legs and hair, and lots of men whizzing round Monaco in expensive cars, dirtying up the air?'

'It's open for debate, I guess, but I'm not a great fan either.' He paused. 'So, do you live locally?'

'Just on the other side of the square.'

'Right. I'm new to the area.'

'It's nice. The area. Kind of … friendly, given that it's such a big city.'

'Good.' He smiled. His light eyes were warm in a sun-tanned face, and he reminded me of someone, but I couldn't think whom. I gave up on Robin and stood now, in my stained white jumper. I nearly pulled on my hat and then decided I might wait until I got outside. I wasn't entirely sure it showed me to my best advantage.

'Well, enjoy! Maybe see you again.'

'I hope so,' he said and for some reason I felt ludicrously pleased.

I paid at the till and left, giving the man a quick smile as I passed, which he returned. He was reading the article about the Grand Prix now himself.

Outside it was bitterly cold but I felt more jolly than I had in weeks. Walking to the shops through the park, though, my happiness quickly deflated. The man had been so nice. Very … attentive. It seemed like a long time since anyone had paid me any attention. But I needed to concentrate on Polly, and Polly alone.

In the greengrocers' mirror, I noticed I had dried cappuccino froth on my nose. Scrubbing it off, I realised the man just felt sorry for me, poor bumbling idiot that I was. And anyway, he was probably married. Most of the good ones were. Leaving the shop, I sidestepped a woman hidden in her furry hood, hissing into her phone. She was stiff with anger, turning away from me for privacy.

I walked home, alone and dejected. I wanted to speak to Polly. Was it all right to call her at Sid's? Would that upset her? What *was* separated parent protocol? God only knew.

I waited for an old lady and her spaniel to cross my path.

Forget the men. Maybe it was time to get a dog.

NOW: HOUR 3

11am

I sit in the lorry's cabin. It's very high up, and for a moment I almost feel safe, in my vantage point above the world. I can see over all the hedges into the sprawling bare fields beyond. Drizzle and churned brown earth belie England's green and pleasant land.

The driver doesn't talk, and I'm grateful for that. He is listening to Johnny Cash, his fingers tapping along on the steering wheel. My mind flickers like the speedometer on his dashboard. I try to assemble my thoughts.

I check the time. It is nearing eleven.

I assemble the facts. I know that my mother was taking Polly to Euro Disney. I try desperately to remember the time they were due back, but in my panic, it escapes me. My mind feels like a giant sieve, or worse, a soup of forgotten facts. I try to concentrate on the things I remember. Emily was taking me away; that's definite. Ostensibly for my birthday, but really, to escape after the disaster at the Lehman Gallery. After Sid lost it. I remember clearly that Sid lost it. Again, and worse than he had for a long time – after I told him he couldn't see Polly for a while. And this is what bothers me now. This is what makes me think he couldn't forgive me.

We have to live life forwards, but can only understand it backwards. Kierkegaard said that some centuries ago; my first mentor John swore by it. I'm still coming to terms with the truth of it now.

I had fallen for Sid's old tricks; I had fallen into *my* old trap. He had sucked me in again, gullible fool that I was. I knew so, so, *so* much better, and still I faltered and ultimately failed in my resolution.

I had wanted to believe, desperately, against all the odds, that this time it would be different. That this time it would work, and it was the right thing, for Polly, to have her parents back together; for me, to be back with the man I'd loved like no one else. The man I could not erase from my DNA, try as I might; he was burnt into my synapses indelibly. The man that I had cared for, literally, since the day I staggered out of bed with him for the first time, already addicted; the man that I— I stumble over the word *mothered*; I hate to admit it even now. Even now it makes me feel nauseous and stupid and weak. But it was true.

The man I had mothered, as well as loved.

But the human heart is fallible. And human flesh is weak.

And Sid *is* beautiful and worse, irrefutably powerful and charming. He learnt charm from an early age, he could switch it on at will. It was his salvation against a lifetime of abuse. Throughout our marriage, whenever he had done wrong, he would wend his way slowly back into my psyche without me even noticing.

Oh, I would defy the strongest character to resist Sid if he decided he wanted you. But he would only ever want you for some deeply personal reason, and it would never be of benefit to anyone but Sid. Only you wouldn't be aware of that – not until it was too late. Not until you were lost.

You couldn't win against Sid. Not really. The decks were stacked; the odds were nil.

The lorry jerks over a pothole. I blink; check the clock again. Add up the hours on my fingers.

How long do I have left?

Maybe I am just panicking. I am in shock, there is no doubt. Then I remember the scene at the gallery – and what came next.

'*I'll kill you, Laurie.*'

'You'll damage yourself in a minute, love.'

I start.

'If you keep doing that,' the driver indicates my hands. I look down. I am jabbing my palm, the un-bandaged one, whilst I've been thinking. 'Don't, love.'

'Bad habit.' I try to smile. I put my hands into my pockets.

'You've been in the wars,' he says.

'Yes,' I agree. It seems pointless not to.

He doesn't ask any more, and I am grateful. I imagine he sees all sorts, out on the road. On the stereo, Johnny Cash is singing Trent Reznor's 'Hurt'. It is the saddest song I think I've ever heard. I itch to turn it off.

'How far are you going?' I ask.

'Turning off at Exeter. I'm headed Exmouth way. Guessing that's not much use to you?'

'No, not really. I'm going to London.'

'I'll drop you at the next junction, before I turn.'

'Thanks.' My heart sinks. I have absolutely no idea where that junction is, but I need to get to London – and soon. 'Thanks a lot.'

He nods. 'Not far now.'

In the wing mirror I watch a red car tearing up the inside lane. I hold my breath.

The car passes us on the inside, cutting across lanes. The lorry driver shakes his head.

'Idiot.'

I remember everything, Cash sings.

I breathe again. I don't want to get out of the lorry.

But how will I get where I need to be quickly enough without calling the police? The police who didn't believe me last time, or the time before …

THEN: MAL

Polly came home on Sunday evening and I was insanely pleased to see her, although by bed-time we were already arguing about Daddy letting her stay up 'much later'. Daddy only had her for a few days every few weeks, I pointed out, which meant he might like to see more of her at night, for a treat, but of course that meant nothing in Polly's world. I didn't add that Sid didn't own a watch, despised time and schedules, and had no inkling or concern about sensible bed-times for small children. That staying up late was far more about him not being bothered to put her to bed than anything less selfish.

Like most parents, I had spent hours of Polly's babyhood yearning for a bit of 'me-time', especially with a husband who often painted right through the night and went to bed at dawn. But as soon as Polly wasn't there, it felt like someone had just chopped my arm off. I'd managed to keep busy: I'd tidied cupboards I never even opened, caught up with my case-loads and my paperwork, tramped round the park wondering if the rather desperate way I wished Polly was with me now meant I was co-dependent with my own child. Sometimes being a counsellor wasn't healthy for one's own psyche. I collected a pocketful of the prickliest horse chestnuts in the vague hope the barbs would make me forget my own pain; I put my headphones on and listened to Maria Callas very loud in the hope she'd drown out the incessant chatter of my mind. It didn't really work.

But slowly, life after Sid resumed normally again. Or rather – a different normal. I avoided my husband as best I could. I missed him too, desperately sometimes, but seeing him was horribly painful, so I tried my hardest not to. I kept our contact to the bare minimum and occasionally on a bad day, when I couldn't face it at all, I would ask my mother or Emily to do the hand-over.

One Sunday I spotted a photograph in the papers of Sid and the beautiful Jolie out on the town. I was incredulous to see their matching outfits, her all eyes and silvery extensions, him beautiful but glowering. Sid hated the press passionately. I gazed at their Hilfiger hoodies and their long leather coats, no doubt designer-wear; it seemed only marginally less stupid than the picture of him on an old Enfield bike the week before, lip curling scornfully before his latest canvas. No doubt a ploy of the pernicious Randolph as award season approached: perhaps Randolph thought it evoked shades of a young Brando. Or was Sid simply trying to recapture his lost youth?

Whatever the truth, I laughed until I caught my reflection in the mirror and realised I looked like a mad woman. I pulled out the photo and threw it on the fire.

Back at the Centre, I was inundated with new clients referred through the NHS; the current recession and bleak days creating a boom time for divorce, anxiety and depression. I'd returned the Spanish house key to Robert along with a picture Polly had drawn him. 'It's the most beautiful place,' I said. 'I really appreciated the mates' rates, Rob, it was so kind.' I pulled a face. 'Bit skint now since Sid and I … since, you know.'

Separated. The word still stuck in my throat.

'You and me both, love.' Glum, Robert searched the cupboard for a teabag. 'That house is a bloody luxury these days. Putting an ad in the Centre newsletter's been a godsend, at least. Got a few bookings through it already from various branches.'

'Is that a good idea?' I raised an eyebrow. 'Do you really want clients out there?' Robert was an acupuncturist who specialised in addictions. 'You could do a special offer I suppose: recovery sessions plus sun and sangria.'

'Don't be daft.' He looked faintly annoyed. 'Boundaries and all that.'

'It was a joke.' I passed him a mug. 'Not a very good one, admittedly. None of my business, of course.'

'Well, it's a fair comment, I suppose.' He dug out a box of camomile tea. 'But we need the income to keep it going. Liz hates the idea, but she's looking at redundancy and I need to drum up some business or it's back on the market – and then we'd both be gutted.'

'Yes, well, I can see why. All that light and air. Good for the soul.'

'And God knows our souls need feeding, eh?' he winked at me. 'As long as we've got it, you're always welcome to rent it cheap, lovie. No problem.'

I found myself going to Robin's Café most days, but I didn't see the man again. After a few weeks, I gave up the idea I'd see him again.

Sid came to collect Polly one Saturday morning. He was driving a Porsche. An old one, but a Porsche nonetheless.

'Given up your *Communist Review* subscription then?' I eyed the car over his shoulder. Sid was unshaven, his old jeans covered in smears of oil paint, brilliant greens and blues, which meant he was in an 'up' period. The down periods saw browns, greys and black; the colours of sludge. I looked closer at him. Handsome as ever, maybe, but his green eyes were slitty and bloodshot and he smelt of cigarettes and stale alcohol. Less up, more wired.

'Daddy!' Polly was there, in her scarlet coat, excitedly hanging off the door handle. 'Can I watch *Kung Fu Panda* again tonight?'

I was surprised Sid would stoop to a cartoon. He was nothing if not esoteric, my husband.

'I should think so.' Sid picked her up and kissed her rosy face. They looked so alike, it sometimes wrenched at my heart.

Soon-to-be-ex-husband.

'Daddy lets me watch telly in bed.' Polly was proud, patting her father's cheek. 'Till I fall asleep, actually.'

I wondered what he was doing whilst she was watching cartoons.

'Yes, well, perhaps she could actually go to sleep *before* midnight.' It was out before I could stop it. Petty bourgeois, Sid would throw at me any second. Quickly, I kissed Polly's mop. 'See you tomorrow, baby.'

Basics Rule One: don't argue in front of the kids.

Sid raised an eyebrow at me. 'Laurie, darling,' he drawled, 'when did you get so fucking pedestrian?'

'Don't swear.' Resisting the temptation to shove him down the stairs, I shot back into the house before Polly saw my face. 'Have fun, Pol. Oh, and, Sid,' I couldn't help it. '*Please* make her wear her seat-belt.'

Five minutes later, the doorbell rang again.

It was Sid. 'I meant to say,' he was lounging against the porch wall, Polly behind him in the car, absorbed in some game on his mobile phone.

'Yes?' For a long time, I thought he still gave me butterflies, but recently I'd realised it was simply cortisol. Not love, just stress hormone.

'I've sorted out an estate agent. He'll be round on Monday to value and photograph the house.'

I stared at the man I'd shared everything with for eight years. He held my gaze and for a second I thought I read guilt, but instead of an apology, he just smiled nastily.

'He'll call you first. If you can ever find your phone.'

I shut the door hard in his face and leant against it, waiting for my heart to slow, waiting until the noisy old Porsche had pulled off. I looked balefully at my phone on the hall table, the phone I could apparently never find. No calls, no texts, no messages: no one.

Resolutely I grabbed my coat and bag, resisting the temptation to switch a computer on and surf Facebook. I would not sit tearfully in the empty house – apparently not mine for much longer – and mourn my bloody marriage.

I stomped over the square to the café, to life and people.

'Haven't seen you for a bit,' Robin was ever cheerful. 'Coffee?'

'Yes, thanks. And a huge piece of chocolate cake please. A really big one. With extra cream.'

'Oh dear,' Robin was sympathetic. 'That kind of day.'

'Yes,' I pulled a face. 'Exactly that kind of day.'

I had lost myself in the cake and a chapter about Freud's professional and sexual jealousy of Carl Jung when a voice spoke above me.

'Hello again.'

I dropped my chocolatey fork on the floor.

'Oh God, I'm sorry.' The man with the light eyes. 'You're very jumpy, aren't you?'

'I am a bit,' I agreed. Nervous wreck, he no doubt thought. He scooped up the fork and went through to Robin, returning with a new one that he handed me.

'Thanks. Please, have some cake,' I said, without thinking. 'I can't eat it all anyway.'

'Really?'

I nodded slowly, already regretting my haste. 'Yes, please – if you'd like.'

'I would like,' he sat down. 'Thanks.'

At least this time the table was bigger so our knees weren't jammed so intimately against each other. As soon as he sat, my mind went blank.

'Do you come here often?' I said, and then felt daft.

He grinned. 'Not really – but I'm planning to.'

'Sorry,' I said, embarrassed. 'I was being … silly.'

'I like silly,' he said. 'Silly's good, in my book.'

Cursing my thin skin, I tried not to blush.

'Mal Cooper,' he offered his hand.

'Laurie Smith,' I took it, looked at him properly. He looked … healthy, somehow. Totally different to Sid, who was pale, interesting and constantly dishevelled. This man was scrubbed and fresh, slightly tanned – and strangely familiar somehow.

'So, you live nearby?'

'Yes, with my daughter.' I felt odd saying that. 'But not with her dad.' Oh God. 'I mean, we used to. Live together.' *Shut up now, Laurie.* I spent my days counselling people in situations like mine, yet when it came to my own life, I could barely speak. 'Have you got kids?' I blundered on. I looked at his finger. No wedding ring. But … was there a slight indent on his left hand? A narrow stripe of paler skin where it should have been?

He was still talking.

I shook myself. 'Sorry.'

'I was saying, yes. One boy.'

'How old?'

'Just seven.'

'Nice age. Polly's six.'

'What school does she go to?'

'St Bede's.'

'Oh, we're hoping to get Leonard in there. We've left it a bit late though. We're having to schlep right across town at the moment.'

We. I popped the most extravagantly-iced piece of cake in my mouth and began to gather my things.

'Well, I must get going actually.' I was falsely bright. 'Please, finish the cake.'

'When I say we, I mean my ex and I.'

Did I relax visibly? I sat back for a moment. There was no rush, I supposed. 'I see. So what brought you here?'

'Work, really. That and the need for a change.'

'What do you do?'

'I'm in IT.'

'Oh right.' Dull. But safe. 'I'm not very …' I searched for a polite way of saying it, 'good with computers—'

'Interested in them, you mean.' He smiled. 'Why would you be? Pretty boring things really.'

'You said it.' I smiled back. 'Not me.'

'Doesn't mean we're all boring though. The IT crowd.'

'Oh, very good.'

'I try my best. And I do love that show.'

'Yeah, it's good. So where do you work?'

'In the city. I'd rather work in the countryside, I think. I must be getting old. The city's so … I don't know. Full on, sometimes.'

'Yes, I know what you mean. So, whereabouts? No, let me guess. Canary Wharf?'

'Bank actually. Near the actual Bank of England.'

'That sounds very posh.'

'It's not.' His hand hovered over the last piece of cake. 'Not posh at all. Just lots of suits.'

'And money. Have it,' I pushed the plate towards him.

'Fake money. If you insist,' he grinned, and polished it off before I could. His phone beeped. 'Sorry,' he checked it quickly. 'Got to collect Leonard. My day.'

'No worries.' I wrinkled my nose. 'Something I'm getting used to, this single parent-dom.'

'It's hard, isn't it? Takes some getting used to indeed.' He stood now, buttoning his jacket. 'It was very nice to meet you properly, er …' he looked abashed. 'Oh God, sorry.'

'It's okay. It's Laurie.'

'Of course,' he clapped a dramatic hand to his head. 'I'm rubbish with names.'

'It's fine, really.'

As he turned to go, I spoke in a splurge. 'Er, Mal, I was just thinking, it just crossed my mind, if you wanted, if you ever wanted to do something with the kids – well …'

'I'd love that,' his ruddy face lit up. 'Why don't we arrange something now?'

'Oh, right.' His alacrity took me aback a little. 'Yes, we could, I guess …'

'Next weekend? Do you have your daughter?'

'Yeah, I do.' I didn't want to come here though. Too small, too intimate, too many people I knew. 'We could go to the Toy Museum. On the south side of the park?'

'Fantastic. I've been meaning to since we moved. It looks fun.'

'Great.' Did my voice sound wobbly? 'Saturday or Sunday?'

'Saturday's better for me'.

'Fine. Meet you there at – what,' why did I feel so flustered? 'Er, just after lunch?'

'Cool. Two suit you?'

'Two it is. See you there.'

As he left, a flurry of rain slung itself against the window. I was glad I was safely inside.

NOW: HOUR 4

12pm

At the service station I thank the driver and swing down from the cab, back into the damp grey day. It is freezing; I wrap the over-sized coat around me tighter.

Inside, glad of the warmth, I buy a cheese sandwich and sit in the cafeteria section. I stare at my new mobile phone, willing it to ring. I want to speak to my mother. At the age of thirty-six, I really want my mother. But I also want my mother to stay wherever she is, with Polly. To keep her safe.

My instinct is bothering me; my head is chattering. I would like to know where Sid is right now. One part of me says: ring him, check. Is he in the vicinity? I think of the last time I saw Sid, and I remember his fury: a blaze of pure emotion, scorching anyone in range.

Has he been called to the hospital? He won't go, I am certain of that. He has a deep dread of the institution, born of his turbulent childhood. I am safe until—

Until someone sees Emily's broken body and realises it's not me …

Until the newspapers pick it up …

Until …

I bite my lip to stop the thoughts of Emily. I need to concentrate. There will be time to mourn – if I make it out of this mess alive.

I twist my ring round and round my finger. I should have tried to sell or pawn it when I had the chance, back in the town, but it hadn't even occurred to me then. A ring worth thousands of pounds; one of the few beautiful things Sid bought for me, after he made his first million.

On Polly's fourth birthday, he made us all breakfast in bed – which was a rarity in itself. We'd been fighting badly. He'd been away so much, suddenly so feted and revered, he just couldn't acclimatise to life at home. And he found the media attention an immense pressure. He was wary, he didn't really trust anyone; my wounded Sid.

That morning, propped up on my pillows in our enormous new bed, still half asleep, I bit down on my spoon of cornflakes and nearly took my tooth out. Polly thought it was hilarious as first I dribbled milk from my mouth – followed by a diamond ring. Turning it over in my hand, wiping the milk away, I couldn't be cross about my sore teeth. It was the kind of gesture so rare from Sid that it mattered a lot. Not ostentatious; Sid was too classy for bling, but wildly expensive; princess-cut diamonds set in platinum.

Today, it's the only jewellery I still wear. I took off my wedding ring – but I can't bear to part with this; I'm still tied to it emotionally. It marks a little pocket of time when I was truly happy.

Maybe that's what life is. Just precious little pockets of time we must cherish, to get us through the grey days.

Gazing out into the grey day, I see a police car parked outside. They must be in here somewhere. I realise I have been panicking; acting like a paranoid fool. I need to talk to someone, explain this mistaken identity. The police are not my greatest fans, apparently, but still …

I make a decision.

I am imagining it all, obviously. I, of all people, know about shock and its effects. Deluded, I've managed to convince myself that someone is after me – but surely that is rubbish. There was an accident. A very horrible accident and my beloved Emily is dead, but that is all it was. *An accident.* Tears start in my eyes. I blink them away and wait by the window for the police to return to their vehicle.

A big black motorbike enters the car park from the far end, driving slowly towards the building in which I am sitting.

I feel a strange tightening in my chest: a flash of memory.

A big bike roaring down the motorway on the inside of our car. Emily is driving. She is increasingly flustered. 'Fuck off,' she's saying to the faceless biker, who can't hear her. She flaps her hand at the window, gesturing for him to go away.

'Emily,' I am saying. The car is starting to swerve. 'Concentrate.'

Now I see a stocky policeman striding out across the forecourt, eating a burger. I have a memory of talking to a different policeman in the last few days. Sitting next to Emily, in a small, provincial police station, drinking tea from polystyrene, talking to him about my fear and feeling indignant; sensing he was simply bored. But Emily wasn't sure either. It was me who was truly worried.

I knew who it was on that bike, chasing our car.

I stand. The blood is starting to pump fast round my body. I feel light-headed.

The motorbike is pulling in, the driver's booted foot on the tarmac now.

My sandwich falls to the floor as I move away from the window so the driver can't see me. My heart bangs painfully in my chest. I *am* correct; something *is* very wrong. It all adds up.

And I need to reach Polly. Before he does.

I leave from the back entrance and into the car park for the heavy vehicles. I look for a driver. Any driver will do.

I need to get out of here – fast.

THEN: MEETING MAL AGAIN

By Friday, I was seriously regretting not having got Mal's number. Our house had gone on the market and Sid still hadn't given me any money for Polly, so I was anticipating problems as I prepared to talk to a solicitor. Worse than that, work had been horrible all week, compounded by two incredibly traumatised Sudanese girls at the Refugee Centre. They had been horribly raped back in Darfur, but were now being threatened with deportation. None of the phone calls I made on their behalf to the authorities were being answered, and I felt futile and hopeless about their situation.

As the weekend rolled round, I just wanted to hunker down in the warm with Polly and watch old musicals. I certainly didn't want to meet Mal; God only knew what I'd been thinking, and I didn't want Polly to have to play with his son, but short of not turning up, I had no way of contacting him to cancel.

So on Saturday we ate a hasty plate of beans on toast and then, with Polly on her scooter, made our way to the south gate of the park to meet the Coopers. I decided I'd tell Mal that we had a sudden new appointment, that Polly had to be somewhere that afternoon that we couldn't get out of, so we would only have time to spend an hour or so together.

But when we arrived, Mal was already waiting – apparently alone.

'No Leonard?' I said as cheerily as I could, watching Polly scoot round and round the naked flowerbed.

'His mother's being difficult,' he said, hands in pockets. He seemed awkward and ill-at-ease now we were outside the café, and I noticed what a sprawling, large bear of a man he was as we stood together, stamping our feet against the sudden cold. 'She gets quite possessive.'

'Well, no worries,' my sense of relief was huge and I tried not to show it. 'We can do it another time.'

His face brightened. 'Can we? Fantastic.'

I wondered if I could get away with leaving immediately.

'Shall we grab a quick coffee?' he said, rather forlorn.

I looked at Polly who, having presented me proudly with some bedraggled feathers 'for your collection, Mummy', was now desperately trying to entice a curious squirrel nearer with half a stale Hula Hoop and some fluff from her coat pocket. I looked back at Mal. He smiled, and I remembered what a nice face he had.

'Sure,' we were near the park's Tea Pavilion. 'Shall we just pop in here?'

After a row with a rather squawky Polly about whether she was allowed fizzy or plain orange juice, during which I tried my utmost to keep my cool and not be the kind of mother who raised her voice or acquiesced immediately just for a quiet life, the three of us settled in a corner.

'It's such a nice park,' Mal gazed out over the bandstand, warming his hands on his mug of tea. 'Kind of cosy.'

'It is, isn't it,' I agreed.

'Much smaller than the huge park we had back home.' He looked almost guilty for a second. 'I mean, back near our old place.'

'I'm bored,' Polly announced loudly. She fixed me with her blue stare.

'Drink your juice,' I returned the stare.

'You blinked first,' Polly guffawed, and turned her attention to her biscuit.

'Sorry, Mal. So, where was home?' Adding a sugar-lump to my coffee, I contemplated a second. Such decadence.

'St Albans.'

'Can I go outside, Mummy?' Polly finished removing the filling from the biscuit and laid the remnants down with disdain, her mouth ringed in chocolate. 'I want to see how many times I can scoot round the café in five minutes. Can you time me?'

'If you promise to stay where I can see you. And wipe your mouth.'

'Promise.' She was already off; banging out of the wooden doors.

'Sorry.'

'God, don't apologise. I know exactly what it's like.'

'Lovely, but exhausting!' We smiled at each other. 'So, that's a bit of a change. From St Albans to North London.'

'Susie – my ex – she forced the issue. It was all a bit sudden – over the holidays.'

'How come?'

'She works for a bank. She transferred branches, and I followed her, basically. To be near Leonard. But I didn't mind leaving, to be honest. It was her family who were near us there, not mine. Her sister, anyway.'

'I know St Albans quite well actually. Nice town.' I resisted the sugar-lump and offered Mal a Bourbon instead.

'No, thanks.' He refused it. 'How do you know it?'

'I did my first placement over there. The Centre was affiliated to the University of Middlesex. This one is too.'

'Training?'

'Yeah, I'm a psychotherapist. A counsellor.'

'Oh really? We did a bit of that once. Susie and I.' He pulled a face. 'When things first started to go wrong.'

'A bit of …?'

'You know. Talking to someone. Counselling. At the Vale Centre, I think it was called. About five years ago.' He looked sheepish. 'Susie had very bad post-natal depression after we had Leonard. Very bad.'

'That's the place I mean. Where I finished my training,' I was enthusiastic. 'The Vale Centre. It's our sister centre.'

'She hated it actually, my ex. She blamed it for our split. The counselling. But I thought it was helpful.' He met my eye. 'In terms of trying to communicate better.'

'Yes, well, it's not for everyone. Sometimes people just aren't ready to look at their stuff.' I did my empathetic face. 'But how funny that you went there. It really is a small world, isn't it?'

My own words echoed peculiarly in my ears. We gazed at each other for a moment.

'Oh my God.' I felt a horrible burning sensation. 'Oh bloody hell. We've met before, haven't we? I *thought* you looked familiar.'

I had a memory of a big light room at the Centre, of sitting behind my mentor John Sheppard; of a couple, a woman, crying. 'Your wife,' I cleared my throat, feeling suddenly hot. 'Is she … does she have long, red hair?'

'Yes,' he nodded. He looked thoroughly rattled. Shaky even. 'Yes, she does. Bloody hell indeed. How… odd.'

I tried to laugh; I didn't want him to feel embarrassed, although I felt ridiculous myself. I had felt I'd seen him before … I just wish I'd remembered where rather sooner.

'It really is a small world,' I repeated pathetically, draining my coffee and standing decisively.

Outside, Polly whizzed round and round without a care in the world, curls and scarf flying behind her.

'Laurie, please. Do you have to go?' he wasn't smiling now, he was just looking at me intently. I looked away first.

'Duty calls,' I pointed at Polly, who chose that moment to go flying head over heels, face-first onto the path. 'Oh God—'

I banged through the doors to pick her up. Her knee was bleeding quite badly, one cheek was grazed – and of course, she was howling.

Mal followed and stood behind us. As I hugged Polly, quietly he handed me a hanky.

I mopped her up as best as I could and then, standing again, slightly panicked, I held out my hand to him, clutching Polly's scooter in the other. He leant forward and kissed my cheek before I could step back. He still smelt of fresh air, just like he had the last time.

'Laurie. Would you …' he stopped. 'It's just, I'd really like to get to know some people in the area. Maybe we could try again—'

'Sorry.' I gathered Polly nearer, propelling her towards the gate. 'I just think, you know, given the circumstances, it's a bit … I mean, normally, I'd love to, but you know …'

He looked sad, but I saw, with relief, he wasn't going to argue.

'Thank you for the coffee,' I said formally. 'We'll see you – say bye, Polly.'

'Bye,' she snuffled.

'Bye, love,' he said, trying to smile convincingly. He failed.

My face was hot as we made our way to the gate, and I felt his eyes on me, though when I finally dared glance behind, he had gone. I kicked myself for my stupidity, although the truth was I hadn't even really counselled them as a couple; I'd only been sitting in on a preliminary session. I hadn't even been qualified at the time. What were the chances of running into him now? It was true; the world was ever-shrinking.

Still, I hoped I hadn't made him feel embarrassed, running away like an idiot.

Along the road by the gate, someone got into a red car and revved the engine loudly, making me jump. I really needed to get control of my nerves. I couldn't wait to get us home.

NOW: HOUR 5

1pm

I jerk awake in the cabin of the lorry, disoriented.

'Sorry,' I say, to no one in particular, looking for Polly. She is not there.

'Don't apologise, love.' This driver is not as nice as the last. He has a huge gut that almost rests on his thighs, pock-marked cheeks and a look in his eye that makes me nervous. Photos of naked, big-breasted girls are taped to his dashboard and ceiling; the ones on the ceiling are not wearing pants. I try not to look up.

'Great view when you're having a quick kip,' he winks at the ceiling, his Welsh accent thick. He smells like he's been on the road for a long time. 'We all need to lie down sometimes, know what I mean?'

'Where are we?' Looking out at the grey horizon, I realise we are not on the motorway anymore; we are on a dual carriageway in an unknown landscape. Panic rises in my chest. 'I need to get to London.'

'Don't worry. You will. I just need to make a quick detour.'

'Why?'

'None of your business, girlie,' he winks again, but his look is less friendly now. He doesn't like being questioned. 'Man about a dog.'

'I need to get to London really soon.'

'Well you should have got the train then, shouldn't you?'

I think of all the refugee girls I have worked with; of how vulnerable they are when they are on the run. Of the predators, mostly male, who hound them constantly.

'Can you set me down somewhere?' I ask. My voice is coming back slowly, but my hand really hurts; my shoulder throbs where I slammed into the hotel door again and again. I realise that my bedraggled appearance is making me appear vulnerable; that to this man, I probably seem like easy prey.

'No, I can't stop,' the driver leers at me. 'You don't want to go anywhere, girlie. Stick with me.'

I visualise my daughter. I have never ever wanted something so badly. I imagine her small, warm solidity; the smell of her hair, the way she sticks her tongue out when she is concentrating, the way she guffaws when you tickle her. I concentrate on her image. It is why I need to keep going.

'Please,' I am almost shouting. 'I need to get to London. Just drop me anywhere. If you don't ...' I fumble for the mobile in my pocket, 'I will call the police.'

But I think about the policemen in that little station on our way to the hotel. I think about the lugubrious duo at the hospital with their list. I think about the police officer in London who didn't believe I had an intruder; the same one who thought I'd invented it when Polly went missing. I have lost my faith in them, I realise.

The driver's mouth clamps shut like a letterbox. The lorry slows. I prepare to jump down.

In the wing mirror, I see a red car behind us.

'Actually,' I hold the mobile so tight my hand hurts. 'Take me a bit further please.'

'Make your fucking mind up,' he snarls.

'Sorry,' I mutter, slithering down in the seat, watching the red car, not daring to so much as blink. 'I'll get out at the next town.'

'Yeah you will, and it'll be good fucking riddance.'

I haven't seen the motorbike again – but the car is still behind us.

THEN: THE CAFÉ

I didn't tell anyone about my encounter with Mal – not even Emily.

I felt deeply embarrassed by it, as if I had done something bad, something I shouldn't have. I buried myself in work; in particular pursuing the Sudanese case. Working with refugees was fast becoming my main area of interest. I had always enjoyed the couples' counselling, but recently it made me feel rather hopeless, and too close to home, watching as yet another relationship sailed perilously close to the rocks. I recognised these feelings were likely to be triggered by my own recent history, and I spoke to Bev, my first supervisor and my mentor, about it, and a little about Sid.

But I wasn't ready really to delve deeper into my own marriage; it still felt too raw and painful. I knew Bev would want to talk about my father again and I couldn't face that at the moment. Let me lick my wounds for a bit, I said, and she smiled and said *When you're ready, Laurie. Just don't leave it too long.* We both knew the implication was that it could affect my work badly.

The weekend after my unfortunate tea with Mal, Sid went to Paris. He didn't tell me why, but one evening driving Polly home, the chirpy Radio One DJ told us that Jolie was playing a gig at Versailles. With a shudder and to loud protestations from my daughter, I turned over quickly to something rather less painful.

On the Saturday morning Polly and I went to collect conkers in the park, and I tried hard to 'stay in the moment': tried and failed. Tried *not* to think of my reconciliation with Sid last year, of the entire weekend we had spent fucking in the George V's most lavish suite after Charles Saatchi had bought Sid's 'Madonna Eats Eve' series for a cool million or three.

The truth was, Sid had slipped away from me ever faster since he'd hit the dizzy heights, winning the Turner Prize two years ago as the rank outsider, immediately generating a media frenzy. He was more bewildered than I'd ever known him, and conversely more angry and haunted, but I simply couldn't give him my undivided attention; immersed in Polly starting nursery and a burning need to focus on my own work more, now I had some time for it.

But there were always consequences when Sid wanted something and didn't get it. He started staying out all night with his cohorts, drinking too much Scotch, smoking too many cigarettes. His work, ever dark, became darker. His demons were chasing him, snapping at his heels; especially since one of his brothers had contacted him after seeing Sid on the news winning the Turner. Ostensibly he wanted a reunion; in reality, he was only after money.

The night after the call, I'd found Sid curled up asleep on Polly's floor at the foot of her bed. I tried to wake him; he punched me in the face. I didn't think he'd meant to hurt me – he wasn't even properly awake, he'd just lashed out unconsciously – but I'd ended up with stitches in my split lip.

The next day, Sid caused the most enormous argument, accusing me of not loving him, of fancying other men, of preferring Polly to him – all provoked by his own guilt. He'd disappeared into the night, came back in the early hours when we were sleeping, packed a bag and disappeared to Paris for his opening at the Galerie Yvon Lambert.

'*You're better off without me*', his note said simply.

I didn't know what to do. I was worried about him, but I was also furious. He was behaving like a child. But he *was* a child really, I had come to understand that during our relationship; an arrested child.

In the end, my mother decided it for me. Out of the blue, she asked if she could take Polly to visit my auntie Val in Leeds. Agreeing, I delivered Polly to school on Friday morning, did my morning clinic, and then on a complete whim, bought myself a Eurostar ticket and arrived unannounced in Paris. Exhausted, mentally and physically, by the time I arrived at Sid's hotel, I tucked myself up in the huge bed in his palatial suite and slept until he woke me around midnight, arriving back from dinner with the dreaded Randolph.

It was a little like the first weekend we'd spent together, although this time there was a sense of absolute desperation about it, an underlying urgency that had not been there when we first met. We knew so much about each other now, and we bore the scars – but Sid was happier to see me than I remembered him being in a very long time. Years, maybe.

I didn't realise it would be one of our last weekends together.

'You can put these with your other nature things on the fire shelf.' She meant the mantelpiece. Depositing another load of conkers into my coat pocket, Polly brought me out of my reverie. 'Can we go for hot chocolate now?'

Going to Robin's on a Saturday morning had long been a family tradition, but right now it was one I felt extremely wary about.

'Gosh, look at this one,' I picked out the shiniest conker. 'We can put it on a string.'

'Why?' Polly looked confused. 'So, can we? Go to the café?'

'Oh I don't know, Pol.' I stroked the surface so smooth it looked polished. 'I'm not sure we've got time before we meet Emily.'

'Please, Mummy. I want to see Bernard.' Bernard was the café dachshund. 'We haven't been for ages. Please!'

She pleaded so fervently that in the end I gave in. Relieved to find the place half-empty, I texted Emily to meet us there and read articles about the bankers' bonuses and what I *could* have been wearing this season if those very bankers hadn't deprived us of half our incomes, whilst Polly, tongue firmly out in concentration, drew pictures of the little dog for Sid.

A new waitress served us, a thin-faced Spanish girl who admired Polly's picture and the fact that she could say '*Cómo estás*'?' I was less enamoured when the girl put on Jolie's new CD – marketed as soulful folky funk by *NME*, and Jolie as an heir to Winehouse, apparently, according to the cover on the counter – and sang vigorously at the coffee machine whilst frothing the milk. I felt even worse when Polly knew the words – something along highly inappropriate and frankly awful lines like, 'Baby I walk alone until you explode in me, then I walk amongst the stars.'

Just as I could bear no more, Robin arrived from the cash and carry. 'I'm glad I caught you, Laurie.' She dumped a box of frozen croissants on the table. 'You have a fan.'

'A fan?' Emily had followed her in, all scarves and long velvet coat. She was in a *Doctor Who* phase, I could tell; ever the drama student, despite her sensible job at the council. She raised an eyebrow at me.

'That nice new guy, Mal. He left his number for you.' Robin scooped a stack of polystyrene cups up. 'Said something about having lost yours.'

'Oh,' I knew I was blushing and I hated myself.

'I'll just find it for you. I put it somewhere sa—'

'Oh don't worry, Robin. I'll get it next time.'

'Do worry actually, thanks, Robin,' Emily shoved me in the small of my back. 'She'd love the number.'

'I really wouldn't,' I mumbled. I'd never given him mine in the first place, anyway.

The problem was solved by Robin not being able to find the piece of paper Mal had written it on. 'Sorry,' she grimaced. 'I'll get it off him next time he comes in.'

'It's fine,' I said, infinitely relieved. 'Really.'

'Brilliant,' Emily said. 'Do that, Robin.'

'I feel sick,' Polly said, who had somehow consumed cake and ice-cream *and* hot chocolate without me really noticing.

I shepherded my daughter out with a growing sense of unease. I had thought Mal would just disappear, and although part of me was flattered by his persistence, a bigger part was increasingly disturbed. And I wasn't used to being 'single'. I wasn't single, was I – I was still married. I caught myself thinking, '*What will happen if Sid finds out?*', and then remembering that what I did was no longer Sid's business anyway.

But my instinct said that it wouldn't be that simple. In his head, it would be fine for Sid to have a new partner, but somehow I didn't see him accepting anyone into my life that easily … And anyway, I couldn't see Mal again, romantically or not. It would be unethical, to say the least.

Of course, I was right about Sid. I just didn't anticipate quite *how* violently he'd hate it.

NOW: HOUR 6

2pm

The lorry veers off at a truck stop just outside the next town, which is called Sherborne, I think, to judge from the road signs. To my huge relief, the red car that's been behind us carries on.

I climb down without a goodbye to the driver; he doesn't look like he cares, mutters something obviously obnoxious in what I assume is Welsh as I slam the door behind me.

I go into the rather smelly caff. I can see from the clock emblazoned with a winking pin-up girl that it's already 2pm. If I have recalled right, I have just six hours to get to Polly before Sid does. It is of the utmost importance to me that I get there first, rational or not.

There is a policeman in leathers at the counter, drinking a cup of tea. I pause in my tracks for a moment, and then I go to him.

'Please, sir,' and I think of Oliver Twist; plaintive, hands extended. 'I need your help.'

The policeman looks at me from his perch on the stool. He is quite handsome, tall and grey-haired, and I feel reassured for a moment. His radio crackles into life. 'Hang on a sec, madam,' he says and stands; steps away. How polite we are, even in a crisis.

I wait. My attention is diverted suddenly as I think I hear my name.

There is a television talking to itself, hung high in a corner in the café. I step nearer to it; *Sky News* is on, the ticker-tape of rolling news across the bottom bears my name. The screen is filled with an aerial shot of a partially burnt-out white building, surrounded by a park and woodland, smoke still billowing gently across the lawns. These shots are followed by stills of two men I don't recognise, and then footage of Sid accepting his award at the Turner Prize two years ago flashes up. I am in the crowd somewhere in front, clapping my husband, but I am invisible. They have no image of me.

'*We have just learnt that the third victim of the Forest Lodge fire is believed to be Laurie Smith, estranged wife of artist Sid Smith. Smith made his name with the* Jesus, Mary and the Sin *sculpture he so famously placed in St Peter's Square, Rome, in 2010, causing his own arrest and an international furore. The Catholic Church took huge offence at the suggestion that Jesus and Mary might have had an incestuous relationship.*

"It's art, not reality," a contemptuous Smith said at the time, although he made his name and a considerable fortune from the first in a string of controversial works. Smith is believed to have recently left his wife for the young blues singer Jolie Jones. Police are refusing to confirm reports, although we know from hotel staff that Laurie Smith was staying at the Spa with friend Emily Southern. Miss Southern is believed to have escaped with minor injuries; so far Sid Smith has been unavailable for comment. The couple have a six-year-old daughter together, Polly Blue ... More news as we get it.'

I stare at the immaculate presenter. At least I have bought myself a little time, I think. But my chest is tightening and I am verging on a panic attack, I can feel it rising in me.

The policeman is coming back. 'Bad business,' he indicates the screen, talking to the raddled woman behind the counter. 'Lucky there weren't more dead.'

'How did it start?' She refills his cup.

'Not sure,' he shrugs. 'One of those two women didn't put a fag out properly, I'm guessing. Pissed, they were, apparently.'

'What women?' She takes a desultory swipe at the grease on the stainless steel worktop.

'The stupid bint that's dead.'

'Bit harsh, Mike,' the woman's laugh quickly descends into a terrible rattling cough. 'Don't speak ill of, etcetera.'

'Well,' he is angry, righteous with it. 'It wasn't just herself that she killed, was it? And if you will smoke …' He looks at her pointedly.

'Point taken,' she chucks the J-Cloth back into the sink behind her. I walk back towards them.

'So, love,' the policeman remembers me now. *Stupid bint*, I think. 'How can I help you?'

'We don't smoke,' I want to shout, outraged. 'Neither me or Emily smoke. We're not to blame.'

But I don't say that: what can I say that will make sense? '*I am that woman they are talking about on the news, I am not dead but I am frightened for my life?*' I see from the speculative way he is looking at me already he will only think I am mad.

So instead, I say, 'My car broke down. I need a lift to the train station please. I need to get to London.'

'Broke down?' he looks at me, still appraising me. 'Where? Shall I take you back there? Have you not got roadside cover?'

But of course there is no car. I re-think my story. 'Actually,' I laugh nervously, 'I had a row with my boyfriend. He drove off.'

'A row?' I can see him wondering now about the scratches on my face, my bandaged hand.

I think of Sid, of the fights with Sid.

'Yes, it's nothing, really, just a silly row, but I need to get home. Back to London. I have to meet my daughter.'

'I can take you,' the woman says, retying her straw-like pony-tail with an elastic band. 'I'm finishing in five minutes. Driving into Sherborne. Early Christmas shopping – before our Richard spends it all on the gee-gees.' She rolls her eyes to heaven. 'Drop you at the station if you like.'

'Thanks,' I say, 'that'd be great.'

The policeman's phone rings: he moves away to answer it. Something about an urgent call from a farm a few miles away. 'Gotta go,' he says, returning.

I wait for the woman who has disappeared into the back now, but I am thinking about Polly. I am thinking that I need to do something urgently.

'Please,' I follow the policeman outside. 'I am ... I haven't been totally honest.'

'Oh?' he reaches for his helmet from his motorbike. 'About what?'

'I am ...' I take a deep breath. 'I was at Forest Lodge. My daughter, Polly Smith ... my husband Sid – he's the ... you know, the artist, and anyway – I think someone's trying to kill me. I need to get to my daughter. She's on the train, I think, coming back from—'

'Stop,' he holds up a hand. 'You're not making any sense. What are you on about?'

'I'm Laurie Smith.'

He looks at me again. 'Laurie Smith is dead.' He points at the tea-hut. 'They've just said that on the TV. She's dead, in the fire. You were listening to it. So, sorry – but *who* are you?'

'*I'm* Laurie Smith.'

'So, what are you doing here?' his face hardens. 'Because if you *are* Laurie Smith, you're wanted for suspected arson.'

And who is Laurie Smith anyway, I wonder. Where did that girl go? The one who fell in love with the man who had been ir-

reparably hurt by his own past, the one who had almost been ruined by her own father's lack of love. The one who always loved
the wrong boys at school, who learnt nothing from Emily's great
confidence; who couldn't see it was the men she picked, not her.
The one who held Sid's hand so tight at her wedding because it
felt like a second chance; a new beginning. The start of something – not a descent into madness. The one who used to feel
hopeful. Where is that Laurie?

It feels like I am dreaming with my eyes open. Any minute
I will wake up.

The policeman's radio crackles again; he speaks into it. 'Six-
seventy, receiving.' He looks at me with contempt, shakes his
head. 'I'd get your story straight if I was you, love. Broken-down
cars, arguments with boyfriends, famous husbands.' He slams
his visor down. 'There's a word for women like you.' He kicks
the bike-stand up and roars off through a puddle. Muddy water
splashes my already-damp legs.

'Sexy git, in't he?' the waitress is standing behind me, lighting
a fag. She coughs. 'I would, wouldn't you? And you wouldn't
blame me if you saw my Richard in his Y-fronts.' She pulls a
face, and without waiting for an answer, heads for her car. 'You
coming then, or what?'

Or what? I follow her to a rusty maroon Capri that looks
older than she does.

Laurie Smith is wanted for arson?

There is no what.

THEN: LEONARD

Dropping Polly at school the following week later, feeling harassed because we were even later than usual, I thought I heard my name being called across the playground.

'I'm going to get a late mark,' Polly's lower lip was trembling precariously and I refrained from pointing out that if she hadn't insisted on changing her entire outfit at the last minute because her woolly tights were too 'frizzy' against her skin, we would have been on time.

'You'll be fine.' Dispatching her up the stairs to her classroom with a kiss, I turned to see Mal and a small red-haired boy traipsing across the emptying playground. My heart sank.

'Laurie! I thought it was you,' Mal grinned. The small freckle-faced boy was holding his father's hand very tight. 'How are you?'

'Good thanks,' I was artificially bright, immediately confused. My pleasure at seeing Mal's friendly face was almost entirely erased by the memory of our last meeting – although I was relieved to see that he did really have a son. I had put his mention of the school to the back of my mind, but obviously I was going to have to retrieve it. I looked down at the solemn little boy. 'Hello. You must be …' the child's name escaped me.

Mal prodded his reticent son.

'Leonard,' the boy muttered.

Poor child, I thought, saddled with such a serious name at such a young age.

'Bit anxious,' Mal rolled his eyes. 'We're hoping he'll get a place but they still can't confirm it. We've come to meet the headmistress again.'

'You're going to be fine, Leonard.' I offered him my hand. 'My name's Laurie. Pleased to meet you. It's a very nice school. And Mrs Webster's a nice lady. She won't bite you, I promise.'

Leonard took my hand limply, but refused to meet my eye, staring steadfastly at his shoes instead.

'Well, look out for Polly,' I gestured at my daughter's disappearing back. 'If they find you a place, you might be in Mrs Evans' class with her. Polly's got long curly black hair and a red coat, and she talks a lot. Girls, eh, Leonard?'

Still no smile. Leonard wasn't giving in that easily.

'I was hoping we could have met her,' Mal gave me a tentative smile. 'I did leave my number at the café. I thought it might have smoothed the transition a little …'

'Maybe.' I tried to smile but I felt inordinately relieved that Polly had already gone inside. 'I think Robin lost your number. Anyway, don't let me keep you.' I pointed up at the office. 'You probably need to stop off there. They'll sort you out.'

'Oh right. Okay.' Mal looked disappointed. 'Well, maybe we could—'

My friend Roz wandered up, all pert and taut in her running gear, intrigued by a stranger.

'Hi,' she was overly bright. 'I'm putting off the trot round the park.'

'I'm so sorry, Mal, but I'm really late for work.' I began to back away. 'Good luck, Leonard. Hope to see you in the playground soon.'

Leonard just glowered at the floor.

'Laurie,' Mal tried to catch my arm, but I sidestepped just in time. I was acting like a jumpy teenager, I knew, but I couldn't help it. I was too busy fighting my inclination to be his friend. It was tempting – but I also knew it was unwise, given the origins of our meeting.

'God, is that the time?' I made a show of checking my watch. 'I'd better get going. Maybe Roz can show you where to go.'

'I know where to—' Mal began.

'Sure,' Roz loved to get involved. 'No worries. Roz Craft,' she offered Mal her hand. 'Come on. I'll take you to our leader.'

But however fast I'd beat my retreat, it was too late to have missed the hurt in the big man's eyes.

I was muttering aloud as I walked across the car park. Frankly, I was relieved that Leonard was real and even more so that Mal's ex-wife hadn't been there too, but it had felt uncomfortable in the extreme.

'Bloody, bloody stupid,' I walked faster. 'Bloody ridiculous situation to get yourself into, Laurie Smith.'

What exactly that situation was though, I wasn't quite ready to admit. Still muttering, I arrived at my old Ford and found that someone had boxed me in, parking across me even though there were empty spaces further down the row. Slamming the door behind me very hard, I derived huge satisfaction from putting my hand on the horn for at least thirty seconds. The noise suited my mood entirely. No one came. After about five minutes, during which my blood pressure rose continuously, I got out again and walked to the parade of shops. I stuck my head round the newsagents' door.

'Has anyone parked a red Audi across my Fiesta?'

No one even bothered to answer. At this rate I was going to miss my first client. Muttering again, I went into the butcher's and repeated the question.

'Sorry, love. I can do you a pound of sausages though, if you like. Best pork?'

Coming out of the shop, I saw the door of the Audi shutting. I rushed towards it, ready to give the driver a piece of my mind.

A red-haired woman was putting huge sunglasses on. She saw me approaching, I could tell from her body language – but she was determined not to look at me. As I neared she revved the engine and pulled out. I felt a nasty burst of adrenaline as I realised that I recognised her.

'Sorry,' she mouthed at me at the last minute, and zoomed off down the road.

There was no sign of him, but it was without a doubt the woman I'd met with Mal all those years ago during their marriage counselling. The woman driving the car that I'd just side-stepped was Mal's wife, Susie.

NOW: HOUR 7

3pm

The waitress drives me to the station in Sherborne. She hasn't stopped talking since she pulled out onto the dual carriageway, but I'm so riveted by her painfully slow driving, willing her to put her foot down, that I've heard little of what she's said. Fortunately she doesn't seem to expect any answers.

I come to when she points at the scratches on my face.

'I had one of those,' she says. 'Bastard.'

'One what?'

'Bloke who used to deal it out.'

I try to hide my wince.

'Takes one to know one,' she glances at me and lights another super-long cigarette off the last. Surreptitiously I wind the window down a little. I think of the policeman's unfounded accusations about Emily and I smoking in the hotel room. But it was Sid who couldn't kick the habit, not me.

'Sorry,' she exhales a long plume of smoke. 'Filthy habit, I know. But it's got me. Well and truly got me.'

'I used to, a long time ago.'

'Gotta have a little pleasure in this dull old life, haven't you?'

'Yes definitely.' I try to smile. The wind rushes through the crack in the window, making my ears vibrate.

'So you've got away from him.' Like an attack dog, she's back on her subject. 'For now, at least.'

'I don't know what you mean.' I look away.

'Your boyfriend. I heard you back there. You said something about having a row.' She changes up a gear. Hallelujah. 'And just look at you.'

'What?'

'You don't need to be so defensive.' A tower of ash is building along her cigarette. I watch it with fascination.

'I'm not.'

'I'm on your side.'

'There's no side to be on,' I say.

How long before the tower falls?

'Nothing to be ashamed of. It's bloody hard to get away from them.'

'I'm not ashamed,' I say clearly. 'How long before we reach the station?'

'Ants in your pants?' she says.

I look at the clock. 'I'm just worried about reaching my daughter in time. She's on her way back from holiday.'

'Don't tell me you're worried about *him* getting there first.'

'Who?' I frown.

'Him,' she gestures at me. The ash falls, speckles the dashboard. 'Whoever did that to you.'

'No one did this to me.'

'So why did you tell Mike back there? I heard you say you'd had a row.'

'I just – look …' I falter. 'Please. I appreciate your concern, really, but it's not me that I'm worried about.'

'It never is,' she says darkly.

'What does that mean?'

'It means women who are victims worry more about their kids than themselves. And because of that, the bastards get away with bashing the mothers.'

'Is that really true?' I consider her words. 'Isn't it just that you get into such a terrible cycle, and a slump, that you can't get out of it again?'

'So you do know what I'm on about.' She's triumphant.

'No,' I say staunchly. 'I counsel women, that's how I know.' I am hugely relieved to see the sign for the station looming up against the washed-out sky.

'I see,' she indicates right to turn off the carriageway. 'And like I said before, it takes one to know one.'

One tiny part of me is tempted to unburden myself. I'll never see her again; her judgement will make no difference to my life. A stranger's empathy can be a tempting lure. But I quickly see sense. I don't have time to share a sob story. And anyway, it's no one's business but my own.

'Please. Can we just agree to disagree on this one?'

She shrugs. 'It's your funeral.'

I shiver. For a moment, I have forgotten Emily, lying somewhere in the dark. Guilt pierces me.

'But you mark my words,' she's off again. Thankfully we are at the roundabout outside the station. 'If you don't get out now, whilst you're still young, you'll never get out.'

I don't answer. She's starting to sound evangelical.

She pulls up; I practically fall out of the car in my haste. 'Thank you so much.'

'And listen. You might end up with a boring one like my Richard, but I'm here to tell you, no make-up sex is ever worth getting clouted for.' She chucks her cigarette out after me. 'The bastards might be sexy but they're still fucking bastards. The nice ones might be boring, but they're safe. Good luck, love.'

I run up the concourse. The monitor tells me there is a train to London's Waterloo in ten minutes. At last, something is going my way.

I stand on the cold platform in the drab day. I am stripped back to basics: no purse, no friend, nothing but survival on my mind. I use the ladies' in the waiting room; there is a girl in the corner in a checked shirt changing her trousers, pulling clothes from a rucksack. Her legs are skinny and mottled, her arms badly scarred. I think of the girls I have counselled at the Phoenix Centre; the ones addicted by sweet sixteen. I feel suddenly overwhelmed by life's horrors, by the bleakness, by the lack of hope. Where are the blue skies, the flowers, the happy endings?

Where is my daughter?

Back on the platform, I pace up and down. Two minutes until the train comes.

I take the risk: I switch my old mobile on for the first time since it died in the early hours. The battery sign flashes; it's about to die again. Maybe I can retrieve my mother's mobile number before it does.

But before I can hit the Contact button, it rings. I nearly drop it in horror.

It is Sid.

THEN: POLLY'S SCHOOL CONCERT

'I'll meet you there.' I doodled a square box on my note-pad. 'If you're actually going to turn up.'

I didn't know why Sid was so intent on coming to Polly's concert, but I was most uneasy about it. Not only was I surprised – he was normally impossible to drag anywhere near the school – I was also worried about presenting a united front when we barely spoke these days. But Polly's Harvest Festival was about her, not me, and I could hardly refuse Sid the opportunity to see his daughter in full singing glory – even if it was while dressed rather ingloriously as a corn on the cob.

'Of course I'm going to turn up.' He was scornful, as only he who had no right to be could manage.

I added a lid to the box. 'Right.' Through the door, Bev was making signs. I mouthed 'Five minutes' at her. Then, lightly as possible, I said, 'Sid. Just one thing.'

'What?'

'You're not … you're not going to bring *her*, are you?'

'Who?'

Why make anything easy for me?

'Your new … Jolie.' Beside the box I drew a jagged heart.

'Don't be stupid.'

I didn't bother to argue. Arranging a time and place to meet, I scribbled out the heart and went to see Bev.

I'd spent hundreds of hours trying to pinpoint exactly where my marriage went wrong, but actually, it was pretty simple really. I'd married Sid too quickly. I thought I knew him – and then it turned out I didn't, at all. I was fascinated by him, by his dark brooding mystery, by his traumatic childhood, but I didn't know him. Yet.

'You can take the boy out of the care home,' he used to say, as if it excused everything, 'but you can't take the care home out of the boy.'

I listened, but I couldn't see. I was blinded by him: I thought I could help him. Change him, I suppose. Impossible to explain, the thrall he held me in. From the moment we met: the way he looked at me; looked *into* me like no one else had. The way his gaze wrapped round me. I cannot explain it, even now. Cannot explain, understand, excuse it. The way he trapped me, as if I was a small, rather helpless animal.

I invested everything in Sid, naïve to the maximum, and I suppose, in the end, I just couldn't face the fact for a long time – too long – that it was so very wrong.

Of course, there were many things that I absolutely did know about Sid. For instance, tonight he would be late. He'd make a big entrance, sighing dramatically, pausing until all eyes were on him – and then he'd be utterly aloof and unfriendly, cleverly drawing attention to himself.

But actually it was me who arrived late and flustered. My last client had been inconsolable and I'd had to calm her down and put her in a cab – and then my own car wouldn't start because I'd left the lights on all day, and there was no one around with jump leads, so I'd got the bus, arriving at the school with minutes to spare.

Making my way across the busy hall, Sid didn't see me. He was studying the little programme the children had made, and in repose his face was almost soft. His dark hair was as tousled as usual, but for once he didn't look sulky or cross, or lit up and euphoric, he just looked … like Polly's father. Like the man I had loved so deeply. And then he did look up, and my heart almost skipped a beat until I remembered that it was too late.

Much too late.

'Phew,' I slid in next to him, sitting on the corner of next-door's anorak; apologising; dropping my woolly hat under the chair.

'Clumsy Laurie.' Hawk-like, he bomb-dived my weakness. 'Nothing changes, does it?'

'Some things do,' I retorted, reaching for his programme.

I wasn't clumsy. I was nervous.

He held it away from me.

'I'm still reading it.'

'Okay,' I shrugged. There was really nothing to read but I wasn't going to argue.

'Appalling illustrations,' he muttered darkly. 'Load of shite.'

The mother in front of us turned round indignantly.

'Sid, for goodness sake,' I gave her a weak smile. 'They're all under eight.'

'So?' his turn to shrug. 'They're not babies. No one has Polly's eye. Not one of them.'

Oh God.

'So why didn't they put her pictures in?'

'Because—' I was saved by Mrs Evans thumping out the opening chords to 'Morning Has Broken' on the piano, and Polly's class entering, dressed as various fruit and vegetables.

'Jesus,' Sid muttered, ever louder. 'Who the hell is that fat turnip?'

If I hadn't been so tense I might have laughed. We did used to laugh, a lot, once, Sid and I. But I couldn't now; I just heard his cruelty. Staring ahead of me, I prayed he would shut up now.

And then suddenly I spotted Mal on the other side of the hall. So Leonard must have got a place after all. I felt a jag of adrenaline: studiously I avoided eye contact and concentrated on Polly.

At the end of an hour of fairly atrocious singing and dancing, Sid was already zipping up his leather jacket during the grand finale that involved Polly lying down at the front of the stage as part of a vegetable tableau, and then not being able to get up again thanks to her unwieldy costume. Sid began to laugh. I shoved him hard in the ribs, already anticipating Polly's tears.

'I'll meet you outside,' Sid shot out as the audience were still applauding, no doubt to smoke.

I collected a thoroughly overexcited Polly who'd already forgotten about her trauma on stage, and we wandered outside. By now it was dark, and Sid was nowhere to be seen.

'Where's Daddy?' Polly was first puzzled, then put out.

'I don't know.' I looked up and down the pavement, filled now with chattering children and their parents. 'But I'm sure he's here somewhere. You did brilliantly, Pol. He was ever so proud.'

'So where *is* he then?' her bottom lip jutted out dangerously.

Opposite, a sleek black car was parked, blatantly across the *Keep Clear* signs, music floating from the partially open window. I knew the tune but I couldn't place it … until suddenly Sid got out, waving at his daughter. As I raised a hand in greeting the far door opened too. A young woman emerged, a young woman I recognised from our brief meetings.

I clutched Polly's hand, glad of the contact.

'Pol!' Sid waved, and Polly's face lit up.

'Daddy.'

He bounded across the road and grabbed Polly, swinging her up to face height. 'I've never seen such an amazing corn on the cob.'

From her place on the pavement, the girl called Jolie smiled and waved at my daughter. Shiny-looking, all huge hair and silver ribbons, wearing a diaphanous skirt, endless legs bare despite the cold night. Polly waved back happily. I watched, dazed, until Jolie turned her head-lamp gaze on me. I tried not to flinch as she positively beamed.

I managed half a rather watery smile and turned away.

My pain was visceral. Sid looked at me.

'What?' he spoke eventually. But he knew.

'Nothing.' His insouciance was a final slap in the face. 'I think we should go now, Pol. It's freezing. You'll see Daddy soon.' I held out my arms for her.

'Haven't you got the car?' Polly moaned. 'Don't say we've got to walk.' It was starting to drizzle. 'Have we got to walk? Please, Mummy, I don't want to, I'm tired. I'm really really *really* tired. Can we go in Daddy's car?'

'Jolie's car, you mean,' I couldn't help myself.

'My legs hurt,' Polly whined. 'I can't walk any more.'

Sid's eyes slid towards the Mercedes.

'Bit of a surprise, I must say,' I muttered. 'Given our earlier conversation.'

He started to say something, then obviously thought better of it. He deposited Polly on the pavement.

'Sorry,' he said eventually. 'I didn't ask Jolie to come. Really.'

I didn't believe him. Not for one tiny iota of a second. I grasped Polly's hand tightly. 'It's fine,' I started to drag Polly away. 'Let's go, Pol, before we get soaked. You'll see your dad on Friday. We'll get a cab.'

'I want to go with Daddy,' Polly began to cry and the knife in my chest twisted. 'My legs *do* hurt. I miss Daddy.'

'Please, lovie,' I begged. This was turning into my worst nightmare. I could see the beautiful girl across the road wafting to Florence and the Machine, oblivious; I could feel Sid's sullen presence and Polly straining to go back to him. 'It's not long till Friday.'

'Daddy,' she started to screech, hysteria building.

'Sid,' Jolie called, 'Laurie. We'll give you a lift, yeah? No bother.'

I would walk across town and back again naked before I would accept a lift in her car.

'Oh yes,' Polly perked up mid-wail, 'a lift!'

And then suddenly Mal was there, Leonard in tow. 'Everything okay?' he asked.

'What's it to you?' Sid scowled at him, ignoring Polly.

'I was just checking,' Mal said pleasantly.

'It's fine, Mal, thanks.'

'Mal?' Sid scowled harder.

This was not the time for introductions.

'Friend of yours?' Sid spat. To my horror, I realised he was actually squaring up to Mal.

'Fellow parent.' Calmly, Mal tucked Leonard behind him and offered Sid his hand. 'Nice to meet you, buddy.'

Sid looked at the extended hand like it was poisonous. He didn't take it.

'Please, Sid,' I said quietly. 'Don't be silly.' I picked Polly up myself now; she was almost too heavy for me to lift.

'Siddy,' the girl over the road waved at him.

I bit back my retort.

Sid hesitated. He was torn, but in the end, the girl decided for him.

'Come on, honey. It's cold,' she called again, wrapping her arms around her skinny frame. 'I'm freezing. If you're not all coming, let's go home.'

Home.

'See you, Pol,' Jolie waved again. 'I'll get that muffin mix you like for next week. And tell your mum nice things about me, yeah?' She winked at me, sliding out of view.

I was breathless with outrage.

'I'll see you after school on Friday,' Sid kissed the top of Polly's head and loped across the road, not before shooting Mal a look of pure malice. He didn't bother with me. Polly sobbed piteously into my shoulder.

'Come on, little one,' I whispered in her ear. 'Let's go home and have some ice-cream.'

There was a pause while Polly debated this internally.

'With strawberry sauce?' she hiccupped eventually.

'And chocolate sprinkles.'

She wiped her runny nose on my jacket in appreciation. The rain was getting harder.

'Can I give you a lift?' Mal asked. Leonard was still hiding behind his legs.

I glanced over at the sleek black car. It was in shadow but I thought I could see Sid and the girl entwined. My stomach felt contorted.

'Do you know what, Mal, that'd be fantastic,' I put Polly back down on the ground and grasped her hand. Fuck all my good intentions. We began to follow Mal towards the car park. 'Thank you very much.'

NOW: HOUR 8

4pm

On the blustery station platform, I stare at the phone, frantically weighing up whether to answer it.

If I do, he'll know he failed – and my cover is blown for good.

It rings off – then rings again.

I don't answer it. Thirty seconds later, the voicemail buzzes.

'Where the hell are you? Why is everyone saying you are dead?' Sid sounds almost hysterical.

Don't trust him, Laurie. You can't trust him.

I have rarely heard him this way. Angry, yes; scared – no.

'Ring me, Laurie. Please. Tell me where you are and I'll come and get you. Wherever you are, I'll come there.'

Every time you've ever trusted him, look what has happened.

I contemplate calling him back, pleading with him to stay away from Polly – but as I twist it in my hand, the phone dies.

The train pulls in two minutes later. I get on.

I think of Sid, of the few times I glimpsed fear in his eyes; of the nightmares he constantly had when we were first to-gether, before he discovered the beautiful peace encased in a sleeping pill. I think of trying to get him to open up about what had gone on in his family when he was small; I think of the rage it provoked if I pushed too hard at the wrong time. I think of the nightmares that began again briefly after his brother phoned and said his mother wanted to see him. And then I can't think about it any more. It makes me almost stupid with misery.

It is painfully true that we are the sum of our experience, but what worries me more is how easily we can be ruined by others' actions.

And sometimes, some days, I feel so angry about something unspoken between Sid and I, a frustration caused by his own damage that meant we couldn't ever work, that I want to punch my fist through a wall. But I have not ever done that. Not yet.

I tuck the phone away and queue at the buffet car. Two swans swoop down together onto the small brown river we cross, and I feel a sadness so heavy it's leaden; quite overwhelming.

It's not until I am paying for my tea and see the guard wobbling down the aisle from first class that I realise I don't have a ticket. I haven't even thought about buying one; I don't even know if I have enough cash to pay for one at all.

I turn quickly and walk away from him.

The cash I do have, I need to save for London. I think of my old Brownie leader. Ten pence for the phone, for emergencies. This is an emergency. I need to save my money to get to Polly.

I walk half the length of the train and linger in the area between two carriages, sipping my tea, thinking; waiting. Eventually I see the inspector at the far end of the next carriage, headed towards me. I slip into the loo. Overflowing, it stinks. God knows when it was last cleaned. Five minutes later, as we pull into the next station, someone knocks on the door.

'Tickets from Sherborne, please.'

My stomach contracts. I really do not want to get off this train now; I do not want to have to wait again; I *must* reach my destination.

I contemplate calling on the guard's good nature. Seconds later, I realise that is ridiculous. He knocks again.

I am clearing my throat, preparing my argument, when I hear voices, and a dog barking, a big dog by the sounds of it. There is some kind of altercation starting outside on the platform. I hear the guard speaking, moving away from the door.

'You can't bring that on here,' he's saying, and someone is jeering and someone else is swearing. A woman shouts.

I open the door and peer out. The guard is on the platform too. A boy slips onto the train as I slip out of the loo. He is tall and skinny with deep-set, haunted eyes, silver rings in his lip and nose; a dark, mottled crew-cut.

Our eyes meet and I experience a strange flash of emotion: recognition of a kindred spirit, perhaps. I pause for a second, and then I move down the carriage the guard has just come from. I slide into an empty double seat; my heart is beating fast. I feel like a fugitive. I *am* a fugitive.

The tall boy passes me; he glances down. 'All right?' he mutters; before I can respond, he carries on walking.

What does he recognise in me? My scratched face, my bandaged hand. I find myself wishing he had stopped and sat with me.

The argument on the platform is winding down. The huge Alsatian is being dragged off by the shouting woman. The man who was trying to board the train is obviously drunk; can of Special Brew in hand, he stumbles against the woman. She pushes at him, furious. They turn on each other now.

The guard is back on the train. He has not seen my face this whole time, I realise. He does not come into our carriage now; he must have gone the other way. An hour or two away from London, I am safe – for now.

THEN: SID

I didn't invite Mal in that night. Leonard was still glowering in the back; Polly was still utterly overwrought, I could tell from the flushed roses of colour in her cheeks, and the two of them hadn't exchanged a word the whole journey.

When Mal pulled up outside the house, I rushed to jump out.

'That was so kind.' I knew I was gabbling slightly. 'Thank you so much.'

'You're welcome. And if you ever fancy a drink—'

'Yes, great, thanks.' I wouldn't look at him; was on the pavement already, opening Polly's door, hoisting her out. 'See you soon.'

I didn't look back; I shut the door firmly behind us and bolted it. There was something to be said for sometimes locking the whole world out.

Polly and I polished off the whole tub of mint-choc-chip, though the addition of strawberry sauce left something to be desired, in my humble opinion. Soon she fell asleep beside me on the sofa. I covered her with the blanket and watched the end of *Casablanca*. And when I found the tears coursing down my face as the beautiful Bergman walked away from Bogart to board the plane, I told myself it was a good thing to cry. All the best love stories are the most painful, obviously. If the star-cross'd lovers ended up together, they'd be arguing about the washing-up before too long.

This was a much-needed release, some form of catharsis.

So why did I feel so utterly wretched?

Around midnight, I carried Polly up to bed. On her chest of drawers was the photo of Sid and her taken in St Ives the year before he finally made it. They looked so happy and, for once, Sid looked carefree, the great golden beach unfurling behind him as he held his small daughter high in his arms, proud and strong. Pierced by a deep and unremitting sadness, I curled up next to Polly in her little white bed, my face buried in her hair, and fell asleep.

Sometime in the early hours, I came to with a gasp. Confused, I wasn't sure what had woken me, but I had the unnerving sense that someone had been watching me.

Polly was still sleeping soundly, her breath a whisper on my cheek. My arm was twisted painfully beneath me. As I eased myself, wincing, from the bed, I heard something downstairs.

I froze.

Somewhere, a door banged. I couldn't tell if it was inside or out in the street.

A minute passed. I forced myself from the bed; paused at Polly's door, listening.

A creak. My heart began to race. I scolded myself. It was just the wind. An old floorboard; this old house.

I tiptoed onto the landing, towards the stairs.

Down the stairs, to the kitchen. Towards some kind of protection? A bread knife, perhaps.

Suddenly, the garden was flooded with the security light's beam.

I stopped breathing.

What was I going to do with a bread knife?

Next door's ginger tom stalked across the patio.

I breathed again. He'd set it off, obviously.

The front door rattled like it did when it was windy – but the night was still. There *was* someone in the house, or trying to get in.

Where was the phone?

In the sitting-room.

I edged towards the corridor.

The front door was still bolted on the inside. The windows were alarmed. The patio doors, I had just seen, were shut and locked.

I ran to the sitting-room, snatched up the phone.

Through the un-shuttered window, I saw a figure walking back down the path, towards the gate, away from the house where we lived.

Love should be simple, right?

X loves Y, who loves X back.

Why wouldn't it be?

Because it takes two people. Two minds, two wills. Two to connect; two to choose a path, a similar if not identical course. Imagine a conversation, then have it for real. Does It go the way you thought it would?

I doubt it, because you don't know what the other person is going to say until they speak.

I met Sid when I first came to London. I was broke, waitressing, not sure what I was doing with my life. After qualifying, I'd gone travelling around South America, met hippies and bandits and shamans; I'd danced in the moonlight and on beaches, trekked through the rainforests and visited lost cities, losing myself briefly. I'd come home only to argue with my father badly, finally finding the strength to stand up to him. I wanted to go to back to college, to finish my training so I could start counselling for real, but my father unequivocally refused to help me, though he was currently solvent, and my mother couldn't afford it at all, though she gladly gave me a bed at her home in East Finchley. Whilst I applied for grants and began my studies again, I needed as much cash as possible. I worked two jobs and then I saw an ad in the corner shop for life models at an off-shoot of Slade Art College in central London.

I was unsure but Emily encouraged me. She was in her free-love, free-will phase, sleeping with a Bob Dylan look-alike and spouting Jean-Paul Sartre. 'It will unleash your soul, darling,' she said, but I wasn't so sure. It was more likely to unleash my wobbly thighs. Still, I was broke; I bit the bullet.

Sid was teaching at the art college. A year or so older than me, he was gaunt, grumpy and curt; all hollow cheeks and permanent scowl. He hardly spoke, showed me the store cupboard where I could change and pointed out the kettle in the corner, though there was no milk. 'Come out and lie on that divan thing. And,' he surveyed me quickly, 'try not to lie like a lump of lard.'

I stared at him, even more appalled now. I'd never met someone so rude. And in the cupboard, shivering, I realised too late that I hated the idea of taking my clothes off with a passion. What on earth had I been thinking? I was totally and utterly wrong for it. I wasn't proud of my body, I was simply mortified by my nudity, and worse, I was freezing, my pale skin unattractively goose-pimpled, the tiny fan heater no solace, simply burning one unsightly patch bright red on my thigh.

Halfway through the first session, during the tea-break, I made a run for it. In the tiny loo, I threw my clothes on, slipping out the back door of the studio whilst the class was grouped round the kettle and a plate of broken digestives.

Sid caught up with me halfway down the path.

'Where are you going?' he caught me roughly by my arm.

'I can't do it,' I shook him off. But something electric pulsed through me; a pure physical thrill at his touch. 'It's embarrassing,' I mumbled. My shirt was still half-unbuttoned.

'Don't be such a little prude.' His eyes – the green of damp moss – narrowed. I read the disdain easily.

'I'm not.'

'You are. Taking your clothes off is the most natural thing in the world.'

'For you maybe.'

'For us all.'

'You do it then,' I retorted.

'No way.' He stared at me. 'Your body's much better than mine.' And then he grinned.

I cringe when I look back. I cringe at how easily I was lost. One smile and I fell in.

I didn't go back. He called the class to an early close and took me to the pub. We ordered whisky macs and were drunk by five. I saw something in Sid that I responded to eagerly; something forlorn that he thought he'd hidden; that he managed to hide from most. But not from me. We drained the final glasses, and then he took me to bed in his artist's garret. And it was a garret. It had a magnificent view of the clouds through the sky-light, a double mattress and not much else; his easel and oils stacked against the wall, a bottle of whisky on a wooden box, no visible food. Some Camus and lots of Ernest Hemingway on the windowsills. I hadn't read Hemingway yet, and I had no idea about Sid's preoccupation with death. I just knew the room seemed romantic in the extreme; it smelt of paint and turps and Sid.

We fell into bed and we didn't get out until the next day.

Now I implore my female clients, 'Don't sleep with them until you are really sure you can handle what comes next.' Old-fashioned, maybe – but show me a woman who can have really good sex and not attach in some way, and I'll show you a genius, a liar – or a broken soul.

I slept with Sid the first day I met him. What did I expect? Certainly not the punishment he meted out.

But even that wasn't simple. Because Sid took me to bed, hooked me entirely – and then vanished.

Hope died a slow and painful death. I yearned for him – and then I pushed the thought of him away, because it hurt. Stupid and naïve, I knew, after just one meeting – but I thought I'd glimpsed more. I knocked on his front door a few times, but the third time, when the landlady let me up the stairwell, I thought I heard female laughter inside, and I turned away, huddled into my own rejection.

Later, I walked past the art college once or twice, dawdled down the road, dolled up to the nines, but when the door opened and a group of tutors came out, I ran the other way.

Just when I had almost succeeded in forgetting him, he reappeared.

Typical Sid. Sticking the knife-point back in the wound just as it was about to heal.

That night he came back, it was sultry. A night when sirens wailed, as they wail continually in the city until we don't notice anymore; a night when the pollution blurred the edges of the tallest buildings, hiding the sky from the ground. A night when the newest skyscrapers stacked light above us, and stumpy tower-blocks flicked into disjointed Lego-brick life as dusk drew in; as the DLR wended *Blade-Runner*-like between concrete and the stark shine of Canary Wharf. As the streetlights hummed and the kids on the corner doused their chips with too much

vinegar and jostled each other in trousers that rested dangerously low: 'G'wan blud', throwing wrappers in the gutter. As the
youths, all-hooded, youths who never cracked a smile, paced the
pavements with their chunky dogs, and the young girls clacked
past skinny-legged in shiny patent heels so high they couldn't
walk, let alone run from their hunters.

As this vibrant life spread out before me, I came alive again
simply because Sid came back.

'Sorry,' he said, simply. And he only said it once. It was a
word he struggled with. That was a lesson I quickly learnt.

'Where were you?' I asked.

He regarded me gravely for a moment with eyes that told me
nothing.

'Getting rid of the last one,' he said, and then he smiled, bar-
ing teeth that were rather wolfish.

Another rarity, smiling; something he was not good at.

I said nothing; I didn't really trust myself to speak. Because
what was there to say? His words floored me; his words were
enough.

Did I wonder then about how easily he did it? Got rid of her
for me, whoever she was?

I don't think it occurred to me, in fact, because it never felt
easy with him. It was more like trying to keep up. Trying to
dodge forwards, one step in front of him, and guess which way
he would go next. It was exhausting.

But then, everything about Sid was difficult. That was what
became addictive. And later, he admitted why he was attracted
to me in the first place. Because I had dared, that first day, to
run away.

I should have kept on running.

NOW: HOUR 9

5pm

The train rattles through the dusk. Far away the sun, invisible all day, begins to set, bleeding into the sky, the clouds to my left stained vermillion, reminiscent of yesterday's fiery heavens.

I think of Sid's work, the paintings that made him famous, a kneeling naked Mary holding her dying son in a desert beneath a clashing sunset, distraught. The idealised mother he had always felt would have saved him from himself; the mother who would never have abandoned him. So very far from his own experience. The other Mary licking the Son of God's feet, sucking his toes, imbued with an eroticism and a bond it felt almost embarrassingly personal to share. When Sid suggested Magdalen for our daughter's name, I'd already seen the sketches for this work. Blanching, I refused flatly.

I push Sid firmly from my mind.

Think, Laurie, think. Who else is out there? Who else can help?

Normally I would find peace on long train journeys, but there is no peace to be had here. Every minute is torturous.

I try to ring my own mother again but there is still no answer from her landline, and no life at all in the old phone to retrieve her mobile number, and as we sway between the high banks and the tall trees, the signal keeps cutting out anyway.

The guard comes back the other way; thank God he doesn't notice as I slink down in my seat. Across the aisle, an old lady pops paracetamol from a box, offered by her doughy-faced son. Like some kind of junkie I watch her gnarled hands on the pills, desperate to ask for some. I don't dare. I don't want to draw attention to myself.

I listen to their conversation. They are talking about her hip operation, and how well it went. Then they move on to whether George will come and collect them, and whether he will arrive on time, which they doubt, because he's always at least five minutes late, and will he have brushed the car seats down because the dogs are so dirty and moulting all the time, and smell, and it's all such a pain.

It's so very normal in its mundanity, I am soothed by it.

The Tannoy announces that we are nearing our next stop and the old lady and her son begin to clear away their clingfilm and their Tupperware; I am about to dial directory enquiries again to see if I can get a number for the Eurostar office when the train comes to a sudden juddering halt; brakes screeching, metal on metal, a hideous jarring sound.

For a moment there is silence in the carriage and then chatter breaks out, spreading down the aisle with a sense of outrage.

I stand up and move to the door to see what is happening, but all that's visible in the gloom are a few cows mooching in the field beyond the hedge. Nothing more.

Anxiety rises.

'Typical,' a low voice says behind me.

It's the tall boy from earlier; the boy with the rings in his face.

'What do you think's happened?' I ask, peering out into nothing.

He shrugs. 'Sheep on the line, probably. Usually is.'

'Perils of the countryside.' But even as I make the innocuous remark, the despair wells up. 'Oh God.' I bite my lip so hard in an effort to quell my impatience that I taste blood. 'I really need this train to keep going.'

Laconically, he considers me. 'Why so desperate?'

'I'm not …' I begin, and then I meet his eyes. In a hard, angular face, they are beautiful; deep-set, long, grey. Why lie? 'I need to get to my daughter.'

'Where is she?'

'With my mother. Coming back from France.'

'Is it?' he shrugs again. 'Is your mum, like, bad news?'

'No,' I actually smile. My bustling little mother, efficient and endlessly kind. I would trust no one with Polly to the degree I trust my mother. 'My mum's great. It's … it's someone else I'm worried about. Getting there first.'

'Right.' He doesn't ask any more questions and it doesn't surprise me. He looks like he understands hardship, this boy; complicated, dysfunctional situations. He has a long scar on his head that runs livid through the crew-cut; tough-looking, maybe, but with an air of something I can't describe. A kind of weary acceptance. The expression 'old beyond his years' comes to mind.

What has he seen, I wonder, in his short life?

The Tannoy announces a '*brief delay whilst we check what the problem is*'. I taste my own blood on my tongue again.

The boy, who on second glance is older than he first looked, holds his tattooed hand out.

'Saul.'

'Laurie.'

I estimate his age: about nineteen or twenty, probably.

'Where are you going?'

'London.'

'Me too. The streets are paved with gold, ain't they?' he regards me gravely, but I see he is joking.

The Tannoy crackles into life again. The sun has set. It is almost completely dark outside, there is nothing to see now but hedgerows.

I look out at them and I have a sudden flash of my first holiday with Sid. *Holiday* might be too grand, in fact; it was more of a camping trip. Sid wanted to paint the sea; I bought us a tent. We were broke but, a few months after we'd met, already inseparable, contemplating a move to Cornwall. A tent seemed romantic. But we arrived on the campsite late because we'd got lost down Norfolk's narrow lanes, following the first real row we ever had. Sid had shouted at me about my map reading, and I'd shouted back at his loss of humour, and then I cried and he kissed me to say sorry. By the time we put the tent up it was dark and neither of us really had a clue what we were doing, but accompanied by a bottle of red wine and some whisky it seemed quite simple. We sat in front of our funny little stove and cooked baked beans and then we went to bed. When we got up in the morning it had rained so hard the tent was practically floating and we were soaked because we hadn't put the ground sheet down properly. Then Sid, wringing wet and foul-tempered, had a fit about the campsite.

'It's so ugly,' he kept saying, marching back and forwards in outrage, 'this bloody campsite – and I hate the bloody hedgerows. I'm all boxed in. I can't breathe. And where's the fucking sea?'

He was so irate about the hedgerows, stomping about in his boxer shorts and his unlaced boots, with his hair all up on end and his sweatshirt on inside out that I started to laugh, and it was one of those Sid moments which could have gone either way, as he glared down at me and I managed to stifle the laughter, just about, until he put both feet in one leg of his jeans and promptly fell over backwards. And then I laughed till I cried and although he debated shouting even louder, eventually he saw the funny side and laughed too. Then we took down the tent, and along with a tiny, delicate animal skull that I'd found in the grass, we shoved everything into Sid's bashed-up old Mini. We found a room in a B&B on a farm on a hill overlooking the sea, and when it rained for most of the weekend we didn't care because we just stayed in bed, ate cheese and chocolate biscuits and made love, though Sid made me put the animal skull in the cupboard before he would touch me.

Sid refused to ever go back to Norfolk, but he did find the sea in the end.

The Tannoy crackles into life.

'*I regret to inform you we may be held here for some time due to suspected damage on the track ahead.*'

Trapped.

Oh God. For the first time today, but perhaps inevitably, tears spring to my burning eyes.

'Laurie,' the boy looks at me. 'Is that your name?'

'Yes,' desperately I try to hold them back, but I fail. One tear escapes, trickles down my cheek.

'Don't cry,' he says. His voice is soft now.

'I'm trying not to,' I smile wanly. But it's always worse when people are nice. 'I really, really am trying.'

He regards me again for a moment as I wipe the tear away.

'If you could get off the train, would you?'

'Yes I bloody would. Though I don't have a clue where we are.'

'We've crossed Salisbury Plain, so probably somewhere in Hampshire. And I reckon I can.'

'What?'

'Get us off.'

'How? The doors are all locked till we get to a station, aren't they?'

I have a flash of last night. Of a room and a door. Of rattling a door frantically, Emily on the other side. I hear my name being shouted … or was it me? It was me, shouting hers, over and over again, slamming my shoulder against the door. And the door was wedged; I am sure it was, something heavy against it on the other side. I had slid the key-card into the slot over and again, and every time it flicked green – and every time, it refused to open, and turned red again.

I close my eyes against the memory.

'Follow me,' Saul says.

Quickly we walk the length of the train, through the grumbling, disconsolate carriages, through the fluorescent light and the smell of too many bodies too close together, knocking into people's bags and feet. After a while I stop apologising.

We make it to the far end; to the guard's carriage. Saul knocks on the door.

'Why don't we just ask?' I whisper. 'If we can get off?'

'Don't be daft,' he doesn't bother looking at me. 'They wouldn't let us, in the middle of nowhere. Health and safety bollocks.'

In the middle of nowhere.

The futility of my situation is hitting me in great waves. I am exhausted, physically and emotionally. My best friend is dead and I am in considerable pain. I don't know where Polly is and I don't know what the killer intends and I am frightened and I am alone.

I hear a voice on the other side of the door.

The boy turns and grins at me.

Not quite alone, perhaps. I don't know why I should trust this scarred, tattooed lad I only met ten minutes ago, but I do. I have little choice. It is, actually, as simple as that.

'Okay?' he mutters.

'I guess.'

'Just follow me, and when I say jump, jump.'

He bangs on the guard's door again. As we wait, he holds out one rather grimy, nail-bitten hand behind him. 'Ready?'

I take it.

'Ready,' I say.

THEN: MAL

The second time I heard someone in the house, I called the police.

They sounded politely uninterested, especially when, after some probing from them, I admitted I had recently separated from my husband.

'He's got rights, love,' the voice on the phone explained wearily, as if he had heard this type of thing too many times before. 'If he co-owns the house, he has rights. You can't lock him out.'

'I'm not even sure that it's him,' I said.

'It is actually illegal to change the locks, if he is on the deeds,' the voice said, ignoring me. 'Your husband.'

But they did send someone round. The someone looked at my expensive alarm system. 'You're pretty safe with that, aren't you? Linked up to the local station.'

Normally I never even remembered to switch the blessed thing on; we only had it installed because of the vast insurance premiums on Sid's work. Some of his art was still here, in the studio at the end of the garden, bolted, triple padlocked. I never ever went anywhere near it. I couldn't bear to. But I supposed someone might want it.

'Where did the "*intruder*"' – heavy emphasis on this word – 'break in?'

'I'm …' I paused for thought. 'I'm not absolutely sure. I just … someone has been prowling around at night.'

'Inside the house?' she frowned. She had a huge gap between her front teeth, I noticed. Big enough to fit a straw through.

'Um – not necessarily.'

'What do you mean?'

'Not necessarily inside.'

'Where then?' she raised one eyebrow now.

'Possibly in the garden.'

She snapped her neat little book shut. 'Right. So you've no absolute evidence of a break-in? You haven't actually seen someone in the house?'

'I did see someone walking down the path a few days ago.'

'Outside? In the back garden?'

'No.' I realised this was sounding stupid. 'In the front.'

'So, no one in the house, or the back, secured garden?'

'Not really. But I'm pretty sure someone has—'

'Mrs Smith.' She stifled an obvious sigh. 'Without any obvious signs of break-in or visual evidence, there is really nothing we can do. Are you sure it's not just your imagination running away with you?' She was kind but patronising. 'It is quite a big house for just you.'

'And my daughter.' And the fish and the rabbit, I didn't add.

'And your daughter. I noticed the *For Sale* sign outside.'

'Yes,' I turned away from her. It was my job to ask the questions; I hated divulging anything personal to a stranger. 'It's on the market.'

Our house. Our first house together as a family. It wasn't grand, not considering what we could have bought once Sid started to make his fortune. Bought after a particularly bad patch; meant to be a new start. It was safe, my haven; four walls against the world. Our home.

'Marriage breakdowns are hard. You're probably under some stress.'

Jesus. Who was the counsellor here, her or me?

'I'm fine.' I locked the back door, and hid the key on the side. 'I am quite sure I have heard someone moving around at night but I understand that if you have no evidence …'

And *was* I quite sure, anyway? I was sleeping badly, fitfully. I dreamt of Sid; I dreamt strange vivid dreams that I forgot again by morning.

I didn't bother to finish my sentence. I walked the policewoman to the front door instead.

'Let us know if you actually see anyone.' She put her hat on. 'Have you contemplated CCTV?'

'No way,' I shook my head. 'I hate all that Big Brother stuff. We probably won't be here much longer anyway.'

God only knew where we were going though.

Against my better judgement, and largely because Emily forced me, I went to the school parents' quiz night at the local pub.

'You have to get out,' Emily said, drowning my protestations over lunch round the corner from work. 'You cannot sit in and mope about Sid forever.'

'I'm not.' I refused to meet her blue-mascaraed eye. She was channelling Farrah Fawcett today apparently.

'Yeah right.' She pinched a chip off my plate. 'And I'm the Pope's uncle.'

'Are you?' I said. 'How's your Latin?'

'Hilarious.'

'You know me. Anyway,' I said stoutly, 'it's absolutely the best thing I ever did. Leaving Sid.'

Emily stared at me until I looked away.

'Best thing, but hardest thing too, eh, kid?'

'Best thing.' But tears threatened behind my pathetic façade. Fortunately she knew me well enough not to comment.

'Well, that's as maybe, but you're hardly a picture of unadulterated pleasure in your new state, and you still need to go out,' she donned her white fake fur. 'I'll babysit. Happily. I need to watch *Mary Poppins* with Polly. It's been ages. I'm in withdrawal from Chim-chiminey.' She made cow-eyes at me. 'That Dick's my idea of heaven, don't you know.'

Laughing, I shoved her out of the café door, a sense of relief washing over me. Of course I would be more than happy to have Emily there. She would stay, and the house would not seem so quiet, with just the two of us rattling round in it, Polly and I; and maybe her presence would allay some of these silly night-time fears that someone was prowling.

And if someone *was* prowling, well then Emily would see them too and, finally, I'd know I wasn't mad.

So I did a deal with the devil and – on the proviso that she would stay for the weekend – I agreed to go out.

At seven I met my friend Roz at the Irish pub on the high street; by eight I was half-cut. I had sworn I wouldn't drink – I hadn't since that night in Spain – but I was a little overwhelmed and nervous, and frankly, I hadn't been out in ages. Literally months; not since Sid and I, on our last legs as the successful couple, had gone on our final outing: a dinner party at his art dealer's penthouse in Holland Park.

Typically of Randolph, I had been seated at the far end of the huge oak table from Sid, at the 'unimportant' end, next to the perfect Russian wife of a gallery owner who spoke no word of English, her mouth so swollen with collagen I was amazed she could open it. From the other side of Sid, Randolph kept saluting me with his overflowing glass. I smiled back, but it was a false and empty gesture. I knew exactly what was really meant.

Randolph and his world were winning.

In the distance, on Sid's other side sat a pneumatic young actress whom I didn't recognise but apparently was in the latest Bond film. She laughed like a coquette at all his jokes, tossing her dark mane like a frisky pony; I'd just had my own hair cut into a severe bob, seeking something missing – a new look, something to excite both me and Sid – but only ending up with something he hated. 'Very school-marm' was all he'd said, and he didn't mean it as a compliment. I was driving that night; remained stone-cold sober whilst all around me the evening descended into bedlam, half the guests not eating as they disappeared into the marble bathroom time and again, exiting with running noses and eyes-a-glitter, fighting to be heard in the cacophony.

Occasionally Sid would catch my eye, and then very deliberately turn back to the pony-girl who whickered with delight as his ruthless eyes bored into her. Very attractive man, my husband. So controlled on the surface, so turbulent beneath. Still waters run deep, and need a lot of soothing. And so very easy to imagine him fucking you …

Eventually, able to stand it no more, I turned away from the Russian doll and began to charm the man on my left, a critic from *The Times*, who responded with alacrity. Sid watched in silence, the Bond girl forgotten.

It hadn't been a good idea to flirt, I discovered later. It never was.

Never quite knew what would happen when we got home.

So tonight, by the time Emily had shoved me out of the door, and Roz had hugged me hello with a 'Whoop whoop, no kids, hey?' and we had greeted the rest of the parents' team and started on the second round, I was already a little wobbly.

And so when, just as the quizmaster asked a question about the origin of the word 'dipsomaniac' and we were giggling girlishly about his enormous red glasses, Mal walked in, I wasn't quite sure how to react. More sober, I would doubtless have been more cautious.

But I wasn't sober.

He bought himself a pint and as someone stood up to go to the bar, he slid into the seat next to me.

'Hi,' he smiled, holding up his drink. 'Cheers.'

'Cheers.' Tentatively I smiled back. 'Are you any good at general knowledge?'

'Completely useless. Memory like a sieve. But I thought it'd be nice to meet some more parents.' Did he look slightly pained? I felt a stab of guilt. 'Get to know some locals.'

'Yes, of course.' I busied myself with my glass. 'Best place to come.'

'So,' he tried to catch my eye. 'How are you?'

'Fine, thanks.'

'Really?' he frowned. 'You didn't seem so great the other night.'

I thought of Sid squaring up to Mal; I thought of him entwined with Jolie.

'No, but that was then,' I drained my drink. I didn't want to discuss Sid with him. 'And this is now.'

'That's a song, isn't it?'

The quizmaster announced the sports round. As one, the women at the table groaned.

'Football not your forte then?' Mal teased. He really was quite attractive. Big. He looked like he would be able to just scoop me up and …

I felt myself blush. 'Er, no, I quite like football actually. All those men in shorts …' I trailed off. Apparently I was drunker than I realised. Then our eyes met and we both laughed, the tension dispelled.

For the next half an hour, I sat with Mal and we worked out answers together and I felt myself slide into a more comfortable place, where I was not worried or bothered by anything other than 'the similarity between Britney Spears and Venus?' – to which I never learnt the answer.

Roz winked at me over Mal's bent head as he filled in a question, and I smiled back at her, and his leg brushed mine, and I felt a brief surge of something that I didn't want to feel. I looked at the clock, and it was nearing last orders and I felt disappointed because I knew the evening was drawing to an end.

And then two things happened.

I got up to go to the loo. As I stood, I heard my phone ring. Plucking my bag from the back of the chair, I grabbed the phone.

'Laurie,' Emily. Voice tight, stressed. 'Where are you?'

'Still at the quiz.' My heart was thumping. 'What's wrong? Is it Polly?'

'Polly's fine. It's—' the line broke up. 'She—'

'I can't hear you, it's too noisy in here. Hang on.' Quickly I pushed the back door of the pub open, walked out into the car park, my breath unfurling before me in the freezing night. 'What's wrong?'

'Did Sid call you?'

'No? When?'

'He spoke to Polly earlier. She told him you'd gone to the pub. He made her cry.'

'Why?' Cold fury pressed down. 'What do you mean?'

'I don't know really. I couldn't hear exactly what he said, but I think he was angry.'

'Did you talk to him?'

'He hung up before I could.'

'Where's Pol now?'

'Tucked up in bed, asleep. She's fine, really. It's just … I thought, I know it sounds silly, but I thought I heard something a little while ago.'

'What do you mean, something?'

'Something upstairs. And then I checked and there was no one. But then I'm sure someone tried to unlock the door, only I'd put the chain on.'

'You should have called me.'

'I am calling you,' she sounded impatient. 'But I didn't want to bother you, really. It's probably nothing. I want you to have some fun. And Polly's fine. You know what Sid's like. He put the wind up me, that's all. It's just that, when the door went, I wanted to check …'

'He's still got keys. And rights, apparently,' I remembered the weary policeman. 'But he won't do anything.'

Would he?

'I tried to phone Sid just now,' she said, 'but he didn't answer.'

'Oh for God's sake. I'm sorry, Em.'

'Look, it's fine. No harm done. Just wanted to know when you'd be back.'

'I'll come now.'

From the pub I could hear the bell for last orders ringing.

'You don't need to rush,' Emily said, but she didn't sound convinced.

'I'll get a cab.'

Someone stepped up behind me. I spun quickly.

'Okay.' Emily sounded relieved. 'I'll see you soon.'

Mal was standing there. 'All right?' He looked worried.

'Yes. No. I don't know, really.' I looked at him helplessly. 'I've got to get home.'

'Shall I give you a lift?'

'Would you mind?'

'Of course not.' He reached out and pushed a strand of hair from my eyes. 'Laurie,' he said quietly.

'Mal. Please, I need to go right now.'

'Sure, let's go. I'll just get my jacket.' And before I knew it, he had leant down, and touched his lips to mine.

There was a commotion behind us as the pub door swung open and I heard Roz's voice calling me urgently. 'Laurie.'

We jumped apart, but not before another woman appeared, pushing past Roz. With a jolt, I recognised the vivid Titian hair.

'I wondered where the hell you'd got to.' Strident, angry. An Irish brogue that suddenly seemed familiar.

'Christ,' muttered Mal.

Christ indeed. It was Susie Cooper. Mal's wife.

This wasn't my mess. My mess was waiting at home.

'Sorry,' I mumbled to Mal, quietly so no one else could hear. 'I've got to go.'

I fled the car park, out onto the high street, flagged down the first cab, heart racing, palms sweating; realising, in my panic, I'd left my coat in the pub. I thought of Mal's face; put my hand on my mouth where moments ago, his lips had been.

I headed home, towards my daughter, my best friend. My empty bed.

I had done nothing wrong, had I?

Apparently, that remained to be seen.

NOW: HOUR 10

6pm

My breath leaves my body as I hit the ground hard. A voice behind us, shouting, angry at the way we have passed, unbidden and unwelcome, through his safe, enclosed world – and worse, endangering his job, no doubt.

'Stupid. You could have been killed.' The furious voice fading as we move, fast, across the tracks, away from the stationary train.

Out in the open; the strong tang of the countryside, animal, alive. I am disoriented again, my face scratched as we stumble up the embankment, though the hedge into the field on the other side.

In the distance, lights. Some kind of built-up area – a village or town, hopefully. We turn towards it. I stumble in the furrows of damp earth; Saul takes my hand and pulls me up.

'This is ridiculous,' I feel a laugh bubble inside me. Verging on hysteria. 'I feel like a fugitive.'

'I am a fugitive,' he says, echoing my earlier thought, and I laugh again, and he stares down at me until I realise he isn't joking. He drops my hand.

'Are you?'

'If you like.' Once again he shrugs eloquent shoulders.

'Fugitive from what?'

He looks ahead. 'This and that.'

'Oh,' I say, uselessly. I wonder, am I scared of him? It takes me only seconds to acknowledge that I am not. And that this is not the time to press for detail.

'So. Where are we going?'

'I thought we'd get a car.'

'I haven't got enough money,' I say. 'Have you?'

'No,' he has started walking now. 'But we don't need money.'

'Don't we?' Like a child, I follow his long stride. His jeans are very low against his narrow hips.

'No.'

It takes me a moment to absorb his meaning.

'Oh God, Saul. I don't know about that.'

He keeps walking. 'Well, I do.'

'I don't want to get in any more trouble than I need to.'

He walks on.

I run to catch him up.

'It's up to you what *you* do.' He has closed to me. I know I've angered him; he thinks I'm judging him. 'You make your own choices.'

What choices do I have, out here in the dark, desperate to get home?

'I understand,' I say. 'Sorry.'

'Do you?' he has turned against me quickly; hardened. I recognise self-preservation. 'I doubt it.'

'Don't, please. It's just …' I stutter, trying to think.

'It's just what?' he stops for a moment. 'Do you want to find your little girl, or what?'

'More than anything in the world,' I say truthfully.

'Well, then. Beggars can't be choosers.' He walks on. 'And it's only an object, and it's only borrowing. They'll get it back. The car.'

The moon has appeared from somewhere, slid out from behind fast scudding clouds into the velvet black night. The boy grins down at me, suddenly illuminated, both devilish and sanguine. 'And I'm a very good driver. Honest.'

I think of the waitress, of the interminable drive earlier, of how she got me there in the end.

'Okay,' I say.

It is time to trust in others. I have never found it easy, but I have no options now. It is a steep learning curve, but a necessary one.

Saul is walking fast. We are two-thirds of the way across the field now. I can see houses, some kind of farm buildings, a cul-de-sac perhaps.

'Saul,' I say, 'a fugitive from what?'

'Never mind,' he says. 'Just know you're not the only one who needs to get somewhere fast.'

'Somewhere?'

'To help someone.' In the darkness, his face is blank, but he clenches and unclenches his fist as we hurry. I want to know who he is thinking of, but there's no time now to ask more.

'Right. And, how do you …' I gulp air, breathless, my poor damaged lungs working hard, my throat still sore. 'How do you, you know, intend to do it? To get a car?'

If we get caught, I am thinking. What then? I remember the hard-faced policeman outside the diner. '*Wanted for arson.*' True or not, if we get caught, that'll be it.

The boy must sense my fear. We are nearing the fence now, a row of tall conifers beyond it. Buildings over to the left; barns maybe. On the road, beneath streetlamps already on, incongruous out here in the countryside, a toy-town in the dark, cars are parked.

Somewhere a dog barks. In the far distance, the hum of a busy road. The rusty caw of a late bird.

'You go down to the end of that track,' he points at a stile. 'I'll meet you there. Just be ready to bloody run fast. To get in fast. I don't know how long it'll take me.'

I take a deep breath.

'Roughly?'

'Five minutes?'

I nod. I can't speak; no air left.

We separate. The boy vaults the gate with the easy grace of an athlete.

Panic surges. What if Saul leaves me here? What if I am left in this dark that smells so pungent, in this freezing night? What if Polly is about to pull into St Pancras any minute and I am in the middle of God knows where, unable to move nearer? What if *he* gets there before me? Fear crawls over me; a sob chokes up through my chest.

I hear a voice. Somewhere to the left of me, a deep male voice, shouting – at me, I assume.

'Are you lost? This is private property.'

A light sweeps the ground; a torch beam.

'Sorry,' I mutter, into the night. I speed up.

I hear an engine turn over to the right of me, on the other side of the trees; a car door slam. I clutch my old phone in my coat pocket; remnant of my old life.

The mud flies up behind me as I start to run.

THEN: CONSEQUENCES

I slipped. Perhaps I didn't actually fall, but I certainly stumbled that night with Mal.

But the best of us have bad days, don't we?

Sid and I arrived on my front doorstep at almost exactly the same moment. It was hardly surprising that it was not a happy reunion. I had tried to call him from the taxi, attempting to calm myself after the unexpected events of the evening, furious that he'd been grilling Polly about my whereabouts. An innocent six-year-old: not her fight. But of course, Sid hadn't answered. He hadn't answered, it became apparent now, because he'd been on his way here.

'Where the fuck have you been?' he snarled, bounding up the front stairs, and I very nearly quailed in the face of his anger, but then I remembered the truth. 'Why did you leave Polly?'

'I don't know why you are here,' I tried to keep my voice level, 'and actually, it's none of your business where I've been.' I turned away, sliding the key into the lock, adrenaline making my hand jump. 'Polly was with Emily, and I've done nothing wrong.'

Of course, I *had* done something wrong, of that I was painfully aware, but not to do with Sid; not his business. I'd half kissed a man I hardly knew, a previous client, drunk, in a pub car park. His wife, ex or not – a point which remained moot – had possibly seen us, as had one of the mothers from school, friend or not. Stupid, stupid Laurie. So why should I get off scot-free?

And it was a red rag to a bull, turning my back to Sid now. I knew that but I had chosen to forget: Sid hated nothing more than not receiving the respect he thought he was due; it made him incandescent with rage. But he didn't deserve respect, so I wouldn't feign it.

'Go away, Sid,' I said softly, as the key turned.

Sid made a grab for me just as Emily, hearing me, opened the door. She stood in the hall, back-lit, reminiscent of the Pre-Raphaelites Sid so despised, long hair tumbling round her face, and she hissed 'Don't you dare,' at my husband, who stopped in his tracks. 'Not this time.'

'It's fine, Em,' I said. I had sidestepped him neatly. After all, I had had enough practice. 'Go back inside.'

Emily hesitated, standing there wrapped in a blanket; dishevelled, eyes narrowed.

'Just give us a minute,' I murmured, pushing her very gently inside.

Eventually she walked back into the house, leaving the door slightly ajar. Sid was itching to barge his way in, I could sense it, but I stood between him and the door now.

'You know, I'm not frightened of you any more,' I said.

'You were never frightened of me,' he was withering.

But we both knew the truth.

'Sid. It's over.' Steadily, I held his gaze. 'You left. So what's the problem?'

'I wanted to make sure my daughter was all right.'

'She's fine. And anyway – really? You're concerned about that, about Polly's welfare, when you're off with Jolie, are you? When you're in Paris having a good time with her, or riding a

stupid motorbike,' I felt breathless, but I pushed on, 'or at the –
the latest premiere wearing stupid matching coats?'

He looked abashed; just enough for me to know it had hit
home. And I was on a roll. 'When you're in your new studio,
wherever that may be, or ordering paint or stretching canvas—'

'I'm not working,' he interjected.

'Why not?'

'I can't.' I could hardly hear him as he looked away, his face
sullen now.

'What do you mean?' I didn't understand.

'I can't paint.'

Sid *always* painted. He painted like a demon, like a man pos-
sessed; sometimes straight through the night. He didn't always
like his work; often he hated it, but it was his life-blood. He hid
in it; he was nothing if not driven. The only time I had known
him to stop was after his brother had called about seeing their
mother. Then he had struggled to pick up a brush until sometime after the Paris trip, when he began to create the most dis-
tressing, dark work of his life; work I could hardly bear to look at.

'I can't work. I've tried a little. But it's gone.'

'What?'

'Just … it.' He shrugged. 'The inclination.'

'Why?'

'Because everything I do now is shit.'

Emily opened the door again. 'Are you staying out there all
night?' she demanded. 'It's bloody freezing and all the heat's escaping.'

'Well, shut the door then,' Sid snapped.

'Er, let me just think about that one,' she glared at him. 'How
about – no. Not till Laurie's inside.'

I walked away from Sid. It got a little easier every time.

'I'll call you,' I said.

'Don't bother,' muttered Emily.

'About Polly.'

I shut the door behind me. But not before I saw the look in his eyes. The look that made me want to scream; that lost boy look. No one else could understand. For all my bravura about Sid, he gave me something too that no one else did. That no other man ever would. A thrill I despised myself for.

And who would take care of Sid now I couldn't anymore?

How can we always get everything right? It's impossible.

I lay in bed that night, hot and restless, trying not to beat myself up for my own actions. I imagined what Bev, or my peers would say: *Don't be so hard on yourself*. Had Carl Jung, father of the psychoanalysts, inventor of the 'talking cure', always behaved correctly? When he was fucking his mistress whilst his wife popped out babies, he knew damn well that, in theory, he *should* remain faithful. Should – but didn't. '*Don't say "should"*,' instructed the humanists, the psychosynthesists, '*don't beat yourself up. Say "could"*.'

I should have, I should have, I should have.

Because reality is *not* theory. Reality is tough, in-your-face stuff; making vital decisions every day when you can barely choose what cereal to eat.

'Why is life so bloody hard?' I heard it all the time from my clients, railing against their gods. I don't know exactly what Jung would have replied, but like most of us, he simply couldn't resist something that salved the wound of living. In his case, the lure of a woman who gave him something he did not find at home.

Theory versus reality. Isn't that what life came down to?

I knew I *shouldn't* have let Mal kiss me, but I'd wanted to, and so I did. Sure, I also wanted to be alone; I wanted, more than anything, to recover from my broken marriage; to heal my horrible scars – but I was still human. Frankly, I wanted some attention. I was bloody lonely. I had been for years.

In the morning Emily made us all blueberry pancakes and then, slopping coffee into our cups, she said, 'I thought maybe I could take Polly up to Mum's?'

Her mother had moved up to a smallholding in Lincolnshire a few years ago with her new partner. Polly loved it there; all the dogs, sheep, ponies, the fresh air, the tractor rides and the muddy fields. 'She's got a new Shetland. And I'm sure Pol wants to ride.' Emily batted her eyelash extensions at me. 'You can have a break, and not worry about that—'

I shot her a look before she swore in front of Polly. Emily pulled a face, but supplicated.

'Her father. I'll bring her back tomorrow night. Please, Laurie. You have a break.' She put the lid on the maple syrup. 'Or you could come too?'

'No, you go.' For once, I made a snap decision. It'd be good for Polly to get out of the city, and I could get my head together. 'Maybe I'll join you later.'

But I knew I wouldn't. I just wanted to lock the doors against the world and retire to bed.

When Sid had moved out, I'd begun to go to bed when Polly fell asleep; not because I was tired, but simply so the day would be over. I had always been a night owl, but these days I practically threw myself into bed, desperate for oblivion. And since I had largely eschewed the booze again since leaving Spain, there was no option but to sleep.

Only, falling asleep at ten usually meant I woke at four, to lie restlessly alert and pray for oblivion again with a futile desperation, listening to the planes track relentlessly overhead, to the birds begin their day too cheerfully at dawn.

Oblivion was a game I'd been playing since Sid; hard sought; a battle I never fully won.

And throughout that day and night, whilst Polly was away, Sid kept ringing, until at last, I switched the phones off and put a pillow over my head.

NOW: HOUR 11

7pm

The car Saul has 'borrowed' is an old blue Volvo; well-worn interior, with just a hint of dog. Empty crisp packets and scrunched Coke cans rattle round the foot well, the ashtrays are overflowing.

Saul jacks the heating up and, after one false start down a lane that quickly turns into a bumpy farm-track, it doesn't take him long to find the main road. At first I find myself sitting almost on the edge of the seat, clutching the leather until my hands sweat, watching in the wing mirror for someone to follow us; for blue lights, the bleat of a siren. But soon I'm nodding off in the comfy leather seat, exhausted, the hiss of tyres on tarmac soporific as we pick up speed.

When I wake, we have stopped; apparently in some kind of lay-by. Saul is out of the car, smoking, I realise, from the tip that glows and dances in the dark – and he's talking to someone.

I sit bolt upright, my mouth dry. Who else is out there?

I open the window a little; the strong tang of manure assails me. Saul is on a phone, I see now. It sounds like he's pleading with someone.

'Please,' I hear him say. 'I promise, this time—'

He runs his hand frenetically over his shorn hair, backward and forwards it goes, I can tell, watching the trail of the orange cigarette tip.

'Yeah I know,' he's trying to speak, but whoever is on the other end is talking over him, I guess, because he stops and starts, his body language jerky and tense. 'Yes, but—' pause, 'yes, I know, Dean. I know she's out of control.' A longer pause. 'Yeah, okay, I get it. Yeah. Right. See you there.'

He chucks the cigarette and heads back to the car. Something tells me I shouldn't have been listening, so I feign sleep. As he gets in and slams the door, I pretend to wake.

'Hi,' I am genuinely bleary. 'Where are we?'

'About fifty miles from London, I reckon,' he says, but he sounds uneasy. Something is not right, I sense, as he pulls tobacco from his pocket and makes another roll-up.

'Not long then,' I say, and I almost sound jovial, but my stomach knots with tension.

He lights the cigarette; edges the car out of the lay-by, biting his thumbnail now.

'Saul,' I say quietly. 'What's wrong?'

'Nothing,' he attempts a crooked smile.

'Please tell me.'

'It's just ...' he trails off.

I know this silence. It is the silence of a tortured soul, the moment before they choose whether to unburden themselves or not.

'You can trust me,' I say.

'Is it?!' he laughs, but there is no mirth there. 'I'm not that daft.'

'You can,' I repeat.

'Laurie,' he glances at me. 'Not now. Go back to sleep.'

I don't mean to; I want to stay awake, to keep an eye on him, to talk him down from whatever it is that's scaring him, but I am so tired, and the car is so warm, and soon I am drifting again.

'We need petrol,' a voice says, cutting through my dream of slicing ham sandwiches for Polly's lunch. I can't think whose the voice is.

'I'm going to have to stop,' the voice says again.

I blink. My sore eye is stuck together with something. I rub it.

'Laurie.' More urgent. 'Do you have any money for petrol?'

'Sorry.' I scrabble to stir myself. I focus on Saul; feeling a little sick, utterly disconnected. Hunger and the effects of the painkillers are getting to me. I pat my pockets, bring out my money. 'This is everything I have.'

Saul casts a disparaging eye over what I hold in my hands, the crumpled note, the few coins.

'Not enough. This car drinks bloody petrol,' he says shortly. He looks ahead again, his hands clenched on the wheel.

The fuel light blinks on the dashboard.

It isn't the painkillers, or hunger. It is fear. My life is spiralling into some madness I do not understand and cannot control.

Ahead, a service station looms out of the darkness. Saul's jaw is set tight; he indicates left. I have a knot of foreboding in my stomach although I am excited to see we are somewhere on the M25 now.

We pull off the motorway and follow the fuel signs. Saul pulls up at the pump furthest from the kiosk; we are masked by a van. He jumps out, and starts to fill the tank. My instinct says this cannot be good. But what does my instinct know? I have lost all faith in it. My heart is starting to hammer. The long-haired driver in the van is re-setting his sat nav. He looks down at me, and winks. I look away. I cannot shake the feeling I am on the run; I shouldn't be seen.

Saul starts to walk towards the building and I feel a massive wave of relief. He's going to pay. I open the window to call for coffee. Suddenly he doubles back on himself, patting his pockets in a show of 'forgetting his wallet'.

He gets into the car slowly and sits, looking around him, and then, just as I am about to hand him my money, he flips the ignition on and, slamming the door, pulls out. My head whips back; the tyres actually screech.

No one in the petrol station seems to react; maybe because we are moving so fast. Despite my racing heart, everything stays the same.

I swallow my protestation. I *am* on the run.

'Saul,' I say as we hit the exit route. 'Lights.'

'I know,' he frowns.

But as we meet the motorway he flicks them on.

I am not sure how much of this I can take.

We drive fast for a few minutes, both of us constantly checking the mirrors. The motorway is quite empty. After a while, I say, 'I don't know if I can do this anymore, Saul.'

'So?' he is tense, irritated. 'What do you want me to do about it?'

'I don't know,' I mutter.

'Laurie,' he glances at me. 'I can let you out. You don't have to come with me. It's your choice.'

Let me out? In the middle of nowhere? I look out into the night. The entire countryside is shrouded by darkness.

'It's fine,' I say. 'Sorry.'

But my heart won't calm again. It clatters away, and I feel nauseous with fear. I am terrified that they will stop us, and then I won't be able to find Polly. But right now, Saul seems my only chance of getting to her. I wish I could think straighter but lack of sleep blurs the lines; makes me delirious. I see things on the side of the road, faces like smudges in the darkness; a plastic bag flapping in a hedge like a white goose. I need coffee. I need sleep.

I need my daughter.

I have a thought, and I rummage through the glove-box. CDs, some old peanuts, an Ordnance Survey map. And a coiled white lead – a phone charger! My heart soars.

I plug it into the cigarette lighter and pull my iPhone out, my old phone that's been dead since the last flicker at the station.

It doesn't fit. Of course it doesn't, that would be too good to be true. It's the wrong charger; it's for a Nokia I see now.

'Wrong phone?' Saul asks.

'Have you got one?' I ask him, without much hope. 'For an iPhone 6?'

'Course,' he grins. 'Where would we be without Apple, eh? Side pocket of my rucksack.'

I lean over onto the back seat, pull open the zip. Various phones and chargers are tucked inside. I glance at him.

'Don't ask,' he says.

'Okay.' I find the one I need. 'I won't.'

'It might be a bit temperamental,' he warns as I plug it in, and I see the split in the flex, already taped-up by some unseen hand. I pray it works. As I fiddle, Saul puts the radio on. An Elbow song finishes; then I recognise Jolie's lilting voice, singing about pure love. I almost laugh, but if I start, I won't stop. I reach out and change stations; something classical, soothing, quiet.

'Not a fan of that Jolie bird?' Saul is trying to make friends again. The tension stretches between us. I read the tattoos on his hand. '*Carpe diem*' one says, only they've left the 'e' off *Carpe*. My heart softens. He is only a boy. I have a weakness for dysfunctional males; the proverbial lost boys of JM Barrie's Never Neverland.

I switch my old phone on now it has a little charge; the voice-mail symbol pings up. Seven messages. My stomach contracts, thinking it will be Sid again, but, listening, I realise the first is my mother, and my heart soars.

They are safe, for now at least.

'*The trip's been wonderful. We're a little bit late though because of the strike this end. Control people or something. Very French, lots of shouting and hand waving at the Gare du Nord.*' I smile as she pronounces the hard 'd'. '*Anyway, love, I'll ring you when we're through the tunnel. Polly's dying to see you. She's been so good. I'm really going to miss her, Laurie. She's given me a new lease of life.*'

The phone dies. For a second, I feel cheered; but I know she hasn't got my messages on her landline and she doesn't realise the danger. I fiddle around again; the charger isn't working any-more apparently. I find myself biting my own thumbnail now. I haven't done that since I was a child.

'Why have you got two phones?' Saul's voice breaks my rev-erie.

'What?'

'Two phones. You've got two. I just wondered why.'

'You've got about five,' I counter. 'Apparently.'

'Yeah. But I'm a good for nothing. You're not.'

'Oh I'm sure you're not.' But now is not the time for moral discussion or rebuttal, I sense. 'I've got them because ...' but I don't know how to continue.

'Because?'

'Because, there's someone I don't want to speak to. On this one,' I hold the old one up.

'Who?'

I wrinkle my face. 'My husband. Ex-husband.'

'Why?'

I lean my head against the cool glass for a moment. 'It's complicated.'

'Isn't it always?' Saul grins. 'Love, eh? I'm rubbish with women.'

Women! He is so young.

'I can't believe that,' I say. He is a little grimy, perhaps, but he is … very male. Slender, maybe, but with a strength I cannot quite describe; as if a fine layer of steel mesh lies beneath his skin. The kind of boy I imagine girls his age would swoon over; those piercing eyes that see right through you. Aloof; alluring.

'I am,' he shrugs, scrabbling in the well for his tobacco. 'I fall too hard.'

I'm surprised. 'Really?' I look at him.

'Yep.'

'Why, do you think?'

'Dunno. Always have done.'

'Is there someone now?' I think of the phone call I overheard; the 'she' he referred to.

'Nope.' He grins again. 'Are you going to analyse me?'

My turn to shrug. 'Maybe.'

'I'll analyse you first.'

'Go on then.'

'I'd say he's a bastard.'

'Who?' I look out at the night.

'You know who. Your ex.'

I'm about to demur, but what's the point?

'Maybe,' I say again, quieter this time.

'Nasty, was he?'

I turn the phone over in my hands. 'Why do you say that?'

'You're hiding from him. It's not difficult.'

'I'm not hiding from him because he was nasty.' But that's not true. Not exactly. 'I'm not hiding from him, really. I'm just ... I'm confused.'

'About what?'

'I think ...' I remember the hotel. I can see Emily and I splashing around in the huge marble pool, laughing in the deep end, her blue mascara adrift beneath her eyes. Was it really only yesterday? 'Well. My friend – my best friend, she just – she died.' The word almost chokes me. 'But I think ... I don't think it was her who was meant to die.'

'I'm sure she wasn't. Though, what is it they say?' he glances at me. 'The good die young?'

'No, what I mean is ...' I take a deep breath. 'I think someone was after *me*.'

'After you?'

'Trying to ...' I swallow. 'Trying to kill me.'

'When?'

'Last night.'

'Fucking hell,' the car swerves as he tries to roll his tobacco at eighty mph. 'Why?'

'I'll do that, shall I?' I say tartly, taking the Rizla and the Golden Virginia from him. 'You concentrate on the road.' Quickly I make a neat roll-up.

'Impressive,' he takes it, raising a pierced eyebrow.

'I have many hidden talents.'

'So. Someone tried to kill you?' Saul lights the cigarette. 'That's heavy. Are you sure?'

I pause. I think. 'Pretty sure.'

Am I though? I feel exhausted suddenly, lean back, shutting my eyes. Last night floods in again.

'Why?'

'I don't know,' I say, slowly, opening my eyes. 'But the door was locked. I remember that. We were in our hotel room, Emily and I, I was in bed and then …' and then what happened? I find my fingers at my temples as if I am trying to force the memory back into my head.

'And then?' Saul prompts.

'And then, it's hard. I'd fallen asleep.' I remember grabbing Emily's hoodie from the back of the door, shoving feet into my trainers, going down the corridor. 'Emily had a migraine. She woke me to ask me to get her painkillers from the car. When I came back from outside, the fire alarm went off.'

'And she didn't come out of the room?'

I can't speak for a moment.

'Laurie? You okay?'

'It was all so … hectic,' I say quietly. People running. Screaming. Thick, acrid smoke. No air.

'And?'

Slowly I try to piece the bits together.

'I ran back to the room but,' I find I am rubbing my sore hand, 'I couldn't … I couldn't get the bloody door open. I had my key-card thing – but it just wouldn't work. It was like, I don't know, Saul. Like the door was jammed by something – something heavy. And she …' I grind to a halt.

He glances at me. 'What?'

'She was inside.'

'Did you tell the police?'

I shrug. 'Yeah, sure, I tried, but it was all so crazy. I think they just thought I was hysterical. Most people were a bit. And anyway,' I think of Sid, and of the threat of injunctions; of the biker on the motorway; of the incredulous policeman earlier. 'Let's just say, my card was marked already. The police are not my number one fans.'

'Sounds familiar.' In the gloom, Saul half-smiles. 'But why do you think he was trying to kill *you*?'

The tobacco smoke is sweet as it fills the car. I don't answer.

'Your ex?' he prompts. 'Why would he be trying to kill you?'

'He was so angry with me. Because I left him. Because I took our daughter.'

Emily was inside.

I think I might be sick. I sit up, open the window. I hear Emily's voice on the wind outside.

'Do you mind,' I whisper, the cold night air lashing my face. 'Do you mind if we leave it for now?'

'Course,' Saul says, and turns the radio up.

We are in Kent now, just below London, about to turn up towards the capital, I presume. My knowledge of this part of the world is extremely hazy. I see a sign for the Channel Tunnel.

I have an idea.

'Saul,' I say, excited. 'Could we go to Ashford? To the station? We can't be far. It'd be quicker than going into central London, wouldn't it?'

I can meet the Eurostar. I can be with Polly.

'Course,' he shrugs. 'No skin off my knob.'

Not long now. I shut the window and close my eyes again. The grief is numbing.

I dream of Emily.

THEN: MY NEIGHBOUR NEXT DOOR

I was woken late on Sunday morning by an incessant ringing on the doorbell.

After Emily and Polly had left for Lincolnshire, I had closed the door behind them and locked it. I hadn't gone out; I hadn't talked to anyone for over twenty-four hours. Never healthy, actually, to lock yourself away, not really. I certainly told my clients that all the time. But it was definitely easiest, given my frame of mind. My own words bored me, on the rare occasions when they spooled out of me; and I didn't want my own pain reflected back at me in anyone's concerned expression.

Heading down the stairs, I caught sight of myself in the hall mirror. I hadn't brushed my hair since I got back from the pub on Friday and my eyes were bruised and puffy with too much sleep, my pyjamas old and scruffy. I looked exactly like I felt.

Tentatively I opened the door.

'Oh, I'm so glad you're in,' the woman looked relieved. 'Laurie, isn't it?'

I don't know whom I'd expected to see, but it certainly wasn't my elderly neighbour, peering anxiously up the hallway behind me.

'Yes,' I agreed. 'Mrs ...' I blanked. 'Sorry, I can't ...'

'Henderson. Margaret.'

'Mrs Henderson.' Something visceral shunted me as I remembered a moment I'd tried hard to bury. 'Is everything all right?'

I hadn't seen her in a while. Deliberately, I acknowledged to myself now. I had avoided her as best I could.

'I'm not sure.' She looked behind her rather nervously. I could sense that she wanted to come in, but I resisted, hand firmly on the door-jamb.

'What's wrong?'

It felt awkward in the extreme. Above all else, I remembered that which I wanted to forget.

'I don't want you to think that I'm prying—'

'But?' Too late, I realised that I'd snapped at her.

'But. I just wanted to check. Your ... your husband,' she trailed off miserably. She had a soft burr about her voice; maybe the West Country somewhere.

'Sid? What about him?'

'I thought ... he did move out, didn't he? I remember seeing him, loading things up. A while back.' She met my eye, she ploughed on anyway. 'A van, I think?'

I rather admired her valour.

'Some time ago,' I nodded bleakly. 'Yes.'

'Only I thought ... I thought I saw him. Yesterday.'

'Well, you might have done. He comes to get Polly.'

'Oh,' she blinked at me. 'You let him see your daughter?'

My hand clutched the door tighter. She blinked again, as if debating whether she'd overstepped a mark.

'Why would I not let him see her?' I bit back my retort; I must be polite. She meant no harm, I was aware. She had seen something that had troubled her, that was all.

'Because ...' her hands fluttered helplessly. 'Because of what happened.'

I had a flash of myself as I would rather forget. A flash of the person this woman standing in front of me *thought* I was;

of what she *thought* she'd seen. I drew myself up a little, met her gaze. Her eyes were kind; watery, the faded blue of denim.

'Mrs Henderson—'

'Margaret.'

'Margaret. I understand your concerns; it was an …' I searched for a word. 'An *unfortunate* incident, and I'm very sorry you had to witness it. But it was a one-off, and I am fine, really, and I would never let Polly go somewhere I thought she might be in any …'

I couldn't say the word. I just couldn't quite countenance it.

'Danger,' she finished for me.

'Yes,' I nodded affirmation, holding the door-frame so hard that my fingers felt numb. 'Anyway, I must get on. As you can see,' I glanced down at my unkempt self, 'I'm not really ready for the day.'

'Of course.' What was she thinking now, though? Single mother, abandoned by husband, lets herself go? 'I'll let you go. It's just … I wanted to say too, I do …' she glanced up into the far corner of my cobwebby porch; choosing words; looking for ghosts. 'I am not sorry I witnessed it. I am only sorry for you. And not … not in a patronising way.' We gazed at one another. 'Because I … I do, well, I have some understanding.'

She reached out and patted my hand, still clutching on to the door for dear life. To my horror, I felt my eyes fill.

'You'd better go inside, Laurie, dear. Before you catch your death.'

She walked down the porch stairs.

'Mrs … Margaret…' I said.

She turned.

'If you do see …' I cleared my throat. 'If you do see Sid at a funny time of the day or night, you could … you could let me know?'

'Of course,' she nodded. 'Of course I will.'

'I'll drop my numbers round later.'

Inside the house, I leant on the closed door, and the tears I had tried so hard to hide spilt down my face unchecked. I cried until I could hardly breathe, and still I couldn't stop.

Just after I got married, before the pain began in earnest, I went to see my father. My father, the charmer. Oh, he had everyone wrapped round his little finger, my pa. Self-made money, get-rich-quick schemes that finally worked. Irish blarney, stories to listen to all night; gold fillings, silk handkerchiefs in suit pockets; the looks and ease of a debonair gentleman – with the spine of a degenerate; a shell-less mollusc.

My mother. Small, dear, worrying. Anxious, cake-baking, making time for the sick and old of her small community, giving up her accounts job at the local brewery at my father's behest. So people wouldn't think she had to work. So people wouldn't see beneath the surface. A little naïve perhaps, my mother; never any soul-searching. Hiding her misery so damn convincingly to outsiders. But flattened long ago. Deadened.

In the end, he left her anyway, despite all her acquiescence; ran off with his business partner's twenty-five-year-old daughter. Frankly, it was a relief. It didn't last, but the family disbanded anyway; not before time, probably. My older brother had already gone; had had enough by sixteen. He couldn't help our mother, he realised, because she wouldn't be helped. He left home, crossed the globe to Sydney; never returned.

Pregnant with Polly, nauseous and swollen with hormones and baby, one sunny day in September I caught a train and went to see my father in Tunbridge Wells.

I wanted to ask why he had refused to come to the wedding. Was it deliberate? Had he tried to spoil my day?

But he wouldn't play ball. He wouldn't answer anything, he almost refused to talk at all. We sat in awkward silence over a cup of Nescafé and some stale, softening brandy snaps, and then I caught the train home again. He never even met Polly.

Before he died, last year, he came to see me one last time, looking horribly old. Then he wrote me a letter.

It was the hardest letter I had ever had to read. He admitted why he hadn't come. He admitted what he'd done; his shame. Trying to make amends.

Too late.

Finally it made sense. Finally I understood myself. My own patterns. The things I'd thought I'd heard as a child, cringing in the midnight shadows. I put the letter away. At first, I thought maybe I should show my mother, but I wasn't sure she could bear it, so I put it at the back of my desk drawer and waited for the right time. It never came.

They were still there; my father's scars. In me. They always had been.

After Mrs Henderson's visit, when I stopped crying, I went and got in the shower, and afterwards, I picked up the phone and resolutely made a call that I'd been debating for a bit. I saw myself at seventeen, laughing, with Emily, matching peroxide hair, cut-off dungarees and long beads, dancing, drinking, with our friends in the local pub. Happy. Happier. Not exactly carefree, but not far off.

I would not keep being this victim I didn't recognise.

I got dressed, and dried my hair; I needed to regain some control. I put on mascara and a spray of perfume. I went downstairs and finished the coffee from yesterday – and then I found the emergency vodka at the back of the food cupboard. I poured a small one and drank it in one. I topped it up.

I would not chastise myself any more.

All these things we fight, and yet, it's impossible always to do everything exactly right. It's just life.

The doorbell rang again. This time I knew who it would be.

NOW: HOUR 12

8pm

The next time I wake, we have stopped again, and everything is definitely not all right.

At first I think, thank God, we must have reached Ashford Station, and I grope around blindly, to sit, looking for the lights – but actually we are in darkness. Saul holds his phone clamped to his pierced ear, the other hand to his mouth as he chews ferociously on that ragged thumbnail. His window is slightly open, and I can hear a strange screeching; can smell something new. It takes me a minute or two to realise it's the tang of the ocean.

This is not good. Why are we by the sea? I squint at the clock. We should definitely be in Ashford by now.

Saul is trying to speak, but someone is shouting at him down the phone. It's a girl's voice, and she sounds hysterical.

'Janie,' he keeps saying, 'shush, love,' but Janie, whoever she is, isn't listening. She is shouting.

'Janie ...' he says again, but another tirade begins. Despite it, I am struck by the tenderness in his voice.

Eventually the tirade ends. Then, nothing. She has hung up, apparently. Saul looks like he is about to smash the mobile against the dashboard.

'Saul,' I say urgently. 'What's going on? Where are we? You said—'

'Shut up,' he holds a hand up. I think for a moment he's going to hit me, and I duck. Then I realise he's listening.

In the distance I hear another sound, a noise that sickens me. It is the roar of an engine that is getting nearer.

Saul has sold me out. I start to scrabble at the door, my fingernails catching on the leather, but he reaches over and stops me.

'Don't,' he hisses. 'For fuck's sake, stay inside the car.'

'Why?' I say. My voice is a cracked whisper.

'Just do it.'

'Did you tell them where I was?' I say.

'Who?' his frown deepens. 'Tell who? I don't know what you're on about.'

Light floods the windscreen.

'Fuck.' He pushes me down so I am slumped, half double, in the passenger seat. 'Stay there. Don't let them see you.'

I am convinced he's done some deal; that he's told them where I am. But he doesn't know anything about me, not really, so how could he? I've never mentioned my surname, or Sid's name, even …

'Where are we?' I struggle to get up.

He bends near me. 'Laurie, please. Stay there. I don't want these nutters to see you.' He opens his car door. 'The key's in the ignition. If I don't come back, just fucking drive.' He looks down again. 'You can drive, can't you?'

I nod stupidly. He gets out. He looks down at me and gives me half a shaky wink.

'Saul,' I say, grabbing for his coat sleeve, but the shingle is already crunching beneath his foot as he heads towards the light.

He has gone.

It's the noise I can't bear. The crunch of shingle beneath boot; the crunch of bone.

I fumble at the door; I almost fall out of the car.

It's hard to make things out on this dark beach, but I know that Saul is on his knees. A smaller wiry man stands above him, a dark figure sits on the back of the bike whose engine still runs. The figure seems to be examining its nails.

The hiss and slap of the waves hitting land; the sucking of the sea as it pulls back out.

I see the wiry man take a run at Saul.

'Stop!' I scream. The figure on the bike looks up. The short man stops in surprise. Saul looks towards me, his face a pale bloodied disc in the darkness.

'Laurie,' he says, wearily. 'Fuck off.'

'Yeah,' the short man laughs derisively. He is not wiry, I see now, but more like a barrel; shaggy, moustached. He spits at my feet. 'Why don't you fuck off, Lau-*rie*?'

'What has he done?' I stand my ground. The stench of rotten fish floats on the breeze.

'What hasn't he done?' Barrel Man snorts. His hands are laden with silver skull-rings that glint in the darkness.

'Can I … please, I … let me help,' I plead. 'How can I help?' The man eyes me.

'Have you got ten grand?' he says, and spits again. 'Laurie Van.'

Funny guy. 'Why?' I ask.

'Have you got ten grand?'

'Not here, no.' I try to laugh, although I've rarely felt more like screaming. Anything, though, to diffuse the tension

The man stares at me and then walks backwards. It is very measured walking. He is going to take a running jump at Saul's head, I can sense it. Why doesn't he get up? *Get up, Saul.*

'But I can get it,' I shout. 'The money. I can get it.'

The man glares at me as if it is the wrong answer. 'You must be desperate,' he says.

'Desperate?' I think of Polly.

'To save him.'

I look at Saul.

'Yes,' I say clearly. 'I am desperate to save him.'

'Fuck,' the man says. 'He must be good in bed.'

I don't respond.

'You, pal,' the man says, derisively, 'you've got one fucking useless bint round your neck like a dead weight, and one desperate to save you.' He glances at the figure on the bike. 'Women. All whores or madonnas.'

God. So tired, this cliché. So over-used.

The woman on the bike looks away; Saul looks up. I cannot read his exact expression, but I think it is one of dereliction. He has given up.

But I have not, I realise. I will not give up.

I feel a flush of my own chemical relief, a wave I can ride for a while at least.

'What do you need?' I ask the man.

'The money.'

'I don't have it here, obviously. What can I give you now? To mark my word?'

'Your word?' he sneers. 'This isn't a fucking gentleman's club.'

'I know,' I can feel myself shaking with adrenaline. Who do I think I am? Lara Croft? Lisbeth Salander? 'But I want to show you I mean it. What can I give you?'

'Yourself?' he scoffs.

The figure on the bike stiffens.

I think frantically. I have nothing. No – I have one thing: the ring. I have been saving it for the real emergency. But they are all bleeding into one now. Get out of this situation and I can get to my daughter, that's all I know.

'My ring?' I slip it off. Maybe it's time it went to someone else. It has brought me no luck whatsoever. 'Take my ring.'

'Laurie,' Saul says. 'It's not your fight.'

'Saul,' I say. 'Get up. Please.'

I hold the ring out to the man. Saul pulls my hand back.

'I won't let you.'

'You haven't got much choice,' Barrel Man says. 'I'd let Mrs Lorry-driver help you, sonny boy.'

He holds his hand out for the ring. I try to step forward, but Saul is still restraining me, although his grasp is less certain than before.

'Saul,' I whisper. 'Who was on the phone?'

He won't look at me. Blood trickles down his face; his lip is split, the piercing has come out.

I shake myself free and walk up to the man. He stinks of old sweat. I hold out the ring. 'This ring is very expensive,' I say. 'It's worth at least five grand alone. More, probably.'

'Yeah, right,' the man says. 'And I'm Charlie's aunt.'

'I'm sure Charlie is very proud,' it's out before I think too hard. He stares. My stomach swoops. 'And it is, actually. It was handmade for me.'

'Aren't you the lucky one,' the figure on the bike says, through her helmet. She sniffs her displeasure.

The man takes the ring, sparks his cigarette lighter to examine it. I watch the translucent stones glint blue beneath the flame. The flame goes out; the colours disappear. He pockets the ring.

I take Saul's hand. 'So, we can go now,' I say.

It's not a question.

The man does not stop us, though I expect him to.

Saul limping beside me, I walk towards the car.

THEN: SLEEPING WITH THE ENEMY

When Emily brought Polly home that evening, I was still a little dishevelled; a whole lot discombobulated.

I put my daughter to bed and then I opened a bottle of Becks for Em at the kitchen table.

'You look funny,' she said. 'Different.'

I flushed. 'What do you mean?'

'I don't know really.' She eyed me quizzically. 'You have a look about you I haven't seen for a while. Have you been drinking?'

'No.' The vodka was tucked safely into the cupboard. Chastely, I sipped tea now.

'Are you sure?'

'Yes.' She knew me too well. I changed the subject. 'I've been thinking. Worrying. Am I wrong to let Sid see her? To see Polly?'

'Why?' Emily took a slug of beer. 'What's prompted this? Are you getting maudlin?'

'No. It's just ... my neighbour came round earlier.'

'So?'

Now I felt reticent. 'I haven't seen her for a while.'

'And?' Emily was impatient. 'What are you getting at?'

I warmed my hands on my mug.

'I was embarrassed,' I said quietly. 'About something that happened a while ago.'

'Why?' She looked at me directly; tiger eyes that took in everything. 'What happened?'

The lump in my throat stopped me speaking.

'Sid?'

I nodded.

'What?' She moved towards me, about to hug me.

'Don't,' I hid my face in my hands, but the tears spilt again.

'What?'

'Don't be nice to me. It makes it worse.'

'Oh, you silly cow,' Emily hugged me. She still smelt of sandalwood. 'It's okay to cry. You hold it in all the time. I see you, so held together, so bloody stoic, but it's bloody bad for you. It scares me, Laurie. You need to let it out, lovely.'

But the tears dissipated quickly, absorbed by the mention of stoicism. I fetched a tissue and blew my nose.

'So,' Emily was careful now, not looking at me. 'What did she see? Your nosey neighbour.'

'What did she *think* she saw, you mean?'

'Okay,' she shrugged, 'what did she *think* she saw?'

Months ago, when Sid still lived here, in the middle of a cold March night, Margaret Henderson saw me half-naked in my front porch, dressed only in a t-shirt. Roused by my frantic hammering on the door for Sid to let me back into the house again, she had walked along the pavement to ask if I was all right, by which time I was crying with rage and frustration and pain. And as soon as she had approached, Sid had opened the door. He must have been watching from a window the whole time. Tormenting me.

Tormented by me.

I didn't speak to the woman that night; I just fled inside when he opened up, up the stairs, checking first that Polly was asleep before locking myself into her bedroom and crawling into her bed. Waking the next morning so bruised I could hardly move,

I pretended I was fine to my sleepy, surprised daughter. Realised this could not continue.

Margaret Henderson had, however, missed the exact moment that Sid had shoved me out of the house, so hard my breath had been expelled from my body. I had fallen down the front stairs onto my knees, stunned and winded, landing on all fours like an animal, frozen for a moment, so dazed I couldn't move. I still remember looking up at the soapy whorls of the camellia flowers before me, and thinking how perfect they were.

Eventually I'd managed to pull myself inelegantly to my feet – almost naked, utterly humiliated, my nose bleeding, my shins grazed. Praying no one had seen me, I'd managed to scramble up into the porch as quickly as possible, alternately banging on the door and flattening myself against the porch wall, trying to hide myself.

'She saw me after I had rowed with Sid,' I said carefully, sitting again. 'Last Easter. When things got so bad. After his mother turned up. Again.'

How the hell had it come to this, I had thought, in between sobs, in between my desperate knocking; the pain in my left ribs sharp, fingerprint bruises already flowering on my arms.

'Bad?' Emily frowned.

The first time he had left real marks on me, intentionally.

'She saw me after …' I cleared my throat. 'After he'd shoved me outside in … in just a …' I trailed off.

If you didn't count the split lip.

'In just a what?' she shook her head.

'In just a … a t-shirt.'

'Why?'

'Oh I don't know, Em. To teach me a lesson, I suppose.'

'Oh right,' Emily's eyes were dark with anger. 'And what lesson would that have been, then?'

'I don't know really. I think it was to do with speaking to someone at school.' I had blocked out the incident as best I could. 'A dad.'

'Oh, that old chestnut. Of course.'

'Yup.' I really didn't want to talk about it – and it was also reminding me of things I'd rather not think about now. Like Mal.

'Best rid, darling,' Emily knew me so well. She saluted me with her beer. 'Best rid.'

'But when she came round earlier, that Margaret woman, oh, I don't know. It just made me think. She said she'd seen Sid and she … she seemed to be worried about Polly,' I feel a suffocating clutch of fear now. 'Oh God. Do you think I'm mad, Em? Letting him see Polly?'

'No.' She was firm. 'I don't think you're mad. For all his faults, Sid adores Pol, we all know that.'

She was right, and that was why I still let him see her. He'd never raised a hand to our daughter; of that much I was quite sure. Apparently, it was only me that riled him. And recently, my solicitor had warned me to 'play nice' if I wanted to retain full custody.

'But, having said that,' Emily finished her beer and stood now, pulling her old Afghan coat around her. 'Well, really, lovely, you're the best judge of Sid's behaviour. It has to be your decision.'

Oh God. Maybe I *was* making all the wrong choices.

'I don't feel like a good judge of anything much right now,' I said quietly, thinking about earlier, after Margaret Henderson had returned to her neat house and I had made my phone call. Thinking about the few hours I wasn't sure yet if I regretted.

I followed Emily up the stairs, watching her flick her hair over her collar. For once, I was glad she was heading home. I wasn't ready to share what I'd done.

Mal was much heavier than Sid. Less fine-boned, less ethereal – more ... male, I guess. I realised that properly when he un-buttoned his shirt that first time, a big, slightly shambolic man, silhouetted in the winter afternoon light slanting through the sitting-room window.

Half-unbuttoned myself, my mouth already burning from his stubble, I had stood and shut the curtains as he undid his belt. The back garden was sheltered and not visible from the other houses, but I was still unnerved by the thought that some-one had been prowling ... and this, here, now, on my old sofa, this was only between us.

Mal was nervous, I could tell; and I was a little drunk. I'd had two large vodkas even before he'd arrived, and when he had finally kissed me, which had taken some time to orchestrate, he was a little clumsy, our teeth clashing for a moment. We laughed awkwardly but the truth was, at first, we weren't a natural fit. I was anticipating already, to be honest, that the sex wouldn't be great.

But it was the first time, I reminded myself. Albeit quite likely the last.

And was it ever great the first time?

I tried desperately not to think of Sid; the fact I hadn't slept with another man since the day I'd met him at the art school. Sid had been enough; more than enough. He had taken every ounce of my energy, and then more; had utterly sapped me.

And my body was different now; marked by him. I had borne his child; no other man had seen me naked since before I had been pregnant with Polly. How had I changed? I didn't know; I was just impatient to get on with it.

I pulled Mal down to me.

At first I found myself thinking he didn't do things quite right. But that wasn't fair really. He just did things differently to Sid.

After a while, I stopped thinking about anything much.

And once I gave into it, it became less about the memory of Sid and more about me and Mal. About this moment, and a moment I badly needed. To remember I was still living. That life hadn't stopped because Sid and I had parted.

Afterwards, I just felt a huge sense of relief that it was done; that the void between Sid and no one had finally been bridged.

Mal pulled me into a rather awkward hug, there on the sofa, my chin almost in his ear, my arm twisted between us uncomfortably. I let myself lie motionless for a moment, before pins and needles set in and I had to move.

'Drink?' I said brightly, grabbing for my dress on the floor.

'Oh,' he said, sitting up. 'Yes. Please.'

He looked a little bewildered, so I leant forward and kissed him on the cheek.

'Thank you.'

He grinned. 'No, Laurie. Thank *you*. That was … well.' He looked around for his shirt. 'Not quite what I was expecting to do this Sunday afternoon – especially after such a— '

'What?'

'Reticent start, I was going to say.'

'Well,' I found his shirt behind the sofa and handed it to him. 'We have to live in the moment sometimes, don't we?

Or that's what all the silly 'mindfulness' experts bang on about, anyway.'

We grinned at each other, rather awkwardly.

In the kitchen, I put the kettle on, found him a beer and put the vodka away. It had served its purpose.

We sat in comfortable silence, looking at the garden, at a squirrel trying to fathom out how to steal the birdseed.

'Cheeky little buggers,' Mal said.

'Aren't they,' I agreed. I wondered what would happen next; surprised by how calm I felt about the situation.

When he left he kissed me on the mouth, and I put my arms around him and hugged him, and felt his arms around my back, and it was nice to feel the warmth and strength of a man. I had not hugged anyone really apart from Polly for months and months; Emily occasionally, maybe, but there is a difference between women and children.

We are animals, I found myself thinking. We need animal things; like touch and sex and brutal force to remind us we're alive. Maybe what I'd done wasn't such a bad thing, after all.

The next day, leaving in the morning for school with Polly, passing Mrs Henderson's glossy-leaved camellias, I remembered briefly that I meant to give her my number.

For some reason, I never got round to it.

Maybe I'd have been safer if I had.

NOW: HOUR 13

9pm

I open the passenger door for Saul and manhandle him into the car as gently as I'm able. He doesn't argue. I get in the other side; look for the key to turn the ignition. My hands are shaking. Of course there is no key. With a grunt of pain, Saul leans over me, and reattaches the wires he hot-wired earlier. I can feel the heat of his body across my legs, the wet of the blood from his lip on my hand.

After a grumble or two, the engine fires.

I don't look behind me, or in the mirror, as I pull off. I try to steady my hands on the wheel, taking several deep breaths, waiting for the roar of a motorbike – but I don't hear one.

'Where are we?' I say after a minute or two, trying to steady my voice. The road is very straight, skirting the coast. Beyond the shingle beach, the sea is a great dark sigh.

'Dungeness,' Saul mutters, his voice indistinct. His lip is split badly, blood trails from his eyebrow and glistens on his cheek, darkening by the second.

'Power station?' I say.

'Artists, my dear,' Saul affects a posh voice. 'Yeah, and power stations and steam railways and BNP.'

Before I can respond, Saul starts to cough. It's an odd, guttural sound.

I glance at him and fear rises in me again. I pull the car into a bus stop.

'Don't let the engine stall,' he says, but pain is etched on his face.

'God, that looks nasty,' I move my hand towards his cheek. 'Let me see.'

He flinches, but still he lets me take his chin gently and manoeuvre it round so I can see him properly. At least he's stopped coughing.

'You shouldn't have …' he starts to say, and then he gags – on his own blood, I think.

'Don't talk,' I say. I search in the car for something to staunch the blood, but everything is grimy and covered in dog hair. I find a serviette from the train in a pocket; I hold it gently to his lip and then his brow.

'I think you need stitches.' The idea of another hospital is anathema to me, but Saul is hurt.

'Fuck that.' To him too, apparently. He coughs, opens the door, spits. Groans, clutches his sides. 'Christ. My ribs.' He looks at me and manages a weak grin. 'Again.'

'Oh, Saul.' I stare into the night, at the Union Jack that flaps in the wind above the pub on our left.

Broken ribs. I open my mouth to empathise; to tell him something – and then—

There is a buzz; a deafening roar.

A flank of motorbikes appears out of the darkness behind us, Harleys, low to the ground; a coterie of scarved and bearded riders. They pull up next to the pub. I search frantically for Barrel Man and his woman, but it's too difficult to distinguish them in this group.

'Let's go, Laurie,' Saul is urgent. 'GO, for fuck's sake!'

We go.

I don't know how it happens, because I must have blacked out. I remember fixing my eyes on the ribbon of road before us, the window open for the cold air; I remember thinking, if I don't sleep, we will crash; watching Saul from the corner of my eye drifting in and out of consciousness; from exhaustion, I prayed, rather than his injuries. He is still refusing to let me take him to the hospital and when I see the look in his eye at my last suggestion, I don't dare argue again. So I keep driving, out of the town, away from the buildings, and then the next thing I know, there is a massive noise in my head and a huge juddering jolt and my cheek whacks against something hard and cold and I rebound; I think I stop breathing for a second just because the breath is knocked out of me and because I am so shocked.

The car is tilted, rammed up against something. I think we're in a ditch, and I hear a scrabbling noise: it's Saul, opening his door. I give my own door a nudge but it's wedged hard, I realise after a minute, and then a hand grabs my arm.

'We need to move fast, Laurie,' Saul instructs. 'Come on, hurry up.'

I resist his pressure. I am so stunned I can't compute anything; I just want to sit here and wait for someone to come and look after me.

'Laurie,' he urges. 'I need to go before the feds arrive. Are you coming?'

And this is the moment I think – it is time. Time to stop running and give up. I've done nothing wrong and they can take me in, the police – think of me what they will, but surely they will help me and it will all be over.

But then I think of the policeman near Sherborne who said I was wanted for arson; I think of the fact that I've been running, which will only make things look worse – and I think about whoever it was who shut Emily's door, who stopped her from escaping from the fire. I could hear them, I know I could, in the room, though none of it makes any sense. I think of the injunction threats and the craziness even before this past twelve hours. And I think – they will lock me up. Like they threatened before: they will lock me up and I will be powerless.

And I think of Polly, my little Polly and I imagine Sid – or someone, if it's not Sid, though I'm convinced it must be – I think of that person getting to her before me, and my mother, what will my mother do, she will panic and she won't know what to do: what if she can't save Polly; what if Polly might not be safe?

It is down to me to save my daughter.

And so I give up the idea of giving in. Instead, I let Saul haul me from the car. Scrambling across the seats, I clamber out, nearly falling as my feet meet the dirt verge, and Saul holds me up. He takes my hand again and we cross the road, and lights are coming on in a house near the car, and then as we take the first turning we come to, as Saul drags me after him, I hear another vehicle pulling up.

'Where are we going?' I say to Saul, but he isn't listening, he's pulling his phone out of his pocket and dialling.

Eventually, someone picks up.

'You need to come and get me,' he says. He starts to cough again. 'My car's totalled.'

Then, 'I don't fucking care. I need your help *now*. I'll text you the address in a minute, but I know we're down by the Broad Marsh.'

The person on the other end speaks; Saul listens.

'If you don't help me now I will tell Dean where you are.'

Pause; he listens again.

'Yeah, I will,' he snarls eventually, 'and you'd better fucking believe it.'

Saul snaps the phone off.

'Wait here,' he says. He lollops off to check the road sign; he's limping badly. I am shivering with shock and with cold that bites into my very bones. My bandaged hand throbs, my shoulder burns.

He returns, texting.

'She'll be here in a minute,' he says.

'Who?'

'Janie's friend.'

I don't bother to ask who Janie is. It seems pointless right now.

'Will she help me too?' I do say, after a while.

'Dunno.' He grimaces, his face flat planes of shadow in the darkness. 'If she thinks it'll serve her. But she'll get us out of here, at least. If she's not so fucked she can't drive.'

'Oh.'

He looks down at me. 'You're shaking.'

'Yes,' I say. 'I'm cold.'

He wraps his arms around me, he leans on me a little. I can feel his heart beating. We stand like that, stock still in the darkness, and we wait.

THEN – SUZANNE O'BRIEN

I grabbed a coffee and my client list from reception and kicked my door firmly shut behind me. I was already running late after Roz had cornered me in the playground at drop-off, trying to extract information about the pub quiz.

'I wanted to say that Mal seems nice,' she started. 'But it was a bit awkward, with—'

'I've got to go, Roz.' I just couldn't face a pow-wow. 'Sorry.'

'But, Laurie,' she had called after me, 'I just wanted to say that if—'

'I'll ring you,' I chucked over my shoulder, almost running to the car. 'So late.'

The morning started with a middle-aged couple I'd seen once before. My small room was quickly suffused with their anger; so furious with each other they could barely talk, unable to countenance the other's pain. Instead, they either spoke directly to me or hissed at one another without turning their heads, her grey-faced and red-eyed and verbose, him taut above his awful striped polo-shirt with shame and embarrassment, either stuttering or monosyllabic. They were both obsessed with blame; with whose fault it was. So many of us are, I realised over my years of counselling: what hurt we inflict on one another because we are not fully conscious of ourselves.

Life could be so simple if we could only fit into our own skins properly.

After they left I saw an older woman called Anna who had come regularly since the summer, literally emanating grief. Her husband had died suddenly and she was struggling desperately to come to terms with her loss. I felt her pain deeply, but I also wanted to try and help her remember the amazing life they'd had together.

When she left, I made a few notes. I refilled the water jug and emptied the bin; found a new box of tissues in the cupboard and checked my book. My next appointment was a new client, an appointment made via reception; a name I didn't recognise, Suzanne O'Brien.

She was late. No-shows were common, especially first appointments; people often lost their nerve.

I ate an apple and filled in my expenses for the month; stared out of the window, watching a pigeon flap into the tree outside, bending a fragile branch of the silver birch. I rearranged the crystals, feathers and pebbles on the windowsill that Polly and I had collected between us, the 'infernal trail of nature that follows you every-bloody-where'; that Sid detested so much. I thought a little about Mal; forced myself to not think about Mal – because what was there to think? It was obvious I was not in any fit state to embark on anything with another man, ex-client or not. End of story. But the thought that someone liked me again was a salve in this winter of discontent, although I was still not quite clear about my own feelings for him.

Finally, I could no longer resist. Against my better judgement, breaking my own rule, I fetched my phone from my bag to text Sid. I tried not to bring my own life into this office, but the truth was Margaret Henderson's visit last night had really rattled me.

I needed to talk to Sid before he saw Polly again, to allay the fears my neighbour had dug from the darker recesses of my mind. I sent a message asking if we could meet somewhere neutral for a cup of tea some time this week. I'd be lucky if he replied though. Sid hated mobile phones.

Half an hour into the appointment time, there was a knock at the door. Putting my phone away, I opened it. A tall woman walked straight past me into the room before I could so much as catch her eye.

'Hi,' I was a little surprised. It was unusual for someone new to be so confident; people normally waited to be told what to do, hovering by the door, anxious and self-conscious, slightly ashamed. Still, nerves do strange things to people. I walked round to my own chair. 'Please, do have a seat.'

And then I looked at her properly, and with a horrible roll of my stomach, realised exactly who this woman was. Susie Cooper, Mal's wife. Or ex-wife. I wasn't even sure how far along the divorce process they were.

She smiled at me – and the smile made me most uncomfortable.

I felt myself stiffen, but I offered her my hand politely. I didn't know what kind of game she was playing, but I didn't want her to see how shaken I felt. Of course, there was no way I could help her – but I was sure we were both aware of that. She wasn't here to be counselled by me.

'Laurie Smith.'

'I know,' she took my hand in her very warm one. 'Suzanne O'Brien. You can call me Suzie.'

'I believe we've met before,' I said carefully. 'Shall we sit down?'

She sat opposite me. She was attractive in a rather washed-out way; vivid hair pulled back tightly from her white face in a kind of plait, many freckles against a pale skin, dark eyes, big shadows beneath. She crossed her legs. Then uncrossed them. I was used to people being uncomfortable at first, fidgeting, delaying. But she didn't seem nervous. She seemed almost lit up. Adrenaline, I guessed.

'We nearly met the other night,' she said. 'At The Three Rams. You were on the quiz team with Mal, weren't you?'

'Yes,' I nodded. 'But I think we have met before that too.'

For a moment, her sang-froid nearly slipped. 'Really?' she said. 'Remind me.'

I gazed at her for a moment, trying to get her measure.

'Mrs O'Brien … Suzanne. Why exactly are you here?'

'Because…' she looked at me hard; a long calculating look.

'Because?'

Wait. Let them talk.

'Because,' she licked her dry lips. She was nervous, after all. 'I've come to warn you.'

I shook my head. 'Warn me?'

'About Mal.'

'Oh really.' I paused, thinking. 'What do you mean?'

'I want to warn you about Mal,' she leant forward now.

I resisted the urge to move backwards myself. She was in my space, far too near.

'I need to tell you about him.'

I cleared my throat. 'In what context, Suzanne?'

'Suzie.'

I ignored this. 'In what context do you want to "*warn*" me about Mal? What are your concerns?'

'Ah, you therapists.' She leant back, something like a smirk playing round her lips. 'Such clever speak.'

I gazed at the woman, trying to get a handle on her. Everything about her sloped downwards, including the corners of her mouth.

Her clothes were well-made, but old and rather dowdy. Her beige chinos were rolled slightly too high, her flat plimsolls no longer white. She wore a belted mac and, I noticed with a sinking heart, a wedding ring on her left hand.

'Did you make the appointment to talk to me about your marriage?' I said carefully.

'No. I came to tell you to watch out.'

'For what?'

Was she threatening me?

'I know you've been with him.'

I could feel the thud of my heart in my chest. I stood now.

'Suzanne. This is highly inappropriate, I'm afraid. I will have to ask you to leave now.'

'I thought you might say that. People never want to hear the truth.' She didn't move. 'Until it's too late.'

I moved towards the door. 'Please. Ms O'Brien.'

'Mrs.'

'Are you?' I looked her full in the face now. 'Are you still Mrs?'

She held out a hand now, showing me her ring. 'What do you think?'

'I don't know,' I opened my door. 'And right now, I don't think it's my business, Ms O'Brien. I really just must ask you to leave. I cannot see you as a client. I know your husband as a friend.'

'Is that what you call it?' she moved towards me now, no longer smiling. 'I might call it something rather different.'

I fought my blush.

'But I am serious, you know.' She stood next to me at the door, taller, thinner, more wiry than me. 'You should be careful. He is obsessive.'

'Really?' I met her eye steadily. I wouldn't let her see that I was rattled.

'Yes, really,' she held my gaze. 'He followed me here. To London. Me and Leonard. I didn't want him to, but he came anyway.'

I couldn't think what to say, so I called to Maeve. 'Is my next appointment here?'

Maeve looked up, startled. It was earlier than I should finish, and I never normally came out of my room during an appointment.

'Er…' she started to scrabble through the desk diary.

'Don't say I didn't warn you,' Suzanne O'Brien lowered her voice so I had to strain to hear her. 'You should be careful.'

And then she was gone.

'Excuse me,' a confused Maeve called after her from the reception desk. 'Miss O'Brien. You haven't paid—'

'Don't worry about it,' I told Maeve. I was trembling as I shut my door behind me.

I didn't know what to do; I really didn't. I sat in the chair in the office for a while, staring blindly at the wall, at the 'Cycles of the New Moon' calendar which Robert had given me last Christmas. I hadn't turned it on to the right month for some time, I realised; it still said July.

And I was thinking fervently, but my thoughts just went round and ended nowhere new.

I thought about phoning Mal, but what would I say? '*Your wife has just accused you of being a stalker*'? I imagined his kind face crumpling with discomfort.

I remembered the meeting in the park when Mal had arrived without Leonard. Why had I felt so worried then?

Mal had seemed so lost. I tried to recollect the conversations we'd had about Suzie and their split, but I just kept seeing us entwined on my sofa, his heavy torso above me.

In the end, I rang Emily.

'Ignore her, she's a nutter,' she said, but I wasn't so sure. A sliver of disquiet had lodged itself deep in my brain.

'But…' I had to say it. 'But … I slept with him.'

There was a very slight pause.

'Oh I seeee,' she drawled. 'Oh, of course. Now it makes sense.'

'What does?' My best friend had the ability to irritate me deeply when she was this knowing.

'Your face last night. It was 'cos you'd got some.'

'Emily!' I reproved. 'For God's sake.'

'Well, you know what I mean.'

'Well, that's not the point.'

'Well, what is the point then?'

'The point is, I shouldn't have slept with him anyway—'

'Why not?'

'Because.'

'Because what?'

'Because he's my … he was my, my sort of client.'

'Okay, back up. Since when was this bloke your client?'

'It's complicated. Not quite a client, but – almost.'

'Complicated? You're telling me.'

'Emily,' I expostulated. 'You're not really helping.'

'Sorry. Look, hold tight, babe. I'll pop round after work for a cuppa. Stop worrying. I'm sure it'll be fine. I'm sure she's just a jealous loon.'

'But how does she know?'

I'd lost her attention.

'Look, I've got to go; I'm late for a meeting. More wrist-slapping for using too many biros and decimating Boris' budget. I'll see you later.'

But how *did* Suzanne O'Brien know? That was what immediately worried me. How did she know I had slept with her husband – if he hadn't told her?

Or maybe she didn't know. Maybe she'd just seen that very brief kiss, in the car park, and was making assumptions.

But her assumptions were correct.

Oh God.

I knew I shouldn't have got involved with Mal. I spent my entire working life telling people to listen to their intuition and then, at the first possible opportunity, I'd entirely ignored my own. And worse, what if Suzanne was actually telling the truth about Mal?

How the hell was I going to extricate myself from this?

NOW: HOUR 14

10pm

A fine drizzle has started to fall. We are still waiting for Saul's friend, stamping our feet against the cold, when I start to panic. I have to go; I am getting sidetracked.

'Saul,' I say carefully. 'I need to meet that train more than I've ever needed anything. Please, do you understand that?'

He looks at me through the eye that still opens. 'Yes.'

'And I don't have much time.'

He checks the clock on his phone. 'It's ten,' he says. 'What time does it get in?'

'I'm not sure. My mum's message was from about three hours ago, I think. She said they were running late. So, I'm guessing ... about midnight.' I look at the ragged wasteland, the scrubby field between road and beach, a shaggy grey pony tethered in the middle, visible in the gloom because of his pale coat. The lights of the town in the distance, the hiss of the sea not really audible; just faintly present like white noise. 'But how am I going to get there?' The panic rises in my gullet. 'Shit, Saul. *How am I going to get there?*'

There's a brief pause. 'I'll take you.'

'Will you?'

'Yeah.'

'How?'

'There's always a way.'

I consider this for a moment. 'Why will you?'

'Because.' He shrugs. 'I owe you one.'

Words. Words are powerful, but actions are the truth. How the hell is Saul going to get me anywhere? He can hardly stand.

I walk to the edge of the pavement and curl my toes over it, staunching the fear. I walk back again.

'Will your friend give me a lift, do you think?'

'Yes. And if she won't, I will find a way.' He starts to cough.

'Saul,' I look at him. 'Look at us. We're a couple of reprobates. And you need help.'

'Nothing new there then,' he tries to laugh through the coughing, but it's a miserable impression.

An old banger rattles round the corner, dubstep thumping into the cold night. Saul holds a weary arm up in greeting.

The girl in the driver's seat looks angry. So angry, the frown-lines on either side of the young mouth are already deeply scored.

'Get in,' she snarls through the open window.

We obey meekly. Saul tries to make me sit in the front next to her, out of politeness or dread, I don't know — but frankly, he is welcome to her wrath. I sit in the back.

'Laurie,' Saul doesn't turn to look at me when he speaks; he is already wincing with pain. 'Binny.'

'Hi,' I say, 'thanks for coming,' but the girl called Binny doesn't bother to answer. She just chews gum frenetically as she pulls out, takes the first left, away from the abandoned Volvo. I don't look back. Instead, from the relative safety of the back seat, I study the girl.

Her long face is an unpleasant and rather mottled grey; skin bumpy and scarred; hair cropped very close for a girl. She wears no make-up, no jewellery apart from some kind of chain round her neck. A tattooed wrist pokes from her long sleeve. I realise it's a similar design to Saul's.

'Fighting again?' she sneers, looking at him, looking away.

'Where's Janie?' he asks quietly.

'Don't know.' She shrugs, staring ahead at the road. 'Your guess is as good as mine. She went out hours ago and hasn't come back. Phone's run out. Silly bitch.'

My hackles rising, I lean forward. 'Can you take me to Ashford Station please?'

'Are you having a laugh?' Only now she does glance back at me.

'Not really,' I resist screaming in her ear.

'Well, I am,' somehow she stretches her cadaverous grey face into a grin. 'I'm going straight home. You're lucky I came out at all. I feel like shit.'

'Clucking?' Saul mutters. 'Again?'

'No!' She is vehement. 'I'm clean actually. Have been for months.'

Saul raises the good eyebrow.

I sit back in frustration. I feel intense dislike for this girl and I've only known her two minutes.

'I'll take the car then,' Saul says. 'I'll drop you first.'

'You fucking well won't.'

'Please.' *Sotto voce.* 'I owe it to Laurie.'

'I don't care what you owe. It's not my problem.'

'Maybe not, but it is Janie's.'

She frowns at him. 'How's that then?'

'Because. I just saw Dean.'

Long pause. She actually stops chewing for a moment. 'I thought he was away?'

'Well, he's back.'

She looks at him again. 'Oh.'

'Yeah. Oh.'

'So *that's* what's happened to you.' As if it was the most normal thing in the world to collect a friend from a field, injured and covered in their own blood. Maybe, for them though, it was.

'And Janie owes Laurie.' I can feel the effort it's taking Saul to speak. My concern for him is building.

The marks on Binny's face deepen as her frown does. 'How's that then?'

'Laurie paid off Janie's debt. Part of it, anyway.'

'Why?' Binny catches my eye in the mirror. 'Are you insane?'

'Very likely,' I mutter. Louder, I say, 'Can you just take me to Ashford Station, please? I need to meet my daughter. It's a matter of ... of...'

'Urgency,' Saul finishes for me.

I was going to say life or death, but I can't get those words out.

'Urgency,' I agree. 'Please. I am desperate.'

Binny regards me in the mirror for a moment. 'Okay,' she says eventually. 'I'll take you to Ashford.' She glares at me. 'For Janie,' she says, in case I have misunderstood her magnanimity.

'Thanks,' I say. I slump back in the seat. Who is this Janie, I wonder, this girl I gave my ring up for, who has such a hold on both Saul and this strange angry girl? Whoever she is, they both really love her.

'Have you got a fag?' she asks Saul. He lights a Lambert & Butler from the silver packet in the car-well and hands it to her. She is relaxing a little; her face is less taut.

'So what did Dean say?' she inhales.

'Not a lot.' Saul's face is white. 'Just ... don't worry about it now.' He closes his other eye.

'You need a hospital, Saul,' I say.

He just grunts.

I will the car on. I will Saul better. I clench and unclench my fists until my palms are sweating.

Binny drives on.

On the outskirts of Ashford, I spot the station and the hospital signs at the same time. I feel a surge of adrenaline and a bigger one of relief.

'We need to drop Saul,' I say to Binny. He is sleeping; snoring with a wet rattle. 'At the hospital.'

'He won't want to go.'

'I don't care.' I am the grown-up here. These two are mere babes. 'He's not in a good way. That man really kicked him.'

Binny glances at Saul. 'Okay,' she concurs eventually. 'You're probably right.'

I wonder if she's thinking about the mysterious Janie. She indicates left, follows the signs to the William Harvey Hospital.

I lean over and gently remove his phone from his *diem* hand. I put both my numbers into it, copying my new one from the display. Binny jerks to a halt in front of A & E.

'Can you take him in?' she says. 'I don't like these places.'

I start to say I'd rather she went but I look at Saul, and I know I should take him. He is my team-mate; he has, as they say these days, my back. He is for me.

'I'll come back after,' she says. 'I promise.'

I get out and open the door.

'Saul,' I wake him gently. 'I'm taking you into the hospital. I have to go to the station. You understand, don't you?'

He opens his good eye. He gazes at me; he hasn't the energy to argue. I feel a knot of anxiety tighten in my stomach. Please God, don't let him be seriously hurt.

'You'll be fine,' I say as brightly as I can. 'Binny will come back for you.'

I help him from the car; we walk under the great red sign. I think of Emily. I think of how it was only twelve hours ago that

I slipped away from the hospital somewhere in Devon. I try not to think about it.

I think about now.

'I've put my numbers in your mobile.' I slip the phone into his hand. 'Both of them. Will you text me? Let me know you're okay?'

'Sure,' he agrees. He can hardly stand. As we approach reception a small Asian nurse comes forward with a wheelchair.

'Sit.' She is brisk and stern.

I relinquish his arm. I feel like I am betraying him; my eyes are stinging with unshed tears.

'Saul,' I lean down and whisper, holding his hand tightly. 'I will see you again. Promise you'll call me?'

He nods. 'Thank you,' he says.

'For what, silly?' I am going to cry. I can't bear it. I shouldn't leave him here; I should stay and look after him – but what choice do I have? I have to find Polly. 'Thank you. For helping me.'

'Any time,' he tries to grin.

'Likewise,' I say. 'I'm so glad I met you.' I turn to leave before the tears fall, then I turn back. I have one more question before I go. 'Who is Janie, Saul?' I say.

He closes his eye again. The nurse is talking to the receptionist, handing over a form.

He opens it, blinks at me. I look at the beautiful grey iris, the pupil dilated, flooded with pain. I see myself reflected.

'My sister,' he murmurs. 'My twin sister.'

Binny drops me in the floodlit car park of Ashford International. Everything seems very bright.

'Thank you,' I say as she pulls the handbrake up with an unhealthy crunch. 'I'm very grateful. But ...' she is lighting another cigarette, not looking at me. 'You will go back to Saul, won't you? Will you text me from his phone? Tell me how he is? Please.'

'No worries,' she shrugs, but I doubt she will bother – and how can I force her? She tears at a fingernail, once painted black. It bears a tiny scrap of varnish still.

I zip my hoodie up and fumble for the door.

'Why were you with him?' she asks.

My first thought is of Sid. It takes a second to understand whom the girl means.

'With Saul?' I say.

'Yeah,' she stares like I am daft. 'Obviously.'

'We met on a train. It broke down. I've got to ... I've got to collect my daughter.'

I look across to the big station: there are no trains I can see at the moment, but I need to get out now. I want to be ready.

'His sister. Janie. She's my girlfriend.' Binny is proud as she says it, though quickly her face darkens. 'But she's not ... she's not very well.'

'Oh dear,' I say. What else can I say? I remember Saul's mention of the 'clucking'. I think of Barrel Man and his big black boot; of his reference to whores. I see, in a flash, a girl who looks like Saul, but more fragile, not so robust. I imagine long grey eyes, half-open, glazed; scorched foil beside her; dropped syringes. I see her lying on her back in a room with no curtains. I see a faceless man above her.

'I'm sorry,' I say.

'Yeah,' Binny nods. 'So am I. Fucking bastard smack.'

'Fucking drugs,' I agree. I snap the door open. 'Thanks again.'

'Laurie,' she says, almost tentatively, just as my foot meets the tarmac.

I turn, surprised she has remembered my name.

'I'm going back. To Saul. I'll get him to text you.'

I put my hand on Binny's arm for a moment. Then I get out.

By the time I reach the station forecourt, she has gone.

THEN: CONFRONTING MAL

It turned out I wasn't going to extricate myself that easily from the Mal situation. Best laid plans, and all that.

I was too disturbed by Suzanne O'Brien's claims to let them go. At tea-time Emily arrived with a DVD of *Black Beauty* for Polly, a giant tube of Smarties, and a stern word for me.

'Retro is the way forward,' she said, popping the DVD into the machine. 'Let me know what you reckon to the riding, Pol. Roger?'

'10-4,' Polly blinked solemnly at her from the sofa, clutching her Smarties.

'And don't forget to save the blue ones for the Martians,' Emily's face was as serious as my daughter's.

'Over and out, roger.'

'Hmm. She hasn't quite got a handle on her CB name yet. Right, come on. I haven't got long. Places to be.' Emily shepherded me downstairs. She leant against the worktop as I loaded the dishwasher. 'I just want to say. When are you going to start taking your own advice, Laurie Smith?'

'What do you mean?' I busied myself for a ludicrously long time with some forks.

But I knew what she meant.

'You can dish it out, but you can't see the wood for the trees.'

'That's a lot of metaphors.' I shoved the forks into the tray very hard. 'I'm not sure they make sense all mixed together.'

'Whatever,' she shrugged. 'You know you have to speak to this guy. Soon. Whoever he is.'

'Mal.'

'Mal. You can't just ignore it. You need to confront it.' She handed me the phone from the side. 'Call him.'

'Really?' I looked at her. 'I don't need any more confrontation in my life.'

'Oh for God's sake.' She rolled her eyes dramatically. 'Really, Laurie. Or it'll be like one of those Medusa heads, growing more problems.'

So I called him. And when I heard the pleasure in his voice at my request to see him tonight, I felt horrible and guilty, like I was duping him, and then I felt stupid, because maybe it was the other way round; it seemed more likely that he was duping *me*.

Emily left. I sensed she was probably waiting for a call, but these days, she played her cards close to her chest when a new man was in the offing. She became cross when I got overexcited that this one would be *the one*. Phone in hand, she lectured me a bit more about how good I was at holding counsel but not taking my own advice, until I shoved her out of the door. Polly and I sung the *Black Beauty* theme tune as I put her to bed, and then I sat in the kitchen, waiting, and I wondered what Sid was doing now.

Mal arrived, brandishing a bottle of expensive Shiraz.

'I don't drink, actually,' I said shortly. 'But thanks.'

'Oh,' he looked confused, 'but I thought … the other day…'

'That was a one-off.' I walked down to the kitchen and switched the kettle on, unable to quite bear facing him yet; rattling china and teabag around. Sid's 'Best Daddy' mug, hand-painted by Pol, that he'd insisted on keeping here for 'stability', suddenly leapt out at me. I took a breath, and stuck it in the cupboard.

'Tea or coffee?' I said. 'Or did you want to open the wine? There's a corkscrew in that drawer.'

'No, no, coffee's good, thanks.'

Poor man. Obviously terrified now I was being so terse and unfriendly.

Mal hadn't been downstairs before. Waiting for the kettle to boil, I was aware he was looking around, at the last surviving photo of the three of us, still pinned to the board, laughing on my mum's seventieth birthday. Then he stood in front of Sid's *Madonna Eats Eve #4* and suddenly I saw the painting through a stranger's eyes, who would not understand it; who would no doubt be in the *Daily Mail* camp; think us odd or perverted for hanging a picture of women licking each other where we ate our cornflakes.

For a brief and utterly piercing moment, I missed Sid so badly it felt like someone had just gouged something out of my chest.

'That's amazing,' Mal said. 'That lithograph. I mean, I'm no expert, but the lines are really … pure.'

'Yes,' I agreed, surprised.

'Is it—'

'Do you mind—' I felt the heat suffuse my face. 'I'm sorry, Mal, but I'm not sure I can talk about it now.' I sat heavily at the kitchen table, the fight going out of me.

'Are you all right?' Mal frowned, stepping towards me.

'Not really,' I admitted, and then I looked up, looked him full in the face – and finally, I began to relax.

This was in my head, surely. He was not a bad man, I knew that. I *knew* he wasn't. Maybe my intuition *was* a little out of kilter, but I could read the honesty in his light eyes as he regarded me, and the struggle going on internally as he tried to work out what was happening. He was transparent. So much more so than Sid, who was so impermeable; so filled up with dark.

In the end, it was Mal who made the drinks.

'There's some biscuits in that starry tin,' I pointed at the shelf. 'Help yourself, please.'

'I just ate.' He plonked my tea in front of me, with the tin. 'Fish and chips. Not so healthy,' he patted his tummy ruefully. 'Need to keep an eye on this!'

'Hardly,' I said automatically. He was about to make a joke – and I interrupted.

'Mal, your wife came to see me today.'

'Jesus,' his coffee splashed on the floor. 'Oh God. Sorry.'

'Don't worry about it,' I pushed a chair towards him. 'Sit down, please.'

He did so, looking shaken.

'She came to "warn me". Her words.'

'Warn you?' Furiously he stood again, chair scraping noisily across the flagstones.

'Apparently so.' I looked at Madonna eating Eve. I felt exhausted.

'The bloody bitch.' Completely rattled, Mal stared down at me. 'Warn you about *what* exactly?'

'She said you are … obsessive.'

'Oh, did she?'

'Apparently,' I repeated.

'In what sense?'

'She said you followed her here.'

He was struggling to contain himself, poor man. 'Well, yeah, she might say that – but I had no choice. Because she upped and took a job and my son, with hardly any warning, making ultimatums.' He ran his hands through his hair, slightly thinning at the crown, until it stood on end. 'But I wouldn't call that obsessive, would you? I would just call it being a good father.'

'Fair enough,' I said carefully. I didn't want to meet his eye, I didn't know how to phrase it. 'But ... she also knew about ...' I cleared my throat.

'About what?'

'About us.' My words felt like boulders rolling down a hill.

'Knew *what* about us?' he stared at me.

'That we'd slept together.'

'No, she didn't.' He was furious, I could see, his face puce. 'She doesn't know that. Not from me, anyway.'

'Well, she doesn't know it from me either,' I sat straighter. 'I didn't tell her anything.'

'That's not what I meant.' He sat down too now. 'I mean, she's just guessing. After she saw us at the pub she had a complete meltdown.'

'Right.'

'And she's insanely jealous, Laurie. Paranoid. That was part of the problem. She couldn't bear me talking to anyone. Man, woman or child, she'd read badly into anything innocent.'

'I see,' I said. I wished I could remember more about that one time I'd met them at the Vale Centre.

'She saw me kiss you in the car park after that quiz, and then she accused me of all sorts. She must have made the appointment then, I guess. I didn't know, honestly.'

'But why didn't you tell me? About her – jealousy?'

'Because. What would I say? "My wife's shouting about you being a harlot." That doesn't bode well really, does it?'

'A harlot?' I grinned. I couldn't help myself. 'How very ... old-fashioned.'

He looked at me warily and then he smiled too. 'Yes, I suppose it is rather. I just – I didn't want to put you off.'

'Oh God, Mal.' For a moment it seemed as if we were a proper couple, united by the madness of our respective exes. 'This is all a bit ridiculous, isn't it?'

And for the first time since the woman had come to see me, I felt better about the situation. Calmer. It made sense; she was just jealous, she was trying to stop Mal and I progressing in any way – not that we were progressing, of course.

'Laurie,' his face went serious in the way that means a man is either going to tell you something bad, or try to get you into bed. Funny buggers, men. He held a hand out to me and I took it and he pulled me up and then he kissed me.

I shut my eyes so I couldn't see Sid in the photo behind Mal's head, and I felt his lips on mine, warm, tasting of coffee, and then he lowered his mouth to my neck – and then I pushed him back quickly because I heard a footstep on the stairs. The spell was broken.

Polly was in the doorway, flushed and sleepy-eyed.

'Oh, Pol,' I rushed to her in the sort of over-protective way I wouldn't normally; flustered, terrified she'd seen me in this man's arms. 'Bad dream, baby?'

She was still half-asleep, blinking at me like a koala bear, staring at Mal with huge eyes as I scooped her up and carried her, a small warm animal, towards the stairs.

'Back in a sec.' I didn't really want to leave Mal alone in my kitchen, I wasn't ready yet, but I had no choice.

Polly settled into bed with no fuss, eyes closing even before I pulled the cover up.

Rushing back downstairs, I found Mal standing by the kitchen door, car keys in hand.

'I should go,' he said.

I felt a strange kick of disappointment. 'Yes of course,' I bowed my head in acquiescence.

He flicked his jacket up from the back of the chair.

'Lovely town, that,' he pointed at a photo of Polly grinning from behind an enormous chocolate ice-cream. 'Vejer, isn't it? I recognise that church. We were there at the end of the summer. About six weeks ago. Last holiday together.'

'That's funny. It must be a place of ...' I searched for the word. 'Of, you know, marking significance. It was mine and Polly's first holiday alone.'

'It was our last hoorah. To say goodbye, I guess.'

'I'm sorry,' I followed his broad back up the stairs.

'It's okay,' I thought he said, but he was indistinct, ahead of me now in the hallway. 'Such a big world, such a small one.'

He opened the door, and then turned, standing slightly below me on the doorstep. I waited, framed by the door. We didn't touch each other. Instead we conducted that uncomfortable kind of farewell where neither party knows quite what to say, nor wants to commit to being the first to bring up the future – so neither of us did.

'I'll speak to her,' was all he did say. 'To Suzanne. I'll tell her not to trouble you. I am so sorry that she did.'

'It's okay,' I said.

'She's not handling it well, this divorce. Not well at all.'

You don't say, I nearly replied – but I restrained myself. 'I understand,' I said instead, 'it's not easy. It never is.' As if I was the great expert on divorces.

Although, in some ways, I was. Just not an expert on my own.

There was a brief pause, during which I realised I was hoping for something that did not then transpire.

'See you soon,' he said, and I nodded.

Mal walked down the front stairs into the cold night and there were no stars, and the moon was a tiny sliver of white high above us. I wanted to say something else, but I didn't know what exactly. I was increasingly confused about the situation, and my own feelings, and I was scared that I was beginning to feel I rather liked this man.

So in the end I just shut the door behind him, as the phone started to ring inside the house.

But when I answered, rushing to pick it up, hoping maybe for my mother or Emily's friendly voice, there was no one there.

NOW: HOUR 15

11pm

The train has gone. I cannot believe it. I look down the track into darkness, the track that heads to London, and I can't believe it. My mother and my daughter float away from me, down the rails, whispering in the darkness – and I scream silently behind them, *Come back*. But of course they cannot hear.

The last Eurostar passed through the station about half an hour ago.

My daughter has gone.

The thought that if I hadn't taken Saul to the hospital spins through my head – but I had to, I know that much, and that way of thinking is futile.

'Are you all right, love?' asks the solitary guard on the station, and I gaze with wide eyes that must reflect my fear, and I want to say no. I want to shout *No no no I am really not all right* – but of course he will just think I am mad and then what will happen? He might stop me, cart me off somewhere – and so I don't shout that. I just back away and sit down on an orange metal seat with tiny holes in it, so cold through my cheap jeans, and I think fervently for a moment.

I check the time; I check my mother's message again … and then it dawns on me. Stupidly, so stupidly, I did not allow for the French time difference. And so they must have reached London by now and I have not. The train has sped down the tracks to the big city – and I am still here. My mother is expecting me to meet them, and I won't be there waiting – and where will she go next?

And worse, much worse.

Who else will be waiting at St Pancras?

I need to catch a break, as Emily would say. Emily. The thought of her makes me almost gasp out loud.

I find out the time and platform number of the last train to London. I have a ticket, bought with almost my last money. I think of Saul. I think of Polly.

I need help. I am delirious with fear and grief and exhaustion.

Digging out the disposable phone, I input the number that has been burnt into my brain for such a long time. There is a moment as my finger hovers over the call button where I think this way only madness lies – and then I hit it anyway. He will know by now that I am still alive – and what choice do I have? None.

My stomach churns as I listen to the ring. But he doesn't answer.

So. That is that. Halfway through the automated voicemail, I cut the call off. There is no point leaving a message. What would I say?

And as I pocket the phone, all I can think of is Polly and somewhere underlying that panicked thought is the idea I will never be warm again, it is so cold; so cold I envisage my blood as ice now, my veins as frozen rivulets. I look for the waiting room and then my phone rings and it makes me jump.

'Who is this?' The tension in his voice vibrates down the line.

'Me,' I mumble. 'It's me.'

Your me. There is no need for names.

'Laurie? Is that you? For fuck's sake, Laurie—'

I was always your me, wasn't I?

For a moment I actually think he's going to cry.

'For fuck's sake, I've been sick with worry.' But of course he doesn't. Anger is his default position. 'Where the hell are you?'

I am trying to formulate sensible thoughts.

'Are you okay?'

I swallow.

'Laurie? Speak to me.'

'Unfortunately for you, yes I am,' I say. 'Where are *you*?'

'At home.'

'Really?'

'Yeah, really. Why? Why wouldn't I be?'

'Did you try to kill me?'

'Are you fucking insane?'

Possibly. Probably.

'No. Are you really at home?' I crane my ears for background noise at his end, but there is nothing to say that he's not telling the truth – about that at least. 'Did you speak to my mum?'

'No.'

He's lying. I'm sure he's lying. I stare at the predictor-board that flickers as I speak. My train is in six minutes apparently. It can't come quickly enough. 'Surely you must have tried? When you ... when you heard what happened?'

'No, Laurie. I didn't. I didn't know what the fuck was going on. I still don't. They said you were dead, Laurie.'

'Well, I'm not. Despite your best efforts.'

'Laurie,' he howls. 'Shut up, for Christ's sake. Why would I want to hurt you?'

'You always hurt me.'

Silence.

'Sid.' I need to know he's not going near Polly. 'So you didn't speak to my mum? Did you go to the hospital?'

'Yes … no. I didn't know what the hell was going on, and I didn't want to panic anyone until I understood, and I set off … and then … I … I didn't get there.' He pauses, changes tack. 'Anyway, she's abroad. They're not back till tomorrow.'

'No, Sid, they're back now—' The instant they're out, I want to drag my words back in. 'Maybe,' I mumble, ineffectually. Too late.

'What do you mean, maybe?'

I can't think quickly enough. I'm too tired, too distraught. What I do think is this: if Sid doesn't know they're coming back, he's no danger to Polly – except now I've laid my lie bare. And he knows I'm lying. He knows me too well and I'm so bad at it.

'What do you mean?' he prompts. 'I thought they got in tomorrow night? From the hell-pit.'

He means Euro Disney. For a moment I feel a blazing hatred for myself; but that is not helpful. Nor is despising him for his antipathy; for not even knowing when his own daughter is back.

I've been so fearful that it was him who set the fire, him who would reach Polly first; but now my fear ebbs a fraction. However much he wanted to punish me, he doesn't even know she's headed for London. He can't be a danger to her: to his, to *our* own daughter.

Can he?

And suddenly, with great clarity, I see what my best course of action is. Of course. I need to get him on side. I need to stop fighting him and make him think I will depend on him for my survival. I see myself from above: exhausted, unwashed, spent. My need will appeal to his delusions of grandeur. If I get on the train, he could meet me. And if I am with him, he can't hurt Polly. Of course. I don't care what he does to me, but I know that I can save her if I am with him. I am so tired, so desperate, so maddened by worry and grief that I can't think straight – but this feels like an epiphany. I take the plunge.

'Can you meet me at St Pancras?' I say. The boards flicker again. Three minutes and I'll be on the train. I'll be speeding towards Polly.

'Sure,' he agrees. 'Whatever you want. When?'

'Thank you. I'll be there in forty minutes or so, I guess. Just call me on this number and tell me where you are.'

'I'll leave now.' I've never known Sid so compliant. 'I'll text you when I'm there.'

'And send me Mum's mobile number, can you? The battery's dead on my own phone. I can't get any numbers out. I need to ring her.'

'I'll send it now.'

His strange enthusiasm unsettles me more. But I have no options I can see.

I hear the train before I see it; the relief I feel is so huge my knees almost buckle as the sleek metal monster slides into view from the darkness.

'Sid,' I yell above the noise. 'I'm getting on the train. I'll see you at St Pancras.'

In my seat, in the warmth I've craved, I'm nodding off, my head wedged between seat and window, when my phone bleeps. I expect my mother's number but it's the girl called Binny.

im bac with saul. He's uncnscs ☹ i'll let u no whn he wakes. Binny xxx

The kisses surprise me. It takes me a moment to decipher the rest. When I do, I text back.

Thanks Binny. Send him all my love & pls keep me posted.

Then I text Sid. Mum's number please.

Two minutes later he responds: I've left her a message for you. Having trouble fwd-ing numbers. On my way.

Liar. I start a terse reply, but I don't send it: it only reminds me of our marital battles. In frustration, I chuck the phone down beside me; close my stinging eyes just for a second. I'll get the number from him when I get there.

Something is tapping at my arm. I can't think where I am; my head's so heavy it feels like my neck won't support it as I come back to consciousness. I pull away with a gasp as I open my eyes.

'You have to get off now, love,' a man says. I struggle to focus.

He is awkward; slightly embarrassed. I imagine it's my appearance that worries him. His breath is bad; rancid; I can smell it from here. Staggering to my feet, he points at something.

'Your phone, love,' he says.

'Thanks.' I scoop it up. There's a text from Sid.

I'm opposite the cab rank

As I near the door, I ring him.

'I'm here,' I say. Stepping down from the train a black woman in silk trousers pulls a case across my path so I stumble and drop the phone. The man with bad breath retrieves it for me.

'Hello?' I say into the phone, but I've lost him.

I walk towards the exit through a station more empty than I've ever known it. Sleepy tourists lie on benches and rucksacks, hats pulled over faces, waiting for trains. A drunk wanders in and is quickly escorted away by a man in an orange fluorescent vest.

I know they are not here, but I scan the station for Polly and my mother. I imagine the euphoria of seeing them.

I don't see them, of course. I follow the signs to the exit and, as I emerge into the night, I see the car across the street.

In my panic, I step out too quickly and a taxi blares its horn and slams on the brakes. I jump back. I look over at his car again.

Something is triggered deep in my brain; something I have buried.

Sid is waiting – but I find I am frozen. I can't take that step towards him. A memory rears from our past: an apparition that I grab at, slipping like smoke through my fingers. If he hurts me before I reach Polly … if he takes me somewhere and locks me away …

I waver, and then I turn away. I am suddenly desperate that Sid doesn't see me. At the cab-rank, I sidestep the drunk, who wants to befriend me, his hair in matted clots around his filthy face. He isn't very old. I climb into the first taxi that comes.

When I've given my mother's address, I sink into the back seat. As we pull out, I turn to look at the car. I imagine him sitting, smoking, impatient, thin fingers tapping on the steering wheel, the ever-present fury building in him.

The city unfurls around me, flashes past the windows. Exhausted, I've entered some realm of hyper-sensation; almost painfully aware of noise, lights, the mutter of the driver's talk radio show. It is nearly midnight, but this city never sleeps. The streets are still busy, Camden's pavements thronged. We cut through North London; we pass not far from the end of my road. Past the shadows of Hampstead Heath, up and out towards the suburbs.

I call my mother's phone again. She must be home now; she must have got my messages. I imagine Polly trailing, exhausted, up to bed. I imagine my mother lugging her neat travel-bag up to her bedroom, disrobing, hanging her best travelling jacket back in the wardrobe; donning her long flowery dressing-gown with the zip right up the front. Bustling back down to her kitchen, relieved to be home, switching on the kettle.

So why doesn't she call? I phone her house for the hundredth time, turn the phone over and over in my hands until it's hot and sticky with my sweat. And then suddenly we reach my mother's street and I crane forward anxiously. I imagine seeing Polly; running up the stairs, picking her up, her spindly legs flapping against me. I crave her like a drug.

I concentrate on Polly; force back the memory, the physical feeling of Emily's loss; of having to tell my daughter her beloved friend is dead.

My mother's house is in darkness. My heart contracts. Maybe they are in the back of the house. The spare room is upstairs, overlooking the Japanese garden my mother is so proud of, that John helped her plan and plant, the tiny wooden bridge, the pagoda he built for her, covered in vine. The kitchen's at the back too. I fumble around: of course I don't have enough money to pay the driver.

'I just have to get some cash from my mum.' I sound like I'm seventeen again. Tears spring to my eyes. If my mother was here, everything would be all right.

He casts a dubious glance at the dark house. 'Really?' he says; old, bald, tired. Too tired for London nights. He's heard it all before.

'I'll only be a sec,' I am out of the door before he can stop me. I run up the front path, the wet lavender bush dampening my cheek. I put my finger on the bell and hold it down. If I press hard enough, someone will come.

But there is no answering kerfuffle, no noise at all. I do not see my mother's shape trundle down the hall behind the frosted glass. I do not hear stirring upstairs. I bend and peer through the letterbox. I find I am praying.

There is nothing. I can see mail stacked on the hall table, which my mother would have picked up to open immediately. So she hasn't been home yet.

I stand again. My heart is racing too fast. I bang on the door now with my closed fist. Nothing.

The driver is still there, the engine ticking in the background.

'Shit,' I say. 'Shit shit shit shit shit.'

I walk slowly back towards the taxi.

'I'm so sorry,' I root in my pocket. I can't give him everything. 'I thought she'd be back before me. Can I give you a fiver now, and send the rest?'

'Send the rest?' he sneers at me. 'Oh come on, love.'

'I will, I promise.'

He appraises me. This is the first time he's been able to see me properly. He looks into my face. Beneath the streetlight, I am aware I look a mess. Bruised face, bandaged hand, mad eyes, mismatched outfit. Why would he trust me?

'I should call the police,' he says. I don't really care what he does: I am just trying to think where my mother and my daughter might be.

He snatches the note from my hand, muttering, and pulls off. And then, as I am about to despair, I have a brainwave! John must have collected them. Of course!

'Hey!' I wave my hand at the receding taxi, but he's turning the corner now and even if he can see me, he's not coming back.

How bloody bloody stupid. And I have a horrible feeling that I know John's away; that he was going to Cumbria with his

walking chums, to tramp the hills whilst Mum did her grand-
motherly thing.

Panic is rising like a force-field when I hear a car pull up beyond the hedge. My heart leaps. They're here after all. The relief
rushes through me like a shot of adrenaline. I rush back to the
pavement.

A dirty white van pulls up opposite and a young couple tum-
ble out. They head towards a house on the other side of the road,
bickering about something in a language I don't know – Polish
perhaps. She hits him lightly on the arm and he turns and grins
at her in a way that says he's not bothered; that he's not taking
her seriously at all in fact. He holds out his hand for her and she
hesitates and then takes it.

And then suddenly another woman's voice cuts through the
night, making me jump.

'Are you … sorry, are you looking for Christine?'

It's my mother's next-door neighbour, blinking at me across
the garden gate. Her name escapes me, but I know we met
over burnt sausages at a street party here last summer. She said
timidly that she liked Sid's work, though of course 'it was very
shocking' and I said nothing much back, got busy with Polly so
I didn't have to talk about him.

'Linda. I'm Linda. From next door.' She knows I don't remember; looks at me anxiously, mole-like, small screwed-up
face peering over gold-rimmed glasses. 'Oh my goodness, it *is*
you. We thought you were … so you're not …' she trails off.
'You're all right then?'

'I'm all right, yes,' I agree, blank. How does she know what
I've just been through?

'We saw it on the news – your poor mother, we thought –
just dreadful, the shock, and I was watering the Japanese pots
– so delicate, actually, those new azaleas – but then, well …'

And then I realise what she means. She thought I was dead. Everyone thinks I am dead. Only Sid knows. Only Sid knows he failed. My brain is slow, so much has happened. Linda blinks at me; almost flushed with excitement. 'Here you are.'

'Yes,' I say again, impatient now. 'But my mum's not. I've just been knocking.'

'She *was* here. Briefly. Poor Christine. She came back and I saw her.' She draws nearer to confide in me. 'The reporters were all waiting.'

Oh Christ. My poor poor mother.

'When?'

'About …' she looks worried. Like I'll hold her to it. 'I'm not sure, exactly. About an hour ago?'

'Did you talk to her? Was my …' I can hardly get the words out. 'Was my daughter with her? Polly?'

'The little girl?' She frowns. 'I'm not … I think so. It was all so quick. It's hard to … I was just going to bed actually, turning in. I get so tired since, you know, the medication, and there was such a clamour, and then …'

'And then?' I prompt.

'And then they were besieged really, it was a little frightening. Swallowed up, almost. I was going to call Stan, but then a man shouted and he got them, he got those reporters out of the way. And they all went off in his car.'

'A man?' I shake my head. 'What man?'

The glare from the streetlamp hits Linda's glasses; they glimmer with refracted light.

'What man?' I repeat. 'Was it John?' Please let it be John. Kind, reliable John: the antithesis of my arrogant father. But I already know it wasn't him. Although, I realise, I also know it can't be Sid. Because Sid was at St Pancras half an hour ago.

'A man with a car like Morse. Well, sort of like Morse.'

'Morse?' I shake my head, uncomprehending.

'Yes, you know. *Inspector Morse*. John Thaw. It was so sad, wasn't it, *Morse* was such a good programme. I do love Oxford, don't you—'

'For God's sake!' I can't help myself. 'Please. I need to find my daughter and my mum. Urgently.'

She looks aghast, whether at my rudeness or her own stupidity, I don't know.

'The car?' I stare at her.

'I don't know the make. A different colour maybe, too.' She presses her fingers to her forehead, conjuring memory. 'I'm not good with cars.'

She is on the verge of tears, I realise. I soften my voice, as I would with a child or a client.

'Linda. Please …'

'I didn't see. Long, grey maybe. But I didn't see the driver.' Linda is tearful. 'Not really.'

So, if it isn't Sid, who is it? Who the hell has taken my family?

THEN: SUZIE'S REVEAL

That night after Mal left, and the cloud covered the moon, my sleep was interrupted by dreams that terrified me.

Around five, I woke sweating and confused.

My body entwined with a man. With my …

With Sid.

Another man, watching. In shadow, in the corner.

I got up and splashed my face with cold water, opened the window a little, lay down again. I closed my eyes but they were hot and sore. Chasing sleep, I turned the pillow, pummelling it into submission, searching for the cool spot, but I never found it.

What was the best part of my marriage?

Before the swing of the accidental punch; the punch he'd learnt at his mother's side.

And when I eventually gave up on sleep and got up just after dawn; boiled the kettle and made some toast which I ate standing against the kitchen counter looking into the garden; pulled the Shreddies from the cupboard and persuaded my best beloved from her bed; sang, 'Polly put the kettle on' at her behest for only the five-hundredth time since she'd been born, I did not think of it. I dropped her off and kissed her rather absently for me, tired and distracted. When I drove to work, and when and when and when, it still did not click.

But walking towards my office, past the big church on the corner where the Africans came in magnificence, in orange and yellow head-dresses, children in snowy starchy frills and patent leather; well then I remembered the woman yesterday, Suzanne O'Brien, and her accusations. I still couldn't quite fathom what the thing was that troubled me so much; it was like a tiny worm in an apple, burrowing away, only I couldn't quite see it – just the browning hole on the outside.

And then there she was in front of me, and the strange thing was, I didn't even feel surprise. That woman, Mal's wife, here again, waiting outside the Centre. I ducked my head instinctively, but still she stepped forward as I drew parallel.

'Mrs Smith—'

'Laurie,' I said automatically.

'I wanted to apologise.'

Smarter today; same raincoat, black skirt, Titian hair pulled back hard from her face. Different expression. Slightly hangdog, perhaps.

'I know – of course, you can't see me as a client. But please … let me just talk to you. To explain.'

I was about to refuse – but something in her eyes made me change my mind.

'I can't right now.' I looked at my watch. 'But I … I think I have a gap in about an hour? If you give me your number …'

'Sure.' She scribbled something on the back of a receipt and presented it before I could change my mind. 'An hour is good.'

'Do you know Cathcart's?' I pointed over the road. 'Meet you there just before – around eleven?'

'Thank you,' she said, and I read relief on her face.

'I'll see you there.'

I found it hard to concentrate on my first client of the day, which in turn made me feel guilty. Mal's anger in my kitchen last night haunted me. My own oblique feelings about him did too. How was I being dragged into this?

But life is not smooth and straightforward, is it? We overlap each other like Venn diagrams. Sid and I split, he'd already met Jolie. They got together; and then I met Mal – who in turn was linked to Suzanne. We take a piece of each other and move on.

Or not.

In the end, everything boils down to choices, doesn't it? And sometimes we are brave and bold and we decide to do something we wouldn't normally; to take a risk.

Other times, we yearn for danger – but we play safe instead. When we are calm and when we tuck ourselves away.

So, I chose to meet Suzie O'Brien – just like I chose to go with Sid when he came back for me. The first time. And then the next time.

I chose to hear her out.

She was already there when I arrived. I ordered a coffee and came to sit opposite her. And waited.

I was good at waiting, it was part of my job. Do not talk over people, let them speak and it will come out, usually.

'I realise,' she clasped her mug of tea between rather mannish hands, 'I realise that yesterday must have made me seem rather mad.'

'A little …' I semi-shrugged. 'A little … extreme, I would say.'

'So I wanted to explain. To make you see that I am not a mad woman. Really.'

'Why did you come and see me yesterday?' I looked her in the eye. 'What did you want to tell me?'

'What I said really. Just more calmly, perhaps. I wanted to tell you not to trust him.'

'And why would I believe you?' I was frank. There was no point beating around any bushes. 'Why would I not just think you had an agenda?'

'Because …' she looked down at her tea. A single leaf floated on the milky surface. 'Because it would be wise to. Mal gets a little … obsessive. Like I said.'

'And are you still together?' I looked at the fat gold ring on her wedding finger. She caught the direction of my gaze.

'Old habits,' she said ruefully, twisting it round her finger. 'It's, like, the final step, isn't it? But, no, we're not. We tried to make it work, and then I threatened to leave him and got a new job, and then he begged me to give it another try, for Leonard's sake he said, and I did. And that's when we went to Spain.'

'Right.' But it wasn't really all right; nothing felt any clearer.

'It was against my better judgement. And then he got all funny about you. It was such a strange coincidence really. Seeing your name, and he remembered it.'

'Sorry,' I gazed at her, at the delta of tiny lines around the hazel eyes. 'What are you talking about?'

'We went to Vejer. We saw your name and address in the book.'

'What book?' I stared at her blankly.

'The guestbook. In that lovely house.'

'Whose house?' I was confused. 'Do you mean Robert's?' She couldn't do.

'I guess so, yes. And by that time, when Mal saw your name, well, it was obvious it wasn't working out with us, and I told him on the last night that I wasn't coming home with him. I'd already been offered a transfer by the bank.'

'Mrs O'Brien—'

'Suzie.'

'Suzie. I don't know what the hell you're on about.'

'He saw your name in the guestbook, of that nice house in Spain. He recognised your name and he started ranting about you and then, well, that was that.'

I had a vague recollection of Polly drawing ice-creams in Robert's book, of her carefully and proudly copying out our name and address, tongue stuck between her lips in concentration.

I suddenly felt sick.

'I didn't understand at first.' She was still talking. 'I barely remembered you, that was the truth. It's been a long time, a busy time since we met you then. But Mal, well. He harbours terrible grudges.'

'I am really confused, Suzanne.' I couldn't compute what she was saying.

'I had already secured the tenancy on a flat in Streatham, but he said he would fight me tooth and nail for custody unless I agreed to move north of the river. And I just wanted to make everything easy for Leonard, I felt so guilty anyway about the split, and so I agreed.'

I understood the guilt part.

'So,' I stared at the clock above her head, hardly seeing it. 'Let me get this straight. You're saying that you and Mal went on holiday to the same place as me, and that you saw my name somewhere and he came to Tufnell Park to … what?'

'To find you.' She sat back in her chair, and she was triumphant, her cheeks slightly pink beneath the freckles.

'To find *me*?'

'Yes. That's why he came here.'

'And that wasn't a coincidence?'

She pulled a face. 'What do you think?'

'I really don't know to be honest. Why?'

'Because. Mal said you ruined his life.'

Jesus Christ.

And the tiny worm of worry that had been niggling at me all morning suddenly appeared from the slash in the apple.

Vejer. Mal had looked at that photo of Polly in my kitchen last night, and he'd known it was Vejer – and yet I hadn't said so. It could have been anywhere; it was a close-up, the church wall behind us could have been any church in the Mediterranean sun. So how had he known? I stared at Suzanne O'Brien in horror.

He couldn't have known. But he had.

NOW: HOUR 16

12am

I am trying very hard to hold back the tears, having just asked Linda if I can borrow some money. She has agreed readily, in on the drama, buzzes off to accumulate all the spare cash she and her husband Stan have in their neat little house. She is glad to lend the money to me, as if it will somehow make up for not knowing where my mother and daughter might have gone. Stan hides upstairs behind the net curtains watching television; they seem to have a set in every room. Occasionally I hear muttering voices, but he doesn't appear.

To my intense frustration, Linda doesn't have a phone charger – but she does have my mother's mobile number. I store it in my new phone, and then I ring it three times, but each time the call goes straight to voicemail.

I call Sid, but he doesn't pick up either. And then I feel like I can't breathe, like all the air is being squeezed out of me, so I ask Linda to excuse me and I go into her bathroom with the coy-faced flamenco doll whose skirts drape coyly over the loo-roll, and I give in to my tears. I sob, mouth opening in a silent scream, until Linda knocks tentatively on the door.

'All right in there, Laurie?' her voice is timid, and amidst my own emotion, I feel terrible for worrying this woman so in the sanctuary of her own home. I dry my eyes on the fluffy pink towel with '*Lady*' embroidered in the corner and notice too late I've left dirt and blood behind.

'Fine, thanks,' my voice sounds gruff. 'Sorry. I'll be out in a sec.'

When I do come out, five minutes later, Linda hands me a cup of tea and a jam tart from a box of Mr Kipling's. I don't like jam much, but I eat it anyway because she looks so pleased when I take it, and because I can't remember when I last ate something.

'Thank you for your help,' I say. 'Could I just use your phone quickly?'

There is one thing I have to do before I go; that I have put off since this morning. I feel sick and ashamed about it.

Fingers hovering anxiously over the keys, finally I ring Pam Southern, Emily's mother. To my enormous and guilt-ridden relief, she doesn't answer, but the answer-phone kicks in and it has her mobile number on it. I scribble it down on Linda's neat telephone pad. I guess Pam is headed down south, to the hospital, if she is not already there. Taking a huge breath, I ring the mobile – but it's dead.

Just like my best friend.

And will Pam ever forgive me for taking her daughter to her death? For being alive still myself, for pretending to be Emily?

Time will tell, I guess.

I hang up as Linda sticks her head round the door. 'Can I get you anything else, dear?' she asks, and again I sense her semi-enjoyment. What a story to regale the bingo club with.

I shake my head, sitting forlornly on her sofa, staring at the television that chatters away to itself in the corner, sound down – and then Sid rings my new phone. I contemplate it for a split-second: I pick up.

'Where the hell are you?' he is angry.

'Looking for our daughter.'

'Why weren't you at the bloody station?'

'I was.'

'So?' Even more impatient.

'So. I changed my mind. I know, Sid.'

'What?'

'That you tried to kill me.'

'For fuck's sake, Laurie—'

'Sid, do you know where Polly is?'

'She's with your mother, isn't she?'

'Apparently. Only I don't know where Mum is either.'

'What the fuck are you on about? You're acting pretty crazy, Laurie.'

'I'm not.' I am. But there's good reason. Isn't there? I am so tired, so blurred, I can't get a grip on much right now. 'Look ...' I start, and then I hear a woman's voice behind him, interrupting. Jolie. 'What?' he snaps. She responds; I can't hear her.

'Sid. I've got to go. Just know this. If you hurt a hair on Polly's head, I will kill you myself. And I will do it by the slowest, most horrible way possible.'

'Christ, Laurie ... this is really infur—'

My phone bleeps and, to my sheer amazement, I see my mother's name come up.

Hands shaking, I try to switch the calls, but all I've succeeded in doing is cutting off both of them. I call my mother back but it goes to the answer-phone. She's probably trying to call me again.

I ring again and again. I hear Linda walking upstairs now, Stan is turning the television down, saying something.

I call my mother again.

A pause ... and then the line goes dead.

'Mum?' I shake the phone first in disbelief, and then frustration and call her back. It goes to the voicemail again. 'Fuck.'

I jump as I realise Linda is there, Stan standing behind her in the shadows. 'Problem?' she looks a little less elated now. 'Can I just say …' She falters.

'Yes?' I prompt; trying not to snap at her.

'I had a thought,' the colour in her face is subsiding a little, but she is still thoroughly overexcited. 'Well, it was Stan actually.'

'What?' She's lost me. 'Stan took my mum?'

'No, no!' her voice is a yelp. 'I mean, it was Stan who caught a glimpse … you know.' She looks towards where he skulks; calls to him, as if to a disobedient dog. 'Come *on*, Stan. We haven't got all day.'

Stan appears, wary, in the doorway; he's wearing a pyjama shirt open over a vest, obviously dressed quickly to come downstairs. He is a scrawny, rather frail-looking man who frankly has seen better days.

'Hello, Stan,' I say, hopefully.

'I saw them. Your mother. She looked very …' he considers the word carefully, 'anxious.'

'Right.' My poor mother. What hell have I got her into?

'And your girl. Pretty little thing.'

My stomach contracts painfully.

'Yes?' I prod him on. 'So …?'

'The man with the car.' Pause. I try to contain myself. I can see Stan's vest under his shirt. 'He was a big chap.'

'Big?'

'And fair.'

Oh God. An unspoken fear that has been circling somewhere high swoops down on me now.

'Did he … what car was it?' I'm useless with cars. I try desperately to remember what he drove. 'A big silver one?'

'I'm not sure.' Stan looks troubled, ponders carefully. Looks up at me, light in his eyes. 'Yes. Possibly.'

Nothing like Morse then.

'And did he, could you see …' I indicate the top of my head. 'Was he slightly balding here? Right on top?'

Stan casts his eyes upwards in thought. 'I'd say so, yes.'

Mal.

But he's in America.

Isn't he?

THEN: AFTER SUZIE O'BRIEN

I didn't think I cared about Mal, not really. I had pushed thoughts of what I felt as far away possible. It felt as if he had just appeared in my life and, if anything, it was me who had used him: for reassurance, for comfort. Only when Suzanne left the café that day, with a sort of rueful but satisfied apology, a twist of that downward-turned mouth, and I sat, staring at the wall, at the clock, at nothing much else except the waitress bustling up and down for a good ten minutes, I realised that I'd been wrong. On top of the shock of Suzanne's revelation, the sense of disappointment seemed doubly huge. Feelings that I'd been hiding from myself began to unravel until there was just me left, revealed and afraid. It seemed, in hindsight, that I had hoped for more from this man – whilst he, apparently, had felt nothing other than a worrying and rather warped hatred.

Blindly I paid for my drink and walked back to the office. At reception, Maeve handed me my messages; there was, unusually, one from Sid.

'Something about school holidays?' she said helpfully. 'Nightmare, the holidays and childcare, aren't they?'

'Thanks,' I took the slip of paper from her and went into my office. Closing the door firmly behind me, I leant against it.

Now what?

I had about ten minutes until my next appointment. Putting Sid to one side, I rang Emily. She was in a meeting apparently.

I contemplated ringing the police; I even picked up the receiver to do so – but what would I say about Mal? *'Please officer, a man I slept with once apparently followed me to live in North London and hates me because I once counselled him and his wife briefly and then they split up? No, he's never demonstrated any threatening behaviour towards me.'*

Without thinking about it too hard, I picked up the phone and rang Sid. A woman answered, taking me aback, even though I knew who it was.

'Put Sid on, please,' I said. Why bother with niceties? She certainly didn't.

There was a pause, a sucked-in breath. I saw Jolie sitting in the gallery window in diaphanous lace at one of Sid's opening nights after she'd had an 'altercation' with her manager outside on the fire escape. I couldn't remember which exhibition exactly, but it might have been the 'Madonna Eats Eve' series. I saw her crying, piteously but prettily, into her Apple Martini, upstaging even the half-naked waitresses in their Vivienne Westwood fig-leaves. I saw Sid standing over the pretty singer, led there by Randolph. *Placed* there by Randolph, who smirked at me across the room as if he'd just won something. Her gallant protectors. Somehow, despite the tears, Jolie's mascara never ran, her kohl-rimmed eyes never smudged.

She knew what she was doing.

I saw the photos the next day in the Londoner's Diary, engineered no doubt by Sid's conniving agent – *'YBA comforts soul sensation after boyfriend fracas'*. But most vividly, I saw her meet my eye over my husband's suede-jacketed shoulder, her lovely face rather too near his tousled curls. No glimmer of embarrassment in the cool, appraising gaze that met mine – only certainty of action. Then she smiled at me, exquisite, gracious; kindly bestowing her beauty on me.

And I suppose I relinquished him. I was beyond fight by that point.

I *was* the fight.

'Hi, darling,' Jolie changed tack now, wrong-footing me. 'How are you? I've been meaning to get in touch about the gorgeous Pol.' My heart beat faster at her gall. She began to say something else, but I didn't let her finish.

'I need to talk to my husband. Now.'

'Ex-husband,' Jolie corrected, pleasantly.

'Husband, actually,' I corrected her back. 'Now. Please.'

There was a silence.

'Of course,' she maintained the grace.

A muffled conversation in the background, a noise I couldn't determine followed by what might have been a door slamming.

'Hello?' Sid, unusually, sounded tentative.

'It's me.'

Pause.

'Hi.'

Nothing more.

'I need to see you.'

'Right. Well, when I pick Polly up tomorrow—'

'Now.'

'Now?'

'Yes. Right now.'

I was surprised by my own nerve. To his credit, he didn't argue.

'Okay.'

I told him when to come and then I did something I had not done since he'd pushed me down the stairs outside. I cancelled all my afternoon appointments, called my mother and asked her to collect Polly from school. Then I went home 'sick'.

I didn't really want Sid to come to the house. I didn't know exactly where he sat yet in the frame of my new life, and so he couldn't slot back into the old one yet. But I couldn't see another option right now. Overwhelmed by the events of the morning, I needed to be somewhere I felt safe, and that was home. So at home we met.

The things that hurt us most are perhaps the things we understand least. For a long time, years even, I could not understand the hold Sid had on me – and so I could not escape it, no matter the damage it caused.

Then my father died. It only served to open up some great wound in me, and slowly, things fell apart, until one morning I arrived at work exhausted after a midnight fight with Sid, scratches visible on my face.

That weekend, my mentor Bev took Polly and me away for a night, to her house by the bleak shoreline in Kent. It was unorthodox, but she was an unorthodox woman and I revered her rather.

In the windswept garden Polly played with the border terrier whilst Bev and I sat wrapped in shawls on the garden bench; the sea beyond the old wall. We drank tea and she began to gently unravel the similarities between my father's behaviour to my mother, and my own husband's.

'Sometimes, Laurie,' she was incredibly gentle. 'Sometimes, you know, people are unable to change.'

'I know,' I said miserably.

'Do you? Really look at him, sweetheart. He may not change because he simply can't. It doesn't mean he doesn't love you, but it might mean he keeps on hurting you.' She pointed at my face. 'In all ways.'

And I suppose it was only acknowledging what I'd always feared: that the damage done to him was scored so incredibly deep there was no undoing it. For all the kindness and the understanding I showed him, it didn't make it better, it didn't make it go away. He still had nightmares at least once a week, thirty years on; the pills worked less and less. He couldn't unbutton himself, he couldn't share his hurt, he kept it all locked tight, tight, tight inside – except on the days when it came out like crackling malevolent energy; when it came out physically.

And so I forgave him: because I thought he couldn't help it. Time and again I forgave him; but all it did was make things worse.

As did this sojourn with Bev: it just made things worse at home, inflaming Sid's anger because I'd gone away without him. But mostly Sid was angry because he knew things couldn't continue this way, stretched to snapping point.

And gradually I understood it all better: maybe it didn't hurt any less, but I saw, eventually, maybe it wasn't me who caused everything to go wrong. It wasn't me who was the letdown … the failure. I didn't deserve to keep getting hurt.

I should never have got the vodka out. Of course I shouldn't, but I did; and by the time Sid arrived, I was half-cut and tearful.

'What's going on?' he looked tired and haunted and still unfortunately, to me, rather beautiful. When the fuck was the hold going to break?

I stood in the kitchen and watched him smoke out on the patio, next to the frog statue he'd made with Polly, painted the most lurid green, and I started to cry and once I'd started I found I couldn't stop.

I didn't want to stop.

I couldn't be strong all the time. It was impossible. I couldn't make the right decisions all the time. I tried so hard; so bloody, bloody hard, but it was impossible to know that what I was doing was right.

And I had started, very slowly to trust Mal, and he was no better than the rest; he was no better – in fact he was, apparently, worse. He had lied to me; he had gone so far as to stalk me, and now I was even more bewildered and, frankly, utterly freaked out.

'Why are you crying?' Sid was terse; never good with tears.

'Because,' I sat on the step and blew my nose loudly. 'Because everything is so unutterably shit.'

'It didn't have to be,' he blew a smoke-ring. We watched the perfect O float skywards. 'It doesn't have to be.'

'What do you mean?' I said. I dried my eyes on my t-shirt.

He muttered something I couldn't hear.

'What?' I shook my head at him.

'You know what I mean.'

'Don't talk in riddles, Sid.'

He chucked his cigarette in the flowerbed and stood over me, blotting out the weak sun. I looked up at him, and I felt a sense of longing I could never express.

He put his hand out; I regarded it for a moment. The thin fingers, the ever-present paint beneath the nails, scored into the very lines of his palms. The old tattoo he'd carved out himself with a maths compass when he was fourteen, running below one thumb; the name of some long-forgotten girl called Nikki who'd broken his teenage heart.

A heart already smashed by his parents' neglect.

I took his hand. He pulled me up so we were facing, and, more drunk than I'd realised, I depended on his grasp to stand straight. We stared at each other. His eyes, the cloudy green I knew so well, were opaque, but still I tried to read them like I'd tried a thousand times before.

I saw pain and self-doubt. Only ever pain in Sid's eyes, really. He could not seem to step over his past.

'Sid,' I said quietly.

'What?' he ducked his head nearer mine.

'This is a really, really bad idea, I—'

'Shh, Laurie. You talk too much.'

He kissed me. Of course he did; that was what I had wanted – but for a moment I did not return the kiss. I felt his mouth against mine and he tasted of cigarettes and coffee; he smelt of turps and oil paint and Sid, and so …

And so, I succumbed. I fell easily into the abyss of longing and familiarity and cool clean feeling that was an illusion; was only to do with the cool clean vodka.

I kissed him back. I wrapped my arms around him, stuck my cold hands into his thick hair. Breathed in the smell of him; a smell lodged deep in my memory, my synapses, in the cupboards where he'd thrown his clothes, in the coat-rack and the duvets, in the very air of the house.

In my broken heart.

We stood entwined on the back step, clutching on to one another. Just like I had dreamt.

And then we went upstairs to bed.

And that was that.

Afterwards, we slept a little. We slept, until the frantic knocking at the door two hours later.

NOW: HOUR 17

1am

Everything speeds up, rather as if I am in some animated toy town. I sit for a moment on Linda and Stan's sofa and, having imparted this latest news about the car, they melt away.

I jump as my phone rings. Mum! Thank God. I scrabble for it.

But it's just Sid.

'Sid, someone has taken my mum and Polly somewhere.' I do not mention Mal at this point. It will only be a thorn to needle Sid more, and I can't risk aggravating him further.

'What do you mean, *somewhere*?'

'Some man picked them up from my mum's house ... and I don't know who.' I have an image of every man I know standing in a line. But mostly, I think of Mal. 'Do you?'

'No,' he says urgently. 'Where are you now?'

'At my mum's neighbour's.'

'I'll come and get you. Just don't do a fucking runner this time.'

'No, Sid,' I say as equably as I can in the circumstance. 'I fucking won't.'

And now, as I hang up from Sid, I will call the police, and the police will have to act, now there are other witnesses to Polly's disappearance; it won't matter now if they think I am mad, because Linda and Stan saw my daughter being taken away.

From upstairs, I hear heated words – and I look up from the phone, and the television comes into focus. Forest Lodge is on the screen, in all its glory before it was burnt down last night, and then I see pictures, like snapshots, of two men and an Asian woman – and then Emily. I stare at her; I recognise it as her graduation photo – it's really old, and she is laughing uproariously at something, chandelier earrings swinging madly; looking past the camera at something behind the photographer. And then there is me. God only knows where they got it from; I look frightened and slightly wild, my eyes too big for my face, my hair twisted up in a severe and unusual style that took a hairdresser and a lot of lacquer to achieve, and I think it must be from the Royal Academy Gala dinner. They've cut Sid out of the picture; his suited shoulder is just visible.

Hands shaking, I fumble around for Linda's remote control, neatly labelled '*Telly*' in red biro, and turn the volume up. The newsreader is saying:

'*Laurie Smith is now wanted for questioning in connection with the death of thirty-six-year-old Emily Southern. Smith absconded from the Royal Hospital in Devon this morning, where survivors were taken some hours after the fire broke out. Police believe the fire was started either in or near the women's room, and that Smith may have some knowledge of this.*'

A cold clutch of fear: are they joking? I had some *knowledge*? I *absconded*?

From the sound of the argument breaking out above me, Linda and Stan may just have heard the same news report.

Incongruous, my first thought: thank God that Pam Southern knows now about Emily and I don't have to tell her.

But my cover is irrefutably blown – although of course Sid already knows I am alive. But if it was Sid who came to Forest

Lodge, why has a man fitting Mal's description taken Polly and my mother?

And it only gets worse as fingers are being pointed. I have to stay free; I have to find Polly ...

And upstairs, Linda's hand is probably hovering above her telephone, itching to call the police ...

It is time to go. And there is only one place I need to be now.

In the distance sirens wail as I slip out of the front door. I cast a last look next door at my mother's house, but it's still desolate; clad in darkness.

And so I run. I summon the little energy I have left, and I jog down the neat little roads, through the back of the cul-de-sac where the kids in Arsenal tops kick footballs against the wall, towards the high street, where there is light and people and the smell of kebabs and diesel fumes; I run until I am gasping for breath. From a neon-signed cubby-hole, I get a minicab driven by a blank-faced African who chews twigs of khat, and he takes me to Mal's neat terrace, to the flat he rents across the park from Polly's school, and I pay for it with money that the mole-like Linda lent me – before she thought I was an arsonist.

When I arrive at Mal's, his basement flat is in darkness, but I don't care. I am almost rabid with rage. I stumble through the shadows in the front garden and down to the door, but of course no one answers. I peer through the front window, through the wicker blinds, and I think I see a light, filtering through from what must be the hallway. Behind me I think I see something move, but when I turn there is only a great holly bush looming lethally over the ramshackle fence. Back at the front door, I ring again and again, banging the letterbox, and then I realise that of course if Polly is in there, if my mother is being held hostage, well, he's not going to answer the bloody door, is he?

I look around the front garden, scrabble around on the path until I find half an old brick, artfully arranged as edging on the motley flowerbed. I pick it up and then, before I hurl it as I am about to, I stop and take my hoodie off. I wrap the brick in it and I put it through the window. As quietly as I can – but I am hardly expert at these things. Hardly expert, just frantic with worry and exhaustion and grief. And I think Saul would know what do, and I wish fervently that he was here now.

A light snaps on upstairs. A nosey neighbour who has not helped my child or parent escape. Fury bubbles up inside.

I start to pick the jagged glass away from the windowpane, and a cat appears noiselessly behind me on the wall and I jump and slice my finger, but apparently I am oblivious to pain.

A siren nears; the sound of tyres taking the corner too fast.

A ghostly blue light flickers round the road, bouncing off the windows opposite, and I hear two doors slam, and then another car pulls up behind the first vehicle; a slamming door again. Another figure behind the police, who saunter across the road towards me now.

Mal.

'Laurie!' he practically shouts, looming up behind the police-woman headed my way. And I don't know who is more shocked now, me or him.

'Don't sound so surprised,' I glower at him over the woman's shoulder. 'I thought you were in America?'

'You know this person?' the WPC asks Mal wearily, as if she's seen this very situation hundred times before.

'Officer,' I say as clearly as I can for someone teetering on the brink. 'I'm very relieved to see you. I have reason to believe this man has abducted my daughter.'

'What?' Mal emits a hollow kind of laugh. 'What the hell are you talking about? I've just landed at Gatwick.'

'Really?' I arch an eyebrow in disbelief.

'Yeah, really. I've been in Geneva at a conference, on the way back from the States. Fifty of the world's dullest IT nerds can vouch for me.'

'Really, madam?' the WPC takes off her hat, smooths her cropped hair with one hand as she considers me. 'And what leads you to believe that?'

'Where's your suitcase?' I say to Mal. I am like Sherlock Holmes; I just need a Watson. A Watson would be good.

'In the car.' Mal puts his carrier bag down, bottles clanking, and unlocks his front door. 'You are very welcome to come in and look.' He motions down the hall with a theatrical gesture.

I'm slightly thrown by his complacency.

'It's a double bluff,' I try to say, but I'm not sure my words are clear to anyone but me. They sound odd, like they are being spoken through a mouthful of sawdust. I am so tired I'm not sure how much longer I can physically stand, and people's faces are starting to morph strangely as I look at them.

'And your name is?' the officer asks me. And then I feel like I'm going down a tunnel very fast.

Mal steps forwards and catches me before I fall. His suit sleeve is scratchy against my face.

'She hasn't been well,' he says quickly. 'I can take care of her. Please. Don't worry.'

The policewoman surveys us warily. I think of the newsreader in Linda's sitting-room. I think of the injunctions previously threatened against me. If I tell them who I really am, will they arrest me? If they arrest me, I will never get Polly back safely.

I cannot take the risk.

The male police officer steps forward. 'If you don't mind, sir, we will just take a quick look inside.'

'Sure,' Mal moves aside to let him pass. 'Be my guest.'

He sits me on the front step with my head between my legs, gulping air. I don't feel very well at all; I can't think straight; I can't work out where the danger is coming from anymore. I am aware of Mal hovering above me. From the corner of my eye, I can see his big hand, the sandy hairs on the back, a tiny scratch near his ring finger. I hear him yawn.

The police return; obviously, they've found nothing.

'Do you want to make a complaint?' the WPC mutters to Mal, indicating the broken window. Mal retrieves my hoodie from the floor, shakes the glass off. Tiny shards patter; glitter on the path.

'No. It's fine. Really.'

I start to say something.

I see the look in the woman's guarded gaze: I see the filter she views me through. Another strange domestic that they would rather not be bothered with.

I stop.

'Are you all right, madam?' the woman asks me.

I nod.

'Well, if you're sure …'

I nod again. 'I'm sure. Thank you.'

Mal helps me stand, propels me gently towards his door now.

'Sorry,' I say uselessly, because I am. About everything.

They leave.

Sorry that Polly is not here; sorry that I can't go with them, that I can't sit in the back of the car and sleep and wake and find everything is back to normal; sorry I can't ask for their help. Sorry that I must press on until I find Polly.

I walk before Mal into the innocuous magnolia hallway, and my phone bleeps. I imagine it will be Sid. But it's not.

The anonymous message just reads GIVE UP.

I switch it off. I will give up nothing.

Mal retrieves his duty-free bag, shuts the door behind us. He turns and leans on it; looks down at me.

'Laurie,' he says, and fear rears again as I read anger on his face. 'What the fucking hell is going on?'

THEN: SID AND MAL

I had fallen into a sleep so deep that when I woke I couldn't think who this figure lying beside me was. I could hear only the beating of the rain against the window and then, somewhere further away, some kind of thunder.

Only it wasn't thunder. It was someone knocking frantically on the door, pounding.

'Oh God.' Sid woke suddenly, sat bolt upright in the bed with a sharp, panicked inhalation of air. The usual for him: night terrors.

'It's okay,' I said automatically – only clearly it wasn't.

I got out of bed, thinking, *Polly, something's happened to Polly*. Pulling on my discarded jeans and jumper, I practically fell down the stairs, tore the door open—

Mal stood there, face white, hair on end, soaked from the rain that was hammering down.

'What the fuck's she been saying now?'

'Who?' I kept thinking about Polly.

'My nutty ex.'

'Your wife?'

He went to step inside the house. I thought of Sid upstairs, glanced nervously over my shoulder.

'Mal. This is a really bad time.'

'I'll say. I'm having a really bad time.' He looked so plaintive, so lost and bedraggled, my heart almost went out to him – and then I remembered Suzanne's words. 'Laurie, I don't know what she's been saying, but please, you must—'

'You were in Vejer,' I said, stepping onto the porch. The ground was cold beneath my bare feet as I pulled the door behind me a little so he couldn't see into the house.

'Yes,' Mal admitted. He looked abashed.

'You followed me there.'

'No,' he shook his head vehemently. 'I really, really didn't. Suzanne booked it. Honestly. She booked the whole thing. She always chose our holidays. She begged me to come.'

'Really,' I said dryly. I was losing my patience with both of them; I had problems enough of my own. From upstairs, I heard the bang of the bathroom door.

'Yes really, Laurie,' he tried to take my hands. 'Please. You must believe me.'

'So why didn't you tell me you were out there?' I stepped back, cracking my head against the door, wincing at the impact.

'Are you all right?' he looked worried. His false concern turned my stomach. I just wanted him to go.

'I'm not doing this now, Mal.'

'But   '

I could sense Sid upstairs, moving around. In seconds he would appear and everything would become even more complicated.

'I need some time to digest everything I've heard.' Swiftly I turned and moved back inside the house. 'Please. Just leave me alone.'

And I shut the door in Mal's face. Which normally would be against my nature, but today felt very much safer.

I stood, thinking for a moment. In the hall mirror, my hair was tangled, eye make-up smudged beneath tired eyes. Lesser

than my normal self, somehow. Then I picked up the phone on
the table, called my mother and asked her to keep Polly overnight. She wanted to chat but I cut her short with some excuse
about not feeling well.

I hung up. I could smell cigarettes; a smell the house had
been free of for a while.

One foot on the bottom stairs, I paused for a moment. Then
I ran up, following the smoke.

Sid was in our daughter's room, lying on the small white bed,
staring at the portrait of her he'd painted when she was tiny. A
wee scrap, she'd been, tucked into my chest, a warm puppyish
bundle. Part of me. Part of him; of us.

I stood above him, looking down.

This time it was me that held out my hand. I knew it was
wrong. I knew it couldn't go right.

But right now, I just wanted to hide in my own past. In
something utterly visceral; something with no thought involved.

Sid tried to pull me down to him.

The burn of his fingers wrapped too tightly round my wrist.

Slowly I pulled my hand back.

'Not in here.'

Not surrounded by the childish innocence of Polly's room,
all pink and white and gingham-curtained.

We were already too tarnished for that.

If you'd have asked me once, a long time ago, I'd have said it was
Emily who was addicted to drama, not me. It was Emily who
made the life-altering decisions in a second. It was she who had
the big love affairs; the gut-wrenching, heart-rending break-ups,
the dashes across country or even continent, and – on one spec-
tacular occasion – across half the world, following an ex to Syd-

ney, only to tire of him precisely one week later. She promptly decamped to an eco site on the Gold Coast in order to help save the planet, which largely involved shacking up with a monosyllabic but very blond surfer for three months, doing little but saving sea turtles and shagging.

'He was thick as shit,' she said cheerfully, arriving back at Heathrow on a freezing February day with a suitcase full of flip-flops, sarongs and Tim Tams, and a tan that made her look almost bronze, 'but the sex was fucking amazing. Until he decided he loved me. Then it got dull. Kept trying to gaze into my eyes, which is useless when you want a good licking.'

'Emily!' I nearly drove into the car in front. She made me laugh so much; she was incorrigible.

But no one did ask, and by then I'd met Sid. Slowly, my life caught up with hers in terms of drama. Less flamboyant, perhaps, but every bit as dramatic – only not in a good way.

Emily and Sid never liked each other. My other friends were drawn by his dark good looks, his enigmatic silences, his untapped talent. Occasional bursts of real charm. His what one university friend called 'Mr Rochester presence'.

Emily just snorted when she heard this last. 'Presence? Arrogance, more like.'

Emily knew me well enough to know I was harbouring a desire to heal Sid, although neither of us could have described it with such clarity back then in our twenties.

'You need to think about yourself *before* you think about him,' she said, about a month after he'd appeared again and we'd started dating properly. 'Not always after.'

'I do,' I protested.

'No, you don't. You can't both be obsessing about him.'

Slowly, my other friends fell by the wayside. Sid would insult them, admittedly unintentionally – usually, at least – but the damage would be done; they'd stop thinking he was mysterious and just think him rude. After the wedding, he rang John Lewis without me knowing and sent all the presents back. We would, apparently, make our own way in the world.

When he realised how mortified I was, he was truly sorry. He wrote to each guest individually on hand-decorated paper, and apologised. It was that kind of gesture that made me forgive him time and again. I saw his behaviour for what it was, a kind of misguided pride, a false belief that wedding gifts were some kind of charity. I understood that Sid felt he'd accepted enough charity in his youth to last him a lifetime; he wanted to be in absolute control now.

But after the wedding, the one person he did not apologise to was Emily, even after he sent the beautiful fish-tank she'd bought back to her. I knew it was because deep down he felt threatened by my love for her, by our bond – and there was little I could do about it. And so gradually, over time and despite her best efforts to like him for my sake, she began to despise him. She thought he was pathetic for being so jealous, and I realised it every time the three of us met.

A small, disloyal part of me wondered if Emily was jealous too – after all, she was the one who generally did boyfriends, whilst I'd always been profoundly single. I'd had the odd fling here and there, but nothing ever amounted to much; they'd be wildly unsuitable, or worse, horribly dull, and it would generally end quite swiftly. Emily was used to having my attention; she certainly wasn't used to me being part of a couple. But I dismissed this when she started suggesting double dates.

We had some uncomfortable and frankly ridiculous evenings out as a foursome, until I came to understand these occasions were more punishment than pleasure. Sid and Emily would glower and snipe at each other whilst Emily's date and I attempted polite and hopeless conversation. Eventually we gave up.

And Emily gave up too, trying to dissuade me from Sid. She saw that I was gone, hook, line and proverbial sinker. She didn't exactly give me her blessing, but she accepted it and I was relieved. I pushed aside any thoughts I had of her reservations about Sid.

But still, nothing quite prepared me for what came next.

The day after Suzanne's revelation, I slipped out before Sid woke and went to work early. I looked at his dark head on the pillow and I felt bereft; almost as if it was the last time I'd ever see him. I knew he wouldn't be there when I got home. In truth, I didn't really want him to be; I knew I was poised for disaster. At the same time, I couldn't bear putting the key in the door and hearing the silence behind it.

I collected Polly from school and went home via the high street bakery, buying sticky doughnuts and Belgian buns dripping with icing so white it was luminous. I had a feeling the blues were about to immerse me.

As I pulled up outside the house, Emily was there already, sitting on the front step.

'Nice surprise,' I waved, opening the car door for Polly who bounded out into Emily's embrace.

'I made soup at Gran's,' Polly was gabbling excitedly. 'It was green and it went everywhere 'cos she forgot the lid of the magic-thingy. She said we were parkners in crime.'

'Partners,' Emily corrected absently. 'Lovely.'

'You're just in time for tea,' I held up the bag of goodies. 'A lifetime on the hips, etcetera.'

I caught Emily's eye above Polly's head, but she didn't return my smile.

In the kitchen I divided the cakes into three, viscous jam oozing like blood onto the white china. As I put the kettle on, Emily clomped down the stairs in her cowboy boots.

'So. To what do I owe this treat?' I focussed on the buns now. 'Bad day?'

'No,' she scowled at me. 'Why?'

I stopped cutting. 'What's up?'

'What's that on your neck?' she glared at me.

'Nothing,' I shook my hair over a faint bite-mark Sid had left.

'*Really*, Laurie?' Emily snatched the knife from me, and pulled my sleeve up, sending me off balance. 'Oh, I bloody knew it.'

Four fingerprints bloomed on my upper arm.

I stared at her and then I wrenched my arm out of her grasp, pulling my sleeve back down.

'For fuck's sake, Laurie.' She jabbed the knife into the table. 'One night, and it's already happening.'

Polly launched herself into the kitchen. I sat down rather shakily at the table and rearranged the cake that had slipped off.

'How's the trampolining going, Pol?' Emily unlocked the patio doors. 'Been working on your backflip?'

'Extremely much, actually,' Polly was grave.

'Why don't you show me?'

'But I want my doughnut,' Polly's bottom lip was already trembling slightly at the horrible thought she might be denied the treat.

'Great gymnasts train first, eat later,' Emily gently but firmly propelled her out of the door. 'How do you think Usain Bolt got so fast, or Beth Tweddle spins so high? First backflip, *then* treats.'

Polly realised she wasn't going to win and gave in, running through the damp garden towards the trampoline at the back. Hands on hips, Emily turned back to me.

'Don't start on me, Em.' I stood to make the tea. 'I'm a big girl now.'

'Laurie, it took you eight years to come to your senses and in one bloody night you've lost it again.'

'I haven't bloody lost it.' The emotion of the last few days was building up inside, threatening to overwhelm me. 'It's none of your business anyway.'

'Oh, really?' Emily's voice was at a dangerous pitch that I recognised as suppressed rage. 'So whose business is it when you call me in the middle of the night, howling?'

'*Once*, I did that, Emily. Once.'

'Whose business is it when I have to take Polly to school for a week because you're too ashamed to show your damaged face in the playground?'

'Ouch.' Boiling water splashed my hand. 'And that was only once too.'

'One whole week.'

'Well, if you're counting the bloody days—'

'Don't be so fucking stupid. No one's counting anything, Laurie, except …'

'Except what?' I met her tawny gaze. She was so cross, her round face was rigid. I'd rarely seen her like this and it unnerved me.

'I'm just counting on still having you as a friend.'

'What does that mean?' I picked up the cake too quickly and the pieces all slid off, tumbling over the flagstone tiles. 'Shit.' I caught Emily's eye, desperate to dissipate the tension. 'Still, no point crying over spilt cake I guess.'

She looked away.

No one was laughing now.

'It means that I am absolutely and categorically not going to sit around and watch whilst you go back to Sid and he ruins your life. *A-gain.*'

She did love to italicise her words for effect, my dear Emily.

'I'm not going back to him. We just had sex. That's all. Just sex.'

'Just sex?' Her voice was flat. 'And you're already bruised.'

'I'm not bruised, Emily. Not really.' I knew what she was getting at; I knew why she was cross – but the intensity of her anger was confusing me. 'Look, I can see what you think. But it's not like that. I'm not going back to him. I didn't plan it. I was having a really, really bad day ...' I realised I hadn't even told her about Mal, about Suzanne's second round of accusations.

'So you thought you'd make it a hundred times worse.' Emily walked away, stood with her back to me, looking down the garden to where Polly bounced and repeatedly failed to execute the requisite backflip, mastering a belly-flop instead. 'Put your tongue in, Pol,' Emily called out of the door. 'Or you'll bite it off.'

'I'm not infallible, Emily. I am doing the absolute best I can but sometimes, yes, sometimes,' I felt tears scalding my eyes now. 'Sometimes, or quite often even, I admit, I fuck up.'

'But there's fucking up, and there's fucking someone who has tried to destroy you.' She wasn't going to give in. 'And *don't* bloody cry.'

'What, like I always cry?'

'That's not what I mean.'

'Well, what do you mean? Why are you *so* cross with me?'

'Because I can't bear to watch him hurt you again. And I don't even mean emotionally. I mean physically.'

'He didn't hurt me last night,' I said stiffly. 'I swear.'

'I don't want to know,' she shuddered dramatically.

I stared at her and I started to lose my patience.

There is undoubtedly a difference between sex that is physically rough, and violence. Sid crossed the line about a year after Polly was born. Delirious still with lack of sleep – Polly was a colicky baby who cried a lot – and Sid, who slept badly at the best of times, became almost psychotic with exhaustion. I had thought it was the new mother's prerogative, but Sid trumped me again. He painted, catnapped, walked the baby round and round the flat we lived in at midnight, round and round the block, singing to her, crooning to her. With Polly, he showed an indefatigable patience and calm.

With me, however, it was a very different story. I was hampering him, apparently; holding him back from his work. Not Polly, whom he loved with a raw, pure emotion; just me. It was all my fault. I'd forced him back from his beloved Cornwall. And my body was different, and, even worse, it wasn't purely his anymore. Sid was never good at sharing. As a youngster, he'd had to fight for everything he owned in his cesspit of a home; hiding any possession he managed to retain; regarding what he couldn't have with a silent, simmering jealousy. He couldn't change.

But we were just about holding it together until I made *the* fatal mistake. Foolishly, in a daze of new and overwhelmed motherhood, I contacted his family in the hope that a grandchild would be a salve to their relationship. I thought it would be a nice surprise for him; to see his own mother again.

How little did I know.

I was out with Polly at some heinous local music group, where Gap-clad babies dribbled all over wooden maracas, and

mothers, counting the days till they could return to work full-
time, sipped their take-away coffees, pretending to derive some
sort of pleasure out of singing 'Row, Row, Row Your Boat' for
the twenty-seventh time that day, when Sid's mother arrived at
our flat. I never really knew what happened, but when I got
home, there was tea all over the floor, a Bells bottle smashed in
the sink – and no Sid.

He didn't come home for two days. I was frantic; calling and
calling and getting no answer. Polly picked up on my sickening
anxiety and proceeded to cry all night both nights he was missing.

On the third day, Sid turned up. He looked like he hadn't
slept at all and the knuckles on his right hand were grazed badly.
The navy cashmere jumper I'd saved up to buy him for Christmas was torn irreparably. He refused to speak to me, though he
took Polly for a cuddle.

'What happened?' I asked.

He lit the first of a packet of cigarettes that he continued to
chain-smoke that night.

'My family.'

I held out my arms for the baby as she almost disappeared
in a cloud of smoke, bit back my words about considering her
health.

'She needs changing,' I smiled tremulously at him. I knew I
had messed up.

'One thing, Laurie,' his voice was horribly low as I reached
the door. My stomach turned over with anxiety. 'Don't ever, ever
contact them again. Any of them.'

I bowed my head. 'I won't.'

That night I slept, out of sheer exhaustion and relief I think,
and so, unusually, did Polly. When I woke in the morning, Sid

had been up all night; had begun work on what was the darkest picture of his career. When it was finished, he called it *Filicide*.

At the weekend, I asked my mother to take the baby for a night. I cooked Sid the most expensive steak we could afford, Dauphinoise and steamed pudding. I put my best underwear on beneath my fanciest frock, and rented a clever French film. I'd hoped that without Polly in the bedroom, we might make love, and that everything might start to look a little more rosy again.

Sid devoured the steak, none of the potatoes or pudding, and far too much red wine. I felt oddly nervous; he hardly spoke. We sat on the sofa with the pinging springs in front of the television, and when I snuggled up to him, he responded – but there seemed little love involved in the sex that followed. I felt odd; was ashamed of my fat, I wasn't relaxed; he made me nervous. I drank too much brandy after dinner, seeking Dutch courage. He drank too much whisky, which was normal by now.

We started to row. We stopped, and started to fuck again. Then we went back to rowing. In the bedroom, at some point in the early hours, Sid pushed me backwards in frustration at some nonsense I was spouting, and I fell onto the bed, banging my head on the headboard. I started to cry. He started to fuck me again. During it, he started to hit my head, quite gently, but deliberately, against the headboard. I was too drunk and too emotional to stop him at first, but then I began to complain, to wriggle and push him off.

He stared down at me and I had the sense that he was absent; had almost left his body. His eyes were dark and wild as he gathered my hair in one hand, so tight I was wincing, yanking my head back – and before I could even protest, without warning, he raised one hand and slapped me across the face so hard that afterwards his palm-print was imprinted on my cheek. Then he stopped and climbed off me and locked himself in the bathroom. When I tried to get in, he begged me to go away and leave him. Forever.

So I took the baby and went to my mother's and we stayed there for three nights.

But I missed him. And he missed Polly. And I knew he needed her, more than anything in the world, for his sanity. He rang me eventually. 'Sorry,' he whispered. 'Sorry I'm such a fuck-up.'

I thought it was a one-off.

So we went home.

Emily and I glared at each other across the stupid floating island thing that had come with my expensive kitchen; the kitchen which had initially made Sid feel like he'd arrived; that made me feel like the world's most un-domestic, entirely failed goddess, and that only heralded a lifestyle that Sid could never settle down to.

I opened my mouth to speak; the kitchen phone rang. It would be my mother or someone automated and infuriating, offering to settle my debts. The answer-phone kicked in.

A woman's voice echoed round the kitchen. At first, I couldn't tell who it was.

'I'm so sorry you're taking it so hard,' the voice said sweetly. 'I know you're a good woman, Laurie. But you have to let Sid go now. It's hard, I know. But it's over. If I can, though, I'll help any way I'm able.'

It was Jolie.

NOW: HOUR 18

2am

Whilst Mal bangs around the kitchen and makes me a cup of black sugary tea, I call 999.

I don't tell them who I am but I report Polly and my mother missing. I tell them Linda is the last person to have seen them, and I give them her address. The woman on the other end of the phone sounds frankly disinterested, but she promises to deal with it. She reels off some lines about missing persons usually turning up, and time allotted before searching. I say, 'Just find them, please.'

Then Mal comes in and forces me to sit down on his horrible beige sofa and drink the tea.

While I do, my eyelids closing a couple of times before I jolt back to reality, I'm aware of him watching me from the table in the window. Then he says, enunciating the words carefully, 'I read ...' he stops and clears his throat. 'I read that you were dead.' And the look that flickers across his face is hard to read, but I would guess that it is a mixture of pain and relief. The anger I saw there before has dissipated.

'Where did you read that?'

He gestures at the duty-free bag flung on the table, newspaper peeping from the top. 'I picked up someone's *Evening Standard* on the terminal shuttle. You were on the front cover.'

I start to explain, and then I start to cry. I am so tired and overwhelmed and frightened, and all I can get out is 'Emily's dead, Emily's dead and I don't know where my mum or Polly are.'

Mal takes the mug out of my hand and puts it on the floor, and then he hugs me. And even though I still don't really trust him, and he hurts my sore shoulder and squashes my sore hand, the feeling of arms around me is momentarily blissful. I could sleep here, standing up, leaning on him.

Then I pull back.

'I must call Sid.'

'Oh,' Mal says flatly. He stands now. 'Must you?'

'He was coming to get me. But then they said I'm wanted for questioning.'

'Why?' For the first time, Mal's eyes narrow slightly.

'Don't look at me like that,' I say.

'Like what?'

'Like I've done something wrong.'

There is an infinitesimal pause.

'Well. Have you?' he asks.

I stagger slightly, shocked, and I knock the mug over, the remnants of the tea spreading in a dark pool across the carpet.

'Don't be stupid,' I snap. I think of his hug a minute ago and I realise it's typical. All these bloody men, with their egos and their hang-ups. 'Something wrong like what? Like murdering my best mate? Yeah sure, that was me,' I start to laugh, and it becomes hysterical and overwhelming, and I clench my fists and practically drum my head with my own fists, and try to think, think, because I must have a plan.

What comes next?

Who wants me dead?

Who hates me that much?

'Laurie!'

Mal is staring at me in disbelief. I stop hitting my head.

'I'd say you need some sleep,' he says. 'You don't look very well.'

I feel horrible; sick and bone-weary. 'There is no time to sleep. Not until I know where Polly is.'

'Your call,' he shrugs. He picks up the mug. 'I'm sure Polly is fine. It's just my advice.'

He walks out of the room and, after a second, I follow him.

'Well, Mal, *you* might be sure Polly's fine but until yesterday everything else was fine.' Was it though? Was it? Not really. But I plough on, my voice rising. 'Everything was fine, I was on a nice little break with my best mate and my daughter was having a whale of a time with Mickey Mouse and her granny, and then Emily and I were nearly killed on the motorway, only no one believed us, and then we had a nice dinner and went to bed in a nice posh hotel room and then,' I am shouting really loudly now, so loudly that I am surprising myself, and I am also thinking, thank God Emily did have a nice dinner before she died, she had some sort of duck, which was her favourite. 'And then, Mal, then she was dead. And now they seem to think that I did it, that I might have killed my very best friend in the world, and I need to tell the police to find Polly, and I can't because they'll arrest me so I need to find Polly first but she's God knows where, and so really, how the fucking hell can you say that anything is fine?'

I go into the bathroom and slam the door behind me, locking it.

'Laurie,' he bangs on it.

'Go away,' I say stiffly. 'Please.' There's a pause. 'Thank you.'

He rattles the door once or twice and then he goes away.

I rinse my face. The cold water will wake me up.

I close the door and wash my face. Then I sit on the edge of the bath for a moment, gathering myself. Finally, I am calm enough to continue on. I will call the police anonymously and leave to find Polly. I stand, looking across the room, and there are women's things on the shelf, I see for the first time. A bottle of some sickly Givenchy perfume, a bottle of horrible blue nail varnish, eye make-up remover, a jar of cotton-wool. My eyes track the room. On the back of the door, a small boy's Batman dressing-gown – and there, poking out below it, the sleeve of something horribly familiar.

My stomach lurches.

Polly's small red cardigan, the one she wears for 'best'.

The feeling that rises inside is so strong that I turn and lean over the basin for a moment and heave, and heave again. I try to calm myself, gripping the basin so hard with my good hand that it hurts; trying not to hyperventilate. So it was Mal, all the time.

Hands shaking, I pull the dressing-gown and then the cardigan off the hook and bury my face in it, searching for the smell of my beloved daughter.

I slow my breathing; think back desperately. The red cardigan. And slowly, slowly it filters through. I rack my brain; think of packing her small bag and of the tears last week. She didn't have that cardigan in her bag for Euro Disney, I'm fairly sure. It's been lost for a while, much to her chagrin. She was upset about it because it has her Hello Kitty badge pinned on one side and because she wanted to take it to show my mother. And I blamed Sid; thought it must be at his place.

It just smells faintly of roses and washing powder. And I think back, and maybe the last time she wore it was to Sid's opening in Cork Street – when everything imploded.

When everything imploded, and Sid half-killed Mal, and Mal drove us to my mother's afterwards, his hands trembling slightly on the wheel and me trying to calm Polly whilst she howled in the back.

But why is it here? And who does the perfume belong to? Is it Suzanne's?

I listen at the door, my heart hammering. It sounds like Mal is still in the kitchen. I pluck the door open quickly and walk up the stairs and into the shabby front garden, fumbling for my phone.

I call Sid.

When he answers, he is incoherent with rage.

'Why the fuck weren't you at your mother's? Are you having a laugh?'

'No. I had to leave. They think I killed Emily.'

He's not listening. 'I went there and you were gone. I seem to be running round London after you, Laurie, and —'

'Sid,' I start to say. 'Who did you tell—'

'I know where Polly is,' he interrupts. 'I'm on my way now.'

'What?' I say stupidly. 'On your way where?'

'To fetch her. Randolph went to get them.'

'*Randolph?*' A tall, fair – if greying – man. Slightly balding. A big expensive car.

'Yeah.'

'How the hell did Randolph know where to go?'

'I don't know.'

'Did you tell him I was alive?'

'Yes. No. I can't remember who I spoke to, to be honest. It doesn't matter now. But they're at his apparently, so I'm on my way.'

'Come and get me first,' I implore.

Footsteps behind me. I turn too quickly, lose my balance slightly. Mal stands there.

'Yes?' I say. I feel a tremor through my body. 'I'm just on the phone to the ...'

'To the?'

He can't kill me whilst I'm on the phone. Can he?

'Where are you?' Sid is saying.

'I'm at …' I choke back the words. I don't dare inflame any-one at this moment in time. Recriminations can wait until later, and it would be best for Sid to get to our daughter quickly. I inch away from Mal; my instinct telling me maybe I should run. 'Actually, look. I'll meet you there.'

'Fine,' Sid says, his voice fading in and out now as his recep-tion falters.

'Just wait for me at Randolph's, for God's sake,' I beg, but I don't know if he hears me before the line goes dead.

Through the fog in my brain, sane thought is breaking. I stand on the pavement for safety, Mal stands in his front gar-den, waiting. He doesn't look dangerous; he looks like a big disordered bear.

'Mal,' I say. 'Why is Polly's cardigan in your bathroom?'

'What?' he looks even more confused.

'Her red cardigan. It was on the door in there.'

'Oh. I'm sorry,' he says, rather helplessly, running his hand through his hair. 'I kept meaning to call you but then … well. I went away. As you know. And really, I'm not sure how it ended up there. Probably it was just with Leonard's stuff. You know.'

We gaze at each other; black spots dance before my stinging eyes. If I don't sleep soon, I am going to lose it irreparably.

'Laurie,' Mal makes his voice gentle. 'I know everything went to crap between us. But I'm not going to hurt you. I don't know what the hell's going on, really, I have no clue. Just as I have no idea where Polly is. And I'm so sorry you are having to go through this – but, please. I'm on your side.'

How many times have I believed that of someone recently?

I calculate. I need to get across town to Holland Park – now. Tucked deep into residential North London at this time of night, there will be no black taxis down these streets.

'Can you call me a cab?' I ask Mal.

'Sure. Will you come back in?'

'No thanks. I need …' I look at the front door, yawning at me cavernously. 'You know. Fresh air.'

Mal looks at me with a mixture of sadness and disbelief. Then he walks inside with a shrug, and calls one.

'Twenty minutes,' he says when he returns. 'Please come inside and wait.'

I don't have two minutes, let alone twenty.

'Can I borrow your car please?' I ask hopefully, and he looks at me with doubt, and says, 'In that state? No way. You'll kill yourself. I'll drive you.'

I consider his words.

'Are you back with Suzanne?' I say, and it's stupid and painful to ask and I don't know why.

'Suzanne?' he laughs bitterly. 'Are you joking?'

'No,' I say blankly. 'Why would I be joking? There's Ysatis on your bathroom shelf.'

'Ysa-what?'

'Perfume. Nail varnish and stuff.'

'Oh. No, it's Dora's. My sister's. She stays sometimes. When she comes down from Lichfield for work.'

'I see.' But I don't see anything, and I don't trust him anymore. 'Anyway. I'd better go.'

'Laurie, this is insane. Let me at least drive you.'

I stand, my plan being to walk in what I reckon is the direction of the main road.

'No, really—' I start to say.

'I'll give you a lift.' He moves towards me, I step back quickly. 'You don't look well.'

I have a strange impression of weightlessness; matter over gravity as I feel myself falling. Then I don't feel anything anymore.

THEN: AFTER SID

Emily and I stared at each other across the kitchen, listening to the silence after Jolie hung up. I hadn't answered the phone to her; I hadn't really absorbed her misplaced offer of some ridiculous olive branch, and God only knew what excuses Sid had given for not going home, or where he was now. Frankly, Jolie was the very least of my concerns. Instead, drawing myself up, I turned away from Emily – my oldest friend – and, for the first time in my life, I asked her to leave my house.

Facing Emily's fury about my behaviour was only a reminder of everything I knew I was doing wrong. I needed to be alone; I needed to regain control. Of something. Of some part of my life. I did *not* need to be chastised. I could do that to myself.

After Emily slammed her way out with mutterings of 'Don't say I didn't warn you' and I put a somewhat confused Polly into the bath, babbling about Emily having to rush off to see her mother, pretending everything was fine – a talent I had honed well over the past few years – I went to my bedroom to change. Throwing my jumper on the bed, I saw that Sid had scrawled, right across the expensive cotton pillowcase my mother had bought me for Christmas, scarlet words:

Come to the opening on Friday. You <u>NEED</u> to be there.

I read his message – and all I felt was irritation that, typically, he had not bothered to find a piece of paper; that he'd ruined my one and only Chanel lipstick by writing with it.

The next day I felt horrible; rattled and murky. All morning between appointments, I wrote texts to Emily and didn't send them. The afternoon was taken up with meetings and a review of the Darfur girls' situation, and in the end, I was a little late leaving work because I'd so much to catch up on after playing truant. I arrived at St Bede's as the last children were straggling out of after-school club, taking the stairs towards Polly's classroom two at a time.

Wendy, the wizened teaching assistant, was clearing up the tables in the empty classroom.

'Forgotten something?' she smiled toothily.

'Er, Polly?' I said.

'I'm sure Polly had her book folder *and* her coat.' Wendy bundled the bright felt-tips together and stuck them in a drawer. 'For once. She did a lovely picture. Taking after her dad already, isn't she? Couldn't wait to show you.'

'Where is she?' My heart had sped up a little. 'In the loo?'

Wendy stopped smiling. 'What do you mean, where is she?'

'I mean, where is she?'

'She's gone already.'

'Gone?' My mouth went dry.

'Yes.' Wendy gazed at me, trying not to show her concern. 'She went with the other lady.'

'*What* other lady?'

'The nice one.'

'Wendy!' I resisted grabbing her and shaking her. 'What nice one?' A cold sweat had broken out across my forehead. 'What woman?'

Emily? But she would never take Polly without telling me. Would she?

'The – the pretty one.' Wendy was frightened now.

'Blonde? Big bosom?'

'No.' Wendy could hardly speak.

Jolie? I remembered her sanctimonious pity for me on the phone last night.

'Dark? The singer? Her dad's girlfriend?'

'No,' Wendy shook her head, her gold chains swinging wildly. 'No, she's a mum.'

'Roz?'

'No. New. Her son's in the other class. She said Polly was coming to play.'

'What's her name?' But now I knew who it was.

'I can't remember.'

'Red hair?' The panic was building.

'Yes,' Wendy's relief was palpable. 'Her little boy's called Leonard.' She looked at me like a lost spaniel, hoping for reassurance, but I was already turning to go. 'Sorry, Mrs Smith. She did say that you knew.'

Suzanne O'Brien.

What the hell did she want with my daughter?

Fumbling with my car keys, I called Mal and left him a message, asking him to call me with Suzanne's address immediately, asking him why the hell his wife might have taken my daughter.

Then I rang the police. I reported my daughter as abducted and gave them a description of both Polly and Suzanne O'Brien. As I turned the key in the ignition to begin my own search, Mal rang.

'I'm so sorry,' he began. 'I really—'

'Never mind about sorry, Mal,' I had no time for sorry, 'just give me her bloody address.'

'It's 23b Greenleaf Avenue. The house on the corner. Middle flat. I've rung her. She's not answering.'

'I bet she's bloody not.' I knew the road he meant, it wasn't far from the park. 'Thanks anyway.'

'Laurie—' he began again.

I hung up.

There was no answer at 23b, nor at any of the other flats in the house. I paced up and down outside, and then I called Sid, leaving him a message telling him what had happened. I was just dialling the police again when Leonard and Polly appeared around the corner of the road, drinking cans of Coke.

I had never been so relieved to see anyone in my entire life.

'Pol,' I ran towards her. 'Oh, Polly! Where've you been, baby?'

Suzanne O'Brien appeared behind them. She was smiling. The mad cow was actually smiling at me.

I scooped my daughter up, spilling her drink down my own front.

'Mumm-y!' she protested. 'My Coca-Cola.'

'Sorry, darling.' I put her down and propelled her back towards the car. 'I'll buy you another one.' Suzanne was nearing. 'Just get in, would you.' I bundled Polly into the back seat and shut the door firmly, locking it behind her.

Leonard and his mother had caught us up now. I leant down to the little boy.

'Can I just have a quick word with your mummy?' I asked him. He blinked sandy lashes at me, looked up at Suzanne for approval. She nodded. 'Wait upstairs for me, Lenny.'

He wandered up the stairs, banging his Coke can methodically against each railing. Checking he was out of earshot, I moved very close to the woman still smiling beatifically at me.

'What the fucking hell are you playing at?'

Her smile froze. She blinked at me like her son had just done.

'Leonard told me Polly wanted to come round.'

'Oh really?' I hissed. 'You let a six-year-old arrange his own social life, do you? Without speaking to me first?'

She shrugged, almost imperceptibly. 'Why not?'

'You're having a laugh,' I said, my fingers tightening around my car keys. I wanted to punch her right in the middle of her stupid smug face. 'You knew full well I had no idea about this. About where you were taking my daughter.'

'Didn't I?' she stared at me. 'Mal said it was okay.'

I stared back, a whisper of doubt creeping in now.

'I don't believe you,' I said. 'I just spoke to him.'

'Oh really.' She grimaced. 'I told you, he's a liar.'

'No,' I refused to go this route. 'You're the bloody liar. Don't ever come near my child again, do you hear me?'

Leonard trailed down the stairs towards us now. 'Mummy? What's wrong?'

I glanced at him. Poor little mite. His mother was quite clearly mad.

'There was just a muddle, sweetheart,' I said, opening my own door. 'But Mum and I have sorted it now.'

She laughed, a high bitter laugh.

'Ha,' she said. 'Have we? I tell you something,' she took a step towards me. 'Mal will never fucking love you like he loves me.'

Leonard blinked once more and promptly burst into tears.

My heart went out to him – but I couldn't stay here. He wasn't my responsibility; this wasn't my mess. I had enough of my own to contend with.

'Sorry, darling,' I said rather uselessly to Leonard. Polly knocked on the car window, waving at her friend. He just sobbed harder.

'Why is Leonard crying?' Polly asked as I got in the car.

'He's just a bit … sad,' I watched a motorbike approach from the other end of the road. 'I'm sure he'll be just fine soon.'

'I hope so,' Polly looked worried. 'Shall I get out and make him better? I can tell him my best joke—'

'No!' I practically shouted, turning the key in the ignition just as the bike drew level with me, and as I indicated to pull out, a red-faced Mal pulled off the black helmet.

My heart racing, I pulled away. In the mirror, as he receded, I could see him staring helplessly after the car, still seated astride the motorbike.

All the way home, I was still so furious that I could hardly speak, so I put Polly's favourite CD on and bellowed along with her and The Tings Tings, watching her in the mirror, happily oblivious in the back seat.

I felt so tense that my face ached. What damage was I doing to my child? I had the strongest impulse not to drive home; to keep going instead, to somewhere no one knew us, right out of London, away from this web of heartbreak and jealousy; away from Sid, away from whatever strange game Mal and his ex-wife were playing.

Opening the front door, a strange smell assailed me. Polly, allergy-prone, immediately started to sneeze.

'It's like flowers,' she said, wrinkling her running nose. 'Old lady's smell.' She meant like at Auntie Val's: talc and pot pourri.

I walked into the sitting-room. Something was different.

Someone had moved things around on the coffee-table, I saw at once. My notes were upside down, Polly's Lego on the other side to where it normally was.

I rang Sid. 'Have you been in the house?'

'No.' He was terse.

'Are you sure?'

'Yes.'

'Right. Well, Polly's okay, you'll be glad to know.'

'What? Why wouldn't she be?'

'Did you not get my message?'

'Oh.' He thought about it for a moment. 'I guess so. Sorry. I've been a bit distracted. We've had a bit of … of trouble here. Jolie's not well. And incidentally, she's upset about your attitude.'

'What?' I was startled. 'What attitude?'

'You know what I mean. Her offer of friendship. Put Pol on, please.'

I called my daughter to the phone. Jolie was obviously with him, and I wasn't up for tackling this now.

I went into the sitting-room and moved things back, thoroughly rattled. I thought about ringing Emily; she had a spare key – but I couldn't face her either. I couldn't see why she'd have come into the house – but hopefully it might have been her, come to make amends. I recognised the smell from somewhere, but it evaded me. I wondered if it was maybe one of Emily's exotic perfumes. It was cloying, and I opened a window.

But really, I had other concerns now. I felt foolish; even angrier than when I'd left Suzanne's. I despised myself.

Once again, after all that had just happened between Sid and I; once again, it apparently meant nothing.

NOW: HOUR 19

3am

I wake in the dark, sweating and confused, my face stuck to something plastic. For a second I don't dare move, and then I panic, realising my arms are bound to my body.

I start to thrash wildly against my bonds.

It takes me a minute or so to realise that, wherever I am, someone has wrapped something thick and heavy around me, and this is what restrains my arms now.

Eventually I manage to free myself. I lie panting and terrified, quieter now, until my eyes slowly adjust to the light, and I realise I am lying on Mal's sofa, my face against the duty-free bag he flung there earlier. For some reason, there's a bucket on the floor beside me and a blanket and a heavy sheepskin coat I've become entangled in somehow. Has he tried to bind me?

Why am I still here? I was leaving, I remember; I was leaving to find Polly. But I am still in Mal's flat; here, in this nasty, dingy basement. Polly is at Randolph's. I have no idea now what the time is, but Sid must have collected her and my mother by now. She will, at least, be safe.

If Sid is … if Sid is to be trusted.

I try to stand but my head is pounding and for a moment I can't see for the pain. I slump back on the sofa.

I take a few deep breaths and try again.

I reach the living room door. I switch the light on and try to open it.

The door is locked.

I pull against it, but with my unwieldy bandaged hand, I can't get any sort of grip. The door won't budge. I hear a sob rip through me. Oh God.

A sob of frustration: my own sob. It echoes round the room.

I switch the light on, and look frantically around for something to attack the door with. I see the coal-scuttle, and I start to pick it up and then I realise ...

It is a ridiculous idea; the door is solid wood, and I have no strength left to smash it in without waking Mal.

I absolutely must not alert him, I am sure of that. I drop it on the sofa, and, head pounding still, I try to think straight.

And then I see the window that I broke earlier, and the board Mal has clumsily put before it to cover the hole. He has only used gaffer or duct tape, I realise.

I bend to retrieve the trainers that Mal must have eased off my feet, trying to contain my nausea. As I lean down, I see the *Evening Standard* on the floor that Mal brought home from the airport. It has slipped from the carrier bag, its headlines screaming:

Artist's Wife Killed in Fire and below it, *Laurie Smith, Dead.* There's a picture of me below the headline; the same wild-eyed photo from the gala dinner I saw on last night's news. And another two, smaller pictures; one, slightly blurred, of Sid from a slight distance, coming out of a building I recognise. The clean white lines of the Tate St Ives, above Porthmeor Beach in Cornwall. I pick up the paper and read the caption. *Husband Sid Smith leaving the Tate in St Ives this morning.*

It doesn't make any sense.

This morning? I check the date: this is yesterday's paper.

If the *Standard* is right, it means Sid was still in Cornwall yesterday morning – and so he must have been there whilst

Emily and I were in neighbouring Devon the night before. But he hadn't told me; not even when I rang him to tell him of mine and Polly's plans. And he certainly hasn't mentioned it since.

Hands shaking, I read the whole story; skimming the details of the fire, of my death.

> *Sid Smith, Turner Prize winner, hellraiser, and*
> *infamous for his 'debauched' art, was in talks re*
> *curating his forthcoming show at the Tate St Ives when*
> *he learnt that wife Laurie Smith tragically perished in*
> *Thursday night's Forest Lodge fire in South Devon. The*
> *artist had no comment to make. Notoriously private,*
> *he's renowned for hating the press; in December 2011*
> *he took out an injunction against Rebekah Brooks'*
> News of the World *for malicious reporting on cracks*
> *in his marriage. Seven months later, this summer, the*
> *Smiths did indeed split.*

The other picture is of Jolie, partially obscured, getting in a chauffeured car. The article continues:

> *Sid Smith's new girlfriend, 25-year-old rising R & B*
> *star Jolie Jones, did take the time to talk to reporters.*
> *'Laurie's death is the most hideous tragedy,' she said,*
> *'I'm well shocked, and very sorry. But she never really*
> *recovered from the impact of Sid leaving her.'*

As if I am better off dead. I swallow hard.

But *I* left Sid.

It was the hardest decision I have ever had to make, but I very much left him. It took me a few years to work up the courage, but I did it in the end. And he begged me to stay, but I took Polly, and I went – before he killed me, either literally or metaphorically, with his dark, twisted love. Whatever he's told Jolie, I know that it was me who made the decision.

> *'Now mine and Sid's main concern is his 7-year-old daughter, Polly Blue. I want her to see me as her new mum.' The little girl is currently believed to be on holiday with her grandparents.'*

They've got Polly's age wrong again, is my first thought. Then I think, the day that Jolie Jones gets her hands on my daughter is the day I will kill the insensitive bitch myself. I can just imagine her granting the journalists this gold-dust: all eyes, lashes fluttering, the press lapping it up – the gorgeous young step-mother saving the tragic tortured widower and his bereft but photogenic daughter.

I throw the paper across the room in disgust. It hits a picture, a horrid copy of a Constable mill, which swings wildly and then crashes to the ground.

I hear movement in the next room.

Sid was only about seventy miles from Forest Lodge, a fact he never mentioned.

Sid was in the vicinity when the fire began.

I don't bother with my laces. I pull the board from the window and use my good arm to swipe the last bits of glass from the edges of the pane. All thoughts of why I am still here, locked in, of whether Mal may have had something to do with the whole desperate and life-shattering situation dissipate: my sole ambition is to free myself.

And the thought that drives me on is that Sid must have got to Polly now.

I think I hear Mal.

'Laurie?' he is calling my name. He sounds angry, I think. 'Laurie, what are you doing?'

My heart is pounding, the adrenaline is back; coursing through my veins. With every last vestige of strength, ignoring the pain in my hand and shoulder, I wrench the wooden table back from the window, and shove it with all my might against the door.

And he is rattling the door now; I see the handle turning—

I almost throw myself out of the window. Like a snake out of its skin, I slither out; somehow, I am through. My hands hit the gravel, I'm pulling myself up, launching myself up the stairs, tripping on my laces, falling, standing again, running. Running.

'Laurie!' I hear the bellow behind me.

I run faster than I ever remember running in my life, smashing through an old rose bush trailing over the garden wall on the street corner, lacerating my face. I push on.

Why did Sid not mention where he was yesterday?

I run until I get to the main road. Gasping for breath; I have no jacket now and I can feel wetness on my back. There's blood on my jeans where I cut myself on the last jags of glass. But at least I know I still have Linda's money in my back pocket.

I hail a cab and ask the driver to take me to Holland Park.

He looks disbelieving, frowning at me. Blatantly, I don't look like I belong amongst the echelons of West London – but, thank God, the man doesn't bother to argue, just clicks the door open and lets me in. I fumble for my phone to call the police again and realise with horror I've left them both at Mal's, along with the hoodie. I have no means of contacting anyone now. I am totally alone again.

'Shit!'

But at least I am moving. I sink back into the seat, willing the cab on. I never go to church, didn't get married in one, don't believe in much other than the fact the earth goes round the sun, and the world keeps turning. But right now, I am praying.

THEN: BEFORE SID'S SHOW

If love was simple, everyone would love the right person – and so life would be simple too.

But it's not, of course. It's not.

Nothing allows for the unequal fractions that don't add up; the chase that ends in disaster; the thwarted passions; the hurt inflicted.

On Friday morning, whilst Polly was still asleep, I tidied away every single trace of Sid I could still find in the house, apart from the photos of him in her room.

The previous evening, Mal had rung a few times. I sent all the calls to voicemail; didn't bother to listen to the messages. I was exhausted and shaken by Suzanne's actions earlier. I didn't know who to believe and I just couldn't get enmeshed any further in the tangle of their relationship.

I sat at the kitchen table, staring out into the darkness, and then eventually I rang Emily. The house felt horribly empty and lonely: we'd had no real interest yet from a buyer but increasingly I was desperate to leave, to start afresh somewhere new. I rattled round in it when Polly was in bed; everything reminded me of something.

I really wanted to speak to Emily – but she didn't answer. I left her a message.

'Sorry,' I said. 'I really am. I know it's only because you care. Please call me back.'

But she didn't.

In the morning, I dropped Polly at the classroom door and then asked to speak to the head-teacher, Mrs Webster. I explained what had happened yesterday with Suzanne O'Brien.

'I'm sure it was just a misunderstanding?' gruff Mrs Webster met me at the door of her office. 'These things can happen, unfortunately.'

'No, it wasn't,' I was adamant. 'I hardly know the family, and she has an unhealthy interest in me and Polly.'

'Why?' the older woman raised a quizzical, bushy brow.

'It doesn't matter. But surely you and your staff are aware that no child should be released to anyone they don't know?'

'Yes, of course. But it's hard, Mrs Smith, in a case like this one, when a parent says she's collecting on behalf of another parent – and the child happily goes along with it.'

I imagined my trusting, gregarious daughter, keen to befriend anyone – and the thought only made me more angry.

'If there's any doubt, obviously you should call the parent first.'

'Well, we will in future, in your case. Though,' she smiled pleasantly, but the smile didn't reach her lined eyes. 'It's not always easy in this day and age to know which parent to call.'

A deft swipe. I opened my mouth to retaliate but in the end there seemed no point.

Sid called. 'You are bringing Polly tonight, aren't you?'

My heart sank. I hated Sid's openings at the best of times, and this was the worst.

'Really?'

'Yes, really,' he snapped.

'You never normally want her there.'

'Well,' there was a pause. 'Things change. Things do change sometimes, Laurie.'

'Do they?'

'If you want them to.'

'Sid,' I sighed. 'What does that even mean?'

'You know what it means. Please bring her.'

Around eleven, Maeve on reception stuck her head round the door.

'Another cancellation?' I finished the notes I was transcribing.

'Er, no,' she looked worried. 'Your eleven o'clock's here but – so is – well, actually, so are the police.'

It was the same gap-toothed officer they had sent to my house when I'd reported the 'supposed' intruder a while ago. I greeted her at the door.

'I thought I should pay you a quick visit, Mrs Smith,' she was courteous, efficient – but there was a definite undertone. 'I know that you reported your daughter missing yesterday. She's home safely?'

'Yes,' I said carefully. 'There was a … the woman who took her, Suzanne O'Brien—'

The officer interrupted me. 'Yes, Mrs O'Brien.'

'Ms,' I corrected, then felt foolish. 'Sorry. Carry on. Have you spoken to her?'

'Yes.' I thought the officer looked longingly at the chair opposite my desk. 'I have.'

'And you've given her some sort of warning?'

'Well, actually,' she shifted the weight from one foot to the other. '*Ms* O'Brien has made a complaint against you.'

'Against *me*?' I gaped at her.

'She says you have been hassling her.'

'Hassling *her*?' I shook my head in disbelief.

'Yes.' She met my gaze.

'Is that an official term – "hassling"?'

'Look, I don't know what's happened between the pair of you but—'

'Nothing's happened between us, except she has visited me here, made various allegations, and then took my daughter from school yesterday without my knowledge. How am *I* hassling *her*?'

'She says …' the woman looked at her notebook. 'That you are "displaying an unhealthy interest in her and her husband".'

'Really?' I expostulated. 'Her husband? Who she's no longer with.'

'That may be the case, I don't know,' the policewoman looked at me coolly. 'But, yes, really.'

'Right. Well, I would like it on record that she is, in my professional opinion, mentally unstable.'

'That's as maybe. But if you continue to visit her at her house, and threaten her, then she may have grounds for some kind of injunction.'

'Threaten her?' I was starting to sound like a parrot.

'One of her neighbours verified that you were indeed seen to be admonishing her severely, in front of her small son.'

'I see.' I felt a strange calm descend on me now. 'And did this neighbour know what had happened prior to my "admonishing" her? Have you spoken to her ex-husband about this?'

'We've left Mr Cooper a message. We will be talking to him, I can assure you.'

'Fantastic. You do that. And now if you don't mind, if you haven't got anything more helpful to say, I'd like it very much if you left my office.'

'Look, Mrs Smith,' the officer softened a little. 'I understand that divorces are very stressful. That emotions run high.'

'You're telling me.'

'Well, yes,' she regarded me for a moment, 'I *am* telling you actually. You have made a couple of allegations that frankly, could be seen as … emotional. And now this.'

'So you think I'm mad.' It wasn't a question. It was a statement.

'Not mad, no. Just … under pressure.'

I opened the door for her. 'I can assure you, officer, that I won't be going anywhere near Suzanne O'Brien, or her family, if I can possibly help it. And that it was her who took my daughter, not the other way round. So if anything ever happens …' I faltered, I couldn't bear to say 'to Polly'; my stomach rolled over even thinking the words, 'I will not be held responsible for my actions towards those who ignored me.'

Which, some might have said, wasn't exactly furthering my cause.

NOW: HOUR 20

4am

'I wondered when you would turn up,' Randolph says, yawning so widely I can see his gold teeth. His rumpled silk pyjama top is open to the swollen waist: I look away from the mat of fair hair on his chest, which is almost eye-level for me and, frankly, stomach-turning.

'I must say, you're not looking your best,' he pushes back the greying blond mane from his once-handsome face, now rapidly going to seed. 'What the fuck have you been up to? Or rather,' he smirks, 'what *haven't* you been up to?'

I look at the tiny broken veins on his nose, and I remember with a visceral thud how much I detest this man. A man whose singular skill is to make money from the talent of others.

'Where's Sid? Where's Polly? And my mother?'

'Your little angel?' he pulls the door back. 'You'd better come in.'

I practically sprint inside the penthouse, yelling, 'Polly, Polly?'

I see Toy Bear on the Eames chair in the corner, and my heart soars and I race to the first door, and wrench it open and—

And then, behind me, Randolph actually laughs. 'They're not here, dear Laurie.'

'What do you mean, not here?' I spin round.

'They left at least an hour or so back. Hence me trying – and failing – to get some beauty sleep.'

I turn and I stare at him and then I raise my good hand and slap him as hard as I can round the face. I put all the anger and frustration and fear of the past twenty-four hours, of the past few months, of the past few years, into that slap and it is so hard, it hurts my own hand more I think than it hurts him. Still, I feel a creeping sense of triumph as I wait for him to hit me back. But he doesn't.

'You little bitch,' he holds his reddening cheek incredulously, and his measured honeyed tones slide. Suddenly he sounds like the Northern bully that he really is. 'You *hit* me.'

'How dare you laugh? How dare you fucking laugh at me?' I run round and round the apartment, opening every door, looking for my family. Looking for a clue. 'I've been going out of my mind. Where the hell is Polly? Where are they all?'

'Sid took them off. What's the fucking drama, you lunatic?' He studies his face in the mirror; my fingerprints lie across his cheek.

'You let Sid take them?'

'Yes of course I let him take them. Polly's his daughter too.' There is malice to his tone. 'In case you forgot.'

I am far beyond rising to his taunt.

'But,' my hand is throbbing violently now. 'Why were they here in the first place?'

'Because. He asked me to collect them.'

'Sid did? Sid asked *you* to collect Polly and Mum?'

'Yes. Sid did.'

I try to compute this. Randolph walks to the Louis XVI drinks cabinet where he pours himself a whisky and downs it in one. For all his sanguine demeanour, his great meaty hand is slightly trembling; I can tell from the way the decanter chinks on the glass.

'Give me one,' I say and I hold my own throbbing hand out. 'Please.'

'Well,' he stares at me and then he does as instructed. 'I'm not going to argue with you. You're stronger than you look.'

Do I sense a grudging admiration as he hands me a glass? Is that what it takes to impress in his warped world?

I drink the whisky, which makes me choke. 'Where did he go?' I demand.

'I don't know. Home, I expect.' But he doesn't look at me now, and I don't believe him.

'Can I use your phone?' The alcohol has gone straight to my head, singing up through my veins, buzzing into me.

'Sure,' he gestures to the handset on the table. 'Go nuts. I'm going to put some clothes on.'

And as I dial Sid, I look at the Hirst on the wall, so right for Randolph. I never liked Hirst, so flashy and false, so very – contrived, and I remember the night Sid and I were last here, about a year ago, celebrating some nonsense, the highest sale ever for a piece of modern art, some obscenity like that, and Jolie had just had her first big hit. She sang right here in the room, using a little breathy voice that she saved for the select few, her pretty Afro glittering and her skin gleaming like licked caramel, wrapped snugly in her shimmering white dress, and then out on the balcony, Randolph introduced her to his beloved protégé; to my husband. It was just after we'd been to Paris, just after Sid had taken off internationally and we might still have had a chance, mightn't we?

Although deep down, I knew it was too late. It was only a matter of time.

And Randolph took Sid out to smoke; to deliberately court the girl as I watched from inside, being bored to tears by some gallery owner who was more bored by me, and I saw that Randolph lit the cigars, one eye on Sid and his other eye steadfastly on me.

And I watched him, offering Jolie a suck of the big hand-rolled Havana, and her taking it, giggling up at Sid, wrapping her voluptuous mouth around the cigar, fully aware it was positively pornographic – and I thought, why would she not fall for him? Slant-eyed, snake-hipped, scowling genius: my beautiful nightmare.

Every part of me knew Randolph meant no good. He thought I had too much power over Sid, which was laughable, because no one had power over Sid – not even Sid, really. When Sid made what Randolph considered a bad decision – like when he turned down the NYC show in favour of taking six months off the merry-go-round, or when he turned down the Sultan of Brunei's multi-million dollar commission to create a work about his racehorse – well, then Randolph blamed me.

So Jolie suited Randolph, in the light of things to come – she was at the top of her game, fashionable and, despite her mockney tones and her street urchin game, extremely well-born and privately educated. And it was only later that I learnt she could belt it out too; belt out the songs with a voice as loud and guttural as any docker, that she would fight mean and dirty for this man whom she had decided that night at Randolph's that she wanted.

I listen to Sid's phone ring out, and with the other ear, I can hear Randolph talking now, quietly, in the other room, and I wonder who else is here. Sid does not answer and the voicemail doesn't kick in and so I hang up the handset and creep towards the bedroom door, and then I realise that Randolph's on the phone himself.

'Yes, of course it's definitely her,' he is saying, 'she's here, right now,' and then I push the door open, and he jumps like a guilty child.

'Is that Sid?' I say, and I hold my hand out again for the phone, and he says 'No' and then snaps it shut.

I snatch it from him, and now he does push me, hard, and he's a gorilla of a man, greasy curls hanging round a degenerate face. He pushes me, and I go flying back across the room, falling, skidding on the parquet floor. His phone drops to the floor and I scrabble for it and look at the display and the last number dialled, I recognise: it's Sid's number in Islington.

'So are they there? Are they safe?' I say, panting with the exertion, and I stand and Randolph comes at me again.

'You know, I never liked you, you jumped-up little tart,' he snarls, and he shoves me again, but it's more than just a push, it contains the venom of violent action. 'You fucked it all up, didn't you?'

And there is force in the contact that makes me remember I am alive still and I feel an overwhelming urge to laugh. Somehow, it seems entirely appropriate that I am here fighting with this man, who represented everything I hated about my life with Sid.

I scramble back up and he slaps my face, and I am stunned, falling back, but I get up yet again, and I lunge for the phone which has gone skidding under his huge ornate bed, the floor beneath which is like some overgrown teenager's, littered with old underwear and plates of half-eaten food.

But he is nearer, and he reaches it first.

'Oh no you don't,' he says, and I think he's going to stamp on my hand, but he doesn't; he drags me up forcibly and throws me onto the bed and for a moment, I lie there limply, winded and confused. Is he going to assault me now too? But he just dials again and then he says, 'Police, please.'

And I suppose that at least if the police come Mal cannot get me and nor can his mad wife, if it *is* her who has ever meant me harm. And if Randolph is calling the police, then perhaps my fears about Sid *have* been my own overwhelmed paranoia.

And in fact, lying here, exhausted, racked with desperation to see my daughter is safe, I am almost incredulous now that I have ended up in this sorry and pathetic state. Incredulous that my best friend is dead – and I still don't know who did it. That I still don't know who it is that wants me out of the way for good.

Randolph and I lock eyes across the vast expanse of his opulent bed, which stinks of him; of his nasty fetid existence.

We lock eyes – and I know that this journey is nearly done.

THEN: SID'S OPENING NIGHT

I put Polly in her best dress, the pale pink one with tiny red flowers sewn round the hem, and her red cardigan, and tried to calm her curls a little; plonked her in front of Wallace and Gromit and went back upstairs to change. I put my smart jeans on with a white shirt and tied my own hair back.

Then I took it all off again and, as a concession to the occasion, I put on my own best dress, sea-green silk from Stella McCartney, cut beautifully on the bias. Along with the ring, it was one of the few presents Sid had bought me after he started to make money. He loved to spend money on Polly, but I was a different matter. Still, two Christmases ago it had sat under the tree, lavishly wrapped. 'It's the best colour for your eyes,' he muttered when I pulled it out of the paper, and he was right, of course. If there was one thing he was sure of, my husband, it was his colour chart.

Emily had still not been in touch, although I'd texted her yet again, along with the address of the gallery, asking her to please come tonight. Safety in numbers, and all that. I was struggling to believe she was still so angry she wouldn't even speak to me – but apparently it was true.

Polly, on the other hand, was thoroughly overexcited, jumping up and down frantically beside me as I tried to apply my mascara in the hall mirror with a hand that shook a little. In truth, I craved a drink, the vodka bottle in the cupboard was all but calling my name – but instead, I had poured myself some fizzy water. Rock and roll.

'Can I have some 'scara?'

'No.'

'Why not?'

'You're much too little.'

'Some lipstick then?' she waved the smashed Chanel lipstick in my face. 'Jolie lets me.'

I bit back my retort. 'No.'

Polly's bottom lip wobbled. I grabbed her and hugged her; sank my own lips into her fat little cheek, and conceded.

'How about a little bit of nail varnish instead?'

So we were late leaving because I had to daub each tiny nail with brilliant polish, keeping the cab that I'd called with great extravagance waiting for a good ten minutes.

From the back seat, I watched North London slide by, clutching my daughter's hand so tight I left my fingerprints on the fresh varnish. This would be the first time I'd been to any exhibition of Sid's since we'd separated. I would stay for one drink – long enough for Polly to see her father – and then we'd leave. And tomorrow – tomorrow I would think about a new life. Tomorrow would be the time to address some serious change. I couldn't continue with this heart-stopping pain; adrenaline flooding my body at all the wrong times; this raw, ugly mish-mash of my life. Polly needed stability and calm, and it wasn't possible here, right now.

We got out on Piccadilly and walked up New Bond Street, past Gucci and Prada and the haunts of the Russian mafia; the hallowed enclave of the pop-star and modern celebrity, heading towards a hum of laughter and chat. Polly admired her reflection in every gilt-rimmed window; I felt less confident in the heels I rarely wore, repeatedly checking my phone in the vain hope Emily might say she was on her way.

The gallery was absolutely heaving by the time we arrived, a few paparazzi on the pavement opposite, contacted no doubt by Randolph's team. A crew from the BBC's *Culture Show* were setting up in the corner and Randolph himself was holding court in the middle of the room, dressed in some kind of Indian kurta suit, a long white tunic covering his bulbous gut, his nose already puce from too much alcohol. When he saw Polly he shouted, 'Aha, little one, come here to Papa,' and everyone around him ooh-ed and ah-ed. I winced at his self-conscious styling as some sort of benevolent guru, some loving relative.

His jolly assistant, Missy, appeared by my side. She grinned apologetically at me through train-track braces.

'So cute! Can I?' Missy held a hand out to Polly. 'Just for a minute. Everyone's dying to meet her.'

'Okay?' I bent to ask my daughter – but she was already skipping off to be fawned over without a backwards glance.

I helped myself to a glass of warm orange juice, eschewing the retro Cava, and tried hard to blend into the crowd. It was a less lavish do than the last; even the art world was not immune to recession, apparently. I recognised a few faces, received some air kisses and said some hellos to people I hadn't seen since Sid and I had split, trying not to meet anyone's eye for long enough to make in-depth conversation. I just wanted to see Sid's new work, retrieve Polly and leave again – but there was such a throng round the small pictures in this room, it was difficult to even determine the subject matter.

Waiting my turn, I heard one over-made-up collector comment: 'This is really quite a departure for Smith, isn't it? I'm quite shocked.'

'Maybe. But not in the way you'd have hoped.'

'Tame, I'd say,' someone else murmured. 'Bit disappointing really. Lost his balls, perhaps. Gone soft.' They laughed. 'Soft balls.'

I felt a surge of anger. His work might be different, but there was no doubt, even without seeing the pictures, that he was a brilliant craftsman.

'Who gives a toss about his family anyway?' they sneered. 'It's hardly original content.'

I turned away before I interrupted. Everything I loathed about the avaricious world of the collector.

Looking around for Sid, I couldn't see him anywhere. Jolie, however, was very present, dressed rather like a mermaid in iridescent sequins that barely covered her bottom, tiny shells in her braided hair, taller than most of the men on whore-ish silver heels. It was immediately obvious that she was quite drunk; her heavy-lashed eyes looked glazed as she staggered slightly on the five-inch spikes.

Still, when she saw me, she waved nicely, and I waved back – but as I turned away, I saw her whisper something to her companion whom I recognised as a radio DJ, be-quiffed and leather-jacketed, friend to the Mosses, Osbornes and Geldofs of this world. They glanced over; both fell about laughing.

God, I wished Emily was here. I drained my orange juice and contemplated the Cava, finally managing to slide into place in front of one of the paintings.

It was a beach. I thought I recognised it; I thought it was Sennen, where Sid and I used to go and swim and surf when we lived in Cornwall.

And then my heart was in my mouth, because, despite the dark colours and the blurred figure, there was no doubting that it was a picture of me.

Sid never ever painted me, not since the first portrait when we got married. I stared and stared at it and then suddenly a voice was in my ear. Jolie.

''Spect you're really proud now, aren't you?' she slurred. 'A whole exhibition dedicated to his family.'

I couldn't quite tell if this was sarcasm or not.

'I'm looking forward to seeing all the pictures,' I said. 'I expect you've seen them already?'

She ignored my attempt to appease her.

'You know, he may disappear sometimes,' she wobbled backwards and then leant into me and whispered, 'but in the end he always comes back to me.'

'Yeah, well,' I said wearily. 'Good luck with that.'

'What do you mean?' I felt the tension exuding from her. 'Are you saying I'm a liar?'

'No,' I said quietly. 'I'm not saying that at all.' People were starting to look; I was deeply uncomfortable. This was exactly why I hadn't wanted to come. And I was aware suddenly of a new dynamic too, presumably because I'd been foolish enough to sleep with Sid again. Although she didn't know that.

'Why don't you just let him go?' she was relentless. 'It's pathetic, the way you hold on. And he'll paint me soon. I know he will. He's started already.'

'I'm sure he has. Please, Jolie—' I started to move away, but she grabbed my arm.

And then Sid was there too, in a sharp-fitting grey suit, his dark mop tamed a little, reminding me of Polly's, and his eyes wary as ever, narrowed in anticipation of trouble.

'Come on, you,' he said to his girlfriend, and he took her arm and led her away, and I was surprised by how gentle his tone was – and then I was more surprised at the jealousy I felt. Immediately, I despised myself for it. I had made a huge mistake coming here. What the hell had I been thinking? I couldn't look at these pictures and I couldn't be here anymore, I had to get out.

I stumbled through the crowd, looking for Polly, looking for a friendly face. My daughter was on the other side of the room being fed crisps by one of Randolph's lackeys; I pushed my way through the crowd to her.

'Come on, Pol,' I said, holding my arms out to her. 'Time to go.'

'But I haven't even seen Daddy yet,' she pouted and then someone else arrived brandishing a bottle of Coke for her, and a pot of peanuts, and I knew getting her to leave quietly was going to be a nightmare.

'Polly, we've got to go, baby. You'll see Daddy on Sunday. He's very busy with his work.'

But my beady-eyed child had spotted her father through the window; he was outside with Jolie, smoking, and quite obviously arguing, albeit in hushed tones. The diamonds on her wrist glinted under the gallery's neon lights but her pretty face was ugly as she snarled at him, and it came to me in a sudden flash; despite the jealousy, despite the loyalty I felt towards him still, why I was glad not to be with him anymore. Because it was *always* like this. Always high drama; too much emotion. Everything buttoned up and yet too much on display; the result of Sid desperately keeping all the pain in was that it then so often imploded publicly.

And as I watched, Polly slipped from my grasp, made her way through all the legs and escaped outside, hurling herself at her father like a small missile. His face lit up as he swung her into his arms and buried his face in her hair.

Afterwards I decided it was this that finally unhinged Jolie that night. I arrived behind Sid seconds later – but she'd already begun her attack.

'You got just what you wanted.' All the sweet-little-girl charm dissipated in a trice. 'You know, I never trust people with jobs like yours. Your nose in everyone's lives. A sancti … sanctimon—' she was too drunk to get the word out. 'Just plain meddling,' she managed in the end. 'Why don't you just *fuck off?*'

I wasn't even sure who she was talking to; Polly or me. Missy came out now, no doubt sent by Randolph to keep a lid on things.

'Jolie,' Sid hissed. 'Mind your language.'

'Why the fuck should I?'

'Daddy,' Polly's eyes were huge. 'She said the fuck word. Two times!'

Missy held her hand out again. 'Polly darling, why don't you come with me?'

'No,' I stood between her and my daughter. 'It's fine. We're leaving.'

'That's right. You run away, you stupid bitch.'

The paparazzi were gathering now, blood lust alerted by the shouting.

'Don't talk to my mummy like that,' Polly said to Jolie crossly, and burst into tears.

'If you publish a single photo, I'll throttle you all with my bare hands and then I'll sue you,' Sid snarled at the press. The flashes continued.

'Please, guys,' Missy turned to them now, arms wide, beseeching. 'This is a private party.'

But they were having none of it. This was their dream; a field day for the press.

I held out my arms for Polly. Sid relinquished her, just as the *Culture Show* presenter appeared at his side.

'Any chance of that interview now, Sid?' she purred, all tawny highlights and perfect St Tropez. 'We're throwing live to the studio in five.'

Missy looked like she was going to have an apoplectic fit.

I started to walk away, my daughter in my arms.

'Walk away, walk away,' Jolie taunted. 'Just like he did from you. Left you 'cos you're all dried up, honey. Knew he was on to a good thing.'

I deposited Polly in the doorway of Nicole Farhi. 'Stay here, baby, just for one second, okay? I've forgotten something.' Polly tried desperately to hold on, but I couldn't contain it any longer, prising her small hands off. 'One sec, I promise.'

I ran back up the road to where Jolie stood, swaying on her Bambi legs, and I stood very near to her now so that only she could hear me. 'No, actually, you stupid cow, it was *me* that left *him*. Whatever he might have told you. So put that in your crack pipe and smoke it.'

And then I gathered Polly back up and hailed the first black cab I saw.

In the taxi, I couldn't hold back the tears that broke after all the tension. I tried my utmost not to let Polly see, shoving my old sunglasses on and giving her my lip-gloss to play with whilst I rang Emily again.

'Please, Em. Where are you? The exhibition was a disaster. I feel like I'm totally losing it.' Hot tears slid down my face no matter how I tried to stop them, but Polly by now was more interested in counting blue cars for the reward I had promised her.

'Eight – nine – eleventeen.' Numbers were not Polly's forte. 'She was very cross, wasn't she? Why was Jolie so cross? She didn't look very pretty when she was shouting,' Polly turned back to me. 'Her skirt was very short, Mummy, wasn't it? I nearly see-ed her bottom.'

'Gosh,' I said and I didn't know whether to laugh or cry, but I found I was sort of doing both. I found some old chewing-gum at the bottom of my bag and gave it to Polly, whose eyes widened at the unexpected treat.

'Just don't swallow it. I'm sure Jolie will calm down again soon.'

And when the cab pulled up outside our house, and I fumbled around for change, another car came round the corner too fast, and my heart lifted because it was Emily's old Jeep.

We stood at the gate and we didn't say anything, just hugged each other. And I couldn't stop crying, but I knew it would be all right now, because Emily was here.

But even Emily couldn't control what happened next.

NOW: HOUR 21

5am

So he's done it. Randolph has shopped me to the police, and actually, I am relieved. They will arrive soon, and I can tell them that Polly and my mother are with Sid, and they can arrest me if they like, I don't care, I am beyond caring now, but it will be all right if they just find my family and make sure that they're safe.

'What did Sid say?' I ask Randolph, and he says, 'Everything's fine. They're all fine.'

'Can I call him?' I hold out my hand for the phone. 'Please.'

Randolph moves the phone out of my reach. 'He says they're all sleeping. They're fine. Really.'

'Why don't you let me decide that?'

'Sid won't want to talk to you,' he smiles his oily smile. 'Come on, Laurie. Face it like the brave little cunt you are.'

Oh God, I loathe this man.

I contemplate trying to wrest the phone off him but frankly I don't rate my chances. I have no energy left; I am so washed out; I am bruised and sore where he has pushed and shoved me; more bruised and sore than when I left the hospital yesterday morning. I am not sure my body can withstand any more damage today.

I contemplate trying to get to another phone in the flat, but I don't know where they are, and I feel his eyes on me all the time as we wait.

And so, finally, twenty-one hours in, I give up.

I sit on Randolph's huge white sofa staring into space and I try to order my mind.

Whatever Sid has tried to do to me, and my one fear that reared up recently after the gallery incident, a fear I'd not felt before, that he might try to hurt his daughter purely to wound me, I am sure now – almost sure now – that she must be safe, if so many people know where she is. I have to believe this – but I am confused too. Everything is so surreal.

Still, images and headlines about suicidal fathers killing their children assail me. But Sid is *not* suicidal. He just hates me. He was so furious the last time I saw him, more furious than I'd ever known him. Literally beside himself with rage about Mal; about me preventing him from seeing Polly.

Randolph turns the television on to check the FTSE index. He flicks over on to the news channel. Stories about Syria and Southern Sudan. A story about the impact industry is having on global warming. Domestic news. A story about Prince Harry's regiment in Afghanistan.

And then the story about me.

I sit up and listen. The facts, spooled out again. The wrong facts. A shot of a weeping Pam Southern leaving the Royal Hospital. Nausea sweeps through me. Comments from Forest Lodge staff about the fire. I dig my fingernails into my palms.

'*The authorities are still investigating the cause of the fire,*' the glossy presenter says. '*Meanwhile, Laurie Smith is still wanted by police for questioning. Initially believed to have perished herself, it later became clear that it was in fact her friend and room-mate Emily Southern who had died. It is thought there may have been some kind of struggle in the hotel room though fire officers refuse to confirm this, given the extensive damage to the building. Smith* has been spotted since, but her whereabouts now are unknown, although it's thought she is in London.'

A gruff policeman from the Cornwall and Devon force appeared on screen. 'It's extremely likely that Mrs Smith is suffering severe shock, as well as any other injuries sustained on the night, such as smoke inhalation. She needs to be treated as soon as possible. We would ask the public to inform us should they see Laurie Smith.'

'How caring,' Randolph scoffs. 'Personally I think they'd be safer carting you off to the loony bin.'

'Oh shut up,' I snap.

Now a woman appears on screen, captioned as FRIEND OF LAURIE SMITH. My eyes nearly pop out of my head.

Suzanne O'Brien.

'I never really knew her,' she is saying to the reporter, all wide-eyed solemnity, 'I mean, I thought I did but it turns out she duped us all. She's a very clever, conniving woman. Quite dangerous, I'd say.'

'Yet another fan, Laurie, dear?' Randolph sneers.

'Jesus fucking Christ,' I mutter. 'Do they actually check their sources? That's libellous.'

'Hardly,' Randolph laughs unpleasantly. 'I can vouch for the punch you pack.'

'So sorry, Randolph,' I smile sweetly at him. 'When you're such a gentleman yourself.'

He snaps the television off.

'The police are taking their time, aren't they?' I am dry-mouthed, empty-bellied, weak. 'Can I make myself a drink?'

'Whatever,' he shrugs. But he follows me into the kitchen area, removing the block of sharp knives pointedly. 'Just in case,' he says nastily.

I don't even bother to comment, but I do look for a phone.

The kitchen is a tiny galley off the main room and, compared to the palatial luxury of the rest of the apartment, it's a mess. The bin stinks and I open the window; the moths that have gathered hopelessly along the windowpane fly out to freedom.

Dawn has not broken yet as I switch the kettle on and gaze out at the plane trees, thinking I have never ever felt this tired in my life, not even after I gave birth to Polly, because at least I got to lie down afterwards – and then my eye rests on something glittery beside the Fairy Liquid. I look more closely; it's a woman's diamond bracelet. Typically brash for any lover of Randolph's, although frankly, I've often wondered whether he prefers men. Men like Sid.

I take the tea and sit back on the sofa and then the door buzzes.

And the police are downstairs and so I walk down to my fate, frankly relieved to be out of Randolph's clutches.

THEN: MAL & SID

We are all the same, us humans, and yet so very different. The same things break our hearts and fuck us up; yet your damage is not mine. I struggle to understand my own story – it will take a lifetime's work – yet yours seems simple. But in the end, if we don't try – and even if we don't ever quite get it – well, we're a long time dead.

I changed out of the green dress as quickly as I could, as if it had brought me all the bad luck I'd experienced tonight, and as I hung it carefully in the cupboard, I remembered Jolie's fury. What exactly had triggered it? Was it just the pressure cooker, the insecurity of living with Sid? I knew what that could do to the soul; enough to break the strongest spirit. But I also knew so little about the girl, other than she'd grown up in rural Gloucestershire, been scouted whilst at the very proper Cheltenham Ladies' College, had done some modelling before almost overnight success with her first single. Oh, and Jay Z loved her.

Downstairs, Emily and I drank tea at the kitchen table and we didn't talk about Sid, or Jolie, or the past few days. We just watched Polly draw pictures of dinosaurs, and then drip butter from her toast and marmite all over the stegosaurus, making her weep plaintively.

'She's exhausted,' I pulled her onto my knee and dried her tears. 'Too much excitement for one night.'

'I'll put her to bed,' Emily offered.

'I need another chapter of *James and the Giant Peach*,' Polly sniffed. 'At least one chapter. And can you read the bit again when Aunt Spiker gets squashed?'

'Come on then, Madame,' Emily picked her up and kissed her. 'We'll see what we can do.'

I tidied the kitchen up a little and then I called up the stairs.

'I might just pop to the shop, Em. We're not going to have enough milk for the morning.'

'Fine,' she called down. 'See you in a sec. Get some biscuits, would you?'

Outside, the night was freezing, but I savoured the cold air. Christmas wasn't far off, and I thought, I must talk to Emily about plans. It would be the first one since Sid and I separated. The horrible anniversaries of a divorce constantly assailed me at the moment; the antithesis of the milestones of a happy marriage.

In the corner shop, I bought milk and some chocolate digestives, and trailed home again. At the end of the next road I stopped for a moment to remove a stone from my shoe, and a car pulled in behind me, dimming its headlights. I walked on.

The car began to move too. I glanced back. I had a nasty feeling it was Suzanne again. I sped up, almost jogging the last fifty metres, ringing the doorbell when I realised I'd forgotten my keys.

Emily looked a little worried when she answered. 'You've got a visitor,' she whispered. 'I tried to get rid of him, but he was so insistent.'

I walked down the stairs to the kitchen, my heart pounding. But it wasn't Sid. It was Mal.

'Mal—' I began, exhausted – but he held out a hand to silence me.

'Please, Laurie, let me just say what I came to and then I promise I'll go. I haven't got much time anyway. I'm going away at the weekend, and I need to say this now.'

I relented. After all, it was me who continually banged on about bloody 'closure' to all my clients.

'Okay,' I slumped at the table. 'Go on then.'

I could hear Emily padding about upstairs and then the murmur of the television, and I was vastly comforted by her presence. Perhaps, I thought, perhaps I should talk to her about getting a place together.

'Laurie, where are you?' Mal half-smiled. 'You're not listening, are you?'

'Sorry,' I looked up at him. 'I'm all ears, Mal, really.'

'I'll be quick,' he leant against the counter opposite me, rubbed his face with his hands. 'I know you're tired, and God, I am too. I just wanted to tell you myself, I'm going to the States for a bit, on secondment. To train some geeks in Wisconsin. I need to get away for a while; I need to let Suzanne calm down a bit.'

'Ah yes,' I said. I picked at a knot in the wood of my chair. 'The fair Suzanne. You know she's made a formal complaint about me?'

'Yes,' he looked deeply uncomfortable. 'And I can't apologise enough. But you know, it's not the first time.'

'It is for me.'

'No, what I mean is, she's done it before. She thought I was having an affair with one of Leonard's teachers in his last school. She made an accusation there too.'

'God,' I thought about Suzanne's calm manner. 'I'm sorry. She really needs some help.'

'Yeah I know,' he said ruefully. 'But she always refuses. And she's almost pathologically jealous. That's why I left her. Or that's one of the reasons.'

I looked at him hard, and he met my gaze calmly. I thought, I have to choose someone to believe between the two of them – one of them must be telling the truth. And frankly, Suzanne had proven herself extremely unstable, and he really had done nothing wrong.

'But what about Vejer, Mal?' I asked. 'How did that come about? It seems such a coincidence.'

'I'm still not quite sure,' he said. 'I think it really *was* a coincidence of sorts. Suzanne saw the ad for the house on the board at the Vale Centre apparently.'

I remembered my chat with Robert. 'But what was she doing there?'

'She'd been referred back for CBT to help with her obsessiveness. We'd been talking about a final holiday, mainly for Leonard's sake. Ease the blow. I swear I knew nothing about you going there—'

'But Polly wrote our address in the visitor book.'

'Which Suzanne must have seen, I think. She remembered you. She'd seen you in the press, I think, with your … with your ex.' He looked away for a moment, abashed. 'She simply hated you.'

'Why?'

'Why expect anything very rational from her? I've learnt not to. I don't know, Laurie. She blamed the couples' counselling for all sorts of things. Said it made things worse. She blamed everyone apart from herself.'

'So why did you come here? To this part of London.'

'She got a transfer, as I told you. It was all very sudden, after the holiday. I just followed her to be near Leonard. She said she needed a change when I moved out, and it made no odds to me what part of England I got a shoddy bed-sit in. As long as I was near my kid, you know.'

The doorbell buzzed. Who the bloody hell was that now? I stood, but I could hear Emily go to the door and open it.

There was a muttered exchange for a minute or two before Emily's voice started to rise querulously.

'Sorry,' I said to Mal, 'I'd better just—'

Sid was standing on the doorstep, and from his stance, it was obvious that Emily was trying not to let him in.

'I just wanted to explain,' he said. Sid looked exhausted, like he hadn't slept for a week.

'Explain what?' I spoke over Emily's shoulder. 'Polly's in bed. Go home, Sid.'

'I will. I just wanted to apologise for Jolie's behaviour.'

'Okay. Apology accepted. Shut the door, Em.'

'I can't believe you're hiding behind your minion,' he snapped.

'Minion?' Emily and I echoed together.

'What are you even doing here?' Sid said nastily to Emily.

'Charmed, I'm sure,' she responded tartly, but she seemed shaken by his venom. 'I'll leave you to it.' Stepping away, she melted into the other room, which was unusual. She normally stood up to Sid.

'I just wanted to say, about Jolie. It's just ... she ...' Sid ran a hand through his hair, no longer as sleek as earlier. 'She just lost a baby. Last week. It's really shaken her. And then ... well, she obviously drank far too much tonight. It's made her a little—'

'It's okay,' I intercepted. I didn't want to hear about it; it was too painful to even imagine Sid and Jolie's child. 'It's understandable. Miscarriages are incredibly traumatic. I'm sorry,' I finished lamely.

'I just ... at the opening. I didn't want you to be embarrassed like that.'

'Oh, Sid.' We stared at one another miserably. 'What a bloody mess.'

'You're telling me.'

'You know,' I could hardly bear to look at him, 'I think it may be better if you don't see Polly for a bit. Until things …' I ploughed on. 'Until Jolie has calmed down.'

'You what?' Sid exploded.

And then his eyes narrowed further and he was looking at something behind me, and my heart sank as I realised that Mal had appeared from the kitchen.

'What the fuck is he doing here?'

'Frankly, Sid, that's none of your business.'

'I'm asking you.'

'And I'm telling you. You'd better go.'

'I'm not going anywhere. This is my bloody house.'

'Which you no longer pay the mortgage on.'

'That's not the point.'

'What is the point? That I'm not allowed to have friends over? Grow up, Sid.'

'You fucking grow up.'

'Don't talk to her like that,' Mal said equably. 'I think she wants you to leave.'

'Oh does she?' Sid's teeth were practically bared. 'And who the fuck asked you?'

'No one. But I don't think that's any way to talk to a lady.'

'Really? I can't see any ladies round here.'

'Oh for God's sake,' I laughed, though I'm not sure what the joke was.

'Mate,' Mal said, a little less calmly. 'You heard Laurie. Please stop insulting her, and please leave.'

'I'll kill you, Laurie, before I see you with this prick.'

And then I was on the floor as Sid hurled himself across me at Mal. By the time I'd picked myself up, Sid's hands were round Mal's neck, and though Mal was the bigger man, Sid's fury was such that he was utterly ferocious.

'Get off him,' I screamed, pulling at Sid, but he shook me off and I fell back against the wall, momentarily stunned by the force of the blow.

Now Mal managed to get one of Sid's hands off his neck, swinging punches blindly, but Sid regrouped. He was relentless, like a demon, like the fighting dogs I saw in the park, goaded on to attack.

And then there was an almighty crack as Emily brought a vase down over Sid's head.

Sid fell back, panting, blood almost immediately running down his face. Mal immediately stood over him and then I heard a whimper and looked up and Polly was standing at the top of the stairs, thumb in her mouth, Toy Bear in hand, just staring at us all.

'It's okay, baby,' I said, and I ran up the stairs to her. 'Daddy just fell over.'

Sid managed a weak smile, lifting his shirt to his eye to wipe away blood. 'I'm fine, Pols. I'll be up in a minute,' he croaked. 'I'm not going anywhere.'

Mal looked up at me. 'I think maybe we should go.'

'Yeah maybe you should,' Sid sneered. ''Cos I'm not moving.'

And something in me snapped. This house, tainted by our ruined love, was no good for Polly or I. Sid was still obviously unstable, more so perhaps than ever. I knew I had to stop him seeing our daughter for a while, though I knew my words had just inflamed his mood. Although it made me want to curl up in the corner with the guilt.

I gathered Polly up, wrapping the red cardigan over her pyjamas and I followed Mal out to his car.

'I've got to go, Em,' I muttered at her and she nodded. Her face was deathly white, and she still held a piece of the broken vase in her hand.

'I'll sort this mess out,' she said. 'And lock up.'

'Thanks. I'll call you from my mother's.'

'Shame it wasn't a Grayson Perry,' I heard Sid say as I led a sobbing Polly down the stairs into the garden.

Mal drove us round the park to his shabby little flat, where we had a cup of tea and Polly had a hot chocolate, quiet now, sitting on my knee in shocked silence whilst I tried to collect my thoughts. Eventually, I rang my mother.

'Can we come round?' I said, and then Mal drove us there.

'Won't have this car much longer,' he said, trying to ease the tension with conversation. 'Now I've got the excuse to get a bike when I come back from the States.'

'Oh yes,' I said absently. 'I saw you the other day.'

'Borrowed it for a test drive. Always fancied a Ducati. Suzie hated the idea, but, well, you know …'

'You're a long time dead,' I said.

'Indeed.' He pulled out into the road.

Behind us, another car turned its engine on. I refused to look. I knew it was that witch Suzanne and I didn't even care.

I couldn't talk to Mal, I had nothing left to say. All I cared about right now was my daughter.

This had to end. This had to end forever.

NOW: HOUR 22

6am

'Please,' I beg, as I walk out into the dark, freezing morning, half-blinded by the street lights, 'can you check on the where-abouts of my mother and daughter?'

And I give them Sid's address and his mobile number. They put me in the back of the police car, although they do nothing dramatic like handcuffing me, and no one in Holland Park takes much notice, though you'd think they'd all be hanging out of their windows. The rich have more to hide than one might expect, perhaps. I am driven past the Royal Opera House to Bow Street, where they seat me in a small soulless room and bring me tea in a plastic cup. Then they question me about the fire.

'I know nothing about it,' I insist with vehemence. 'All I know is, we went to bed, and then I went to get some painkillers for Emily from the car. And by the time I got back to the room, the fire alarms were going and I couldn't open the door.'

'What door?'

'The bedroom door. It was locked, or wedged – like, from the inside.'

'It's too early to say why the door wouldn't open, if indeed we will ever be able to tell,' the thin-haired policeman called DS Kelly says. 'The fire played havoc with the automated locking systems.'

'Whatever the reason, the key-card didn't work.'

'Are you sure?'

'Yes I'm sure.' But the truth is it's hard to remember things clearly about the terrifying chain of events. The truth is, Emily and I had shared a bottle of wine at dinner that night; I was a little drunk by bed-time.

One thing is clear though: my guilt now is all-consuming.

'And you say you left the room of your own volition?'

'Emily asked me to get her pills from the glove-box of her Jeep. She had a migraine. Too much red wine, probably.'

'So why did you run away?' DS Kelly asks. He has a lot of dried egg-yolk on his tie, I notice. 'Why run when all it makes you look is guilty?'

'Because I think … thought …' I am so tired, I can't even think in correct tenses. 'I thought that someone was trying to kill *me*, and I needed to get to my daughter.'

'Who would want to kill you?'

'I … I don't know.' I don't want this man to think I am any crazier than he already does. I want to get out and get to Polly and then I can deal with the accusations and suspicions. 'Lots of reasons. It's been a very stressful time. And on the way to the hotel, someone tried to run us off the road.'

He refers to his notes.

'Yes, I can see that you made a complaint about that in Tavistock. Two days ago?'

'Yeah, I did. Which no one took remotely seriously.'

'You mentioned your husband.'

'Yes, I did,' I say reluctantly. 'But they just ignored me.'

'We'll look into it.'

'What's the point?' I shake my head with incredulity. 'It's a bit bloody late now.'

There's a knock at the door and a small wiry man sticks his head round the door.

'A word, Sarge?'

DS Kelly excuses himself and goes outside for a moment. When he comes back in he says, 'You'll be relieved to know that my colleagues have seen your daughter, and she is safe and well.'

I feel an uncontrollable tremor pass through my body and my hands start to shake.

'And my mum?' I ask.

'Your mum is fine too, I believe, but she is being checked over at the Royal Free.'

'Why?'

'I'm not entirely sure. Just a precaution, I think. We'll see what we can find out as soon as possible.'

I stand up and then I quickly sit down, as I feel the blood drain from my head again.

'Get a can of Coke from the machine,' Kelly tells the WPC seated in the corner. 'And some chocolate.'

'Look, Mrs Smith,' he says, when I have myself under control a bit better. 'I understand this is all traumatic. And there is no evidence at the moment to show you were directly involved with the fire.'

'Because I bloody wasn't,' I am furious. 'Do you really think I wanted to kill my very best friend in the world? Why would I?'

'There is that, of course. But—'

The policewoman returns with a Twix and a Coke, which I tear into, suddenly starving.

'As I was saying, there is a suspicion of arson still,' he continues carefully. 'Until the fire chiefs locate the exact cause, there is an element of doubt.'

'Why?'

'The fire is believed to have started in the vicinity of your room.'

So I was right. 'How do you know?'

'I'm not at liberty to say at this moment in time.'

Why do all policemen speak like a textbook? 'So? What does that mean for me now? Am I under arrest?'

'No,' he says. 'You're not. But running away didn't really help your case. I am obliged to release you now, but I advise you to stay where we can contact you if we need to.'

Suddenly I don't want the rest of the Twix. 'I ran because I was scared. I ran to get to my daughter.' I am so tired, and I don't care anymore if he believes me. I just want Polly. 'Please. Where is she now?'

'At her dad's in Islington, from what I understand.'

'What?' I say and then I stand again. Anger surges. 'Well, she shouldn't bloody be. Like I said before, it's him you should be talking to, not me.'

'Why? What evidence do you have?'

'Because he was in St Ives that night. Because I'm sure it was him on that bike.'

'Right.' DS Kelly looks, frankly, almost as tired as I feel. 'Sid Smith was in St Ives at the time of the fire. So what does that prove?'

'Yeah, which is less than one hundred miles from the hotel we were staying at.'

'I mean, why would he want to hurt you? Or your daughter?'

'Because I told him he couldn't see her. Because he was furious with me. Because he's got a terrible temper. Because … he's a mess.'

'Mrs Smith,' he says wearily. 'We are continuing our investigation, I promise you that. Everyone relevant will be questioned.'

'Please,' I say, 'can I phone my daughter? I really need to speak to her.'

Jolie answers.

'Where's Sid?' I ask.

'Out,' she says dryly.

'At this time?'

'He had to take your mother to the hospital,' her tone is cold.

'He took her?' My world shudders on its axis yet again. 'Did you see her? Is she okay?'

'She's fine I think. Just had some palpitations. She's knackered, I reckon, and just a bit ... you know. Old.'

'Right,' I took a deep breath. 'Can you put Polly on, please?'

'She's sleeping.'

'Please, Jolie. I just need to make sure she's okay.'

I hear Jolie call Polly, and Polly comes to the phone, her voice blurred with sleep.

'Pol,' I say, and as she says a bleary 'Yes?' my eyes fill with tears and I have never ever wanted anything so much as to be able to pull her down the phone-line to me. I bite my lip savagely to stop myself weeping at her.

'Where are you, Mummy?' she says. 'I meeted Minnie Mouse. And I got a lollipop about the same size as my head, but then I dropped it and it cracked in half.'

'Brilliant. I'm coming now, darling. You go back to bed, and I'll be there in no time.'

I get off the phone and there's blood in my mouth, my own blood. DS Kelly jumps guiltily because he's been trying to cram down the remains of a Scotch egg that he thinks I haven't noticed.

'Can I go now?' I ask, and he nods his thin-haired head.

'Just don't disappear again, please,' he repeats. 'We need to be able to contact you.' I'm sure he's eyeing up the end of my Twix as I leave.

They offer me a lift, which I accept.

And it's only as I get out of the police car on Upper Street and thank them, and walk down Cross Street towards Sid's house, and stand outside the door, finger on the bell – it's only then that it dawns on me.

That bracelet lying on Randolph's windowsill. The diamond one. I'd seen it before. It was Jolie's.

THEN: THE GREAT ESCAPE

The day before I told Sid that it was finally over, just after I'd been away with Bev to Kent, it was my mother who said to me, 'You're frightened of your own shadow.'

And then my bustling efficient little mother, who *never* cried, who always managed to hide her tears from me as a child, sat at her kitchen table opposite me, and she wept. 'I am not prepared to watch it, Laurie. I'm not prepared to see him do to you what your father did to me.'

'He's not as bad as Dad,' I said quietly.

'Not yet.' And she shrugged, wiped her nose on the tissue she always had balled up in her sleeve, and said 'But it'll ruin you, lovie. It'll ruin you, whether it's a pinch a night or a slap a fortnight.'

'It's not that bad, Mum.'

'Isn't It! I can see it in your eyes. You've started to jump when someone walks into the room.'

Did I? I was so immersed in the misery of my marriage I couldn't see straight any more.

'But, I just think … he needs me,' I said miserably. 'You know what a mess he is. How will he survive?'

'He'll survive,' she said crisply. 'He *is* a survivor. Look at what he's been through already. He made it to thirty without your help, Laurie. He'll be just fine.'

She stood and put the tea-cups in the sink. 'You think you can't live without him, but the truth is, and I know this, Laurie, believe me. The truth is, you're not really living now. You're just existing.'

I covered my face with my hands.

'And anyway,' she turned back, 'he's got Polly now. Polly is his salvation, I think.'

And that much was true. Which was what scared me so much later.

The Saturday morning after the exhibition and the terrible fight in my house, I left Polly with my mother and went home to survey the damage and pack a bag for us.

I had tried to call Emily before I'd gone to bed; later she had texted me to say that all was okay and she'd locked the house up after Sid had finally left, and she'd speak to me tomorrow.

The house had a strange mournful air as I walked into the hall, as if it knew the glory days were over. There was little sign of the altercation other than a few scuff marks on the wall, and Sid's blood-stained jacket was thrown over the banister, but other than that, and the broken vase that Emily had wrapped in Tesco bags and left downstairs on the kitchen table, it might never have happened. Mal had left me a message on his way to the airport, and I had texted him back to thank him for his help last night.

I picked up Sid's jacket and looked at the blood on the collar. I sat holding it on the stairs, wondering how the hell it had come to this, and I tried to think what the best course of action was. My overwhelming sense since the fight had been that I didn't want to be alone now, that Polly and I would stay at my mother's for a while. I sat for a minute or two longer, and then I rang Emily, arranging to meet at Robin's Café.

When I was heaving the bag into the back of my car, Margaret from next door appeared at her gate.

'Oh, thank goodness you're all right,' she said. 'Can I offer you a cup of tea?'

'That's so kind,' I was embarrassed, 'but I have to get back to Polly. I've left her at my mum's.'

'I was very worried last night. I'm afraid I nearly called the police.'

'I'm so sorry if you were disturbed.'

'I must say, I've never heard such language.'

I slammed the boot shut. 'I can't apologise enough. It won't happen again, I promise. I think I'll be moving soon anyway.'

'That is a shame,' she didn't look like she thought it was a shame though. 'I must say, though, after you left, and that other girl arrived. Well, really. The language.'

'What girl?'

'Tall-ish girl. I didn't want to stare. She stood in the street and screamed blue murder.'

I was confused. 'Really? Did you see what she looked like?'

'Sort of.'

'Was she pretty? Mixed-race?'

'Black, you mean? No, I don't think so. It was difficult to see, and I didn't want to be nosey …' she trailed off, a little flustered.

'But it's hard not to look at that kind of thing going on right on your doorstep,' I prompted.

'Well, exactly.' She seemed relieved. 'She was definitely white. Long hair.'

'What was she saying?' I opened the driver's side.

Margaret Henderson flushed slightly. 'What wasn't she saying? A lot of very bad words, the gist of which, I'm afraid, was that she wanted you to rot in hell.'

'Oh dear.' I wasn't even surprised any more. 'And then what happened?'

'She kept smashing at the door but no one answered. She sat down and cried for a bit on the step. Then she went away. Very sad, really.'

'I'm terribly sorry,' I repeated again. 'It's been a ... a strange time. You'll be glad to be rid of us.'

'Oh no, dear,' she said, and I felt oddly like crying again in the light of her empathic gaze. She patted my hand as she left.

Emily was already at Robin's, sitting in the corner, nursing a cappuccino and wearing shades and a fringed suede jacket.

'Still in the Calamity Jane phase, I see,' I sat opposite her. 'Just need a horse. You look done in.'

'I think I drank a bit too much last night when I got home,' she said ruefully. 'I must say I felt a bit ... stressed, after all that drama.'

'Yeah, you and me both. I'm so sorry I left you there but I had to get Polly out.'

'It was fine, really.'

'What happened? I've just had my neighbour banging on about someone shouting in the street?'

'Really?' Emily looked puzzled. 'I just tidied up a bit, after Sid slunk off into the night and that was that, as far as I know.'

'I think it was probably Mal's loony wife.'

'Ah yes,' she said, 'the valiant Mal to the rescue. He seemed ... well, nice, yeah?'

'When was that then? When Sid tried to murder him?'

We looked at each other and started to laugh.

'God, poor bloke,' she said. 'Didn't know what he was letting himself in for.'

'Yes, well, I don't think he's going to be the next big thing in my life – 'specially after last night. He's gone to America, anyway, for a bit. And I can't deal with old Looney Tunes on top of everything else.'

'Looney Tunes? Which one?'

'His ex-wife Suzanne. She's nuts.'

'No, well, I guess a bit of calm would be good. But he did seem like a nice man, I thought. You could do with a nice man.'

Robin brought my tea and we sat in silence for a moment. I thought about Mal. He *was* nice, but it was so bloody complicated. I wasn't ready, much as I craved companionship. Nothing should be this complicated. And I still didn't know if I really trusted him.

Trust. It seemed a curious concept right now.

'I might have to eat cake,' I said after a while.

'Well, what's good enough for French queens. Look, Laurie,' Emily took her sunglasses off. Tiger eyes, unmade up for once. 'I think we should go away. You need a break from all this shit.'

'Go where?'

'I don't know. Just a weekend somewhere. There's some brilliant offers on Discount Vouchers. I fancy a spa. Nice massage, nice dinner.'

The idea of getting out of London, away from all this conflict and heartache, was immensely appealing.

'Sounds lovely. I'm a bit broke though,' I said, sadly. 'Sid's not giving me anything at all at the moment towards the house or Pol.'

'My treat. Early birthday present,' Emily said, and then she flushed slightly. 'Please. I'd really like to. To say sorry too, for being all moody the other day. I'm sure your mum'd have Polly.'

I considered the idea. 'Okay,' I said impulsively. 'Yeah! Why the hell not? We deserve some downtime.'

'Yes we do. Well.' She looked sad. 'You in particular do.'

'Cheer up,' I said, feeling suddenly more enthused than I had in months. 'I've got a feeling things will turn a corner now. I wanted to talk to you about maybe getting a flat together too. Shall we share some Death by Chocolate?'

NOW: HOUR 23

7am

There is no answer at Sid's. I cannot believe it, but no one comes to the door. And I have an increasingly unpleasant feeling in my gut, as I press the bell again and again.

Then I run back up the road to where the police car dropped me, but of course they are long gone.

And then Sid pulls up in the battered old Porsche, nearly writing off the car in front. He is such a bad driver, although this time there is some excuse.

'Thank God,' I am practically weeping with frustration. 'Open the door, will you? I can't get an answer.'

And he unlocks the front door, and we go running up the stairs, and I am praying that they are just both fast asleep – but the flat is totally empty.

Polly's little case lies on the floor and her jumper is there on the sofa where she has obviously been lying under a plaid blanket, but there is no sign of her or Jolie in the flat.

'Where's that mad bitch gone now?' I say. 'Oh Christ, Sid. I can't take much more of this. I need to get to Polly. Where is Polly?' I pace up and down, up and down, until Sid stands in front of me to prevent me walking.

'Calm down.'

'How can I be calm? Have you got any idea what the last twenty-four hours have been like?'

'No, but you look like absolute shit.'

'Sid. Emily is dead.'

He turns away. 'Yeah, I know. I'm sorry.'

'And your girlfriend has vanished with our daughter.'

'I'm sure they're absolutely fine,' Sid runs his hand through his hair. 'Probably just to get some food, or something. They often go out to brunch round here.'

'Call her,' I shove the phone at him. 'Find out.' I sit on the arm of the sofa. 'How's Mum?' I bite my fingernails as he dials the number. 'Is she okay?'

'She's fine. She just had a few palpations and they're keeping her in for observation for a few hours. But she's fine. You can call this number,' he fishes a bit of paper out of his pocket and hands it to me. 'They should put you through.'

'Is Jolie answering?' I say – but she's blatantly not.

He leaves a message. 'Call me, please, Jolie. Laurie's here to get Polly and we don't know where you are.'

'Sid,' I say carefully. 'Why didn't you tell me you were going to St Ives?'

'Why would I? We've hardly spoken in the past few weeks.'

'But,' I clear my throat. 'You knew Emily and I were going to Devon.'

'So?'

'So. I saw you on the motorway.'

'What? When?'

'Oh come on. On that bike.'

'What bike?' he feigned ignorance.

'That motorbike.'

'I don't know what you're on about. I haven't ridden a bike since before Pol was born.'

'I saw you in the *Guardian* mag on one. Bloody great Enfield.'

'Oh, that,' he has the good grace to look embarrassed. 'It was only for some poxy photo-shoot.'

'Whatever. Did you come to the hotel?'

'What?'

'Did you come to the hotel? Where Em and I were staying?'

'No,' Sid looks nonplussed. He sits beside me on the sofa arm. 'Why would I? I don't really know what the fuck's going on, Laurie. All I know is, you went away, I went to see Pete Mann at St Ives about the exhibition next spring, and because Jolie was playing at the Eden Project—'

'What are you talking about?'

'Jolie had a gig.'

'Jolie was playing down there? In Cornwall?'

'Yeah. We were meant to meet up but we didn't manage it in the end. Things ... things aren't going so well between us.'

I'm not interested; I'm starting to panic again.

'Call her again,' I say. 'Sid, for God's sake!'

And then we hear knocking at the door, and I hear Polly's voice calling through the letterbox.

'Hellooo?'

'Polly,' I scream, and I run down the stairs and tear open the door; I grab my daughter who is standing on the doorstep alone, hugging her so tight that she starts to bang me on the back.

'Mumm-y,' she squeaks. 'I can't breathe.' Then a minute later, 'Mummy, you look funny. Why are you crying?'

'Where's Jolie?' Sid has followed me down; he runs out into the street to look for her. 'Pol, where's Jolie?'

'I don't know,' Polly pushes at my knee. 'She was crying too. She drived off.'

Sid runs down the road as I take Polly into the house and shut the door; it's freezing outside and a half-hearted sun is only just coming up now. I sink down onto the stairs and pull her onto my knee.

'Where've you been?' I say, kissing her over and over again. 'I was so worried.'

'We got in a car and Jolie kept crying. Why is everyone crying?'

'And then what happened?'

'And then she took me up the road to near where we live, to the big trees, and then we were going to get out but she started crying and then she cuddled me and we came back instead.'

'And do you know where she's gone?'

'No,' Polly looks sad and serious. 'She just kept saying "I'm so sorry, I'm so sorry." I think it was 'cos Toy Bear got lost.'

'I expect so. But I've got Toy Bear. He's upstairs.'

Polly slides off my knee and runs upstairs. My mind is racing now. Why is Jolie sorry? What was she talking about? I have a horrible sick feeling in my stomach that nothing good can come of this.

'Is Granny okay?' I ask Polly, following her upstairs.

'She just got a bit – like, funny, fast breathing. When we went to the man's flat. Daddy's man. Papa.'

'Was he … Daddy's man. He was nice to you?'

She looks at me, puzzled. 'Nice?'

'He didn't …' I choose my words very carefully. 'He didn't … shout? Or try to … hurt you?'

'No. He just gave me chocolate and told me to be a good girl. So I was. But I didn't like the chocolate 'cos it had nuts in.' She looks grave. 'I don't like nuts, do I?'

'No,' I agree. 'You don't like nuts.'

'So I put the chocolate under the cushion not to be rude. He didn't see.'

'Right,' I grin. 'Well done. Shall we go and see Gran in the hospital?'

Polly nods, yawning, clutching Toy Bear. I zip her bag up.

'Let's go home first, shall we?' I say. 'I think I'd better put some clean clothes on.'

'Yes, Mummy,' Polly gives me the once-over. 'I think so too. You do look quite dirty.'

And the relief I feel as we wait for a taxi is stronger than anything I remember feeling before. A feeling of peace, despite all the sadness and the exhaustion; a feeling that nothing, in the world, will ever matter as much as holding my daughter's small damp hand safely in mine.

THEN: FOREST LODGE

I dropped Polly at my mother's the day before Emily and I left London. She had decided to take Polly to Euro Disney using the Nectar points she'd saved for years now, and I had hardly ever seen Polly so excited.

'We're going to meet the Little Mermaid and Tinkerbell,' she said, hopping from foot to foot as I packed her bag. Then she had a meltdown because I couldn't find her favourite red cardigan. 'But it's got my Hello Kitty badge on it,' she wailed, 'I wanted to show Granny.' I promised to drop it off if I found it before she left.

I had finally had an offer on the house, and it felt like a huge weight off my mind, although I wasn't sure yet where Polly and I would go. Emily had seemed vaguely enthusiastic about the idea of flat-sharing, but I hadn't seen much of her in the week before we went to Forest Lodge. She was very caught up with work, and I had a feeling she had some new man on the go, but she was playing it typically close to her chest.

I was toying with the idea of leaving London permanently, though I hadn't yet mentioned it to Sid. In fact I hadn't spoken to Sid at all since the night of the fight at my house; I was still furious and rather nervous of him again. Fortunately, he hadn't asked to see Polly after my decision to keep them apart for a while and I was relieved that I didn't have to deal with the situation immediately.

Mal had left for America, texting me once or twice from there with funny little updates. I hadn't seen Suzanne since the last time I'd thought she'd followed Mal and me to his flat in her car – although every time I walked through the gates of St Bede's I braced myself, scared I'd run into her.

The night before Emily and I went away, I delivered Polly to Mum's. Roz and I had pizza together and then I went home to finish a supervision report.

Very late, the phone rang. When I picked it up, no one spoke, but I could hear breathing before it was slammed down again.

I went to bed, only to be woken by the phone again. I answered it automatically, eyes still closed, but again, no one spoke.

I slept fitfully for the rest of the night.

The morning dawned clear and bright, if freezing. Emily arrived to collect me, wrapped in a trusty fake fur, a copy of *The Mirror* on the seat beside her.

'Not your standard fare?' I said, moving in to get in.

'No,' she looked faintly embarrassed. 'Just grabbed it when I was buying provisions.' She indicated the array of sweets and chocolate on the back seat.

'Wow!' I glanced at the front of the paper; at a huge photo of Jolie literally falling out of a nightclub in London in the early hours, being scooped up by minders, showing her G-string. 'Not a good look.'

'No,' Emily agreed, turning on the radio. 'Not a good look at all. Poor girl.'

'No sign of Sid,' I scrutinised the picture. 'Not really his cup of tea, Mahiki in Mayfair.'

'No,' Emily agreed again. 'I expect not. Have you …' she glanced at me warily, nervous since our fall-out about him last month. 'Have you guys spoken yet?'

'No, and I don't want to,' I stared ahead. 'I'm avoiding him really. Don't want to go down the whole Polly access road at the moment. He's absolutely furious with me.'

'You're not really going to stop him seeing her, are you?' Emily indicated left.

'Why?' I looked at her, surprised. 'Don't you think I should?'

'It's your call,' she shrugged. 'Not my business. But I really can't see him hurting her. He loves her too much.'

Before I could answer, Nirvana came on the radio, and Emily whacked up the volume. 'Anyway. Let's forget about them. This is all about you and me, babe.'

Somewhere on the M4 I woke from a deep sleep to hear Emily hissing *Fuck off* to someone.

'What's wrong?' I sat up groggily. At first I thought she must be on the phone, but I realised she was glaring in the rear-view mirror.

'This bloke keeps tailgating me,' she was flapping her hand at the window as a black-clad biker roared up the inside of us, cutting her up badly. 'For God's sake,' she said. 'The guy's got a bloody death-wish.'

He disappeared off in a trail of smoke, only to appear again at the next junction.

'This is really stressing me,' she said.

'Just ignore him. He's trying to get a rise out of you.'

'He's bloody well succeeding.'

He pulled up alongside us and started to make gestures that could only be described as crude.

Emily veered dangerously, the old Jeep rocking as she righted the wheel again.

'Em,' I put my hand on her arm. 'Just ignore him.'

But it was easier said than done. For the next ten miles he played cat and mouse, until Emily was tearful. 'I'm going to pull off at the next junction,' she said. 'He's properly scaring me.'

'Okay,' I said, watching him intently in the mirror. He was tailing us again now, and I was feeling increasingly worried myself. I had a nasty memory of Mal on his bike that night outside Suzanne's, although this figure definitely looked a little lean to be Mal.

'What bike is that?' I asked Emily.

'A big horrible one.'

'Is it a ...' I struggled to remember what Mal had said the other night. 'Is it a Ducati?'

'Fuck knows.' She pulled into the slow lane to turn off at the next exit, and the bike zoomed beside us again. I read the name Yamaha on the tank as it passed, saw the arm of his leather jacket as it flashed by, his gloved hand, then as Emily approached the roundabout at the top of the slip-road, the biker accelerated, nipped in and braked right in front of us, before speeding off again – causing her to wrench the wheel to the right so hard that we hit the grass verge.

We sat in stunned silence for a moment, and then the ever-stoic Emily started to cry. 'Oh my God. I thought we were going to die.'

'I'm calling the police,' I said. I had a horrible feeling I had recognised his jacket; the paint-spattered leather, but I didn't speak my fears now. 'In case he comes back.' Emily didn't argue.

Within ten minutes, a police bike had arrived, and we followed it to the town's police station where we were given tea and a poor impression of sympathy. The officer we spoke to obviously thought we were just neurotic, deluded female drivers. I gave him the bike's number-plate and, when Emily went to the loo, I told them of my fears that it might be my husband following us. The officer was polite but obviously dismissive; disinterested in imagined domestics; wrote something down and dispatched us again. The check on the number-plate had brought nothing up; the suggestion was it was either foreign or stolen.

Fortunately the Jeep hadn't sustained any serious damage apart from a slow flat, which a handsome constable changed in the car park whilst Emily fluttered her eyelashes at him.

'I do love a man in uniform,' she said as we set off again, and I laughed, relieved to see her regain at least a little of her sense of humour. 'I'm so sorry, Laurie.'

'It's not your fault.'

'I wanted it to be perfect for you.'

'It is, Em.'

But she was definitely a little subdued after the run-in with the biker – and not surprisingly. We'd both been terrified, and it was hardly the start to the weekend we'd planned.

The sun was streaking the sky as we neared Forest Lodge about an hour later, reminding me of the Magdalen series of paintings; the lurid skies of Sid's imagination. I tried to thrust him as far from my mind as possible as we arrived in the hotel reception.

'We were expecting you a little while ago. I hope your journey was all right? I told the gentleman who rang, Madame,' the elegant French receptionist told me.

'Oh? Did he leave a name?'

'Unfortunately not,' he bowed his head sorrowfully, 'I expect he will call back.'

'Really?' I was surprised. No one apart from my mother knew I was here. 'Definitely a call for me?'

Emily gave me a sly look. 'Secret admirer?'

'Yeah, right,' I tried not to snort in disbelief. 'I'd be lucky.'

'Sid?' Emily said rather sullenly.

'I doubt it,' I really didn't want to start down this path with her now. 'We're barely talking at the moment, he's so cross. So, tea or …' I looked at the champagne bar with some longing. 'Tea?'

The hotel was a beautifully converted old mansion on the edge of a small thicket of trees, almost a wood. Our spacious airy room was on the ground floor, French windows leading on to a small patio that overlooked lawns rolling down to the tree line.

The sun was low and the winter sky a deep blue as we explored a little; swam and used the spa. I dozed on the bed for a while before going down to the most exquisite Michelin-starred dinner, during which the mad biker faded from memory, and my fears that someone was stalking me receded somewhat.

When we returned to our room, giggly, slightly drunk, Emily had a few missed calls from a number she didn't recognise.

'I'd better call back,' she said, suddenly serious. 'It might be work.' She slipped out onto the patio whilst I lay on the enormous bed and watched the end of *Mad Men*, already half-asleep.

'Who was it?' I asked her sleepily as she came back in and headed for the bathroom.

'Don't know,' she said, 'didn't answer.' She looked a little flushed from the wine.

'You okay?' I said, stretching pleasurably under the goose-down duvet.

'Head's hurting a bit. Hope I'm not getting a bloody migraine. Probably just tired,' she called from the bathroom as I drifted into sleep. 'Been a long day, hasn't it?'

I didn't bother to answer.

And that was almost the last thing she ever said to me.

NOW: HOUR 24

8am

I ring the hospital again when I get home and they assure me my mother is fine, that they are just keeping her in for observation after an erratic ECG, but she is sleeping, and there are no serious concerns 'at this point'.

Polly and I sleep for a while in my bed.

When I wake, and see my daughter's sleeping face beside mine on the pillow, the little nose spattered with freckles and the dark lashes sweeping such round cheeks; dribbling slightly, one sodden curl in her mouth; and even though she has hogged most of the bed as usual and I am practically falling off the edge, and her feet are firmly pressed into my side, one sharp toenail piercing my flesh, I think I have never been so happy. This one pure moment of joy, that's what life is; that's as good as it gets. Grabbing on to the ephemera of happiness when it comes.

And then the phone rings, and the spell is broken.

It's DS Kelly.

'Can I pop round this afternoon?' he says. 'About three?'

'Yes sure.' My stomach lurches again. 'Am I—'

'It's not ... it's not about you, no. It's just to put the lid on some things now. Please don't worry yourself.'

I try to call Sid, but he doesn't answer. So I get in the shower and Polly and I go to the hospital, we take my mum grapes and flowers and magazines, but when we get there she's sitting up in bed, right as rain and moaning that it's not clean enough, and the nurses say she'll be out tomorrow and they look, honestly, like they'll be glad to see the back of her. And we don't really talk about what happened, because Polly is there, but when I leave, I bend over to hug her, and she holds on to me very tight.

'I was so scared,' she whispers. 'When I thought you were, you were ...' she trails off, clutches me tighter. I think about my own frantic pain when I didn't know where Polly was and I hug my mother back harder than I remember ever hugging her.

On the way home, I try to call Sid again, but still nothing. I have a very bad feeling in my gut now.

DS Kelly is outside the house when we arrive, finishing a packet of salt and vinegar crisps he quickly tucks away as we approach. We go inside, and I ask Polly to play upstairs for a while, which she moans about until I bribe her with a promise of a Happy Meal for tea, and she gives in.

And I offer DS Kelly tea, just to keep busy really, whilst he's talking, and then he explains what seems to have happened at Forest Lodge. He runs a hand over his wispy hair, belying his own nerves.

And I find my hands are shaking so much I can't even fill the kettle, and he comes over and takes it, and sits me down.

'I am so sorry about your friend,' he says, and I bow my head and the tears I've held in start, pattering down onto my knees.

'It should have been me,' I say after a second or two, wiping my face, and he shakes his head, and says, 'Please don't say that, Mrs Smith. It should have been no one.'

'What will happen now?' I ask, and he says, 'Well it's one for the CPS really. Obviously there is some further investigation to be done, and that will be carried out by the Devon force. You'll be kept informed.'

And then he leaves.

And I go back upstairs and I sit on the sofa and watch Polly carefully setting out all the Playmobil that Emily bought her for her last birthday, and I think I have to tell her soon, that her best friend is gone – but not yet. Not quite yet. And so I just sit and watch her, and the day draws in and the light fades outside, and eventually I stand and shut the curtains.

AFTERWARDS: JOLIE

If you hold on to something too tight, it will break.

If you hold on to someone too tight, then you risk breaking them. You strain the bond to its utmost breaking point.

Jolie found that out the hard way.

She wanted Sid so badly, but he wasn't ready, and she was too riven with her own insecurities to see that it was him who couldn't do it, and not her fault. Then she miscarried her baby, and after that, she couldn't see straight any more.

That morning, Sid found Jolie out in the woods at Hampstead Heath, hysterical, suicidal. She wanted to be found, I guess, and so he talked her down and took her back to his.

Then he called the police, because she told him what had happened. Jolie was now in custody.

She couldn't live with the guilt, she said, and she had wanted to die herself, although she said it had been a terrible accident.

But it still didn't really add up for me.

I went to see Sid at his studio. He wasn't expecting me; he looked shocked when he answered the door.

'Can I come in?' I said, pointlessly, for I was in already.

'Why did she want to kill me?' I asked him, and he shrugged.

'Because she'd found out that we'd slept together again.'

'How?'

'I don't know.'

'Really?' I eyed him suspiciously. 'And that was enough to push her into such – such violent action?'

'Seems so.' He lit a cigarette and then ground it out again. 'I'm trying to stop,' he said.

'Good for you.' I didn't care anymore. 'And how did Randolph get involved?'

Sid pulled a face. 'He always had a thing about her. I think they might have even slept together once or twice,' he stood and started to clean a brush. I thought about the bracelet on Randolph's windowsill.

'Do you mind?'

'Do I mind?' he wiped the brush carefully on a rag. 'About Randolph and Jolie?' He gave a bitter dry laugh. 'Frankly, my dear, I don't give a damn. I'm done with relationships now.'

I watched his thin back, the way his shoulder-blades protruded slightly through his jumper, like the stubs of wings.

My fallen angel. I stared at his back, as if I'd never see him again. 'You know, I always thought it was you that he loved,' I said to Sid. 'Randolph, I mean.'

'Me?' He raised an eyebrow. 'Christ, I doubt it. I don't think Randolph knows the meaning of love. I was just a cash cow, I imagine. It suited us both, didn't it?' He shoved the brush in a jar with vehemence. 'Me and him. A marriage made in hell.'

'I went to Randolph's, you know. When I was looking for Polly and Mum. He was foul. He hit me.'

'He hit you?' Sid looked round now; incredulous first, angry second.

'Well,' I admitted, 'I went for him first, I guess.'

Sid grinned. 'Now that I wish I'd seen.'

'But I don't get it, Sid. Why did he pick my mum and Polly up?'

'I suppose he thought he was being helpful.'

'He said you asked him to.'

'*Me?* I didn't. I absolutely didn't. I hadn't even spoken to him.'

'So ... who ...' But it began to make sense now. 'Jolie?'

'Yes. Jolie asked him to.'

'So how did he know where they were?'

'Because Jolie told him, I suppose,' Sid shrugged. 'Does it matter now?'

'And how did she know?'

'She was in the room when I spoke to you, I guess.'

He looked weary; he didn't want to talk any more, I could tell.

Still, I needed to know. I took a very deep breath. 'How did she do it, Sid?'

'What?'

'You know. How did she start ... start the fire?'

'I really don't know, Laurie. I don't want to know, actually. It sickens me.' He shook his head. 'She said something about cigarettes. The police will tell you, won't they? If you ask them.'

It didn't quite make sense yet; I was struggling with this new truth.

'But you know, when I spoke to her the morning she confessed, well, she didn't sound surprised to hear from me.'

'Well, she knew you were alive then, didn't she? Why would she be surprised?'

'Because she wanted me dead? Because that must have been her aim?' I thought about it for a minute. 'I guess she must have known by then, yes. That she'd killed the wrong woman.'

Sid turned his back to me, running water into the sink to finish cleaning up.

'I thought it was you,' my voice broke. 'I thought it was you, Sid.'

'I know you did.' He wouldn't look at me. 'God knows why.'

'I thought you wanted to kill me because of Polly. Because I said you couldn't see her.'

'Laurie,' and now he did look at me, his eyes dark with sorrow. 'I am not proud of things I've done; of the way I treated you in the past. I owe you an apology or three, I know. But I could no more kill you than Polly. I love you both.' It still hurt, to hear him say it. 'You are all I've ever loved.'

He looked away, out of the window, out at the dying light, and then he picked something up from the windowsill.

I couldn't quite follow what he mumbled then, but he turned, handed me a blue feather.

'Thank you,' I said, a little surprised as I took it from him.

'I think it's from a jay. I found it in the park,' he said. 'Polly would like you to have it, I thought. For your collection.'

I think it was the first time since she'd been born he'd given me something for my collection.

Then he turned back to finish the brushes, signalling the conversation was over.

And I was sure he was hiding something. But then, he was always hiding something.

I left the studio soon after that. I didn't look back.

There were still too many unanswered questions, and I couldn't rest until I understood it better. I was still ravaged by guilt over Emily's death; I was utterly convinced that I could and should have prevented it – and all the time, I missed her more than I could have ever imagined possible.

Every morning when I woke up, I had to remember that Emily was dead all over again, and the guilt never seemed to lessen, and nor did the grief.

I had told Polly now. A few days after we returned home, I took her to the park and bought us both hot chocolate in paper cups, and then we'd walked to the playground. She'd picked up a 'funny stone' she found for me, 'Look it's got a face,' she said, and then I'd sat her on my knee on a bench and told her.

She didn't speak; she didn't cry. She just went totally silent and owl-eyed and then she slipped off my knee, leaving her hot chocolate on the bench, and run on ahead to the big slide. I found her sitting up there, waiting for me. She slid down once, hair flying, small red wellied-feet planted on the ground at the bottom of it. Then she stuck her hands deep in her pockets and asked to go home. When we got there, she went to her bedroom and sat in the corner with Toy Bear and asked me to put her story tape on. So we listened to 'How the Leopard Got His Spots' and other stories, holding hands in silence. My best beloved.

Since that day, she'd refused to talk about Emily at all. I thought it was best to just leave it for a while.

I'd also spoken to Pam Southern on the phone, sobbing my way through some kind of garbled apology, to which she had responded as stoically as someone in her position could, assuring me that the blame didn't lie with me. She didn't want to talk about Jolie and I didn't mention it, but it had been all over the news since she was charged. No one could miss it; the story of the year.

I promised to go up and see Pam before the funeral; I thought maybe I should take Polly too. The inquest was looming and then we hoped the police would finally release Emily's body back to the family.

At least my mother was safely out of the hospital again, back home, watched over by an anxious John who now refused to leave her side. I was infinitely relieved for selfish reasons; my world was not completely shattered.

Only partially so.

DS Kelly rang and told me that Jolie had asked to see me. I contemplated how sensible a visit was, given my emotional state, but in the end, the chance to ask the questions that addled my brain each day was too strong to resist.

I went to see her at the police station where she was still in custody.

We sat opposite one another in a bare room with a very young policeman staring at the beige wall opposite, Jolie pulling her sweatshirt sleeves incessantly over her hands, nails no longer glittering, but scraggy and bitten. Without a scrap of her usual make-up or insouciance, she seemed a different creature to the exotic, wild one I'd known before; now caged and ordinary.

She asked me how Polly was.

'Fine,' I said flatly. 'Thank you.'

We sat in silence for a while. From my own work, and since she'd asked to see me, I knew the best thing was probably to wait for her to start talking of her own accord.

Sure enough, eventually, Jolie began to speak. Her voice was a curious monotone, the street-smart lilt gone as she stared first at me and then at the wall behind my ear.

'It was an accident,' she said. Then she looked at me very directly, challenging me to disagree. I thought her pupils looked dilated; I wondered what medication she was on.

'Right,' I said.

She seemed surprised that I didn't dispute this.

'I was on my way back from the gig at Eden.'

'How did you know where we were? Me and Emily?'

'Sid mentioned it,' Jolie shrugged. 'He said Polly wasn't coming that weekend 'cos you were away and she was in Euro Disney. I asked him where, and he said he wasn't sure but it was some flash place in South Devon. I read Sid's text, it said where.' She actually looked proud of herself.

'So you always planned to come?'

'No way,' she stared at me, affronted. 'I had a car after the gig. Record label offered me a chopper, but I bloody hate flying.'

'Okay.' I needed to wait for her to offer the information.

'I was meant to meet Sid after in Cornwall, but it all went to shit.'

'Because?'

'We had a massive row on the phone in the car 'cos he was being all weird.' She bit her pretty lip so hard I could see teeth-marks.

'Weird?'

'Didn't want to see me,' she frowned at the memory. 'He said we should cool it. And I knew exactly bloody why.'

'Why?'

'What is it with all the questions?' she glared at me. The shadows beneath her eyes were huge.

'Sorry,' I sat back a little, giving her space.

Eventually, she started to talk again.

'So then I started knocking back the champagne. Was planning to come straight back to London and go to Rita's do at Whisky Mist.'

'But you didn't?'

'Nah. We were on the motorway, and then I remembered the name of the hotel. I saw the signs to Forest Lodge and I couldn't resist it. I got my driver to take a detour. No bother.'

'I see.' I didn't really see, but I had to play along with her.

'It wasn't planned. It was just a ... you know.' Jolie blinked at me. 'A spur of the moment thing.'

She made it sound like she'd just decided to go and buy herself a new designer dress, or book a holiday.

'I wanted to check he wasn't there,' she explained. 'I rang her, and she said go away.'

Something wasn't making sense. But I remembered the missed calls when Emily and I got back from dinner; Emily stepping outside to check her messages. 'How did you get in the room?'

'Through the French windows,' she shrugged. 'It was easy. Just climbed over that funny little wall. You hadn't shut them properly.'

'Oh,' I said, remembering the phone ringing in my dreams before Emily begged me to get her pills.

'But how did you know what room we were in?'

'It's not hard to get information,' Jolie stuck her jaw out defiantly.

'When you're you.'

Jolie didn't reply.

'I just wanted to talk,' she looked at me plaintively. 'Honestly.'

'To me?'

For a second, she didn't meet my gaze, twiddling a curl round her finger. 'Something like that.'

'Something like that?' I shook my head. 'I don't understand.'

'I just wanted to get it sorted. Know why it was going on.'

'Why what was going on?'

'Why Sid was fucking her.'

'Fucking me,' I corrected.

'No,' she stared at me. 'Fucking *her*.'

'Fucking … who?' I stared at her. 'You mean … Emily?'

'Yeah. Fucking your best mate. Surely,' Jolie sat up a little straighter. 'Surely you knew that was going down?'

The policeman in the corner shifted slightly.

We gazed at each other. She looked so incredibly young without her make-up, so indefensible. I couldn't speak; words stuck in my throat.

'No?' she half-smiled. I couldn't tell if she was crowing or not. 'You didn't?'

'No. I didn't. I don't …' I shook my head slowly. 'I'm sure … I think you've got that wrong.'

But she wasn't wrong.

Of course she wasn't wrong. And it all started to fall into place now. Emily's strange behaviour during the last week of her life; the way she'd been with Sid during the fight with Mal, not standing up to him as usual. The fact she'd disappeared that night and then the next morning, had been so hung-over and rueful in the cafe. Racked with guilt; insisting she took me away. The fact she'd hardly been around that week before we went to Devon, always a sure sign there was a man in the offing.

It all made horrible and clear sense now. How had I not seen it?

'I didn't mean to kill her,' Jolie said, and she grabbed my hand across the table. 'I swear on my mother's life, I didn't mean it. Please believe me. It just got out of control, you know? I was so angry, and I was a bit … like, pissed. I just came to talk to her. I said if she didn't tell you, I would. I rang her and warned her I was coming.'

Jolie's fingers were very warm, her skin clammy. I pulled my hand back but I could still feel her flesh on mine. I thought of Emily begging later for the headache pills. A ruse to get me out of the room? It seemed so.

'What did you do?'

'She fucking begged me not to tell you.' Jolie wore such a strange look on her face. Not quite triumph, perhaps, but a near relation blazed there. 'She said she'd have done anything.'

Vindication, perhaps.

'But you killed her instead.'

'I didn't kill her.' Her voice rose with petulance. 'It was her. It was self-defence. She went absolutely mental with me.'

'Mental?'

'Yeah, mental. She came at me, when I said you deserved to know. And … well, I hit her.' She shrugged thin shoulders inside her grey sweatshirt. 'I just whacked her, not even that hard, because she was telling me to "shut up, silly little girl" and go away. She was so worried about you coming back and hearing what I was saying, I think. She even wedged a chair under the door handle.'

'Emily did?' I thought about trying so frantically to open the door, feeling something solid and heavy against it. 'Why? Why would she? I don't believe you.'

'Well, believe!' For a second the old Jolie was seated there. 'Think about it, Laurie. She wanted to stop you getting in if I was still there. And I laughed at her; said I wasn't going anywhere till she 'fessed up. So then she just came at me, and I just … I panicked. I hit her in the face, and …' she trailed off.

'And?' I urged her.

'She fell back. She must have banged her head on the corner of the chair, 'cos she fell like a bloody tree. And I couldn't wake her up, she was, like, unconscious then and I panicked even more.'

'But … the fire?'

'I was smoking and the fag must've fallen when I hit her and the next thing I knew, the curtain went up. So I ran.'

'You ran?'

'Out of the French windows. I shut them behind me and I ran.'

'*You locked her in.*'

It wasn't a question.

'No. *She* locked that door. *She* put that chair there. I couldn't move her. She was too heavy.'

I stared at her. 'But the fire … you knew the room was on fire—'

'I didn't. Not really. There was just a bit of smoke at first. And I thought she'd wake up.' For the first time, I thought she might cry. 'She should have woken up.'

We sat in silence for a moment.

'So,' gradually I was processing everything she'd just said. 'It wasn't me you were trying to kill?'

'I wasn't trying to kill anyone,' Jolie moaned. 'I wasn't, I swear to God. I just wanted to tell her to leave my man alone. I read their texts and it made me sick to my stomach.'

'So *that's* how you knew which hotel,' I said slowly. 'Emily told Sid. Because I never did.' I was hiding from him – but Emily wasn't.

'Yeah well. Everyone wanted my man.' Jolie looked at me again, tears in her limpid eyes. 'Only Sid wasn't my man, was he? Bloody bastard.'

'He wasn't anyone's,' I said quietly. 'He never will be.'

Soon after that, I left.

Jolie didn't react to my departure; just kept sobbing quietly and swearing she 'never meant it'. The sophisticated woman had vanished; only the little girl remained.

I made it to the loo just in time to throw up my breakfast.

There was no solace to be had from anything Jolie had told me. I didn't know how much to believe of her story anyway, and wearily I accepted that it was best to leave it for the courts to decide now. Jolie's driver had come forward to confirm that he had driven her to the hotel briefly that night. He swore that they had left under her instruction before he knew the fire had taken hold.

Slowly my anger was beginning to dissipate. Mostly, I felt sorrow.

The only small comfort I could derive at all from the conversation was the knowledge that, at the very least, Emily hadn't died *instead* of me. I hadn't been, as I had believed, the sole architect of her demise.

But in the grand scheme of things, it didn't make it any better.

Later, I remembered Emily's fury when she'd discovered I'd slept with Sid again. Was that before or after she'd fallen into the abyss of betrayal? Of what must have been a horrible and guilty lust? And had it been only once, Emily and Sid? Or had it been ongoing? Is that why Sid had tired of Jolie? Because he'd started up with Em?

Was it never about me?

I remembered something else that had niggled at the time. I hadn't even told Emily about me and Sid, the time he and I had slept together, that one day and night after we'd split – and yet she'd known. She'd arrived at my house, all guns blazing, and she'd known already. Was that anger fuelled by her concern for me – or was it fuelled by jealousy?

I chose to believe the former.

AFTERWARDS

I dreamt my dad came to see me.

When I woke, I realised it was less a dream and more a memory, about our final meeting. Then he had looked old, stooped, incapable of harm to anyone. We had little to say to one another; he told me he just wanted to make sure I was 'all right', mumbling something about getting to know his grand-daughter, who was at school that day. And we both knew that was unlikely to happen, because we both knew he would disappear back into his own life, closeted and afraid of his spectres.

Sometime during that meeting, I asked him why. He sat silently for a long time, and then eventually he said, 'I wasn't good at words. I got angry. It came out wrong.'

I considered this for a moment.

And what I said was this: something I had waited a very long time to say. I said 'I forgive you, Dad' and he started to say 'What for?' – and then he thought better of it.

After he left, I sat for a very long time in the dark.

He had made me think of before.

Of when I had hope, when life seemed fresh and exciting; of when I first met Sid. Of a time when I returned from visiting friends in Wales, filled with the thrill of being back in the big city and knowing, somewhere out there, waiting for me, was the love of my life: as I sat on the tube in somnolence, as I boarded the bus and swayed within centimetres of that fat man's sweat, that *he* was out there, my love, in London town, old London town. Back where I have felt most alive.

It was what I always loved, when we first lived together: the thought that somewhere in this huge city, there was him. And he was going about his business and I didn't know what exactly he was doing – it could have been any one of a hundred things, and it didn't matter what it was, it just mattered that he was out there, and yet I couldn't see him.

As if I'd dreamed you into being.

It took me a long time to realise that maybe I *had* dreamed Sid into being. Into being what I thought he was, what I wanted him to be. Not what or who he actually was.

But one part of me will never ever be sorry. Because I was living. Until the very last part, I was living every inch of life. I tried it, and it didn't work, but Polly came from that deep dark love, and in the end, I had lived to my fullest degree with Sid, every nerve and fibre alert and sentient.

We are born searching for something. Food, warmth, comfort. If we're lucky, life is one long voyage of discovery – and then we die. It may sound harsh, but it isn't really. If we're not lucky, we just exist.

I had done more than exist. I had fully lived life, in all its pain and glory, and then I got out, just in time, before it killed me.

EPILOGUE

I only ever saw Sid cry twice. Once was at Emily's funeral, which was both a tragic but also a strangely joyous occasion. Joyous because she was so loved, had so many friends. The church was packed; the eulogies were utterly heart-felt; the songs were sung with passion and force by those otherwise numbed or lessened by her death. Nirvana, The Charlatans; all her favourites blared out afterwards.

Pitifully sad because if anyone should still have been here, vivacious and bursting with life, it was Emily.

I sat next to Pam Southern, who wore red because it was Emily's favourite colour, with my mother on the other side. I put my arm around Pam's sloping shoulders every time it got too much to bear.

I'd asked Polly if she wanted to come; I thought, six or sixteen, she had the right, because no one had loved Emily the way my daughter had. But on the day, she decided not to. 'I'd rather go and play with Bernard at Robin's,' she said flatly, and I knew she was scared of the dark place she thought Emily had gone to.

'Come to the party afterwards?' I said to her. 'Auntie Pam would like to see you.' She pondered this for a moment. 'All right, Mummy,' she agreed eventually. She didn't say much else.

I didn't think Sid would come, but in the end, he did, and it did feel brave. He must have arrived late. I spotted him sitting at the very back of the church as I walked out after Emily's family, following the brightly painted coffin.

Afterwards, he found me outside.

'I'm sorry, Laurie,' he said, and his eyes were very dark. He'd cut himself shaving, so unused to the blade, a nick of blood beside the handsome hard mouth.

About which bit? I nearly said, but in the end, I didn't. I just said 'Yes, me too.'

I couldn't really be angry about him and Emily. I didn't want to taint my love for her with jealousy over him, and the funny thing was, I *wasn't* really jealous. Mistakes happen; all the time. We are only human. It almost seemed natural, the fact they'd briefly been together – which was impossible to explain to anyone else; would only sound warped to those who couldn't understand. I knew Sid loved me above all else, I knew he was only trying to fill the void. I knew his attraction was powerful, even if you half-hated him.

Jolie was still in police custody; awaiting a date for trial for manslaughter, still hoping for bail. It seemed unlikely, apparently, that she'd get it.

I reached up and kissed Sid, and even in his smart Paul Smith suit – the trousers perfectly pressed, his blue shirt immaculate – he still smelt of paint and turps and cigarettes, and his unusually clean-shaven cheek was wet with tears – and we both knew it really was the end this time.

'Take care,' I said, and then I walked away. And this time, it was easier.

We buried Emily, alongside her feckless father, and I cried so hard I couldn't see the trees behind, the sky, the ground that Emily went into.

I forgave her her small slip. I just wanted her back.

Afterwards I went home, where Mal waited with Polly and Leonard, and together we all drove to the restaurant in Kentish Town where we'd organised a wake Emily would have been proud of. And the saddest thing was that she would have bloody loved it, my darling Em. She would have been in her element, earrings swinging, hair flying as she laughed uproariously and dosey-doed to the Country and Western we had carefully chosen. We didn't play any Johnny Cash though. We didn't play 'Hurt'.

I went to one more funeral that winter, driving down through deepest, bleakest Kent to Dungeness on the bitterly cold Tuesday just after Christmas. I was grateful that Mal had stayed the night with me before, insisting he accompany me for 'support'.

And as we drove, I recollected the last time I'd been on these roads, heading the other way, racing to find Polly, and I remembered how frantic and delirious with worry and grief I was then.

Now I just felt a heavy sadness – but no panic any more. The adrenaline and stress had stopped the day we buried Emily; the day I'd said goodbye to Sid.

Still, I was dreading this funeral, I could hardly bear more grief – but I knew I had to be there. It was the right thing, entirely.

On this morning, I walked into the tiny grey crematorium, and I clutched Mal's hand harder. And finally my heart lifted just a little as I saw my friend.

Saul looked good in pin-stripes, even if the suit was a bit short in the leg for him. Binny looked, frankly, odd in a dark purple gothic dress. But the outfit didn't matter. She was totally distraught.

'I'm so sorry,' I hugged Saul, feeling his ribs as I put my arms around him, and he muttered 'S'all right', because he wasn't the kind of man to show his feelings if he could help it – but the pain was scored clearly across his face.

Binny fell on me as if we were far better friends than our brief acquaintanceship would suggest, sobbing damply into my neck. 'I couldn't save her,' she wept, 'I tried so hard, but I couldn't reach her. She just wouldn't bloody listen.'

'Sorry, lovie,' I said, because I truly was, and because there was little else to say. Although perhaps more than most, I understood the true desolation of that feeling; of being unable to change the path of someone's self-destruction.

And so I never met Janie, who had no doubt been some kind of feisty firecracker, if her brother was anything to go by. Janie, blank-eyed and beautiful in the photos they'd put up as posters on the walls, who had succumbed aged just twenty to the fierce dragon that she'd chased with absolute futility.

But I had hope for Saul. I knew he would be all right. He was one of life's survivors, and he looked infinitely better than he had the last time I'd seen him, when I'd truly feared for his life. He was better fed now; had filled out a little, the hard angular planes softened somewhat – though he bore a new and permanent scar over his eyebrow from where Barrel Man had kicked him.

Fortunately for Saul, it only added to his tough but boyish charm.

After the cheap coffin slid through the cheap curtains to the strains of a song about diamonds, a song a weeping Binny informed me later was by Rihanna, chosen ''specially, in memory of her beautiful Janie', and that I just thanked God wasn't one of Jolie's classics, we went to a pub on the beach. There we ate curled-up ham sandwiches and Pringles; toasted Janie with beer and vinegary wine. Saul's uncle got his accordion out and they sang Irish ballads and cried a lot and hugged each other with a sort of fierce desperation. It was more than a little different to Emily's wake.

Later, Saul and I stood on the shingle outside the pub so he could smoke. It was freezing and the vast rolling sea was a dark grey, the sky hardly any brighter. But amongst the stones, pink and green lichen still grew.

'Come and see me, won't you?' I watched a valiant blue buoy bob up and down far out amongst the choppy waves. 'We're moving down to Sussex for a bit. Giving the rural thing a go. It's not far. You've got my number.'

'I will,' he tried to smile, and my heart bled for him – this boy-man, old before his time.

'Promise? I'd really like you to meet Polly.' I absolutely meant it. 'Please do come.'

'Yeah, I will. I'd like to meet her too.'

Saul gazed out at the forlorn sea, and I guessed he was thinking about his twin, about how they'd played down here as kids, chasing one another between the boats and the fishermen's huts; deriving comfort in happy childhood things like ice-creams and sea-shells and daring each other over the little trainline from Hythe; drinking Merrydown on Camber Sands, and getting served in the local where their mum *didn't* drink, aged just fourteen – before it all got too dark. Before Janie descended into a place Saul couldn't quite reach her; couldn't haul her up from.

I slipped my hand into his and squeezed his long fingers, and I felt him shudder slightly, desperately stifling a sob.

I held his hand a little tighter.

And then Mal came out with more drinks, coffee for me, and a pint of shandy for Saul – and Saul straightened up to his full height, clearing his throat. He wouldn't show his tears to another man. He took the drink, thanking Mal politely. Inside, Binny was very drunk in the corner, singing along to sad songs they put on the jukebox, and crying all over Saul's poor mother.

Soon after that Mal and I left.

I strip it back to where it began. Naked want; unadulterated lust. A love that grew from that want, becoming something too complex, too tangled and sinuous to do us anything but harm in the end.

But in its purest form, my love for Sid and his for me was not a bad thing.

Sid was my love story. It might have been wrong, but it was my decision; *my* wrong.

My dad broke something in me; so in turn, I chose Sid, who only made the injury worse, and was broken too.

I knew, very soon after I met him, that I would never love anyone again the way I loved him. That I *could* not. I knew it even after he raised a hand to me.

And I knew too that he couldn't help it; that he was so destroyed by his past, by his family, by his demons, that it wasn't me he was hitting. It was them he struck out at.

'I see the goodness in you,' Sid said to me the first night we got the keys to the Cornwall studio. Long before the violence began, when it was new and fresh; setting out on our adventure.

It was January and well below freezing. We had one electric heater approximately the age of Moses, that smelt constantly of burning; we had to keep unplugging it in case it blew up. Shivering, we lay in one thin sleeping-bag, beneath a scratchy blanket, on the floorboards of the studio, wrapped round each other in the vague hope of warmth. The window was vast, the wind rattled the loose panes and moaned around the house, but from where we lay, we could see the stars; the vast cavernous sky. The gales had blown the clouds away.

It was infinite outside.

I'd never seen a sky like that before. I haven't since.

Sid lay on his side, staring at me, staring at the sky. Absently, he wound a strand of my hair around his finger, gentle enough not to hurt me – but only just.

'I never met anyone like you before,' he said.

Sometimes, I can still feel his fingers.

'You are good,' he whispered it again. 'You are my salvation, Laurie Smith.'

In the darkness, he was crying. He tried to hide it but I knew; his face was wet.

That was his proposal. The 'Smith'. It went without saying. It would be him. I would be his.

So.

Sid was my love story.

But Mal is *my* salvation.

Different. Safe, steady. Not dull, I realised in time, but calm. I am done with the fear and the rollercoaster ride of that dark love. I have learnt too much about myself. I have travelled away from that path, and I cannot go back.

I have travelled here, and it is the right place, I find.

LETTER FROM CLAIRE

Hello!

Thank you so much for reading 24 HOURS. It was a while in the brewing and it's good to be back. I really hope you enjoyed it because that's the entire aim of the writing game for me!

Laurie has quite a journey to make, both physically and emotionally, and I hope you felt like you were on her side whilst she battled to retain her sanity and reach her most precious goal. I also hope you didn't feel quite as exhausted as Laurie does by the end!

And if you did like the book, I'd be eternally grateful if you felt like recommending it to your friends, or even writing a review. It's always great to know what gets readers going.

And having said that, hearing from you has always been one of the best bits of my very solitary job, so please, do get in touch through Twitter, Facebook or Goodreads ☺

www.bookouture.com
www.claireseeber.com
www.twitter.com/@claireseeber
www.facebook.com/claire seeber author

Lightning Source UK Ltd.
Milton Keynes UK
UKOW06f0114080616

275785UK00015B/297/P